Ruth was sitting rigidly, white-faced; Gregor tried the door handles; *the doors were locked!* Ahead, the edge of the cliff was coming closer and closer as the heavy car picked up momentum, the sea below frothing over rocks beneath a sheer drop.

Suddenly Gregor leaned back in his seat, raising his two feet, jamming his shoes through the glass that divided the empty front seat from the enclosed rear; a moment later he had forced himself through the shards of broken glass still embedded in the frame, unaware either of the ripping of his clothes or the shredding of his skin as he slithered on his stomach across the seat and under the dashboard, pulling with all his force on the emergency brake. The car responded slowly, as if resenting this interference with its unexpected freedom.

Gregor blanked his mind to the thought of the approaching cliff, or of Ruth sitting petrified and frightened in the rear of the car; he gritted his teeth and pulled on the emergency brake with all his power....

THE GOLD OF TROY

ROBERT L. FISH

BERKLEY BOOKS, NEW YORK

This Berkley book contains the complete text of the original hardcover edition. It has been completely reset in a typeface designed for easy reading, and was printed from new film.

THE GOLD OF TROY

A Berkley Book / published by arrangement with Doubleday & Company, Inc.

PRINTING HISTORY
Doubleday edition published 1980
Berkley edition / February 1984

ISBN: 0-425-07043-3

A BERKLEY BOOK ® TM 757,375
Berkley Books are published by The Berkley Publishing Group,
200 Madison Avenue, New York, New York 10016.
The name "BERKLEY" and the stylized "B" with design are trademarks belonging to Berkley Publishing Corporation.
PRINTED IN THE UNITED STATES OF AMERICA

In Memory of
My Father
David Fish

PROLOGUE ‖

BERLIN—April 1945

The fighting had reached the western edge of the city; the shattered buildings, the burning trees of the Gruenwald, the tilted telphone poles, dangling wires, all testified to the ferocity of the battle, now approaching the Elbe. The troops under the command of Captain Mikhail Sudikoff had borne their share of the attack, and the captain heard with relief from his radioman that his battered company had been detached from the fighting and were to retire to the larger of the two bunkers at the Berlin zoo, now firmly in the control of Russian troops, for rest and what little recreation they could find.

The bunker lay like a huge obscene blister on the crater-filled area of the zoo; the last of the many paintings that had been stored there by the Nazis—depriving residents of the city of precious space during the air-raids—were in the process of being removed. The young Russian lieutenant in charge of the operation smiled at Sudikoff and made a welcoming gesture.

"It's all yours," he said, and climbed on the truck bearing the paintings away.

The organization of the bunker fell to the quartermaster, Sergeant Fedor Kolenko. Sergeant Kolenko had been a university professor in the days before the war, but now he was satisfied to serve a younger and more military-minded captain as quartermaster. Under his direction a first-aid station was set up as being the first priority, followed quickly by the establishment of the field kitchen near the huge ventilation ducts that fed air to the half-buried bunker. Then the troops were distributed the bedding that had been abandoned by the fleeing former occupants. A hammock, which was discovered, was taken by the sergeant and hung in the room selected by the captain for his headquarters.

These essentials to normal military operation completed, the sergeant moved on to the next task. He assigned Corporal Leon Sokolov and Private Dmitry Boldin to go through the many rooms and warrens of the huge bunker and make some sort of inventory of anything they might find. Not, the sergeant had to admit, that there was apt to be anything of much value left either by the retreating population, or the troops under the young lieutenant who had liberated the paintings. And also, of course, anything left over would have been instantly commandeered by their own troops before any meaningful inventory could be taken. Still, if there were any food supplies, they would have to be turned over to the quartermaster for equal distribution, and it was not unknown for important personages to see to it that proper food supplies, and even liquor supplies, were available to them in their enforced incarceration while enemy bombers made life on the surface untenable. Both the corporal and the private were more than willing to undertake the important survey, even though Sergeant Kolenko added ominously, "And anything you find, you bring back here!" Soldiers, after all, he felt, were not all that different from students. They needed to be kept in line every now and then. "Understand?"

This last, of course, being rhetorical and requiring no comment, the two nodded happily and went off, the corporal's rifle from habit accompanying him hooked by its webbing over his shoulder, while the private's machine-pistol—his pride and joy since he had only captured it that morning—swung from an arm strap. The two started at the foot of the steps leading up the Tiergarten and the almost-decimated zoo, and followed the many passages and corridors of the bunker to their ends, finding little more than their comrades settling in, soldiers who resented the thought that they might be asked to give up this acquisitioned chair or that liberated table. But there was no sign of food, and the corporal and the private were about finished when by pure accident—Private Boldin kicked at a pile of rubbish more in frustration than for any other reason—they discovered a small recess in the wall. Apparently the recess had once been covered with plaster, but the plaster had crumbled under the bombardment. The corporal bent down and studied the interior of the small cavelike opening. Then, with a sigh—for he had small expectations of finding anything either useful or valuable or even edible at that late date—he dragged a small trunk into view.

It was a small trunk, less than three feet long, several feet wide, and several feet high, with an old-fashioned rounded top. The two men examined it with increasingly diminishing interest. It was simply a small traveling trunk of an earlier era, made up either of cheap wood or imitation board covered with wood veneer, that had been, in turn, inexpertly covered with some sort of faded and malodorous artificial leather, and with bands of greenish copper riveted about it to give it the appearance, if not the actuality, of security. As if to add to this charade of invulnerability, someone in the past had fastened a heavy, efficient-looking padlock through the cheap hasp. Private Dmitry Boldin sneered openly at the padlock and raised his machine-pistol; he loved firing at any excuse, and this seemed like a reasonable time to test his newly acquired acquisition once again. But just as quickly Corporal Leon Sokolov knocked the private's arm up before he could fire.

"Idiot!" he said reprovingly. "What if there are bottles inside?"

Private Boldin had the grace to blush. He lowered his machine-pistol as Corporal Sokolov reversed his rifle, preparing to bring the butt down on the padlock. At this point Private Boldin retaliated.

"Or if it's booby-trapped?" he asked.

Corporal Sokolov managed to restrain his downward thrust in time, and stared at the small trunk with a frown. Then he did what he should have done in the first place; he simply pulled his bayonet from its sheath, slid it through the hasp, and with an easy twist removed the hasp entirely, padlock and all. For a while he hesitated about opening the trunk, but the temptation was too great. He reached down and tipped the lid back, stepping back quickly. There was no explosion. The men stepped forward again and stared inside.

There were four packages there of approximately equal size. Corporal Sokolov put aside his rifle, picked one up, and began to unwrap it. The contents seemed to have been protected with exceptional care, the outer wrapping being of fine suede leather, and the inner one of sheet after sheet of tissue. The corporal's hopes of a rich discovery began to increase as he noted the care with which someone had packaged his find. But his face fell when, after peeling away the final sheets of tissue, there only appeared to be some poor examples of buttons and beads made from what seemed to be a poor-quality brass. With a disappointed grimace he put the package aside and began to unwrap a second.

Private Boldin could not understand this waste of time with something obviously Germanic, especially since nothing edible or drinkable had been discovered.

"Let me put a couple of bursts through the entire works," he said, his finger caressing the trigger of his machine-pistol almost sensuously. "Let me shoot it up. Whatever that junk is, let's make sure no German bastard ever has a chance to use it. Although," he added, frowning down at the opened package with the profound judgment of a Ukrainian expert, "whoever on earth would want to use garbage like that, is beyond me."

Sokolov shook his head. He had finished unwrapping the many folds of tissue that protected the contents of the second package, and while the contents were made up of larger pieces, the same cheap or inexperienced labor had apparently been employed, as well as the same inferior material. Still, the corporal had been sent on a mission, and about the only thing he had found that the troops hadn't already taken over was this one small trunk, and he would have a hard time explaining to the sergeant why he had permitted Private Boldin to use it for target practice without at least first reporting it.

"No," he said with finality, and roughly wrapped the pieces back into their original coverings, thrusting the packages back into the trunk and closing the lid tightly. "No. We'll take it back to the sergeant. Maybe some of the guys will want to take some of this junk home with them for souvenirs." He grinned, exhibiting large stained teeth. "They can tell their friends these are samples of the handiwork of the master race."

"My old grandmother," Private Boldin said critically, "half-blind and crippled with arthritis, could do better. With mud."

"I'm sure," Corporal Sokolov said politely. He picked up his rifle with one hand and one of the end straps of the trunk with the other, while Boldin picked up the other end. Even with its cargo of the four packages of metal the trunk was not very heavy, and the two men had no trouble bringing it to the room adjoining the captain's quarters, where they set it on the floor before Sergeant Kolenko. The sergeant considered them quizzically.

"It's all we found, at least all we found that the other guys weren't already using, like benches and chairs and tables and stuff," Corporal Sokolov stated, and sounded a bit shamed by his failure to bring more loot to his superior. He shrugged apologetically. "No food of any kind. It's obvious this bunker was used just as an air-raid shelter, plus to store those paintings, and not as headquarters for any group who might have left any supplies behind. There's no sign of continued occupancy."

"I see," the sergeant said, and studied the trunk. Its appearance was certainly not very prepossessing. He raised his eyes. "Where did you find it?"

"Boldin, here, was kicking at a pile of rubbish and this was behind it, in a little hole in the wall. Apparently it had been plastered over, but the barrage must have shaken the wall and the plaster broke."

"Was there anything else in the hole?"

"No, sir. It was just about big enough for this trunk, as a matter of fact."

"I see," the sergeant said, and raised the trunk lid. He knelt down and opened the package Sokolov had rewrapped loosely and had placed on top. The sergeant stared at the contents with a frown upon his face. He unwrapped a second package, followed by his rapid unwrapping of the final two packages in the lot. His hands began to tremble. With an effort he kept his face expressionless as he came to his feet and carefully closed the lid.

"Boldin, here," the corporal said into the vacuum, for the sergeant seemed at a loss for words, "he wanted to shoot the stuff up, just for the hell of it, I guess, or just for fun, or to make sure no German ever got to use the junk again, although why anyone would want to, I can't imagine. But I figured that even if it's garbage, maybe some of the guys might like to have pieces of it to take home for souvenirs—"

"You"—Sergeant Kolenko restrained himself with an extreme effort. He had been about to say "Idiots!" but managed to change it at the last moment—"are to be congratulated on your restraint. And you, too, private. That will be all."

And when the two soldiers had left, the sergeant stared at the closed trunk lid for several minutes, sighed deeply, and then walked into the captain's quarters. The captain was lying in his hammock, staring at the arched ceiling of the bunker.

"Captain—"

The captain rolled over in his hammock, almost pleased with the interruption; he had been thinking of the duties that peace would impose upon him and others of the occupying forces, condemned to try to clean up the mess their own artillery had produced. They were not pleasant thoughts.

"Yes, sergeant?"

"Captain," the sergeant said, and took a deep breath, trying to keep his voice from trembling. "Captain, have you ever heard of the Schliemann treasure?"

1

As she did every working day, Dr. Ruth McVeigh spent the hour between nine and ten o'clock in the morning, when the Metropolitan Museum of Art opened to the public, to walk around her newly acquired domain. It was not so much to see that everything was in order—for its nearly six-hundred employees saw to it that it always was—as it was to bask in the heady feeling of achievement, or fulfillment. The vast galleries of the museum with their wealth of rich treasures were the tangible evidence of that. Ruth McVeigh had been the new director of the Metropolitan for two months now, the first woman director in the long history of the museum, and it was more than a sense of power that made her daily inspection trip so rewarding; it was the knowledge that she was fully capable of assuming the responsibility for the vast and complex operation. And that others, in selecting her for the position of director, had recognized that ability.

Ruth McVeigh was a handsome, in fact extremely beautiful, well-built woman in her mid-thirties, whose life had been dedicated to archaeology, learned from her earliest days from her father, the noted archaeologist, James McVeigh. Her childhood had been chiefly spent in exotic and therefore uncomfortable places, with demanding climates and strange tongues. Her earliest schoolhouse had been a shaded bench someplace under an awning, for trees were rare in the places her father and his crews chose to dig; her teacher had been her martyred mother, a woman to whom the arcana of yesterday had come only to mean the suffering of today. And when at last Sarah McVeigh had gone to join the sand that had been her prison for too many years, she left behind a personal failure, for despite her dire warnings and her attempts to teach odium for all things connected with archaeology and excavations, her only child found herself dedicated more and more to the earth and the many things hidden beneath it.

College was a necessary evil, as was graduate school— merely a means of obtaining the degrees vital in these academic years, to advance her in her chosen field. But each day in classroom or library, she felt, was a day stolen from working beside her father in the field. Even her unhappy and soon terminated marriage to one of her professors had been done, consciously or unconsciously, from the desire to wed herself closer to her field by sharing her body with one whose knowledge was greater than her own. It did not work. One of the reasons for the failure of the marriage, other than a surprising lack of passion on the part of her husband, was her early recognition that he was a book scholar, three pages ahead of his class, but many chapters behind her in both perception and experience.

Nor, when her father died—not from any mummy's curse, but from overwork and a lifetime of self-neglect—did her ambition waver. She spent four years in the field, digging in various Luxor sites with several groups financed by various institutions, spent three more as assistant curator for Egyptian antiquities at the Cleveland Museum, three more as curator for Greek and Roman antiquities at the Smithsonian. Now, at thirty-four years of age, Ruth McVeigh had found her niche. She was director of the Metropolitan Museum. Her ambition went no further. She knew she would be satisfied with the job forever, forever content to walk the huge galleried halls quietly glorying in their contents and her relationship to them, before buckling down each day to her desk full of papers. The job kept her more than amply busy, and more than compensated— she often told herself at night in her large empty bed—for the lack of male companionship in her life.

She came down the high-arched corridors, nodding at the guards neatly suited in their blue uniforms, her eyes subconsciously searching for the slightest sign of vandalism from the previous day's guests—there had been nearly thirty-thousand visitors the day before by the time she had left for the day—or any exhibit that seemed the least bit out of place. Or even with the faintest mote of dust upon it. I'm getting to be a crotchety old housekeeper type, she said to herself with a wry smile, and moved into the Egyptian galleries last. They were her favorite. Some of the exhibits there had been brought from their age-old hiding places by her father. Her tour now complete, she walked into the huge rotunda of the main entrance just as the doors were about to be opened to the public. She smiled at the eight receptionists at their octagonal station, and was about to pass on toward her second-floor office, when one of the women there called to her.

"Dr. McVeigh—"

She turned. "Yes?"

"There was a package for you, Doctor. It came yesterday, just at closing time. You had already left, and your secretary as well, so I kept it here for you."

The woman reached under the counter of her station and came up with a flat package roughly five inches square and an inch or so in depth, handing it over. Ruth McVeigh took it, noting that the package had been carefully wrapped in brown paper, bound tightly with twine, and closed by two red seals. Her name appeared to have been machine printed, rather than handwritten or typed. Someone seems to have gone to a lot of trouble, she thought, and turned the package over. There was nothing on the back. She looked up, frowning.

"Did you happen to notice who left this for me?"

The woman looked a bit nonplussed. She shrugged.

"You know how it is at closing, Doctor. Everyone seems to be around here at once, asking questions, wanting folders, or programs. I—" She paused to think. "All I can remember is a hand reaching through the crowd and laying the package down in front of me. When I got a chance I called your office and nobody answered, so I just put it away and held it for you for today. Why? Is it important?"

Ruth McVeigh smiled. "No, of course not. I was just curious." And any archaeologist who is not curious, she said to herself, ought to be in another profession. Still, sealing a simple package with sealing wax?

"I could ask the guards if they saw anything—" the receptionist said tentatively.

"No, that's all right." At closing time, Ruth knew, the guards' attention was on arms and packages, not on clothing or faces. She smiled again to convince the woman no harm had been done. "Thank you."

She walked along the corridor leading toward the staircase that led to her office, considering the package as she went. Behind her the museum was beginning to fill with the sounds of another busy day. The strange package, she noticed, was very light, and the outer wrapping appeared to have been carefully glued shut. Someone had gone to a lot of trouble, indeed. Could it be that the contents were so fragile—a rare manuscript, perhaps, a bit of ancient parchment—that prolonged contact with air could damage them? Or that the contents were so valuable that this extreme care in packaging was warranted? But valuable contents simply laid upon a desk with no message, and no address other than just a simple name? The detective in Ruth McVeigh wondered if possibly the watermark of the paper, or an analysis of the sealing wax could give some clue as to the identity of the sender. Then she smiled to herself. You've been reading too many mystery stories, my girl! she told herself sternly. Undoubtedly the contents of the package would resolve that problem.

Still, it was doubtful that the package contained anything intended for the museum. Such mail and packages were normally properly addressed and delivered to the museum's mail room, not to the reception desk. And as for personal mail for her, or any unexpected gift, what could the occasion be? This was April and her birthday was in September, and what other occasion was there for a gift? Or from whom? Most of her friends were off distant places around the globe, busy with their small hammers, scoops, and brushes. Many had not had a chance even to hear of her new position. And she knew she had not ordered anything from any store, and if she had she would have had it delivered to her home, not her place of work. Besides, no store she knew went in for sealing wax on the corners of their packages.

Of course, it was a puzzle easily enough resolved, and all

her prior detective reasoning had probably been wasted. In all probability it was a new sales gimmick, offering her a free copy of a new woman's magazine for a lifetime subscription or a Florida condominium at a reasonable price at her advanced age. She smiled at the thought as she reached her office. She nodded to Marge, her secretary, and went inside. She sat at her desk, pushed aside the pile of incoming mail awaiting her attention, studied the exterior of the package a few more seconds, and then reached for her letter opener, inserting it carefully at one corner, prying the wax seal loose. One would think I was opening a mummy's tomb, she thought with an inner grin. The grin faded. Or a letter bomb. It was a disturbing thought and she put it away, instead slitting the paper neatly and folding it back. There was an inner wrapping which she removed with equal care; too many years of being taught to open all things with circumspection prevented her from tearing or even wrinkling the wrappings. She removed the cover.

Inside was another box. For a moment she wondered if possibly one of her practical-joking acquaintances had gone to all this trouble just to send her one of those sets of nesting boxes that ended up containing something quite minute and utterly useless. It would fit in with the type of mentality that would go to the trouble of machine printing her name and sealing the box with paraffin wax. With a sigh she removed the cover of the inner box, but inside, rather than any more boxes, was a translucent envelope through which she could see photographs, and on top of them, clipped to the envelope, was a letter. So at least it was no practical joke, she thought with a touch of relief, and then smiled; it also was no letter bomb. She took the envelope from the box and then noticed one further thing at the bottom of the package, in one corner. It was wrapped in cotton-batting and appeared lumpy. She picked away the cotton and stared at the small ring that was enclosed. With a frown she picked up the letter and read it.

When she was done she stared at the ring for a moment, a deep frown on her face. Then she reached for the telephone, pressing the button for her secretary.

"Marge, would you ask Dr. Keller to come in? And ask Jed Martin to come along, too."

She replaced the telephone and leaned back in her chair, staring at the letter. Then she opened the envelope and removed the photographs, studying them intently. Could it be that, after all, she was still being the victim of a practical joke? Or of a bomb of a different type? Well, this day, at least, had not started off in its usual manner, and she had a feeling that many of her days would be changed as a result of the strange package; a feeling similar to the one you got when you dug carefully into the earth and encountered the resistance of something and knew, just *knew*, it was not a stone, but something that could lead to an exciting discovery—although this package with its letter most probably was just a stone. She looked up at a rap on the door; a moment later it opened to admit Dr. Robert Keller and Jed Martin.

Dr. Keller was the director in charge of special projects. He was a large, handsome man in his late forties whose rumpled clothes looked as if they had been slept in. He sat down, crossed his heavy legs carelessly, dug a pipe from one pocket and a sack of tobacco from another, and began filling his pipe with slow, methodical movements while he waited for the subject of the meeting to be broached. Jed Martin, in sharp contrast, was wearing a neat, spotless laboratory jacket over a conservative vest. Jed Martin was the curator of Greek and Roman antiquities. He was thin almost to a point of emaciation, and dapper to the point of being a dandy. He also chose a chair, looking almost as if he would have liked to dust it before offering it to the seat of his neatly pressed trousers. Ruth McVeigh looked at both men appreciatively. Although completely different in temperament as well as appearance, both men shared one faculty; they were both excellent in their fields.

Keller finished tamping his pipe and carefully set a lit kitchen match to the bowl, puffing slowly, his steady gray eyes watching Ruth McVeigh as he waited. Jed Martin, however, was not the type to wait.

"Well, what is it, Ruth?" he asked impatiently, and glanced at his wristwatch in a rather pointed manner. "I've a million things to attend to."

"You may have one more," Dr. McVeigh said quietly, and picked up the letter. "I want to read you both something. This came inside of a package that was delivered last night, after I left for the day. Together with some photographs I'll show you later. I just got it this morning. Let me read it to you."

Jed Martin shrugged and sat back, his small birdlike eyes

watching Ruth almost suspiciously, as if she might be using the letter merely as an excuse to waste more of his precious time. Still, he knew that the new director seldom wasted words and never wasted time, neither her own or anyone else's. Bob Keller's expression didn't change in the least. He puffed steadily and watched Ruth McVeigh, liking what he saw.

"This is what the letter says," Ruth began, and glanced down. She paused to look up a moment. "There is no salutation, and no date. And, for reasons I'm sure you'll understand when you've heard the letter, there is, of course, no signature." Her eyes went down again as she began to read.

"The enclosed ring is from the collection of gold objects discovered at Hissarlik in the Troad in Turkey by Heinrich Schliemann and his wife, Sophie, in early June of 1873. The entire collection, consisting of approximately nine thousand separate items, and with a net weight of approximately 8,600 drams, will be held for auction to selected bidders of whom you are one, beginning October 1, 1979. Instructions for submitting bids will be furnished before September 1, 1979. Bids will be secret, as will the identity of the winner.

"The photographs attached will prove the authenticity of the statements made herein. Further proof can be obtained by examination of the enclosed specimen taken from the actual collection.

"No opening bid below fifteen million dollars will be considered."

Ruth McVeigh put down the letter and looked at the two men across the desk from her. No muscle moved on Robert Keller's phlegmatic face, but his eyes looked interested, and momentarily he had stopped puffing on his pipe. Martin, on the other hand, was staring at the director incredulously; he had come to the edge of his chair and was perched there, almost birdlike.

"What absolute and utter rot!" he said, and snorted. "Let me see that!" He took the letter Ruth handed him and read it again, quickly, before tossing it back disdainfully. "The Schliemann treasure! It's been in the hands of the Russians for donkey's years! Everyone knows that!" He picked up the photographs, leafed through them quickly, and tossed them beside the letter, sneering. "Someone got hold of Schliemann's book, simply had some duplicate pieces made up that look like the objects Schliemann had pictures of—probably made them out of tin and painted them with dime-store gold paint—and then took photos of his fakes. With an up-to-date calendar alongside to show the pictures were taken recently. And they expect to get away with it?" He reached over and fished the ring from the box. "And this—" For the first time he hesitated a moment and then frowned. "Well, I expect he did read up enough on the subject to know the rings that Schliemann found were made from gold wire, not from the solid slabs of the stuff in those days..."

"You'll still check the ring for authenticity?" Dr. McVeigh's tone made it an order, not a request.

"Oh, of course," Martin said. "We'll check it for age, for purity of gold content, for the rare earths that were found in the gold of that day, and everything else. We'll have it done in our own laboratory, and we'll send it out for further checks if we have any doubts as to its—well, its un-authenticity, I should say." He snorted again, eyeing the small ring malevolently, as if it threatened him somehow. "The Schliemann treasure! Really!"

Bob Keller cleared his throat a bit self-consciously. He had gone back to puffing his pipe and was frowning thoughtfully at the ceiling. "You know," he said slowly in his deep voice, speaking almost as if to himself, "I've wondered for years about that gold treasure Schliemann found..."

"Wondered what?" Martin demanded, as if the statement was a challenge to his judgment.

"I've simply wondered if the treasure really *was* in the hands of the Russians," Keller said quietly, and watched the smoke from his pipe weave its way upward. He sighed and sat more erect, bringing his attention back to the others in the room. "What do we actually know about the treasure? What does anyone really know? We know that Heinrich Schliemann and his wife, Sophie, discovered it at what Schliemann was convinced was the original site of Homer's Troy in June of 1873—whoever wrote that letter is right about that, at any rate."

"Which has been no great secret for the past hundred years," Martin said argumentatively. "Any more than the number of pieces and the troy weight of the stuff. What does that prove? That your letter-writer has an encyclopedia, that's all.''

"Probably," Keller said agreeably, and went on. "We also know that Schliemann, over certain objections of his wife, donated the treasure to Germany toward the end of that decade. His wife wanted it to go to Greece, which was her home country, and since she was almost certainly the one who first noticed the treasure, and almost certainly was the one instrumental in getting the treasure from the discovery site to their cottage without anyone's knowledge—carrying it under her skirts, you see—her word might have carried some weight. But in those days"—he cast a mischievous glance at Ruth McVeigh—"the man in the house was the boss. So the treasure went to Germany, where it remained in some museum or other until the Second World War, when, for safekeeping, it was hidden in a bunker at the Berlin Zoological Station." He took his pipe from his mouth, examined the bowl as if to be sure he had enough ammunition in the form of tobacco to finish his discourse, and then, satisfied, returned the pipe to his mouth and began puffing again. "And that," he said, "is all we know."

"Wait a second!" Martin said, swiftly objecting. "Not quite. We know a lot more. We know, for example, that the Americans foolishly allowed the Russians to capture Berlin, including the bunker under the zoo. And we also know the treasure has never been seen since. Are you suggesting, Bob," he asked sarcastically, "that there is no connection between those two facts?"

"I'm only saying we don't know," Keller pointed out mildly. "If the Russians have had the Schliemann treasure all these years—how many is it? Since 1945? Thirty-four years, over a third of a century—why haven't they ever exhibited it?"

"Because they have no legal right to it," Martin said triumphantly. He made it sound as if the statement in itself proved the correctness of all he had said before.

"Besides," Keller went on, quite as if Martin had not spoken at all, "according to your theory, this person"—he pointed to the letter with the stem of his pipe—"has gone into quite a bit of research in order to attempt this swindle." He frowned, but his eyes were twinkling. "I don't care for that word 'swindle'— not for something as big as this, something involving a sum as huge as fifteen million dollars. There should be a more expensive title for a ploy that grand. This *project,* I suppose, would be better. If this person has gone to all this research, not to mention trouble—copies of articles, photographs—then he obviously would also know that the Russians have possession of the real treasure. Right?"

Martin was eyeing him suspiciously. "So?"

"Then how can he hope to take anyone in? If he holds his auction—and he is not trying to sell it to an individual collector, but to a museum—then the whole world will know of it in a short time. Including the Russians. And they could easily prove the man is a swindler—I mean, a project director," he added with a smile.

"Except I'm sure he has no intention of delivering."

Keller shook his head decisively. "Then I'm sure he has no hope of collecting. I know those of us in the musuem field are thought to be woolly-headed, but we're really not so stupid as to buy that pig in or out of a poke."

Martin thought a moment and then smiled craftily.

"Unless," he said slowly, slyly, "it's the Russians themselves who are offering the treasure for sale!"

Keller smiled sardonically.

"So now the treasure is suddenly authentic, is that it? Only now it's the Russians who are peddling it! I suppose you can also come up with a good reason why they would do a thing like that? After all these years of sitting on it?"

Martin shrugged, but there was a gleam in his eyes. The more he examined his new theory, the better he liked it.

"That's simple. Because as I said before, they have no legal right to it. What good is a treasure like the Schliemann gold if you can't exhibit it? So they probably feel they might as well get some money out of it, at least. And they have to go about it in this anonymous way because otherwise there would be a stink if they sold something they didn't own."

Dr. McVeigh had been listening to this exchange quietly. Now she shook her head.

"No," she said. "I seriously doubt if this letter came from the Russians. They've been returning tons of material to the East German museums, and this would certainly fall into that category. After all, the legal ownership of material donated to the Kaiser's government back in 1887 or 1889 is certainly open to a good deal of question, especially when there have been several completely different governments since, including the late unlamented Third Reich. Lawyers would have fun with that one. And also especially since the material was donated by a man whose own legal right to the treasure has been certainly questioned often enough."

"Overlooking that fact for a moment," Keller said, "to sell the Schliemann treasure for a mere fifteen or twenty million dollars? I know," he added, smiling. "A minute ago I described the sum as huge, and now it's merely mere. But, really, for the Russians to peddle the Schliemann treasure for less than the cost of a medium Illyushin bomber? Or one of those missiles they parade around Red Square at the drop of a hat?"

"Then it's a fake, a swindle," Martin said positively, and came to his feet, holding up the ring and reaching for the photographs, "and if you'll let me get on with it, I'll prove it!"

"Do that," Ruth McVeigh said, and pushed the wrapping paper and sealing wax across toward him. "Take these along and see what you can do about finding out where the package came from, at least." She watched the small man pick them up with an expression of distaste, add it to his other burdens, and dart through the door. Bob Keller knocked the dottle from his pipe, blew through the stem to clear it of the remains of smoke, and tucked it carelessly into one sagging pocket. This ritual completed, he looked across the desk at the museum director and sighed.

"All right, Ruth," he said quietly. "I recognize that look in your eye. Let's get down to it. Let's take it a step at a time. Let's suppose the letter is genuine, and Jed Martin and his laboratory prove the ring is from the era of Troy. And let's suppose the best photographic analysis indicates the pictures are genuine."

"So?"

"So let's go a bit further. Let's suppose someone actually has the Schliemann treasure in his hands—"

"The Russians?"

"No, let's suppose it's an individual, not the Russian government. And let's suppose this person, after all these years, has either just discovered the value of what he has been holding—"

"Or just recently came into possession of it."

"Which could mean, of course, a recent robbery at one of

the Russian museums, although you would think we would have heard of something like that. Still," Keller said, nodding his big head, "I like that idea better. Whoever he or she is, or wherever they got their hands on it, it's hard to believe a person could have held the treasure all these years and not known what he had, or tried to capitalize on it before. So what do we have? A man or woman, unknown, is offering the Schliemann treasure—the real article, no substitutions—for auction." He paused and looked at Ruth McVeigh. "Question: Who is going to bid on it?"

Ruth frowned. "What do you mean?"

"Exactly what I say." Keller shrugged and brought out his pipe, but not to light it, merely to stroke it, as if the feel of the smooth still-warm wood aided him in choosing his words. "I know that we won't bid on it, and I seriously doubt if any other musuem will. In fact, I'm sure they won't. Jed Martin was right in one thing, at least. Whoever has the treasure, whether it be the Russian government or Joe, the hot-dog man at the corner, the legal ownership of the Schliemann treasure is definitely in doubt."

"If it's in doubt—" Ruth began.

"Wait." Keller held up his hand. His half-humorous smile remained, but his voice was serious. "Look, Ruth. I know your history as a collector, an avid collector. We all are, or at least we'd like to be if the circumstances warranted. We wouldn't be doing what we do if we weren't. But this is the Metropolitan Museum of Art, and you are its director. We do not, I repeat *not*, touch anything in the least dubious as to ownership. You know that as well as I do. It's merely the smell of acquisition battle in your nostrils, my dear war horse, that has made you forget it. Temporarily, I assume, or at least hope."

Ruth McVeigh smiled.

"Robert Keller, if you are going to tell me that after nearly a hundred years, and after almost that long in the *legal* possession of another country, the Turkish government will be able to successfully present a case for ownership of the Schliemann treasure just because it originally came from a section of that country that happened to be Turkey—"

"I'm telling you precisely that," Keller said forcefully, and then weakened his argument a bit by adding, "or if not the Turks, then the Germans, or possibly even the Greeks—"

"Exactly. Which merely means the ownership is not clear."

Keller ran a hand through his unruly hair in frustration. "Not clear to you because you're stubborn. If the title is not crystal clear, we won't touch it. This isn't the first time we've been offered antiquities that we've had to refuse. We've even bought some and had to return them. Ruth, listen to me! Not only will the board never give you permission to even consider bidding on something like this, but no museum in the world will bid on it. Whoever is offering it to museums is an idiot. To private collectors, possibly, although fifteen million is far more than he'll ever get from them. But museums? Never. You see—"

He paused as the telephone at Ruth McVeigh's elbow rang. She shrugged her apology for the interruption and raised the receiver. It was her secretary.

"Dr. McVeigh, I'm sorry to interrupt your conference, but you have an overseas call from Spain. Dr. Armando Lopez is calling. Will you take the call?"

"Of course." There was a brief wait and then the familiar tones of Dr. Lopez, an old acquaintance if not exactly a friend, of both Ruth McVeigh and her father. Dr. Lopez was the curator of Greek and Roman antiquities at the Museo Arqueológico Nacional in Madrid. He was speaking his usual English, which Ruth McVeigh always referred to as Obscure Florid.

"Ruth, my dear one? How are you?"

"Very well, thank you. And you?"

"At the best. The new position runs itself along well?"

"Very well, thank you." She looked at Bob Keller and shrugged humorously.

"Good!" There was a brief pause. When Dr. Lopez spoke again his usual profuseness had abated to a degree. "Ruth, my dear one," he said slowly, "a most unusual affair has lifted its head. By private messenger a package comes after my director with a letter withinside of it together with some photographs and two *botónes*—"

"Buttons."

"As you say. They are of *oro*. They are from—but I dash ahead of myself. This letter—"

"I'm sure I know what it says," Ruth said to speed the conversation; among his other annoying habits, Dr. Lopez had a tendency to go on and on. "My letter had a ring in it. Purportedly from the Schliemann collection."

"Ah? This is what I wish to know. But of course they would never overpass such a prestigious musuem such as the Metropolitan." There was the briefest of pauses. "I wonder who more? Possibly you might know?"

"I beg your pardon?"

"I mean, which more museums receive this letter, do you think?"

"You're the first I've heard from, but on the basis of the letter I expect to hear from others."

"Yes, of this I imagine. Soon we shall know who are involved."

Ruth frowned at the telephone. "Dr. Lopez, are you convinced of the genuineness of the offer?" She could almost see the indecision on Dr. Lopez's face as he debated his answer. Then, with a sigh, he obviously decided there was nothing to be lost at this point with the simple truth.

"Our laboratories are checking in deep, of course, but for me, myself, I have no doubts. I know these *botónes*, my dear one, I know them too well. I did my study in Berlin, you know, and how do you say? I cut my tooth on that collection. Every day, almost, I see it." There was a slight pause. "So, my dear one, what do you think?"

"Think about what?"

"I mean, my dear friend"—this time Dr. Lopez wished to be very clear—"will the Metropolitan bid?"

"Will the National Museum bid?"

Lopez laughed in what he thought was a delighted manner. "Now we are friends no longer, but now competitors, is that the situation at the moment, my dear one?" His laughter faded, his tone became sad. "There is, most sadly, the question of legal ownership—"

"True," Ruth said noncommittally. She looked at Bob Keller and winked, a gamine grin on her face. She straightened her expression, almost as if Lopez could see her. "Sad, but true."

"It forms itself into a complication, there is no doubt. And also, of course, there arises the question of money. Our small museum does not have the funding backlog of the wonderful Metropolitan—"

"The Metropolitan also does not have such funds," Ruth said, and tried to sound equally sad. "No museum sits around with fifteen or twenty million dollars in its bank account waiting for something to buy."

"But you are possessed of such wealthy patrons, my dear one!"

"And there are no longer any wealthy Spaniards since Franco?"

There was a pause. "A few, there is doubtless," Lopez said and sighed. "But with no artistic sense, no responsibility sense, I fear me." Another slight pause. "Ah, well, I merely only wish to learn if the Metropolitan has been touched on, and I see they are. A shameful pity the question of ownership prevents us all from bidding, is it not? But there it is. It would be a nice acquisition. Well! We must meet someday soon and speak of many things. And please to take good care of yourself, my dear one."

"I shall do my best. And you do the same."

There was a final exchange of regards and they both hung up. Bob Keller raised his bushy eyebrows inquisitively. Ruth McVeigh smiled her gamine smile. It made the man across from her realize, not for the first time, what a desirable woman she was, and why he, a very eligible bachelor, had not put in his bid before now.

"That," Ruth said, "was Dr. Armando Lopez of the National Archaelogical Museum in Madrid. They also received a letter and the photographs, plus a sample from the collection. Which he is sure is quite authentic."

Keller brought his mind back to the business at hand.

"So I gathered from the conversation. I also gather," Keller said, "from the look on your face while you were talking, that the good doctor is not one of your favorite people. But, more important, did he also tell you that his museum wouldn't bid on the collection, or rather couldn't because of the legal position involved?"

Ruth McVeigh's smile became even more mischievous.

"Dr. Armando Lopez is not the most able dissembler in the world," she said. "But I'm sure he told me, even though he wasn't aware of the fact, that he will definitely be working day and night to find some way to raise the money, and in one manner or another, not only to bid, but to win the auction and get his grubby little hands on the treasure to keep . . ."

2

LONDON—May

"It's quite insane, I agree, Maurice," the director of the British Museum was saying into the telephone. Dr. Harold Gordon, the curator for Greek and Roman antiquities sat beside his desk, listening politely. "Fifteen million dollars merely as a starting bid. That's over seven million pounds! Not that it really makes any difference, good Lord! With the legal question being what it is, obviously the British Museum has no intention of getting involved in any bidding scheme. Oh, yes, I certainly agree that whoever sent those letters has the real collection in his possession. I think there is no doubt of that. Our laboratories made quite sure of the authenticity of the piece we received, and when you add it to the pieces the others, including yourself, have received, there can be no doubt. Besides, obviously no money would change hands until the authenticity of the entire collection was assured. What? No, no! Of course this doesn't mean we will be bidding! It would be stupid, and we try not to do stupid things at the British Museum. I do admit, if the title were clear—but of course it isn't, you see, so that more or less takes care of that, what? What? I quite agree. I'm afraid when this entire affair is over the poor man will still have the collection in his possession—or the poor Russian government, whatever. No museum on earth will get involved, I agree. The man must be mad. Ah, well, I suppose in time we'll know who he is and how he came to get his hands on the collection, because I just can't see the Russians being this foolish, although I wouldn't wager heavily on that either, I assure you. Still, it will make a rather good tale to pass on to students in years to come, to entertain them. And possibly to teach them a lesson about buying—or even selling—something in the archaeological field that does not have proper title. What? Yes, indeed, we really must get together one of these days! I get to Paris so frequently, and you must get to London about as often, I should imagine. Of course, of course! We'll have to do it soon. And my very best regards to your lovely wife . . . What? You're divorced? I'm terribly sorry . . ."

Sir Mortimer Edgerton did not sound in the least sorry; moreover he thought the ex-Madame Dupaul a bore and a monster. When he hung up the receiver and turned to Dr. Gordon, there was a heavy frown on his face.

"That Maurice Dupaul! Saying without the slightest tremor in that squeaky voice of his that the Paris museum has no intention of bidding, when I would wager every penny I possess that his bid will be the first out of the starting gate! Really!" He heaved a sigh. "One can't trust a soul these days!"

"But—" Dr. Gordon was a bit confused. "We—I mean, the British Museum—won't be involved in any bidding, will we, Sir Mortimer? As you said, the legality—"

"We? The British Museum? Good God, no!" Sir Mortimer said stiffly, and then added more slowly, "and neither will Dupaul. He'll do it though some private collector, some individual, and the two of them will gloat over the collection in private! If they get their hands on it, that is. The thought is sickening. Ah, well. I say," he added, "be a good chap and on your way out ask my secretary to ring through to Sir Isaac. See if possibly he might be free for lunch with me sometime in the next week or so, eh?"

Sir Mortimer, as Dr. Harold Gordon knew full well, could just as easily have rung through to his secretary himself. He wants an accessory, the doctor thought sourly, and walked from the room. And then brightened a bit. It *would* be nice to be able to gloat over the collection, at Sir Isaac's and a few other's expense. . . .

*   *   *

ABU DHABI—May

Prince 'Umar ibn al-Khoury sat quietly listening to the man seated on a chair slightly lower than his own before the gold-inlaid table that faced them both. At each side of the two, others sat even lower, on cushions, silent, respecting the interview. When at last the man had respectfully finished his statement, Prince 'Umar tented his neatly manicured fingers and stared at the man over them.

"I am afraid it is my ignorance rather than a lack of eloquence on your part," he said politely, "but the truth is I do not understand all of this. You are asking me to pay a large sum of money, which you estimate may be as much as twenty or more millions of American dollars, *not* for something you wish for the museum, but"—he shrugged—"exactly for what?" He reached over to the table and picked up the small bead the man had offered for his inspection at the beginning of the interview. "Certainly not for this, or even for a great many hundreds or thousands of these." He replaced the bead, tenting his fingers again.

"Your Highness," said the man, undaunted. "It is not the value of the actual gold in the Schliemann collection that is of interest. The entire collection weighs less than nine thousand drams, and even at today's elevated market the gold, if pure, would be worth less than one million dollars. No, your Highness, it is as a collection, one of the most famous collections in the world, that it must be considered."

"But I am not a collector," the prince said, his tone inviting the other man to reason, and untented his fingers long enough to pick up a sweetmeat and convey it to his lips. He wiped his fingers delicately on his robe and folded them in his lap. "And even if I were a collector, you have informed me that at present, at least, the collection may not be shown." He shrugged. "Of what value is a gold collection that must be hidden?"

The man paused a moment to put his thoughts into words that might convince the prince.

"Your Highness," he said at last, "the Schliemann collection is much like the oil beneath your Highness' kingdom. There are those who would say that the oil in the ground is worthless until it is brought to the surface. The Schliemann collection, these people might argue, also has no value until it is brought to the surface, so to speak—until it is exhibited. But this is not true, your Highness. As your Highness knows, the oil in the ground not only has value, it has a value that increases with time. And so it is with the Schliemann treasure, your Highness."

He paused to see how his argument was being taken, but the prince's expressionless face gave no indication. Still, the fact that the prince was still listening was a plus, the man felt. He went on, not making the mistake of hurrying his statement, but continuing to maintain the same even cadence.

"Your Highness, the Schliemann collection cannot be acknowledged, cannot be exhibited today, because of foolish rules made by foolish people. But, your Highness, rules change. At one time the oil, even when brought to the surface, had a value that was not proper for your Highness and our people, but today that rule has changed, thanks in major part to the strength and foresight of your Highness. The rules of ownership will change. And as it has been said, ownership truly lies with he who possesses. And your Highness will possess."

Prince 'Umar shrugged slightly and reached for another sweetmeat. "But in reality," he said quietly, "it will be you and your museum who will possess."

"Our people will possess," the man said equally quietly, for the museum and all it contains is of your Highness and his people. And even as the oil beneath the surface has increased in value while remaining unseen, so shall the Schliemann collection until the day it may be brought forth and exhibited."

The prince nodded slowly and came to his feet, dusting his fingertips lightly against each other.

"It shall be considered," he said with quiet dignity, and walked away, followed by his retinue.

NEW YORK—May

The meeting in the conference room of the Metropolitan Museum was not going well, and Ruth McVeigh realized that a good part of the fault lay with her own presentation. Her emotional enthusiasm put against the cold businesslike attitudes taken by a large majority of the board members, emerged looking almost gauche. Bob Keller did not like opposing Ruth and felt sorry for the defeat he knew she would face in a short while, but his responsibility in reporting to the board demanded that the full facts regarding the legal aspects of acquisition be presented, and he had done so. Ruth McVeigh, asking for the floor and receiving it, came to her feet in a final attempt to get her point across.

"You all apparently do not understand," she said, and shook her head at their obtuseness, her impatience with them quite evident. "Or apparently you do not want to understand. You all seem to be under the impression that if we do not bid on this acquisition in some manner—if only under a proxy as I'm sure many museums will bid—that then the treasure will remain where it is, in the hands of a person who was foolish enough to try and sell something that wasn't rightfully his to a group of museum trustees who were far too brilliant, too intelligent, to be taken in. That thought is probably the most ridiculous I've heard in a long time!" There was a shocked sound from someone on the board, but Ruth plowed on, her temper now getting the best of her. "It's simply stupid! Believe me, the collection will be sold. It will be sold to a museum under one guise or another, and I would not at all be surprised to later find we were the only musuem permitted or at least asked to bid, who did not do so. You think I'm wrong in this, and that you all know better. You could not be more mistaken!" She paused for effect. "I know, and I mean I *know*, at least six museums who will bid, one way or another."

"And if they do, let them," someone said disdainfully. "What will they get for their money? A collection they cannot exhibit! A collection they will not even be able to acknowledge!"

Ruth waited until the murmur of voices had eased. "For the time being, perhaps," she said angrily, "but most likely only for the time being. The question of ownership of this collection is far from being as free from challenge in my mind as it seems to be in yours. I have a strong conviction that anyone, museum or private collector, who gets this collection, will find very good arguments not only for keeping it, but for exhibiting it as well. If it were put up for grabs today," she said hotly, not caring about her language, "there would be so many arguing their right to it, that in the end it would come to anyone's right! I still think we should—"

Someone on the board yawned quite audibly. Ruth McVeigh clenched her jaw and glared down the table. The offending member regarded her quite calmly and then turned to face the chairman at the head of the long conference table.

"Mr. Chairman," he said, "I think we've discussed this subject more than amply. Ad nauseum, I should say. I suggest we put it to a motion."

"Mr. Ainsley? Would you care to—"

"I would, indeed. I move that we do not, under any pretext, under any subterfuge such as 'proxy' or 'private collector' or in any other manner, even faintly consider the acquisition of the Schliemann treasure, authentic or not, by the Metropolitan Museum of Art."

The chairman looked down the table, gavel in hand.

"Do I hear a second?"

"Second!" It came from most of the board members present.

"Before we vote on the motion, is there any discussion?"

"Mr. Chairman!" Ruth McVeigh came to her feet, blaming herself for her previous ill-considered attack on the staid members of the board. Different tactics were needed and she now kept her voice emotionless, under rigid control. It was, she knew, her last chance. "Mr. Chairman, members of the board, I should like to ask your indulgence in one thing. Before you vote on the motion, I should like to pose a question I want each of you to answer honestly. Is the problem here the question of legal ownership of the collection, or is it the matter of the fifteen million dollars?"

"Both!" someone said. There was a brief laugh from someone and then silence.

"If, for example," Ruth McVeigh went on evenly, "it was a matter, say, of one million dollars, or half-a-million dollars, would you be more willing to chance the questions of legal ownership?"

Dr. Keller raised a hand and was granted the floor.

"Definitely not," he said flatly. "Speaking for myself—and I'm sure for the majority here—definitely not. It isn't a question of the size of the amount. It's still a question of legality."

"Besides," someone said in a puzzled tone without waiting for permission to speak, "how can we talk of a million dollars, or half a million, if the starting bid was supposed to be fifteen million?" It was one of the few supporters Ruth had in the room and she appreciated his giving her the opportunity to explain.

"Wait, please." Ruth was examining the explanation that

had come to her and finding it more and more to her liking. Even her tone became more confident. She looked from one face to another down the long table, suddenly sure she could convince them, or at least most of them. "Suppose we were able to get the fifteen leading museums in the world, say, to agree to each put up one million dollars—or thirty museums to each contribute half a million—and the treasure would then be owned jointly by all of us. And suppose those museums were to include the Turkish, the Greek, and German—all the possible claimants to ownership. Suppose they all agreed not only to share the ownership, but also agreed on a period and a schedule for each one to exhibit the treasure?"

There was silence as this new concept was explored. Then Bob Keller shook his head.

"The claimants would never agree."

"How do we know?" Ruth was looking at him, a faint smile on her lips. "How will we ever know unless we ask them?"

The chairman cleared his throat. The discussion had taken a distinctly different turn and the looks on the faces of the board members indicated their changed attitudes as well. The chairman looked at the museum's new director.

"Exactly what are you suggesting, Ruth?"

Ruth McVeigh took a deep breath, sure now she would win her point.

"I'm suggesting that I arrange a meeting of the directors, together with the interested curators, of the leading museums at some central location—say London—where we can discuss the entire matter of the auction in detail. No matter what any individual museum may have been aiming for in the way of a bid—and I assure you I was telling the truth before when I said they were—still, the matter of money has to have been a problem. If we can co-operate, at least the question of finances can be overcome. And, without competition, we can keep the price down to at least the original figure of fifteen million, if not less."

She looked around the table. Everyone was watching her evenly, listening to her words carefully. She kept her inward smile from appearing on her lips and continued quietly.

"As to the question of ownership, if the major claimants can be induced to go along with us, that problem can be solved as well. Possibly we may even discuss paying the share of the major claimants; most of them are precisely the museums with the least ability to finance any bid of any kind. Such a proposition certainly should interest them—to have at least a partial claim to ownership, rather than none as at present. And to be able to exhibit the treasure at least for a limited period, rather than never, as at present." She sat down.

There was silence, then a hand was raised. The chairman nodded, "Mr. Ainsley?"

"Mr. Chairman," the man said, his voice now more respectful, "I should like to withdraw my last motion and replace it with another. I move that Dr. McVeigh be given instructions by this board to pursue her suggestion, as well as all the necessary resources to do so. I further move that after she has met with these various representatives of these other museums, that she bring the results of her meeting back to the board for consideration."

"Second!"

"Any discussion?" There was silence. "If not, all in favor?"

"Aye!"

"Opposed?"

There was silence. The chairman tapped his gavel and spoke.

"The motion is carried. I will see Dr. McVeigh tomorrow to make arrangements." He paused a moment to look down the table, and then went on in a different tone of voice. "As I'm sure we all know, the discussions we have in these board meetings are for the benefit of the Metropolitan Museum and are not to be handed out to the press or other media without the permission of the chairman. It is not that there is any particular secrecy to our meetings"—he smiled—"any more than there is strict attention to Roberts Rules of Order. But our discussion today is a good example of the reason for care in these matters. The negotiations we have authorized our director to undertake could easily be compromised by any undue or premature publicity. There has been enough idle speculation in the press over this auction as it is, and I'm sure there will be more when the London meeting—if that is where the meeting takes place—becomes public, as it undoubtedly will in the very near future. Thank you. If there is no further business, I will entertain a motion to adjourn . . ."

*   *   *

Bob Keller was waiting for Ruth in the hallway after the meeting broke up. He smiled at her.

"Well, congratulations, war horse. You don't give up easily, do you?"

Ruth smiled back. "Bob, we're either going to get the Schliemann treasure, or we're going to give it a good try. Part of it, at least, if not all of it."

Keller shook his head.

"It won't even be a try. I didn't oppose you in there because I think a meeting with the other museums may be a good idea. It may finally convince you of what I've been trying to tell you. Nobody will touch the bid under the present ownership arrangements. And certainly the real claimants will dig in their heels at the thought of sharing ownership."

"Even at the cost of losing it altogether?"

"Even at the cost of losing it altogether."

Ruth shrugged. "Maybe. We'll see."

"I'll make you a bet," Keller said. "Loser buys the other dinner. And to establish my good intentions of paying off if I lose, why don't we have dinner together tonight as a preliminary?"

"Good enough."

Bob Keller wet his lips and took the plunge. "At my place? I'm a pretty good chef—"

Ruth McVeigh looked at him and inwardly sighed. It had been a very long time, and Robert Keller was a very attractive man, but she knew he was not the one. Keller recognized the signs and also sighed, but aloud.

"Ah, well," he said, and smiled ruefully. "The restaurant of your choice, then. Seven o'clock?"

3

WASHINGTON, D.C.—May

As the chairman of the board of the Metropolitan Museum had so correctly stated, there had been, indeed, speculation in the press regarding the mysterious auction of the Schliemann treasure, to the point where it caught the attention of the government. A meeting to discuss some of the possible aspects of the matter was therefore arranged between Frank Mayberry of the State Department, and Thomas Wilson of the CIA. The meeting took place in Wilson's office in Langley, and Mayberry led off the discussion. He was a tall, thin man, impeccably dressed in dark blue, who spoke softly and slowly, but effectively.

"I assume, Tom," he said, "that you've been reading about this Schliemann treasure and what the newspapers are pleased to call the 'Auction of the Ages'? Or is it the 'Sale of the Century'? Plus the speculations about this meeting that is scheduled for next month in London?"

"It would be rather difficult to miss," Wilson said dryly, and shrugged. He was a gray-haired, stocky man in his late fifties. "What's State's interest in it?"

"There are several angles that interest us," Mayberry said slowly. "For one thing, our United Nations desk is interested in the possibility that there may be some discussion, some attempt, to overturn the UNESCO ruling regarding the ownership of national archaeological treasures. That could open up a tremendous can of worms—"

"And," Wilson said, with a faint smile, "I imagine your United Nations desk will decide on what position to take once they know who stands to gain most from any change in the rules?"

Mayberry laughed delightedly. It transformed his normally stern-looking face into the gleeful expression of a small boy getting away with something.

"I should certainly hope so." His laughter faded, his usual almost lugubrious expression returned. "But there is a far more serious problem with the auction of this collection—or at least a potential problem, I suppose I should say." He paused and frowned at his companion. "Tom, do you honestly believe the Schliemann treasure to be in Russia?"

Wilson seemed surprised at the question. "Yes. There is every indication it is."

"Why do you say that? You'll undoubtedly tell me something I already know, but I'd like to hear, anyway."

"Of course. Well," Wilson said, leaning back and twisting a paper clip as he spoke, "the OSS investigated after the war, and I was part of that investigation. I was young then, I know, but not so young I didn't know what was going on. There was supposed to be an agreement between the Allied powers that all art treasures found would be turned over impartially to an Allied Art Treasure Commission for disposition when the war was finally over—" He paused, smiling.

Mayberry frowned. "What's the smile for?"

"It's because it's doubtful if any of the Allies carried out the provisions of the agreement one hundred percent—too many officers and enlisted men thought they knew a good, or anyway, a valuable souvenir when they saw one—" His smile faded. "But I should have to say, in general, that the other Allies kept their part of the bargain better than the Russians. The Schliemann treasure, for example, was hidden in a bunker under the Berlin zoo; the Russians took the city, including the zoo, and the treasure hasn't been seen or heard of since. Also, when the city was divided up into East and West zones, the part of the city where the zoo was located—it was in the Tiergarten, a park area—ended up in the West Zone, and a search for the treasure was made. It was gone. I know. I was one of those who looked."

"You never made representations to the Russians?"

Wilson smiled wryly.

"Of course we did. They said they didn't know what we were talking about. Treasure? What treasure? If there had been any treasure it would have been turned over to the Allied Art Commission; that was the agreement between the powers, wasn't it? They had turned over other finds, hadn't they?"

"Had they?"

"Well—yes, as a matter of fact. But they didn't turn this one over, and that's a fact!" He frowned and tossed the twisted paper clip aside. "It's hard to believe the troops stationed in the bunker before the British moved in there divided the treasure as souvenirs and not one piece has surfaced since. The only conclusion we were able to come to at the time—and nothing has changed since—is that the treasure went to Russia. And is still there."

"Then," Mayberry asked, leaning forward a bit, "you think this auction is being conducted by the Russian government?"

Wilson shook his head, tapping his fingers restlessly on his desk.

"That's the problem! Why would they sell it? A collection far more valuable, just for having it, than any intrinsic value it might have? And if they were going to sell it, why just now? I'm sure," he went on, smiling faintly, "that they don't need fifteen or twenty million dollars to balance their budget. They're probably like us—fifteen or twenty billion wouldn't do the trick."

"Precisely," Mayberry said seriously. "And *that* is our interest in the matter. *Why* are they selling it? And why just now? After having it for well over thirty years?"

"And those questions bother you?"

"Of course they bother us. Don't they bother you?"

"Not particularly," Wilson said, and thought a moment. "Unless—"

"Unless what?"

"I suppose the stealing of art treasures isn't unknown, even in Russia," Wilson said slowly. "Suppose they had the treasure and recently some enterprising thief simply walked in, packed it up, carried it quietly out of Russia—because if it's in private hands I'm sure it's not in the country, not the way packages and letters have been scattered about—and is now offering it for sale."

"What then?"

"Then I'm sure we would be interested," Wilson said. *"Very* interested. If the security can be so easily breached—not just by someone stealing what I'm sure was a well-guarded treasure, but by managing to get it out of the country and then blatantly offer it for sale without the Soviet KGB being able to trace the man or his loot—then I should say we would be extremely interested. It would certainly say something about their security arrangements that would definitely be in our interest to know."

Mayberry nodded. "Agreed. Then, between us, we seem to have an interest. You'll do something about it?"

Wilson sighed. "I suppose we'll have to. But at least it should be interesting." He came to his feet, holding out his hand. "We'll be in touch, Frank."

And when his visitor had left, Tom Wilson went back to his chair and reached for his telephone, asking to be connected with Personnel.

"Vic?" he said into the telephone. "Someone who knows something about archaeology, and preferably someone who is familiar with the Schliemann collection. Sure, I suppose a stringer would be all right for this one. What? I'll spell it for you, although I would have thought you were sick of seeing it in the papers by now. It's S—what? S as in Sherlock, C as in Conan Doyle, H as in Holmes, L as in Lestrade—" Both men were members of the Baker Street Irregulars.

LENINGRAD—May

A meeting was in progress in the offices of the Soviet State Security Committee, Leningrad branch, in the Zherinskaja Ul-ica in the Petrogradskaya Storona section of the city. Present were Colonel Ilya Berezhkov, head of the Leningrad section, Major Serge Ulanov of the Scientific section of the KGB, and a visitor from KGB headquarters in Moscow, a rugged, gray-haired man, Colonel Vasily Vashugin, Ulanov's superior. From the tall windows of the office, the spires of Peter-Paul fortress could be seen sparkling in the bright spring sunshine beyond the open stretches of Lenin Park, with a glimpse of the broad Neva beyond, separating the area from the city's principal buildings on the south side of the river. At the men's elbows empty tea cups were being used as ashtrays.

Vashugin was speaking slowly, thoughtfully. "The question is a very simple one. *Why?*"

"The question is a simple one," Berezhkov said dryly. "It's the answer that's so difficult."

Vashugin did not smile. Instead he nodded his head vigorously as if in recognition of the basic profundity of the other man's statement.

"Exactly! Why is the American OSS—CIA now, of course— after all these years, and after all the secrecy with which they have surrounded their theft of the Schliemann collection, suddenly deciding to put it up for auction? Why now?"

Ulanov stirred in his chair. He was a stocky man in his early sixties with a shock of short white hair that seemed to stand on end. He crushed out his cigarette and frowned.

"I wonder . . ."

Vashugin stared at him. "You wonder what?"

"I wonder if it really is the Americans who are offering it for sale? The American CIA, I mean. After all, there are no truly national museums in America. Oh, I know they have the Smithsonian, but that's not the same thing—"

Vashugin was looking at him with a frown. "What's that got to do with it?"

Ulanov lit another cigarette while forming his answer. He tucked it in one corner of his mouth as he spoke; blasts of smoke came out with the words.

"What I'm driving at is that it was the then OSS who stole the collection—or at least that's the best conclusion we've been able to come to in all the years. Where would they have kept it all these years? Not, I'm sure, at the Smithsonian. In some vault at their Langley headquarters? And if they did, why would they be selling it now?"

"Exactly the question I've been asking," Vashugin said shortly, quite as if wondering whether Ulanov had been paying attention.

"I'm sorry, but you apparently still don't understand the point I'm trying to make," Ulanov said, a bit stubbornly. "What

I'm suggesting is far more important. Suppose—as we've supposed all the years since the war—that the OSS stole it from our bunker in Berlin, and that the treasure has been in their possession, the possession of the CIA, now, in Langley, Virginia, ever since. In one of their vaults there." He paused to shake ash from his cigarette, immediately tucking it back in place. "Now, we can be rather sure that the CIA doesn't need fifteen or twenty million dollars suddenly—they have an almost unlimited budget."

Vashugin was watching him with narrowed eyes. "So?"

"So it is very possible that it is *not* the CIA who is offering the treasure for sale. It is possible that someone else has the treasure and is offering it. And if that is the case, then they must have managed in some fashion to get the treasure from Langley, or from wherever the CIA has been holding it. If there had been a theft of this size from the Smithsonian, for example, I'm sure it would have been impossible to keep it quiet. But from the CIA?" He smiled, a humorless smile. "Exactly as we kept the theft from the bunker quiet. Out of pride, if nothing else."

Vashugin was nodding his head slowly. "I see. You are suggesting that someone was able to breach the security of the CIA, is that it?"

Ulanov shrugged. "It seems to me to be at least a possibility."

Berezhkov wrinkled his forehead in thought, and then shook his head, not so much in denial, as in wonder.

"I'm not so sure. Let's not underestimate the CIA. When they were the OSS they managed to steal the stuff from under our noses, so to speak. We had taken Berlin and were in the process of organizing it. Then the area was divided into zones. That was the first mistake. Allowing the city itself to be divided was the second mistake. You can see where it's gotten everyone today. A city belonging to one country inside the borders of another country. Ridiculous!" He shrugged, realizing he was complaining about something he could do nothing about. He also seemed to realize he was getting away from the point. "However, that was the political decision at the time, and as a result there were soldiers from one country, one army, one zone, wandering all over every other zone. And a few days later the treasure is stolen. Who else would the Germans have told about the treasure, or where they had hidden it? The British?" Berezhkov sniffed. "The French? Us?" He sniffed louder. "Never. Only the Americans. And who else could have, or would have, been able to arrange it in those confused days? The forged papers? Everything? The OSS, that's who."

"We're fairly certain of that," Vashugin said, seeing in his mind's eye the ancient investigation, such as it was. "We're positive the man who forged the papers that released the Schliemann collection from the custody of the officer in charge of the bunker, was Petterssen, the Swedish forger. Our experts studied the forged documents and made careful comparisons with other forgeries known to have been done by Petterssen, and there was no doubt he was responsible. In addition, he answered the description of the man who was one of those who removed the crate at Bad Freienwalde; even though both men were dressed as NKVD—or at least that was what the idiot trainman assumed they were. A black suit, a white shirt, and you're automatically NKVD!" He laughed, but without humor, looking down at his own neat gray herring-bone tweed, and then to Ulanov's sport shirt, open at the neck, and then shrugged. "In any event...the guard said Petterssen and the man with him had documents, but of course it would be no trouble to a man of Petterssen's ability to also forge these documents."

Vashugin considered the other two men. His voice was quiet, as if asking them to point out any faults in the logic of the analysis he had presented to his superiors years before after the desultory investigation of the case that had been made.

"The man with Petterssen said nothing from the time he got on the train in Berlin until the two got off in Bad Freienwalde. But the guard said he looked quite Anglo-Saxon. The trainman was sure—after a bit of interrogation by a pair of rather over-efficient NKVD men," Vashugin added dryly, "that he was undoubtedly American. I believe he was, despite the overenthusiasm of the interrogators. But the important question at the time was, where did Petterssen disappear to? He didn't go to Denmark or Sweden, because we certainly looked hard enough and long enough for him in those and the other Scandinavian countries. And it wasn't all that easy for him to get out of Germany in any normal fashion, because he was watched for, and he was easily identifiable. No, there's no doubt in my mind that Petterssen ended up in Langley, Virginia, where he prob-

ably forged Russian rubles or Chinese currency until he died
or was retired." He shook his head. "No, I don't underestimate
the CIA. They did a good job in stealing the Schliemann treasure from us."

"They did even better," Ulanov said dryly. "They also managed to convince the entire world that we have the collection
ourselves. Possibly in the basement of the Hermitage here in
Leningrad, I expect." He shook his head, almost in admiration,
and crushed out his cigarette. "And I also am not underesti-
mating them. I merely mention it as a possibility. I don't see
any others. I simply cannot see the CIA behind this auction.
It wouldn't be the way they would handle it, any more than
we would handle it in this open fashion."

"I agree it's a possibility," Vashugin said slowly, and suddenly smiled, a broad smile that lit up his face. "That would
be something, eh? Someone robbing the vaults at Langley?"
He looked around, his smile disappearing. "So? How do we
handle the matter? What do we do about this so-called auction?
And this meeting next month in London that has attracted so
much attention in the western press?"

Berezhkov looked to Ulanov to make the first suggestion;
he was closer to the archaeological field than either of the two
colonels. Ulanov shrugged. He had fully expected the responsibility and would have been put out otherwise.

"To begin with," he said slowly, "I should think we would
want to be able to enter this auction ourselves, whether we
were invited to, or not. If only to discover who has the treasure,
who is selling it, and—if it isn't the CIA, and I have a feeling
it isn't—then who it is and how they got their hands on it.
And to what extent it reflects on weaknesses in the CIA security
system. And how that knowledge can be of use to us." He
paused and then added, "And if it *is* the CIA, to try and discover
why."

Berezhkov leaned forward. "And as to the meeting in London?"

"That I suggest we attend. I'm sure there will be many there
who have not been officially invited, and more than the museums asked to bid at the auction. In fact, I know there will
be. Turkey, for example, was not asked to bid, but was asked
to attend the London Meeting. I'll go and I'll take along Dr.
Gregor Kovpak, of the Hermitage. He's quite knowledgeable,

I hear. And we'll keep our eyes and ears open and see what we can learn."

Vashugin thought it over and nodded.

"It's a logical first step, at least," he said, and came to his feet, indicating the meeting was over.

Dr. Gregor Kovpak was a tall, well-built, handsome man in his middle forties. His field experience had been detailed in many technical papers published throughout the archaeological world, and his expertise in archaeological matters acknowledged by his fiercest rivals. At the moment Dr. Kovpak was engaged in something far from his true field; he was attempting to produce imitation bones to complete the authentic ones he had discovered in the Ruthenian slopes of the Carpathians while digging for something quite distinct. When assembled, he hoped to have the first skeleton of a baby dinosaur ever found in the Soviet Union. It was not his field, but the doctor felt that by right of discovery he hated to see someone else, even more qualified, complete the job.

He frowned as the telephone rang, held up his hands to the anthropological professor assisting him to indicate the plaster of Paris that covered them. The professor, rightfully resentful of playing second fiddle to a mere archaeologist, and this on the premises of the Zoological Museum, mind you! held up his own hands, equally covered. With a muttered curse for the interruption, Kovpak wiped his hands on his smock and picked up the telephone with two fingers.

"Yes?"

"Gregor?" He recognized the high tones of Alex Pomerenko, the director of the Hermitage Museum, the museum to which he was properly attached. "Are you still fooling around with that zoological thing? Would you drop it and come over to my office? It's taken me quite a while to even locate you!"

"No, damn it, I can't! I'm casting baby dinosaur bones and my hands are full of plaster of Paris!" He glared through the window at the Hermitage across the river, almost as if he could see its director at the window there.

"Disregarding the fact that we pay your salary, not the Zoological Museum," Pomerenko said dryly, "those bones have waited over seventy million years, ever since the Mesozoic

Age, so a few minutes won't hurt. Right now, Gregor. It's important."

The director hung up the telephone to avoid further discussion. Kovpak stared at the receiver a few moments in frustration, considered disregarding the order, and then also hung up, coming to his feet. It would only mean further interruptions, and it was probably better to get the matter over and done with.

"I've got to go over to the Hermitage," he said to a smiling professor, and stalked over to the sink to wash his hands. He dried them, shrugged his way out of the dirty smock and pulled on his jacket. "I'll be back as soon as I can. And leave everything alone until I get back," he added direly, and closed the door behind him. Zoologists! he thought blackly; museum directors! and stamped down the steps of the museum and across the Palast Bridge, feeling the wind from the river on his face and beginning to feel better for it. It was hard to really be angry with Alex Pomerenko, especially on a nice spring day. But not too hard . . .

He pushed into the door to the New Hermitage, where Alex's offices were, and climbed the steps of the broad stairway, walking down the long corridor past the many exhibits he had grown to feel a part of, threading his way through the dense crowds that always filled the museum, wondering as he did so what monumental problem on the part of Alex required his attention so urgently. He probably wants to know what I think he should have for lunch, Kovpak thought dourly; Pomerenko was attempting a diet to counteract the effects of having stopped smoking a few weeks before. Or else it would have to be something equally vital, while my poor little baby dinosaur remains there, all in pieces, waiting for me to put him together and give him birth . . .

The thought made Kovpak smile, and he was in a better mood by the time he came to Pomerenko's office and closed the door to the secretary's cubicle behind him. The secretary smiled and motioned that he could enter without bothering to be announced. It must *really* be important, Kovpak thought. Alex's tailor must be in there with a choice of materials for a new suit Alex wants me to help him select. He bit back a grin, his normal good humor restored, ran a hand through his thick curly hair in a vain attempt to straighten it or give it order, and walked in.

Pomerenko was standing by the window, staring out across the river, obviously passing time until Kovpak arrived. Before the director's wide desk, seated in comfort, was a stocky man with a strong lined face, and a crew cut of pure white hair. An impressive visitor whoever he is, Kovpak thought, and waited to be introduced. But first Pomerenko walked over and closed the door to the outer office, before returning to his desk.

"Major Ulanov," he said, "this is Dr. Gregor Kovpak. Gregor, Major Serge Ulanov."

In mufti, Kovpak thought, and therefore not army. Most probably KGB. And what does the State Security Committee want of us poor scientists at the Hermitage? He came forward to shake hands; the major's handshake was firm and dry. He indicated a chair beside him, waited until Kovpak had been seated, and then took out a package of cigarettes, offering them around. Both men refused, Pomerenko obviously with an effort. Ulanov lit up and came right to the point.

"Dr. Kovpak," he said, "what can you tell me of the Schliemann collection?"

Kovpak frowned, surprised at the question. He was also quite sure that the man facing him knew as much about the Schliemann collection as he did, and most probably a lot more. Still, he was here, presumably to answer questions, not to ask them.

"Well," he began, "it was first discovered by Heinrich Schliemann and his wife, Sophie, in Turkey in—"

Ulanov's hand came up trailing smoke. "No, no. I'm quite familiar with the details of the discovery, and the subsequent history of the treasure, at least up until 1945. I put it badly. What I meant to ask you is, what is your professional opinion of this auction that is being proposed?"

"Auction? What auction?" Kovpak looked at Pomerenko. The museum director shrugged.

"The collection is being offered for auction, Gregor."

"What! When did all this take place?"

"In the last two or three weeks. It's been widely reported."

"And who's offering it?" He turned to the major in apology. "I've been busy with a special project of mine. In fact, I just got back from Uzhgorod on the Czech border a day or so ago. Some bones we found may make us change many of our concepts regarding the life forms of the Mesozoic—" He realized he was straying. "What I'm trying to say is I'm afraid I haven't been paying much attention to the journals lately." He glanced at Pomerenko. "Who's had the collection all this time?"

It was Major Ulanov who answered. "No one knows. In your opinion, Doctor, who do you think has had it?"

Kovpak grinned. "I haven't the faintest. But I can tell you that all my colleagues in the field are convinced that we have it, here at the Hermitage. Either under the sink in my laboratory, or in the desk drawer of my office. And since denial of this idiocy seems pointless, I've let them think what they want." His smile faded as the importance of the major's question came to him. "Why? Doesn't anyone know who is offering it?"

"No," the major said quietly. "It's a blind auction. So far," he added grimly.

Kovpak frowned. "But you must have some ideas—"

Ulanov shrugged and leaned over to brush ash from his cigarette. "In our opinion, Doctor, the treasure has been in the hands of American intelligence ever since the end of the war."

"Based on what evidence, Major?"

"Someday I'll tell you. But for now, it's what we believe. However, I, personally, think it is no longer in their hands. I think someone was clever enough to steal it from them, as they stole it from us. And we are extremely interested in learning how it was done. We think you can be of help to us in this regard."

Kovpak's eyebrows went up. "Me? How?"

"First of all, because of your knowledge in the field. We would like you to read all the news regarding the auction in the journals, speak with friends in other museums, get what information you can. Secondly, there is a meeting to be held in London in a week or so, of directors and curators of many museums around the world. The meeting is to discuss this most unusual auction. Your presence there would not be at all unusual. We would like you to attend."

"I'd be very willing, except I'm in the middle of a project—"

"Gregor!" Pomerenko said threateningly.

Kovpak sighed. "All right," he said at last, sadly. At least it would make a zoological professor happy, as well as the director of the museum where he did, after all, work. And London was a very charming city. "But I'm not—" He paused.

Ulanov smiled, a surprisingly friendly smile from one of such stern features. "An intelligence agent? Well, I am. And I'll be with you." He crushed out his cigarette and came to his feet. "Gentlemen, thank you . . ."

PART TWO

1945

4

BERLIN—April

"The Schliemann treasure?" Captain Sudikoff said. "No, I'm quite sure I never heard of it." He smiled at the elderly sergeant. He was fond of his quartermaster, even if the old boy's head was up in the clouds half the time. "Should I have?"

Sergeant Kolenko also smiled. He took a deep breath, bringing himself back from the euphoria the amazing discovery had brought to him. He was aware of the captain's background and had a profound respect for the younger man despite the other's lack of university education.

"No, I suppose not," he said.

"And exactly what about this treasure of yours? What is it?"

"One of the most valuable collections in the world," the sergeant said, his voice unconsciously taking the tone of a professor at his lectern.

The captain slid from his hammock and took a seat on the corner of a bench that had been added to his quarters; the sergeant also sat down. The captain was pleased with the interruption. As sleep had avoided him, it had been replaced by a feeling of frustration at the many problems peace would bring to the occupying forces, and particularly to their officers. War, whatever its other faults, was relatively simple, the end clearly understood. Still, while war was also horrifying, the discus-

49

sions he and his quartermaster had often had on many odd subjects had tended to lessen that horror. The captain had no notion of what Sergeant Kolenko had in mind with all this talk of a treasure of some sort, but the conversation, at least, had the advantage of postponing thoughts of peace and the problems that came with it.

"Yes?" the captain said in his most encouraging tone.

The sergeant paused to pack a battered pipe with tobacco. He waited until it was burning to his satisfaction, then he crossed his legs comfortably and began.

"The Schliemann treasure," he said, "is supposedly the treasure accumulated by Priam, King of ancient Troy at the time of the war with the Greeks. Homer—" He paused. "You know who Homer was?"

"We're not totally ignorant in the provinces," the captain said dryly, and smiled. "I know who Homer was."

"Good," the sergeant said, not at all abashed by the captain's response, and once again was the professor. "However, what you may or may not know, was that Homer apparently lived— I say apparently, because there is no definite proof of exactly when he did live—in the eighth century before the modern era, that is, before the birth of Christ. Scholars base this fact on references to Homer and his writings in the seventh century B.C.—Archilochus credits Homer with authorship of the *Margites* at that time—and the fact that the Greek alphabet is considered to have been invented about the ninth century B.C. The oldest inscriptions found to date written in the Greek alphabet are those that were found on the island of Thera in 1896, and these are thought to date from the eighth, or at most the ninth century before Christ. Since Homer wrote in the Greek alphabet, it is therefore assumed he lived in the eighth century B.C., give or take fifty years."

"And this has something to do with that treasure?" the captain asked.

"I'm coming to that," the sergeant said in a slightly chiding tone. "As I was saying, prior to the time of Homer, history, or legends, or stories, or poems, were handed down from generation to generation, from father to son, or by professional storytellers, all by word of mouth. Homer, in his *Iliad* and the *Odyssey,* was relating events that took place five or six centuries earlier, and the history of which could only have come down by word of mouth. Many people, therefore, believed the stories to be pure fiction, products of Homer's admittedly brilliant imagination, and that while there probably was a city in the Troad that had had a war with a city in what is now Greece, the facts of that war, or the personalities, were not facts, but merely legend."

"Interesting," the captain said, because to him it was interesting. He always learned something in these conversations with his sergeant quartermaster, and he wondered briefly if, after he was finally released from the army, he might be too old to apply to the university. But he knew it was a dream; the work necessary at home would be even more demanding than the work in Berlin. He brought his attention back to the sergeant.

"Yes. Very interesting," the sergeant said, and puffed thoughtfully on his pipe. "However, there was one man who believed completely in Homer, who believed that Homer, while undoubtedly a man with a great imagination, was still basing his poems on hard fact, even though that fact had undoubtedly suffered somewhat in being repeated as it was being handed down all those hundreds of years by word of mouth. That man was named Heinrich Schliemann, and he dedicated the last quarter-century of his life, and a considerable fortune, to prove that Homer's tales were historical, and not fictional."

"And?" the captain asked, pleased that at last the name Schliemann had come into the story.

"And Schliemann proved it." From the sergeant's triumphant tone one would have thought it was Professor Kolenko who had made the discovery. "He not only discovered the site of the ancient city of Troy, but he found weapons conforming to Homer's description, found the city walls where Homer had said they were, and in general proved—at least to his satisfaction, as well as to the satisfaction of many others, while others still doubted—that Homer had been writing fact."

"And the treasure?" the captain asked.

"Ah, yes. He also discovered the treasure—Priam's treasure—the part that was left after Priam had ransomed the body of Hector and brought it back to Troy for proper burial."

"He found a treasure, eh?" the captain said. "And when did he do all this?"

"In 1873, over seventy years ago."

"And what happened to it?" The captain's initial enthusiasm for the story was waning a bit. He thought the conversation, while certainly educational and interesting to a point, was going no place. It wasn't like the philosophical or even practical discussions he had had in the past with his quartermaster, nor did it seem like a conversation to delay thoughts of future distasteful duties for very long. His mind began to wander to thoughts of burial details and other unpleasant subjects.

"What happened to it was that Schliemann donated it to a German museum," the sergeant said, and now he was beginning to feel pleased at how neatly he had worked the story up to this point. "The museum was here in Berlin. And when the bombing began to destroy museums as well as other govern-ment—not to mention private—buildings, it was apparently decided it would be safer hidden under good, strong concrete. In a bunker."

The captain's eyes widened, his attention now fully caught. The sergeant continued, a faint smile on his lips.

"Under the zoo . . ."

Now the full import of what he had been hearing suddenly struck the captain. "What! No—!"

"Yes, sir," the sergeant said, and grinned widely. "It's out-side your quarters right now."

"I can't believe it." The captain's eyes narrowed. "Is this some sort of joke, Sergeant?"

"No, sir! I don't joke about—"

"Well, if it isn't, bring it in and let's have a look at it!"

"Yes, sir!" The sergeant went out and returned dragging the trunk easily by one handle. The door was closed, the lid thrown back. Captain Sudikoff stared as the sergeant carefully, almost reverently, unwrapped each bundle, placing their contents on the tissue paper along the bench. The captain frowned.

"That's gold?"

"Yes, and almost pure, too. To make the fine wire they had to work it very soft. They didn't have the tools or the techniques for doing delicate work in metals in those days unless they were very soft. They could work metals like bronze—copper and tin—for larger and harder pieces—spears, shields, weap-ons—but for the fine wire used in some of the delicate gold ornaments, they had to work it almost pure."

The captain was still staring at the bench, loaded with brace-

lets, beads, masks, buttons, ornamental singlets. He seemed
dazed by the enormity of the discovery. He also looked as if
he hadn't heard a word of the sergeant's explanation, as indeed
he hadn't. He looked up, staring at his quartermaster.

"What do we do with it?"

"Captain?"

"I said, what do we do with this—this—this stuff, now
that we've found it? Incidentally, who did find it?"

"Two of our troops. I had them looking for food, and they
came up with this trunk."

"Do they know what's in it?"

"Yes, sir." The sergeant suddenly understood the possible
import of the question. "But they have no idea of what it is.
They were going to destroy it, or hand it out for souvenirs to
the others. They won't think anything about it."

"So what do we do with it?" The captain thought a moment
and then shrugged. His first reaction at seeing the treasure was
abating. "Maybe the two had a good idea. Handing it out to
the troops for souvenirs, I mean."

Sergeant Kolenko was shocked. He looked at the captain,
aghast.

"Captain! You can't be serious! You can't do that! It's a
world-famous collection, one of the most valuable that exists!
Break it up? Hand it out piece by piece like—like—" Comparisons failed him. He was rescued by a remembered fact.
"In any event, it's not ours to hand out or to do anything else
with. We have instructions to turn it over."

The captain frowned. "Turn it over? To whom?"

"To the Allied Art Commission. You remember the order.
All recovered art treasures are supposed to be reported and
turned over to the Commission for final disposition after the
war."

Captain Sudikoff snorted. "Nonsense!"

"But our government agreed to it," the sergeant said, and
now that he was at least in what could be construed as partial
disagreement with his superior, he added, "sir!"

"Nonsense!" The captain shook his head in cold determination. "Turn something this valuable over to who? To the
Americans? Who held up helping us in the war until we had
almost bled to death? Who pushed Germany into the war against
us in the first place? And now give them the spoils? Because,

you know, this Allied Commission of yours will never give it back to Germany. No, sir!"

"But—what will we do with it then, sir?"

"I don't know..." The captain thought a moment and then suddenly smiled. "Or, rather, I do know. I'll do what every good army man would do in the same circumstances," he said. "I'll pass the decision up the line..."

BERLIN—May

Hitler was dead, the peace had finally been signed. Those Germans in uniforms, or those whose papers looked too recent to be true, or those recognized by former camp inmates, were on their way to prison camps. The others had been commandeered into clearing the rubble from the shattered streets of Berlin. Even some restaurants and bars had been permitted to open, bringing from their dungeon cellars hidden foods and bottles. The war was over.

But for some the war could never be over, and among them was Hans Gruber. Hans Gruber was an old man, but he was a dedicated German and devoted to Adolph Hitler and his cause, dead or alive. Gruber was uneducated and he knew nothing of politics, but he did know that only under the Nazis had he known a feeling of self-fulfillment, of being part of something he sensed was important.

Before the beginning of the bombings, when the zoological station in the Tiergarten was still in normal operation, Gruber had been a porter there. When the need for bunkers beneath important buildings was evidenced by the increased death and destruction that were beginning to rain upon the city despite the promises of Reichmarshal Goering, Gruber willingly helped in the construction of the one that had been constructed in the area of the elephant cages, poking its bulk in the air. And when the Schliemann treasure had been brought to the bunker and stored in its little niche for safekeeping, Hans Gruber had helped, and had even been the one to cover the hole in the wall with plaster to hide any evidence of its location. And when the final hour had come before fleeing with the others before the Russian advance, it was Gruber who had hastily piled rubbish against the niche. The bombardment had shaken the walls and brought down the thin shell of plaster that had protected the cavelike opening. It was a poor attempt and Gruber was aware of it, but one could scarcely go running down the rubble-strewn streets with a trunk in one's arms. Carrying one's life down those dangerous streets was task enough.

Now, as one of the workers pressed into the gargantuan job of clearing some of that rubble, Gruber was aware that the treasure, while it had been discovered, still remained in the quarters of the Russian captain. Each day, as he lined up with the others to receive his shovel, he would peer past the issuing quartermaster and see the trunk still in the corner of the captain's room. Its hasp had been repaired and rope had been wrapped around it in profusion, but there it was. Gruber did not understand why the trunk remained, why it had not been removed to a safer place. Still, it never occurred to him that he might do something about it.

Until one day, while piling broken building stone into a truck, he noticed that a new member of the work crew was Major Schurz. Gruber walked over, amazed to find the other man alive, and not only alive, but free, not in prison as a war criminal. Still, Gruber knew when he stopped to think about it that hundreds, no, thousands of SS had simply changed clothes and were now utilizing identity cards they had prepared long before.

"Major!" he said, but before he could say more, the other man had glared him to silence. He dropped his voice. "I'm sorry. I didn't think. Don't you remember me? Hans Gruber. I was a porter at the zoo. I was there in the bunker, when you brought that trunk. Don't you remember? I was the one who plastered over the hole."

"I remember," Schurz said shortly, and began to turn away. He didn't remember at all, nor did he want to. Idiots who called out his former rank in the SS with Russians all over the place, were people he could do without.

"Maj—I mean, what do I call you?"

Schurz was on the point of telling the old man he would rather not be called anything at all by the old fool, but one of the Russian troops overseeing that portion of the clean-up operation was staring at them. It would not do to start a discussion or an argument at this moment.

"My name is Kurt. Now, leave me alone."

"But, Kurt—"

"Later!" Schurz said savagely, and walked away.

Gruber looked after him, sighed and went back to his job. But after work, when they had turned in their equipment and been given chits for their labor, he followed the major down the street and caught up with him a short distance away.

"You said, later—"

Schurz shook his head in irritation. Was he going to be plagued by this maniac leech all his life? He looked around. At least if he had to talk to this incredible cretin, they were alone and unobserved.

"What do you want?"

"The trunk, you remember? The one you brought to the bunker for hiding? The one I helped hide?"

"What about it?"

"It's still there. Oh, they found where it was hidden, I don't know how, but it's still there. In the captain's quarters. It's all tied up with rope."

"So?"

Gruber looked around and then wet his lips. "I thought maybe—" He paused, realizing how absurd his thought had been.

"You thought what?"

"I thought—maybe you could figure a way to get it away from them." Even as he said it he knew he sounded ridiculous and tried to give the main reason he had attempted such a foolish comment. "It's valuable, isn't it?"

Schurz laughed, a short, humorless laugh.

"It's more than valuable. It's invaluable. What do you suggest, old man? That I just go in and ask for it? Say it's an old trunk that has sentimental value for me? Or ask for it instead of a work chit? Say I could use it to keep my extensive wardrobe of old uniforms in?" He shook his head in disgust. "You're a fool, old man. Go home."

"I just thought—"

"Don't think," Schurz said harshly. "Go home." He turned and walked away. Gruber looked after him a moment, sighed, and also started slowly walking toward his room.

But while he had admonished the old man for thinking, ex-Major Kurt Schurz could not help but think, himself. It would be a great coup to get the treasure from under the noses of the

Russian pigs! Was it possible they didn't know the value of what they had in their possession? And if they knew it, why was it still sitting in the bunker? Why hadn't it been shipped east with all the other things, captured arms, the factories that were being dismantled and piled on freight cars for Russia, the tons of other goods that left the city for the east each day? One thing was sure; the treasure wouldn't remain in the bunker forever. The Russian troops were being rotated. It was only a matter of time, and probably very little time, before the crew in the bunker would be relieved and sent home, and it was almost positive that when that day came, the trunk would go with them. If it didn't go sooner.

And it was pointless, and even stupid, to think the Russians might not know the value of what was in the trunk. Otherwise why would it be in the captain's personal quarters, all bound up with rope? Certainly not for the trunk itself—it wouldn't serve as a portmanteau to carry anything very heavy, the bottom would fall out. No, the trunk still contained the treasure, and the Russians were waiting—for what? Orders, probably, Schurz thought with a grim smile, remembering his own army days. Which could come any day. Would it be possible to take it by force, to hijack it, say on the way from the bunker to the train when those orders finally came through? Schurz smiled sourly at the thought of himself, possibly aided by Gruber and others of the shovel brigade, attacking a troop-carrier full of armed soldiers. Ridiculous. No, the only way to get the trunk would be by guile, not by force.

Assuming the Russians were merely waiting for orders to move the trunk, when would those orders come? If they should come—Schurz stopped dead in his tracks. *If they should come from us! If the orders should come from us!* But then the euphoria occasioned by the daring idea began to fade as the practicality of the situation took hold. First there was the matter of locating the man he needed before the real orders came through. He put aside all thoughts of supper and hurried toward the small bar where he and others of his friends met for an occasional drink, and to speak—softly—of plans, or, rather, hopes for the future.

The bar was fairly busy. It was one of the few permitted to operate by the occupation forces as a means of reducing the pressures of the horrendous task facing the remaining residents of the battered city. It was a place where food chits could be traded for whiskey or beer or vodka or even cigarettes, although these were never smoked, being more valuable for their barter worth than for the remembered pleasure of tobacco. It was a place where the spoils of barter could be exchanged for articles which the Allied troops held dear; German helmets, bayonets, even pistols, even though pistols were not supposed to be in the hands of any German except the police; anything that might serve as a true souvenir of the city and its fall. Schurz pushed through to a corner, leaning over the occupants, and then slid in beside them as being less noticeable. He spoke in a low tone.

"Petterssen," he said. "Is he still around?"

"I think so," someone said, and shrugged. "It's almost impossible to leave."

"And getting worse," another voice said gloomily.

Someone else laughed. "You'd think Petterssen would have no trouble. That Swede could write his own exit permit with his eyes closed, using a nail and piss for ink, and the border guards would pass him through like royalty. Why do you want him?"

"Important business," Schurz said, and wondered with a sudden touch of panic if possibly Petterssen had already left the city. But there was no point in thinking of that. If Petterssen was gone, or could not be located, the entire scheme was up the chimney in any event. He waved aside the offer of a drink from one of the men. "How do I get in touch with him?"

"You mean, if he's still here. I haven't seen him." The man shrugged. "Well, we can pass the word, that's about all we can do. Where are you living?"

"I have a room in the Goeringstrasse"—Schurz smiled grimly—"what *was* the Goeringstrasse. It's probably the Trumanstrasse, or the Stalinstrasse by now. Number 18, first floor in the back on the right. Make it fast, can you? It's very important."

"Important for you? Or for the party?"

"For both," Schurz said, and started to stand up. He thought a moment and then sat down again. There was also the question of money. The people who had formed ODESSA, the organization dedicated to helping keep the party alive, were all big industrialists and had plenty of it, but it might be difficult to

contact them. And there would be need to contact someone
trustworthy in Wismar, or Barth, or any one of the Baltic
ports—but he could be doing all this while waiting for Petterssen. He stood again, this time to stay on his feet. "Very
much for both," he repeated, almost to himself, and walked
from the bar.

It was three nights later, when Schurz had about abandoned
hope and was cursing Gruber for ever having put the idea in
his head, that Jan Petterssen appeared at Schurz's room. He
was a very thin, extremely tall man with a horselike, long, sad
face, and a shock of bright yellow hair that needed cutting
badly, tucked out of sight under a ragged stocking cap. Schurz
could hardly conceal his relief at sight of the man; by now he
had been sure that Petterssen was either dead or long gone from
the country. He sat his guest down, brought out a bottle of
vodka traded for a genuine Nazi officer's peaked cap, lightning
insignia and all—his own, but the drunken Russian soldier had
had no idea of that, of course—and asked Petterssen why he
was still around. Petterssen shrugged sadly.

"My face," he said wearily. "My height. My hair. They
must be looking for me. It is easy enough to forge papers"—
Petterssen had forged all the pound notes and the dollar bills
printed in Germany, he spoke five languages fluently in addition to his native Swedish, and could handle any one of them
on a bit of paper so that one would swear it was authentic—
"but at every border crossing they are looking for me. They
must be looking for me! They will want me for a war criminal,
can you imagine? Me? An artist?" He shook his head at the
patent unfairness of it all and took a healthy drink from the
bottle. "I almost didn't come here. I go out very little. But it's
only a question of time before I'm caught, I suppose. Very
unfair . . . anyway, they told me it was important, so I came.
Bent over to look like an old man to look short. It hurt my
back." He shrugged again and took another drink from the
bottle.

Schurz was quite sure the occupying forces had more important people to search for than Jan Petterssen, but he could
see no advantage to telling the Swede that. At least it had kept
the forger in Berlin.

"It *is* important, very important," he said and leaned forward, gently removing the bottle from Petterssen's fingers. He wanted the man sober, at least until they had discussed the matter thoroughly. "I can get you out of the country with me. We'll have to take a small case with us—"

"A small case? What will be inside it?"

"A treasure in gold." Schurz did not feel it necessary to explain that it was not bullion, not something readily transferable into cash. "All you have to do is to forge some papers. In Russian. Can you do it?"

The vodka had taken a bit of the lugubrious expression from the narrow equine face. The sadness there was replaced with the pride of the artisan.

"Of course."

"You still have your pens?"

"Not on me, for God's sake! They'd shoot me on the spot if they ever caught me with those in my possession."

"But they're safe?"

"Yes."

"And paper?"

"I have enough if you don't want a book written."

"Good!" Schurz took a deep breath and then thought a moment. He had long since thought of the possibility that Petterssen might also be useful in the matter of the financing of the project. "Do you also still have some of that counterfeit money—pounds or dollars, or whatever?"

Petterssen shook his head. "No. Not even samples." Schurz bit back his disappointment. It would mean trying to locate one of the industrial members of ODESSA, and that would take valuable time. He should have been doing that before, but his time had been taken up with the matter of the boat, and besides, he hadn't really believed in the true possibility of the project. Damn!

Petterssen reached over and took the bottle of vodka from Schurz's hand, drinking deeply.

"But I've got plenty of good money, real money," he went on. The vodka had relaxed him completely, made him expansive. He grinned. "I insisted upon payment in American dollars before I forged the foreign currency. Otherwise I would have been working for myself, if you see what I mean." The smile disappeared as quickly as it had come, replaced by a thoughtful frown. His eyes narrowed as he studied Schurz. "But if you've got gold—bullion—"

"We need a boat," Schurz said flatly. "It's the only way to go and take the gold with us. I have someone who can travel from here to the Baltic without suspicion. He arranges the purchase of fish for the commissaries. He can arrange a boat for us for when we need it. But he says he knows the fishermen up there. They won't rent or sell a boat for gold. Most of them have no way to tell if the gold is genuine or not. They've never seen any in their lives. They want American dollars or English pounds. I thought—"

"You thought they might be taken in by my counterfeit. They would have, too, with my stuff," Petterssen said with pride, but then his face fell. "Only I have none."

"You have dollars," Schurz said and his voice was cold. "I want enough of them to arrange the boat. You'll be paid. With interest."

Petterssen looked at him. "How can I be sure?"

"Because I say so." Schurz was beginning to get irritated. "Besides, you want to get out of Germany, don't you? As you say, it's only a question of time before they pick you up, and then—" He made a gesture, his hand across his throat and then swiftly raised in the air. Petterssen winced. There was a profound tone of truth in Schurz's tone of voice, as there should have been since the threat was true for himself whether or not it was for the tall Swede.

"I know," Petterssen said. The sadness had returned to his face. He raised the bottle; Schurz made no attempt to stop him. The tall Swede drank, put the bottle down and pushed it to one side, ready to properly discuss the matter. "Where will we be going?"

"Sweden," Schurz said with assurance. "Your home." In the past few days he had done a good deal of planning, even if most of it was ephemeral, depending as it did on locating Petterssen. "ODESSA has members there, and there is still sympathy for us and our cause among many influential people there. We can both be safe there."

Petterssen wet his lips. "And rich." He made it a statement, not a question.

"And very rich," Schurz said, agreeing, and wondered that a man as clever with his hands as Jan Petterssen could possibly not realize he would never get off the boat in his country. "And very rich," Schurz repeated.

The tall Swede nodded and leaned back, narrowing his eyes, concentrating on the paper he was about to begin forging in his mind's eye.

"All right," he said, once again the artisan. "What papers will you need, and what do you want them to say?"

5

The Russian soldier-messenger was on the verge of descending the few bunker steps when he turned at a tap upon his shoulder, one hand automatically falling to the butt of his service revolver, staring suspiciously at the ragged, cringing figure who had stopped him.

"What is it?"

The man smiled an obsequious smile that clearly indicated he did not understand the other, and held out a small bundle of official-looking papers, neatly tied with ribbon. "You dropped this." He pointed to the dispatch bag and then to the ground.

"Oh." The soldier understood the gesture if not the language. He shoved the papers into the dispatch bag. "Thanks." Without another word he turned and trotted down the bunker steps. Behind him Schurz watched him turn a corner and disappear, then with a shrug he returned to his shovel. Now all he could do was to wait. And hope the real papers for the disposition of the treasure did not come through in the next two days. A sudden chilling thought came—if the real papers did come through before then, he hoped the soldier-messenger would not be able to remember who had given him the bundle of dropped papers. Possibly they should have included in the instructions an order to disregard any other directives . . . but that, too, could have been risky, inviting suspicion. Ah, well, Schurz thought with a rueful smile, stealing something this important could scarcely fail to involve risk of some sort.

"And about bloody time!" Sudikoff said aloud with a combination of relief and irritation. "My God, how did we ever manage to win this war, anyway? With all the bureaucracy? Three weeks to get a simple answer to a simple question!" He studied the orders again. They were written in a crabbed longhand, and signed with a scrawl that was impossible to decipher, although the neatly printed title of Colonel General L. Schvicheva was easily seen below, as well as the title and command printed on top of the sheet. Fortunately the instructions themselves were clear and understandable. The captain nodded and called out to the sergeant in the outer office. Sergeant Kolenko hurried in.

"Close the door," the captain said. He leaned back, smiling broadly. "We've finally gotten our orders to ship out that treasure of yours, Sergeant. Thank God! I was getting nervous about having the stuff here."

"Oh," the sergeant said, interested. "To the Allied Art Commission, I suppose?"

"You suppose wrong," the captain said, and laughed. "To Russia."

"But—"

The captain's smile faded, replaced by a frown. "Would you care to go against the orders of General Schvicheva? Who apparently agrees with me about who the treasure should belong to? And who is going to get it? Eh?"

"No, sir!"

"I thought not," the captain said dryly. He tapped the instructions. "Now, the orders are clear enough. And will require a little hustle on your part. They want the treasure handled with extreme care, to be protected against any contingency. They want it placed in a case made of thin welded sheets of steel. This case is then to be fitted inside a wooden box of approximately the same size, and in addition to being securely nailed shut, they want it banded about with steel bands for shipping. Is that all clear?"

"...bands for shipping..." the sergeant said, and busily

scribbled the instructions on a bit of paper he had taken from his pocket.

"And tear up that paper!" the captain said testily. He had already decided to destroy the instructions themselves once they had been carried out. While such orders had not been included in the General's crabbed handwriting, Captain Sudikoff imagined he could read between the lines. He looked at the sergeant with authority. "This matter is to be kept completely secret, no notes, nothing in writing. There's been too much loose talk among our men and the other Allied troops as it is. Camaraderie is all well and good, but it's no way to keep secrets. Which means that all information about the treasure and the shipment is to be kept from our troops and our officers, as well. There are to be no telephone calls regarding the matter, and no telegraphed inquiries or questions. Nothing! Is that clear?"

"Yes, sir." The sergeant had been tearing the paper he had been writing on into shreds; he dropped those into an ashtray and lit it with a match, watching the flames. He then tucked his pencil into his sleeve pocket. "But I'll have to get one of the men to make up the steel case—"

"You get the steel sheets cut to the right size, and get the welding equipment from the engineers," the captain said, "and I'll make the case. We do learn something in technical school," he added with a smile, "even if we don't learn when Homer was born."

"Yes, sir." The sergeant paused. "And when the crate is ready for shipment?"

The captain referred to the instructions again, and nodded.

"The case is to be marked 'Captured Medical Equipment' and is to be shipped out on the train that leaves around six tomorrow afternoon from the Stuttgartbahnhof for Leningrad. It is to be placed in the guard's van—*not* in any of the regular freight cars—and it is to be released only to a Colonel Major Boris Golobev or his representatives, on written indentification, at whatever point the major cares to take delivery. Those instructions are to be given to the train officials verbally, understand? But impressed upon them."

"Yes, sir. Impressed upon them. Verbally. Golobev or his representatives."

"*Colonel Major* Golobev," the captain said reprovingly.

"Yes, sir."

"And now," the captain said, pleased to be nearing the end of his custodianship of the treasure, and happy that it was not being sent to the Allied Art Commission, "get a move on having the proper steel sheets cut to size, and getting the welding equipment in here. And start looking for wood for the crate."

"Yes, sir!" said Sergeant Kolenko, and left the room to get on with it, secretly pleased, despite his previous objections and also despite the Allied agreements, that the treasure was actually going to his country.

To Kurt Schurz, the scene at the Stuttgartbahnhof with its appearance of total confusion, was very reassuring. Lorries of all sizes had violated the once-privileged platforms where only passengers had been allowed, and were drawn up before the gaping doors of freight cars discharging into them every imaginable type of matériel; men and women were busy on the different platforms hoisting smaller bundles into similar cars; soldiers being recycled were milling about before the trains roughly marked in chalk as being destined for Moscow, for Kiev, for Leningrad, trying to locate their units; officers with lists were frantically attempting to keep track of the various items being crammed into the cars. Above, the sun's final rays crept in through the open spaces where the glass cover of the station had long since been blasted to bits. On the platform for the six o'clock train for Leningrad, Kurt Schurz walked slowly along, hoping that in that atmosphere of kinetic anarchy, he and his tall companion might pass relatively unnoticed.

At his side Petterssen shuffled along resignedly, almost as if he were walking into assured capture and execution. Had the Russians really been actively looking for the man, Schurz thought dourly, that look of guilt on the horselike idiot face would almost be enough to guarantee capture. The stocky ex-major also thought how happy he would be when his association with the tall Swede was finally ended—and the tall Swede ended as well. While forging the necessary letters, releases, passes, and other papers Petterssen had been fine, but once that work had been completed, the big man's nervous fears had come close to driving Schurz to distraction. Well, Schurz thought as he approached the train, one way or another it will soon be over. He didn't know if that was a comforting thought or not.

Both men were dressed in neat dark suits, black polished shoes, white shirts and dark neckties, and each wore upon his head a black homburg. The outfits, purchased on the black market and tailored by an ex-corporal in the SS, had cost nearly as much as the boat Schurz had arranged in Warnemünde on the Baltic coast, almost as much as the car he had gone to so much trouble to arrange to meet them in Bad Freienwalde; the members of ODESSA, while dedicated, still wanted as much as they could get for taking chances. Still, Schurz was certain, the clothing was vitally necessary; the men they wanted to look like wore just such identifying clothes. And if the ploy failed, what difference did it really make what the clothes cost, or the boat, or the use of the car? In the first place the money had been Petterssen's; and in the second they would not require money in the place where they would end up. The dead spent little.

Freight doors were being slammed; troops were hurrying into the nearest cars. An official was standing looking at a pocket watch, almost as if the trains ever departed on time. Schurz frowned. Where was the crate? Had it been loaded into the guard's van before his arrival? But he had been there for some time, walking about looking very official himself, and had not seen it. He swallowed. His appearance with the abnormally tall and tragic-looking Petterssen on the rapidly-emptying platform was beginning to become noticeable. Should they board the train in the hope that the crate was already in the guard's van? And if it wasn't? Then everything would have been lost; the crate would leave on a train while they were being carried to a different place. Plus the fact that their masquerade could well be discovered when they came to the guard's van to collect a crate that was not there. *Damn!* Where the devil was the *verdamnt* crate?

The official was looking rather pointedly in their direction; he made a gesture clearly indicating that the train was about to leave and that they should board. Schurz put one foot on the lower step of the car and then paused. The official began walking purposefully in their direction. And then, at last, a lorry came charging through the makeshift entrance of the Bahnhof with a roar, blasting its horn. The official paused and turned in the direction of the disturbance. The horn blasted again, echoing in the huge domed hall, directing him to pay attention. He moved toward the large truck. There was a conference at its side, and then Schurz saw three men descend from the cab. Two of them began to drag a heavy crate from the tailgate of the lorry, while the third, a sergeant with a pipe, spoke to the official. A few minutes of conversation and the official nodded. The crate was shoved into the guard's van and the door closed. Schurz tried not to show his relief. He tugged at Petterssen's sleeve and the two men climbed aboard.

It was almost unnecessary to show their identity cards; the soldier-guard easily recognized the black suits and homburgs for what they were supposed to be, and glanced at the cards perfunctorily. He led them without words to a crowded compartment. The sight of the two men was enough. The soldiers within knew authority, and dangerous authority, when they saw it. They got up, wearily dragging their gear from the overhead racks and filed out to search for other accommodations elsewhere on the crowded train.

If the guard thought it strange that the two men had no luggage, he said nothing but was about to leave when Schurz cleared his throat loudly and pinched Petterssen painfully through his sleeve. The tall man looked surprised for a moment, and then remembered his instructions.

"Bad Freienwalde," he said, trying to keep his voice from breaking. "Advise us when we're near."

"Right," the guard said, and backed out, sliding the compartment door shut. Shurz waited tensely for an outcry, for some action from the officials who would have been advised by the guard that the two men were fakes, probably spies, but nothing happened. He wiped his sweaty palms on his trousers and sat down at the window. Petterssen sat across from him for a brief moment, and then got up to sit beside him as being more conducive to quiet conversation.

"Now what?" he asked nervously.

"Now we keep to the plan," Schurz said in an equally low voice. "We get off at Bad Freienwalde and take the crate with us. And try not to look as if you were climbing a scaffold—" It had been the wrong thing to say; Petterssen looked even more frightened than before. Schurz tried to make amends; Petterssen was still necessary. "Look," he added in a conciliatory tone, "everything is working fine! When we get to Bad Freienwalde, just say what you were told to say. Understand?"

"It'll never work . . ."

"What do you mean? It *is* working, damn it!" God, if only

he spoke Russian and didn't need the services of this monstrous idiot any longer! "It's working fine. You're on a train heading out of Berlin, aren't you?"

"Heading toward Russia..."

"Except we're not going to Russia! Good God!" Petterssen knew as well as he did exactly what the plan was, but the maniac insisted upon acting as if there wasn't any plan at all, or as if it hadn't been working fine up to then. If the idiot managed to ruin things at Bad Freienwalde, Schurz promised himself, he would see to it that the bastard hanged, if he had to occupy the adjoining gallows himself! Schurz brought his temper under control. One undisciplined conspirator was enough—was too much. "When we get to Bad Freienwalde," he said quietly, "just say what you were told to say. Don't embellish. Don't invent." Petterssen opened his mouth; Schurz spoke again before the big man could say anything. "And keep quiet now," he added coldly, "until we get there."

The two leaned back, with Petterssen trying his best to block from his mind the terrifying thought of facing the Russian train official in the guard's van, wondering how he could possibly say his little piece without stammering and giving the whole show away. What was he doing here, anyway, dressed up like a Russian security man? He was not an actor. He was an artist, one of the finest engravers in the world! The Americans, or even the Russians, should have welcomed him with open arms, as they did Von Braun and the other scientists that the two countries had divided up like a loaf of bread. What had he done that was so bad in comparison to what the scientists had done against the Allies? It was all very unfair...

Outside the train window the shadows darkened across the battered city and its outskirts, throwing jagged ruins of buildings in stark silhouette against the fading sky, and with a light every now and then from some room, high up in some destroyed building, rehabilitated by some energetic or adventurous—or desperate—soul who had not only managed access to the aerie, but who had also managed to run an electric line from some main somewhere. Survival! Schurz thought, and felt proud of his fellow countrymen. In time, with the help of finances from treasures such as the Schliemann gold, they would come back. It would take time, but time was the one thing that never ran out.

The soldier-guard put his head in the compartment. "Bad Freienwalde in five minutes."

The two men nodded and came to their feet. Petterssen took a deep breath and at Schurz's urging, led the way through the crowded train toward the guard's van. Soldiers lined the corridors, drawing back from the dark-suited civilians unconsciously, as if contact with them might somehow contaminate, or at least compromise. Card games were in progress in the compartments, the air was full of smoke. The advantages of victory, Schurz thought bitterly; the ability to smoke cigarettes rather than the need to hoard them, or trade them for food, or use them for currency! He put the unproductive thought aside and reached past a paralyzed Petterssen to rap sharply on the door of the guard's van, a peremptory knock that advertised authority. The inquiring face of the train official peered out. He recognized the two men from the platform and his expression froze into one of polite immobility.

Schurz poked Petterssen sharply in the back. The tall man seemed to waken, as from a dream, wetting his lips nervously. "A crate . . ." he began, and swallowed the next words, pointing instead to the box near the outer door.

The official, fortunately, found nothing wrong. He had been expecting to be approached regarding the mysterious crate, and he was only too happy to be rid of it and any responsibility it might represent. And also to be rid of the men from the NKVD, as these two were bound to be. Still, there were the necessary formalities.

"You have the proper papers?"

Petterssen managed to find them in a pocket and handed them over. The official checked them carefully and then nodded. He made a move to tuck them in his pocket but Schurz reached around his taller companion, picked them from the official's hand, and put them in his own pocket, instead. For a moment the train official thought to object, but then he shrugged. Let them take their "Captured Medical Equipment" and be damned to them, although the official knew very well that while the contents of the strange crate had undoubtedly been captured, or at least liberated, they were certainly not medical anything. More probably they were things taken from a chalet or castle and were about to decorate the apartment of some NKVD official, or more likely the apartment of his mistress. Although why, in that case, they would be getting off in Bad Freienwalde only a short distance from Berlin, was a mystery. Still, to ask too many questions of the NKVD—or any questions at all—was to invite disaster. And, after all, they did have the proper papers, which was the important thing. His skirts, at least, were clear. The official nodded at the other two and began to wrestle the heavy crate to the door sill itself, while beneath their feet they could feel the strain as the train began to brake.

The three stood, swaying with the motion of the slowing train, and then almost lost their balance as the train came to an abrupt stop. The door slid back. A dark sedan, very official looking, seemed to appear out of the blackness as if by legerdemain. Behind it, four or five railway cars back, the faint lights of the small station could be seen flickering uncertainly in the night. The car came to a stop across from the open van door. Its lights were extinguished and a man, also dressed in dark clothes but with a peaked cap instead of a homburg, stepped down and approached the train. Petterssen hurried down the steps, eager to be done with the affair, and went to pull the heavy crate from the platform of the van. Schurz gave him another sharp and painful poke in the kidneys. Petterssen turned, surprised and a bit angered by the unwarranted blow, and then found that in the meanwhile the trainman and the chauffeur between them had managed to get the crate down and were carrying it toward the car.

"Idiot!" Schurz said beneath his breath, and walked quickly to the car, climbing into the rear seat. Petterssen finally seemed to realize his near-gaffe and followed Schurz to the car, getting in and closing the door after him. Behind them they could hear the sounds of the crate being stored into the large trunk of the car. There was the slam of the trunk lid, the chauffeur returned to the front seat of the car, his headlights came on revealing the small flags of a general officer mounted on the front fenders. His motor started; the car slid into the darkness. Behind them they could hear the tortured scream of the engine's whistle as the train began to move again.

In the car there was silence for a moment, then Schurz burst into laughter, clapping his hands in glee. *They had done it! They had actually done it!* He looked over at Petterssen sitting in one corner of the seat, squeezed there as if to hide from his own thoughts, and punched him lightly on one arm.

"Well?" he demanded triumphantly. "Well?"

"We're not there, yet . . ."

"Oh, my God!" At least, Schurz thought, there was the satisfaction of knowing that before long he would be finished with this pessimistic clown. Once the lights of Trelleborg in Sweden could be seen from the boat, one stab and the chains he had asked to be put aboard would be used to weight down the idiot's body. And for Jan Petterssen there would be no more worries, no more fears. Schurz knew it would be work getting the big man's body over the rail, especially with the chains, but it would be a labor of love. He leaned forward, pushing back the glass between the driver's seat and his own, speaking in a low voice.

"Heil Hitler . . ."

"Heil Hitler."

"Any trouble?"

"No. Only the car must be back before dawn. Lucky you weren't too late." The man smiled, a mischievous smile, etched by the lights of the dashboard. He spoke over his shoulder. "The General will be bouncing up and down on his girl friend till then. Any trouble at your end?"

"Not so far." Schurz could not help but glance at Petterssen as he spoke. The tall man was staring from the car window into the night as if totally oblivious to the coversation. Schurz turned back to the driver. "You spoke to the captain?"

"Sneller? Yes. He came through two days ago with a load of fish on his way to Berlin. He'll meet us at the *fischer landungsplatz;* the boat's called the *Linderndsee.*"

"The Balmy Sea, eh? A good name," Schurz said. "Let's hope it's an omen."

"Yes," the driver said, and added, "You have the balance of the money?"

"We have it."

"Good. As I understand it, the boat has enough fuel, but nothing extra, so I don't imagine you can be joy-riding on your way there." The driver glanced over his shoulder at the still figure in the corner of the rear seat. Petterssen had closed his eyes. There was a grimace as of pain on his equinelike face. The driver lowered his voice even more, as if Petterssen might be asleep and he did not want to disturb him. "Has he been all right?"

"He's been fine," Schurz said expressionlessly. "No problem."

"That's good," the driver said, and turned his attention back to the road. They sped through the darkness toward Warnemünde on the Baltic coast, four hours away.

6

THE BALTIC—May

The outskirts of Rostock rose about them in the dark; they sped through the cobbled streets, past the university and the darkened dormitory buildings, so recently barracks, and took the road that headed along the estuary to Warnemünde, eight miles away. Their trip had been undisturbed by road checks, although Schurz with his false identity papers had been fully prepared for them; the war was too newly over for the Allied forces to be able to organize the proper controls at any but the accesses to major cities. Both Schurz and Petterssen had napped during the journey. Now they both came awake, Schurz refreshed by the brief respite. Petterssen seemingly made more dubious as to the success, or even the fitness, of their venture the closer they came to the sea.

The car crept past the deserted Warnemünde ferry dock, not yet back in operation to Denmark, and took a side road that led eventually past net-hung docks. In the distance behind them the faint lights of Warnemünde itself could barely be seen, throwing into shadow the few dock cranes that had not been damaged or destroyed in the war. The car edged along, its headlights dimmed, its driver looking anxiously about him. A sudden beam of a flashlight, instantly extinguished, gave him direction. A moment later they had pulled up before a small

74

nondescript boat swaying against its stays at dockside. A man came from the shadows, examining them by the lights of the lowered headlights as they climbed from the car. The driver also got down and together with Schurz managed to get the heavy crate from the car's trunk and across the narrow gang-plank to the dock of the boat, while Petterssen stood helplessly by. This done, the driver returned to his car and with a brief wave of his hand and a whispered "Heil Hitler," backed around and sped off for the main highway and the road south. Their contact beckoned. Schurz, trailed by a dazed Petterssen, fol-lowed the man to a tiny cabin located forward and below decks.

Inside the cabin, with its close-fitting door closed and the blackout curtains tightly drawn, the man lit a small lamp con-nected to a gas bottle, blew out the match, and then turned to face the two of them with a smile on his bearded lips. Schurz returned the smile.

"Hello, Captain Sneller. It's been a while."

"Hello, Major. It has, indeed."

Schurz glanced around the small cabin and then sat down on a pivoting pilot's chair set before a small table, swivelling about in satisfaction. Across from him Petterssen sank down on the cabin's single bunk, holding his head in his hands. Sneller considered the tall man a moment and then looked at Schurz queryingly.

"A touch of nerves," Schurz said disinterestedly. "It'll pass." He dismissed the question of Petterssen and smiled at Sneller. "How do you like being a fisherman, Captain?"

Sneller shrugged lightly. "I was a fisherman before I was a U-boat captain," he said, and smiled. "And lucky for you, or you'd still be shoveling bricks in Berlin. And lucky for me, too. Our idiot conquerors can't picture a U-boat commander working with his hands, or with fishing nets." His smile faded. "Major—"

"Yes?"

"I could go with you, you know. Bring the boat back. It would be much cheaper for you—"

Schurz smiled a cold smile. "That wasn't our deal, Captain."

"I know, but do you think you can make it across in this boat with only—?" He jerked a thumb in the direction of the tall man on the bunk. Petterssen was paying no attention to the men or their conversation. He remained, head in hands, staring disconsolately at the deck.

"I can do it alone," Schurz said, confidentially. "I've had experience with boats or I wouldn't have chosen to go this way. I can read a chart and it's a simple gasoline engine, isn't it?"

"It is, but—"

"No buts, Captain."

Sneller shrugged, as if refusing any further responsibility.

"If you say so, Major. Now, the controls are on the bridge"—he pointed to the overhead of the cabin—"up there. I'll show you when we're through in here. There's enough gasoline to get you there, but none to spare. Fuel is hard to get. But there is a full tank of cooking gas here for the lamp or the stove, if you want to do any cooking—"

"We won't."

"If you say so, Major. Then I think that's all. Now"—Sneller cleared his throat—"there's the matter of the balance of the money . . ."

"No problem," Schurz said expansively. He leaned over, taking Petterssen's wallet from the other's inner pocket without asking permission. Petterssen made no move. Schurz opened the wallet, extracted some notes, counted the proper amount, and handed it over.

Sneller also counted the money, and smiled as he tucked the bills into a pocket of his heavy pea jacket. "You have a walking bank with you, eh?"

"More or less." Schurz tucked the depleted wallet into his own pocket and looked around. "Any schnapps on board?"

Sneller pointed. "There's plenty in the locker, there. But I'd take it easy if I were you. It's a long trip in a boat this small, and there are Danish patrols I know of, and undoubtedly Swedish ones as well."

"It isn't for me—" Schurz tilted his head toward the silent figure on the bunk. Sneller nodded in understanding. Schurz dismissed the subject and looked at Sneller calmly. "Now, what were you saying about patrols?"

"Let's go up on the bridge—"

The two men left the cabin, closing the door behind them. In the cabin Petterssen raised his head to stare after them a moment, and then put his head back in his hands.

The two men climbed to the deck. A short companionway took them to the small bridge mounted above the single cabin.

Blackout curtains had been strung over the glass before the wheel. Sneller pulled them shut and flashed his flashlight around in the blackness. It stopped on a button.

"There's the engine starter. Next to it is a choke if you need it."

"Good. Now, about those patrols—"

"The accelerator, there. It pulls in and out. Too far in for slowing and it stalls."

"I'm impressed," Schurz said, trying not to sound savage. "Now, about those patrols?"

Sneller bit back a superior smile; his flashlight moved to the chart table at the left of the wheel. Captain Sneller leaned over it, pointing.

"Here's where we are: Warnemünde. Now, the Danes have a small fleet of patrol boats, at least four that we know of, or that is to say, four that patrol in this area. They come every six hours, right on schedule. You'd think they were German the way they stick to routine! Anyway, one comes from the north every six hours, and another from the west. They all turn at Gedser lighthouse—here"—his finger rested on a small spit of land almost directly across the narrow arm of the Baltic from the estuary where they were—"and then go back the way they came."

Schurz frowned. "They meet here? At the Gedser lighthouse?"

"No." The captain smiled, a rather grim smile. "They're foolish, but not all that foolish. They arrive at alternate periods, three hours apart. Somehow they seem to feel that covers all possible conditions." Sneller sounded as if he wished the ships that had come under the scan of his periscope during the war had been that accommodating.

Schurz looked at him. "You know their exact schedule?"

"Of course." The captain sounded disdainful. His finger went back to the chart. "The one that comes from the Lille Baelt—here, to the west—comes around Lolland and reaches Gedser very close to one, seven, thirteen, and nineteen hours." He glanced at his watch, and then verified the hour with the chronometer mounted at the binnacle. "He would have already turned at Gedser lighthouse and is on his way back by now. But he wouldn't have been any danger to you in any event. You'll be too far east for him to have been any threat. It's the boats from the north, the ones that come around Falster, that you would have to worry about."

"And what are their schedules?"

"As I said," Sneller said patiently, "there is three hours' difference in the times they get here. In other words, the patrol boats from the north show up roughly at four, ten, sixteen, and twenty-two hours. And at four hours again, of course." He checked his watch again, even though he had checked it a moment before. "It's a little after one, now. Figure it will take you an hour or so to be off Gedser. If you leave now you should easily be out of sight of any patrol boat that is due to turn at the Gedser lighthouse at four hours. You should be well on your way by then."

Schurz nodded. "In that case we'd better be off."

"I would say so. I'll help you cast off."

He turned off his flashlight, pulled back the blackout curtains, and led the way down the narrow companionway. Spurning Schurz's help he dragged the gangplank from its hold on the dock and dropped it onto the deck. He stepped on the rail, prepared to jump the small distance to the pier, and waved a hand.

"Good luck. Heil Hitler."

"Heil Hitler!" It was said in a whisper.

Sneller jumped down lightly to the dock. He unwound the ropes that held the boat both forward and aft from the dock bollards tossing them lightly toward the *Linderndsee* already drifting from the dock, waving a hand in a last good-bye. Schurz waved in return and then dragged the ropes aboard, tossing them in a heap against the rail. He then hurried up the companionway to the small bridge, Sneller already forgotten. He pulled the blackout curtains farther to one side and studied the binnacle a moment. Then he pressed the engine starter, pleased to hear the engine catch at once. He brought the speed to SLOW and headed the boat for the entrance of the estuary to the sea. As the first slight wave of the Baltic lifted the prow of the *Linderndsee*, Schurz raised the speed and headed the ship toward Gedser, across the narrow arm of the Baltic. Then, for the first time that long, long day, he took a deep shuddering breath, feeling himself begin to tremble.

He had done it! He had actually gotten away with it! And he had done it alone. There was no point in even counting

Petterssen, who not only had been more of a handicap than a help, but who would shortly be dead. He tried to control the trembling, but it seemed to be a thing outside of himself. For a moment he wondered if he should lash the wheel long enough to go below and take a stiff drink of schnapps to settle his nerves, but he knew this was no answer. He also felt a sudden desire to sing at the top of his voice, or to yell his exultation, but he knew how sound carried over water. And he still had seventy miles or so to go to reach Trelleborg in Sweden, and in this boat that would mean at least six hours at sea. Time to sing or yell when he had beached the boat at his final destination.

The trembling slowly abated under the constant need to keep an eye open for the sign of any ship, or any light; the steady burbling sound of the engine's exhaust had a hypnotic effect that also needed to be fought against. No, schnapps was the last thing in the world he needed. He settled himself at the wheel, forcing his mind to forget the successful events of the day, even forcing himself not to think of the future. All there was, was the present, the boat and the sea and the many miles to go. The Linderndsee headed steadily out across the waters.

Below in the small cabin, Petterssen raised his tragic-looking face at the sound of the engine starting. The rumble of the gasoline motor, transmitted through the small boat in vibrations as well as sound was, he knew, a knell for him. There was no doubt in Petterssen's mind that Schurz had no intention—had never had any intention—of allowing him to live to share that treasure in that crate on deck. Why, then, had he come along? Petterssen did not know. He only knew that he was tired of hiding, tired of running, tired of being afraid, tired of everything.

Should he turn the tables and kill Schurz before Schurz killed him? But to what end? He could not go back to Germany, and Sweden held no future for him; to his family and his friends he was a traitor. And what would he do with the treasure if he had it? He would have no idea where to go to dispose of it, to turn it into kroner, or any other currency. Besides, he didn't want the treasure. If it hadn't been for the treasure he wouldn't be here now, waiting to be killed. Yet, maybe it was better to let Schurz kill him. Maybe that was the answer. He wondered exactly how Schurz planned to kill him. By gun? But the German had not had a gun on the train, he was sure of that; unless, of course, the captain had given him one when the two of them had gone up to the bridge. By knife? The thought was distasteful. He felt a shiver go through him. He hoped it was not by knife, although that was a distinct possibility. Certainly the German could not be considering attempting to throttle him, since he could break Schurz in two if he had a mind to. Still, by whatever method, he was sure that Schurz was fully prepared to handle the matter as efficiently as he had handled everything else in connection with getting the treasure.

And after he was dead?

Then Schurz undoubtedly planned to dump him overboard. That, at least, was not distasteful. The sea would be warm this time of year, and soft and comforting. Yes, letting Schurz kill him was one solution to the pain he was feeling, a pain that had no source and therefore no cure. In fact, it was undoubtedly the only solution.

But it would certainly go better all around if he had some of that schnapps the captain had mentioned. Otherwise he might resist, might even avoid being killed, and that would never do. He came to his feet, bending a bit under the low overhead, and suddenly staggered as the ship dipped. They had entered the Baltic, then. He only had a few hours left of life. There was a certain satisfaction in knowing that. How many people, he suddenly wondered, would have been relieved to know the exact hour of impending death? Probably more than one imagined.

He crossed the room and opened the lockers there one by one until he found the one the captain had referred to. He nodded as he considered the many bottles within. Yes, there was certainly enough schnapps there to drink oneself to death if one cared to, he thought a bit sadly, or if one had the time. Unfortunately, he always either got sick or fell asleep before he had had anywhere near enough to cause death. It was a pity in a way. It would have been the ideal way to cheat Schurz of the satisfaction of killing him. Still, one could always try. And in any event, enough schnapps to numb the thought of death when the moment came could do no harm. He took a bottle back to the bunk with him, opened it, and drank deeply.

The schnapps was of top grade, and it occurred to Petterssen that possibly in the past he had gotten sick or fallen asleep because he had never been able to get his hands on liquor of such fine quality. Maybe with this he could get enough down to never wake up. But the bottle was not even half-finished when he had to suppress a deep yawn and knew he would never make it to death in this fashion. It was such a pity; life was so unfair! He felt a lump in his throat and felt tears begin to roll down his cheeks. What a shame! A man of his talents, and he couldn't even choose his own way of dying!

He looked around the cabin with reddened, swollen eyes, taking in the effects one by one. If he had gone to sea as a boy, as many of his friends had done, he would not be in the position he was in. Maybe he would have ended up the owner of a boat such as this, not big but big enough. In the evenings, after a hard day's work, he could have come to a cabin such as this one, and instead of waiting for death could have rested, or read by the light of the lamp . . . the lamp! *The lamp!* He set the bottle at his feet and moved unsteadily to the table with the lamp on it. He studied the bottle of gas and then watched the steady flame of the lamp burning within the glass enclosure. He smiled and then began to giggle. He reached over to the tank and slowly turned the valve, watching the lamp begin to flicker and dim. One final twist and the light disappeared completely, leaving the curtained cabin in total darkness. Now Petterssen opened the valve fully, sniffing at the aperture over the glass enclosure. For a moment he felt a touch of panic— there was no smell! But the sudden wave of dizziness that washed over him convinced him that the gas was pouring out, smell or no smell. He groped his way back to the bunk and sat down, feeling for the bottle on the deck. He found it and raised it to his lips. Just one more drink and then to sleep, he said to himself. Just one more drink and then . . . He lay back on the bunk, inhaling deeply, and smiled at the thought of Schurz's surprise and undoubted disappointment.

Before the war, and even during the early years of it when the enemy to the south pretended to respect its neighbor's neutrality, Eric Hansen had been captain of a Danish destroyer—

the *Hval*, the Whale, and it was a bitter day for Captain Hansen when, together with other naval commanders, he was ordered to scuttle his ship to prevent it from falling into the hands of the Germans. But Hansen was a man who believed in obeying orders, and he did not hesitate. Opening the sea cocks of his beloved vessel and watching it slowly sink did nothing to further endear the hated Germans to him, nor did the years he spent in internment as a result of the sinking. Only his escape when the building in which he was held was bombed by the British air force in March of 1945 made the outraged mariner feel there was any justice in the world at all.

Now, a mere two months later, the war was over and Captain Eric Hansen was once again the master of a ship. It was not a very large ship, and while it was supposedly a naval vessel of sorts, it was merely a coast-guard cutter, and the only weaponry it carried was an old 40-mm Bofors cannon mounted forward at the narrow prow, plus the rifles issued to the crew when the necessity for them arose.

The mission of the cutter was a simple one, to attempt to prevent any smuggling, or—and more important to Captain Hansen—to prevent the illegal entry of the hated *tyskerne* wishing to escape a country devasted through their own insanity, to the far more stable and prosperous Denmark. It was not the same as commanding a destroyer, of course, but far more satisfying. In the one month Captain Hansen had commanded the *Elritse* he had seen more action than in the eight years he had had the bridge of the *Hval*.

The area patrolled by the *Elritse*—the *Minnow*, named by Captain Hansen in a rare moment of black humor, for he was basically a humorless man—was along the eastern shore of Sjaelland Island, leaving Copenhagen from its base on the Öresund, then around Amager to skirt the shores of the Køge Bugt, past Møn and Falster to the lighthouse at Gedser, and then to return. When not stopping and searching suspicious-looking ships, Captain Hansen was proud of maintaining a rigid schedule of patrol. But tonight it was certain that no schedule was going to be maintained. A bit of flotsam off Ølbylyng in the Køge Bugt had caught the ship's propeller, twisting it badly. The inspection and attempted repair by the ship's engineer, sent below with scuba gear and a light, took an hour from the schedule, and the slow speed required to avoid damage to the propeller-shaft bearings, brought the Elritse around Falster a good two hours late. Captain Hansen had just about decided to abort his patrol and return to the base for definitive repairs, when there was a whistle from the speaking tube on the bridge. Hansen moved over, picking it up.

"The captain here."

"Lookout here, sir. A small boat, two points off the starboard bow, distance between three and four miles. Running without lights, sir . . ."

Hansen picked up his night glasses and trained them in the indicated direction. The small boat that came into his sights seemed to be the perfect example of a smuggler's vessel, undoubtedly expecting the patrol would have already been well on its way on its return trip. Hansen had always known holding a rigid schedule was foolish, but orders were orders. And now when he was sure he had a smuggler in his sights, he had to be with a crippled ship! Still, the smuggler couldn't know that. He picked up the speaking tube.

"Lookout—"

"Sir?"

"Signal that ship to lay to and await our boarding party."

"Aye, aye, sir." The flasher on the lookout platform went into action. The captain turned to his mate.

"Have a gunner stand by the Bofors."

"Aye, aye, sir."

The mate hurried out. Captain Hansen trained his glasses on the ship running at a slight angle to his own course. Was it possible it was not a smuggler, even though running without lights? Certainly there seemed to be no fear of the cutter, well-illuminated though it was. Nor did the other ship make any effort to take any evading action. On the other hand, there was no reply to the order to lay to nor any effort to do so. The small ship was clearly visible now in the brilliant arc of the Gedser lighthouse as it swept around on its steady path. Captain Hansen frowned and swung the wheel a bit, setting a course to intersect the other's path, reaching with one hand for the speaking tube.

"This is the captain. Fire a shot across his bow!"

"Aye, aye, sir!"

On board the *Linderndsee* Schurz had been dozing. The steady drone of the engines, the even vibrations of the ship, the soothing hypnotic rising and falling of the ship as it easily breasted the slight waves of the calm sea, together with the fact that he had not had any decent rest for several days, all combined to induce a lethargy beyond his ability to control. His head rested between two spokes of the wheel, unconsciously holding the ship on course. He had been dreaming of his days as a lieutenant in barracks, trying to sleep, when suddenly some *schlaumeier* started to play a flashlight across his eyes to try to wake him up. He turned his head a bit to avoid the irritating clown, and bumped his forehead on one of the spokes. He started to come awake and then sat erect, frightened by the loud *boom* of a cannon. Ahead of him a spout of water incredulously rose in the air.

Schurz stared, trying to get his confused senses to explain to him what was happening. There, approaching him all lit up like a Christmas tree, with a flasher working like crazy from somewhere above the bridge, was what had to be a coast-guard cutter! He glanced quickly at the chronometer, awake at last. He was less than an hour from Warnemünde! How did the damned patrol boat happen to be here when it should have been halfway back to its base by now? Damn himself for falling alseep at the wheel, but double damn that lying traitor Sneller! Schurz promised himself that if he came out of this alive he would personally see to it that information went to the Russians telling them exactly where they could put their bloody hands on Captain Ernst Sneller of the *Unterseedienst!*

He thrust the throttle to the maximum, turning the ship away from the cutter, and then knew he was wasting time. He forced himself to think clearly. The cutter was no more than two miles away, fifteen or twenty minutes between them at the most. If he turned and ran they could easily send him to the bottom with a well-placed shot from their cannon. As if to prove the point another waterspout rose even closer to him, the echo of the *boom* reverberating over the water. He pulled back the throttle and reached for the switch controlling the deck lights. What happened to him was unimportant. What was vitally important was that the treasure not fall into the hands of the enemy. He hastily lashed the wheel to keep the ship from swinging and presenting a broader target if they decided to sink it despite his surrender, and ran down the companionway. He paused at the chest containing the treasure, looking about him wildly, seeking some sort of orientation. There! The lighthouse itself gave one direction! He swung about, frantically searching for some other marker to give location to his instant triangulation. There were a few lights from the village, strung along what seemed to be a dock of sorts. It would have to do. Someday, somehow, he would recover this chest, but the most important thing was that the treasure *must not fall into enemy hands!* Not now, not after all the work and risk and fears and triumphs—or at least near-triumphs! No, not now!

He bent to the Herculean but urgent task of raising the heavy crate to dump it over the rail, but the strain was too much. The patrol was now only a mile or so away, and while it seemed for some unknown reason to be merely creeping, they were still only minutes away. He bent to the task again, but he could barely budge the heavy case. Damn! Damn, damn, *damn!* Why had he demanded the treasure be put in a steel case? Did he subconsciously know that it might have to be dumped? But what if it had? Gold didn't suffer from salt water. No, it was just one more thing to frustrate him!

He paused, panting, thinking furiously, and then looked up. Petterssen! The big ox was useless, but one final task he would be given—to help put the crate overboard. And if he refused? Schurz promised himself that Petterssen would not refuse, not with a knife in his ribs! He abandoned his efforts with the crate and glanced up. The patrol was even closer; there was no time to be lost. He dashed down the companionway to the cabin below decks, and shoved open the door.

No light! So Petterssen was sleeping, eh? Well, he'd wake the big ox in a hurry, and there would be no nonsense from him, either. Or he wouldn't live to die later! A sudden dizziness seemed to bother Schurz, but he put it down to his lack of sleep and the shock of awakening to find the patrol cutter bearing down on them. No time now for ailments! he told himself sternly, and reached into a pocket for a match, lighting it.

From the log of the Danish cutter *Elritse,* entered by her captain, Eric Hansen:

23 May, 1945: Propeller shaft twisted after hitting unknown object at 2315 22 May necessitating delay and reduced speed thereafter. At 0205 today encountered small boat running without lights off Gedser light. Flashed orders for it to lay to and when it did not obey, fired several shots across her bows. In our crippled condition she could have outrun us, but unaware of that fact, elected instead to self-destruct. The Elritse *cruised the spot where she blew up and foundered until 0300. There were no signs of survivors or anything to indicate what cargo the ship carried so precious as to cause the smuggler to blow the ship rather than lay to and submit to search . . .*

PART THREE

1979

7

Winter storms on the Baltic are not uncommon, but the one that raged down from the north that day in late January surpassed any of the long, bitter season. Knud Christensen, standing at the window of his farmhouse outside of Gedser, stared with concern out over the sea. Ahead was nothing but a wall of white sweeping over gray waters lashed by wind. The small dock at the end of his property was barely visible, with the high waves washing over it, foaming as they tried to sweep away the dory anchored under it. But it was not the vulnerability of the dory that concerned Christensen. He was worried about his two brothers, out in the storm. They were both seasoned fishermen, both excellent sailors, but this storm had come up so suddenly, so viciously, that any boat caught in it could be in danger.

It was odd that Knud had not been the one to take to fishing, leaving either Niels or Gustave to handle the farm. As a boy of fourteen he had been the most attracted to the sea; the oldest and biggest of the three brothers, the best swimmer, the best diver, the one most at home in or on the water. But as he grew older, Knud Christensen realized he preferred the quiet, almost stolid life connected with bringing things slowly from the earth. Sailing, as well as fishing, required the making of instant de-

89

cisions at times, and Knud would have been the first to admit
he was ill-equipped for this. Now, at twenty-eight, he knew
he had made the right choice. Farming permitted a man time
to think, to ponder, to consider problems in depth; either the
middle brother, Niels, or Gustave, the youngest and the family
favorite, were quicker and far better in general for the life at
sea they had chosen.

But now his two brothers were out in a storm and Knud
was worried. For once he wished he had gone with them; the
sea held no fear for him. He might not have been the quickest-
witted, but he was by far the strongest, and muscle was needed
as well as brains in a storm of that magnitude. But here he
was, chained to the land, warm and safe in a house, helpless
to do anything but wait.

The snow ceased as suddenly as it had come, but the winds,
if anything, seemed to intensify, whipping about the old house,
raising the waves even higher. The light of the lighthouse could
be seen once again; under its probing eye the huge waves
twisted and lashed at each other, battering their way to fall
with fury on the shore. Christensen strained his eyes. In the
dim light cast from the dull sky he could see a boat, and then
another, heaving on the waves, trying to beat their way into
the harbor and safety, but it was impossible to distinguish or
identify any particular boat at that distance. He stood there until
darkness finally blocked everything from the sea, and only the
eye of the lighthouse, revolving endlessly, could be seen high
in the dark sky, the beam it threw lost in the night. Then, at
last, he left the window and went through the house turning
up the lights.

There was the possibility, he suddenly realized, that they
had managed to reach another haven, another harbor, but in
that case surely they would have telephoned. A thought came;
he went to the telephone and raised it. There was no sound.
The storm had interrupted service. Christensen felt a sudden
wave of relief. That was it. They had put into another harbor
and had been unable to get in touch with him. He was beginning
to act like an old mother hen with his two chicks. They were
fine and could take care of themselves. Hadn't he himself taught
them to sail? Pleased with his solution to the problem he went
into the kitchen to start supper. The two would be starved when
they got back. It would have been impossible to have managed

anything in the small galley in that storm.

A sudden knock on the door and Christensen mentally kicked himself for having waited so long to start cooking. Then he paused, frowning. His brothers never knocked, why should they? He hurried to the front room, swinging the door wide, stepping back against the wind that rushed in. Jens Krag, a neighbor and a fisherman, came in, shaking drops from his sou'wester, standing on the entrance mat, dripping, his face wreathed in misery. Knud stared at him blankly, wondering at the visit. Then, slowly, the other's silence, his expression, brought understanding.

"Gustave . . . Niels . . ."

Krag stared at the floor, unable to look into Christensen's gaunt face. He swallowed. "The storm came up so suddenly . . ."

Christensen grabbed the man by the front of his slicker, shaking him savagely. "Where are they? What happened?"

Krag allowed himself to be shaken. He seemed to feel that anything that could relieve the other man's agony was permissible. Christensen suddenly seemed to realize what he was doing, but there was no thought of apology. He released the other man and pointed abruptly to the sofa. "Sit down. I'll get something to drink. You will tell me what happened."

He shoved Krag onto the sofa and walked into the kitchen. It seemed to him he was walking in a dream, or standing to one side watching someone else walk into the kitchen and cross to the cupboard to take down a bottle. He stopped and stared at the wall without seeing it. No. *No!* Jens Krag was a liar! He wouldn't give the bastard a drink. Instead he would beat the truth out of him! It was impossible that Gustave was dead, that Niels was gone! He would make that miserable liar admit the truth—it was a vicious joke, and Knud Christensen was not one to be joked with!

But Jens Krag had told him the truth, or would when he gave him a chance to say anything at all. Krag was not a liar, and he knew it. He walked back into the front room with a bottle and two glasses, fighting the tears that stung his eyes. He filled the two glasses, threw his own drink down his throat without waiting for the other. It might have been water for any effect he felt. He refilled his glass and stood over Krag, a menacing figure.

"Now—what happened?"

Krag took his drink down gratefully. It brought color to his face and made the telling of the tragedy, while not easy, easier. He was relieved that Knud Christensen had not gone completely berserk at the news. He had known Knud since the Christensen child had been the only one. He had seen him grow and knew the boy who was now a man, while slow to temper, could be frightening when finally aroused. He looked up into Knud's white face and then looked down at the carpet, his heavy veined hands slowly twisting the empty glass, speaking hesitantly.

"The storm came up so suddenly . . . It had looked threatening, but we were sure we would be back before anything serious. The herring were running, we were netting them like mad, our lockers were almost full, and nobody wanted to leave until we had filled them completely. It hasn't been so good lately, the fishing I mean, and—" He seemed to feel Christensen's increasing impatience and hurriedly went back to his story. "When the storm really struck, we all pulled our nets and headed in. We were off the lighthouse when it really hit. We were within sight of each other when the snow came, but in that blizzard we couldn't see a thing. I was afraid we'd run into each other, but we had to keep moving. Without the engines we would have been swamped in a minute. Then, suddenly, the snow stopped and I saw we were almost on top of your boat. I veered away and then I saw they were in trouble. The engine must have failed. They were losing way and bouncing around completely out of control. There was nothing we could do to help them in that sea. Then—" He paused.

Christensen's eyes were cold on Krag, as if accusing the man of the crime of surviving when his two brothers had not. "Then?"

"Then I saw Niels starting to raise sail—"

"Raise sail? In that sea?"

"There was no choice! He had to try something, didn't he? Without power he wouldn't have lasted a minute—" Krag suddenly seemed to realize they still hadn't lasted. He swallowed. "Anyway, he had barely started when the wind caught the sail and—and the mast snapped." He spoke hurriedly now, anxious to finish and be done with it. "It threw Niels overboard. He was swept away in an instant. There was no chance to do anything to save him. He was gone almost at once—"

Christensen's voice was like doom. "And Gustave?"

Krag swallowed once again; he knew Knud Christensen's feeling for his youngest brother. But it had to be said. "The wind took the boat into a trough, swinging it, tangling Gustave in the shrouds, and then—then it seemed the boat just seemed to open where the mast had split the deck, and—and the next thing she was gone, just like that." He seemed to be relieved to have finished the painful and thankless job of telling Knud Christensen the story. He sighed and filled his glass, drank gratefully, and then set the glass down carefully on the floor. He came to his feet, still avoiding Christensen's eyes. "I'm sorry, Knud. Everyone's sorry."

"Sorry..." Christensen was staring past Krág through the window at the blackness beyond. The storm seemed to have abated. The sound of the wind had died down. "Everyone is sorry..." It was all his fault if they foundered because the engine failed. They had discussed the need for the new engine, but he had felt the farm requirements came first. His one vote against their two, and he had won. A great victory... He spoke, still staring through the empty window. "They were the only boat lost?"

"Yes. I'm sorry." Krag retrieved his sou'wester, pulling it on, moving to the door. "I have to be going..."

"Wait." Christensen brought his attention from the window to the man at the door. His face was expressionless, carved in granite. "Do you know where the boat went down?"

"Fairly close," Krag said, pleased to be on more familiar ground. He was sure he understood the reason for the question. "We could see both the light and the harbor entrance. She wouldn't drift much with her lockers full the way they were, and it's too deep there for much undersea movement from the waves. As soon as it's calm I can locate the place well enough for Father Rasmussen to hold a proper service."

"A proper service," Knud repeated. "A proper service..." he said once more, and turned without another word to climb the steps toward the bedroom. Krag sighed and went out into the windy night, closing the door softly behind him.

It was not the first service of its kind that Father Rasmussen had held nor, as he sadly knew, would it probably be the last.

He stood in his own small dory, bobbing lightly on the calm sea; about him the boats of the other villages were grouped. The air was bitter cold, but calm. Above, the sky was a deep blue, as if the heavens were compensating, this fine Sunday morning, for the two lives that had been taken in fury a few days before. Everyone standing silent at the rails of their boats was bundled in sweaters. Father Rasmussen wore a heavy pea jacket over a turtleneck sweater. Some of the villagers had managed to get some hothouse flowers; others had brought small wreaths woven from fir boughs in their own homes. As the final sad words of Father Rasmussen's all-too familiar service ended, they leaned from the rails of their boats and tossed their offerings from gloved fingers into the pulsing sea. There were a few moments' silence, all eyes following the drifting flowers, the men all aware that but for the grace of God it could be they, themselves, under the sea and the floating wreaths above them; the women thinking how fortunate it was, in a way, that the Christensen boys never did marry, for at least now there were no grieving widows to suffer loneliness and loss. Then there was the sound of Father Rasmussen's outboard being started, and the other boats followed suit, slowly pulling away, heading back to the village.

Krag moved to his boat's controls, happy to no longer be standing beside the silent and somehow frightening Knud Christensen. He pressed the starter, revved the boat's engine, and swung the wheel in the direction of the harbor. And then became aware that Christensen had moved silently to stand at his elbow.

"Jens—"

"Yes?"

"Pull into my dock. I have to get something. Then I want you to take me out again."

"Of course, Knud." A personal gift to the dead, Krag thought; something too personal to be offered to the sea before the audience of the villagers. He wondered how long Christensen intended to grieve. "What is it you want to get?"

"My diving gear."

"*What!*" Jens Krag took his eyes from his boat's way a moment to stare incredulously at the man at his side. "That's crazy! What do you think you'll find?"

"My brother."

"But that's mad! You couldn't live five minutes in that water! This is January, for God's sake!"

Christensen calmly reached over and changed the position of the wheel. The boat obediently changed course, chugging evenly toward the Christensen dock. "When we get there," Knud said conversationally, quite as if Jens Krag had not spoken at all, "you will wait for me and take me back out to where the boat went down. Do you hear?"

"But—not only is it too cold, but the water's at least eighty feet deep there!" Jens was almost frantic. "It's insane, don't you understand?"

"If you say so. I'll try to get my gear from the house as quickly as I can," Christensen said, and moved away from the wheel, walking stolidly to the stern of the boat, hands deep in pockets, staring back at the spot he had marked during the somber ceremony. That service was for you, Niels, he said silently to the waves. Somewhere in this vast sea you are resting, and that service was for you. But Gustave shall rest in Gedser cemetery, beside our mother and father. I know you would both want that. I shall recover his body and see he has a proper burial, that I promise all of you. One brother for the sea is enough. Gustave shall be properly buried on land with the Christensens, in a place where I can go and mourn when I want . . .

The boat tacked, the engine was cut, the boat coasted with practiced precision into the dock, nudging it quietly. Christensen stepped to the dock, warped the ship's rope to the bollard there, turned and walked quickly toward the house. Jens Krag stared after him, frowning. The man was patently mad, totally insane! Should he go off and leave him? Go and get men from the village to subdue him, get the doctor to give him a hypodermic, put him in hospital, maybe in restraint, until he regained his senses? Or maybe the man simply wanted to commit suicide, to join his two brothers in the sea. That, of course, was his prerogative, but making Jens Krag his accessory, his accomplice, was vastly unfair!

On the other hand, if Krag should take his boat and leave, he had no doubt that Knud Christensen would find him and make him sorry he had not waited. And his far greater age would not prevent the younger man from beating him unmercifully. There was nothing to do but to obey and wait. But it was truly insane! In that freezing water? My God, they had ice in parts of the Baltic farther north! And at that depth? And he, Krag, could have been a hundred yards or more off in his estimate of where the *Kirsten Christensen* had gone down! How would he ever explain that when Knud came up empty-handed! *If* he ever came up . . .

He watched with a feeling of dread as Knud Christensen came tramping down the path, heavily laden with his gear. He dumped it over the rail, untied the boat, and jumped in. Krag hesitated in starting the engine, trying desperately to think of some further argument that might dissuade the other from the dive. Christensen seemed to read the other's mind. He took partial pity on Krag.

"Jens, I'm not committing suicide," he said quietly. "I have compressed-air equipment, not oxygen. It's good for well below a hundred feet. I've worked with it myself. And I've worked in cold water. I've got a wet suit and a good lamp. I'll be all right."

"But, Knud—"

"Get moving." There was no longer any understanding in the big man's voice, only implacable command. Jens Krag sighed and started the engine. The best thing to do was to get the affair over with. If Knud Christensen didn't come up, he refused to take the slightest blame. He started the engine and headed out to sea, aware that he was probably being watched with curiosity by villagers along the shore, and possibly from the tower itself. At the approximate location he slowed and allowed the boat to drift, checking the position of the lighthouse tower and the harbor entrance, trying to picture their relative locations as they had appeared the night of the storm. The truth was he was far from sure, but would Knud Christensen accept that statement if he dove and failed to locate the *Kirsten Christensen?* Undoubtedly not. The man had gone completely crazy! He sighed and became aware of Knud's harsh voice.

"Well? This is where we held the service." The large man had climbed into his wet suit; he was strapping on the compressed-air equipment.

"I think—I think it was about here . . ."

"You *think?*" He glared at a subdued Krag. "You *think?*"

Krag swallowed. "It was a storm, a bad one, don't you understand?" he said helplessly. "One minute we were halfway up to the sky, the next down in a trough like a mine! We were bouncing all over. Who could try and see—?"

Knud Christensen took a deep breath and held back his temper. There was only one solution to the problem. He pulled on his flippers, picked up his lamp and walked to the railing, putting his back to it.

"Be here when I come back," he said quietly, and put the breathing tube in his mouth. One enigmatic look at Krag's unhappy face, and he leaned over backwards, falling into the water.

8

The water was cold, shocking, numbing, deadly cold, and despite his wet suit, and despite his great strength, his iron resolution, and his almost fanatical stubbornness, Knud Christensen realized he had only minutes in that icy water in which to locate his brother's body. He sank like a plummet, brought to the bottom by the heavy weights he had attached to his belt, front and back. They would have to be jettisoned for him to rise quickly when his search was finished, but they were there to enable him to reach the bottom as rapidly as possible, and give him that much more time underwater for the job he had given himself.

The beam from his electric lamp cut weakly through the dark waters as he sank, and when at last he was on the bottom it illuminated only a small patch before him as he began a circular search, widening the arc of his path with each succeeding circuit. He had never before explored this particular section of sea bottom, but he was not surprised to find it a mass of broken rock, in sharp contrast to the chalk, sand, and marl so common elsewhere in the area. His brothers and the other fishermen had always avoided deep trawling here; a history of torn nets lay in the past experience of the older men.

Knud pushed ahead, hoping that by the very effort needed

to propel himself through the freezing waters he might generate enough body heat to keep him going a few extra minutes, give him that much more time before he would be forced to abandon the search. The rocky bottom displayed only the normal detritus of an area within sight of land; discarded food tins, the remains of broken and discarded fish crates, an abandoned skiff, its torn bottom the reason for its being there. Christensen forced himself on.

The deadly cold suddenly seemed to be abating. He almost had a feeling of increasing comfort, of warmth, in fact, and he realized he was rapidly coming to the end of his endurance. Many more seconds of the satisfying torpor and he would lose all control and quickly die. One final circuit, he promised himself sleepily, and then came awake with a start, staring into the gloom. Ahead of him, looming out of the darkness, was an obvious wreck, but it was much larger than the small fishing vessel, the *Kirsten Christensen*. It was only as he approached it that he saw he had come upon the wreckage of two boats, locked together on the rocky bottom. He circled, seeking some identification. The nearest boat had obviously been down for many years; the other was beyond, and he swam about the first, sweeping his lights from side to side. A small case momentarily blocked his path, perched between two rocks, forming a slight barrier. He held it in the beam of his lamp as he swam about it, pushing against it to hold his turn to a minimum. The rotten wooden cover fell away, almost disintegrating, revealing a metal inner shell, rusty but apparently still solid. He swam past it, pushing himself to the other side of the combined wrecks. There, faintly seen in the dimness, was his brother Gustave. The body hung from the shrouds, seemingly relaxed, still in the still waters, as if it had come to terms with its grave beneath the sea and was waiting patiently for Armageddon.

Christensen forgot the strange metal case in an instant. He dragged his knife from his belt, somewhat surprised at the difficulty he had in commanding his fingers to obey even this simple chore. He swam over the crushed gunwale and hooked a leg about the stub of the mast, forcing himself to slash at the ropes above his head, knowing his time was rapidly running out. Still, he refused to even consider surfacing, resting, and then returning to the task. He was here and Gustave was here, and it only required a few more seconds, a little greater effort, to free the body and take it up with him.

The rope seemed to be made of steel; his knife seemed merely to be sawing at it aimlessly, helplessly, uselessly. And then it seemed to Knud as if in slow motion he could see the rope part, see the individual fibers wave slowly in the motion of the sea caused by his frantic thrashing about. Gustave seemed to hesitate a moment as if reluctant to leave the safe harbor of the shrouds, and then the body slowly began to rise. Only the most convulsive thrust of his flippers allowed Knud to catch up with Gustave before he rose out of sight in the dimness of the sea. With a curse Christensen remembered the weights at his waist. Rather than attempt to unloosen them from his belt he flipped the belt buckle, feeling the weight and his knife and all his other gear fall away; and then he was free and rising, his brother's arm clasped as tightly as possible in his numb hand.

The boat with Jens Krag seemed far away as they broke surface. The waves washing over him seemed unnecessarily rough, and he prayed he could hold onto his senses long enough to attract Krag's attention. He tried to call out, to shout, but his voice was a mere croak that barely carried to his own ears. At his side Gustave lolled, uninterested. For a moment Knud Christensen felt a touch of panic; not that he might die but that he might fail. Had he come this far only to freeze to death within sight of Krag's boat? But the old fisherman had been searching the sea for him, or for his frozen and dead body, and he had seen Knud surface with his lifeless cargo. In seconds he had brought the boat to Christensen's side and was dragging the semi-conscious man aboard. Knud tried to protest, to insist that Gustave be taken aboard first, that Gustave not be abandoned now. And then at last he lost consciousness.

He awakened, sputtering, choking, the warm bite of sharp aquavit in his throat, its wetness dribbling down his chin, aware that he was alive, swathed in blankets, lying on a bunk before a gas fire. Krag's boat was uncommonly steady, he thought, and then stared through a porthole to realize they were tied at dock. Krag was sitting next to him, a beaker of spirits in his hand, waiting for his response before feeding him more of the potent liquor. Christensen looked around and then tried to sit erect. Krag gently pushed him down.

"His body's on deck," he said quietly, and shook his head

in wonderment. "How you ever managed in that water . . ." He reached out with the beaker. "Crazy . . ."

Christensen fell back, pushing away the hand with the aquavit. Now, at least, one brother would have a decent burial in the cemetery on the hill next to their mother and father. Now he, Knud Christensen, would be able to sleep a little better, knowing he had done what little he could do to save at least one brother from slowly rotting in the sea. It was, if nothing else, the fulfillment of a promise he had made to himself. It was not much, but it was something. He closed his eyes and drifted into restless sleep.

GEDSER—April

Spring came early and swiftly to the Gedser peninsula and to all of Falster that year. One day it was still winter, with the threat of snow, and with blustery winds whipping in from the west and north, and then, suddenly, the winds swung around to blow softly from the east and south, and the smell and feel of spring was there.

The sleep that Knud Christensen had promised himself would be eased by the discovery and proper burial of his brother's body, had not materialized as he had hoped. Though he deliberately tired himself out during the day with the many winter chores necessary to prepare for the spring plowing and planting, the nights still brought the incubus of seeing himself standing at the window staring out at the storm, wondering where his brothers were, even though knowing them dead; of seeing again Jens Krag standing in the doorway fumbling with his sou'wester, stumbling through his story, while the wind shook the shutters and slashed at the roof.

And then one night the nightmare did not come, but before he could feel his relief he knew it was going to be worse, much worse. He found himself swimming underwater and was aware of the cold and he knew he was searching for the *Kirsten Christensen*. In the dim light filtered down through the ninety feet of green sea water he could somehow see the ship clearly, but no matter how desperately he attempted to swim to it, it remained the same fixed distance ahead of him. Gustave could be plainly seen, locked helplessly in the shrouds, staring at him intently, as if pleading with him to hurry, hurry. But a box of some sort seemed to stand in his way, and whenever he tried to swim around it, it seemed to move in some subtle fashion to block him anew. Somehow he knew he would have to remove that damnable metal case if he ever wished to reach Gustave.

He woke feeling a bit dizzy, rubbing his head furiously, trying to recall just what dream he had had that had so disturbed him. A box, a case of some sort. He frowned, suddenly remembering. It was the metal case he had seen, had pushed aside, when he had dived for Gustave's body, when the wooden cover had almost disintegrated at his touch. Beneath there had been the gleam of a metal case. Well, what of it? What of it was, of course, that the case might contain something of value. Or, equally of course, it might not. Still, someone had gone to a good deal of trouble to encase whatever it held in metal, and nobody went to all that trouble for something that was worthless. Unless it held medicines, or papers, or—he realized the case could hold any number of relatively worthless items. And to dive again in that area, to see again the remains of the *Kirsten Christensen* and realize it had taken his two brothers to their deaths? Money was important—among other things it would buy the memorial to his brothers he had often thought of but could not afford—but, still . . . It was a problem!

It was when the nightmare of the metal case blocking his passage to Gustave continued for another week that he awoke one morning knowing he had to bring up the case if only to appease whatever devils were forcing him to picture his youngest brother just beyond his reach night after night. Maybe with the case out of the way the dream would disappear and he could go on with his life in peace, albeit with loneliness.

Still, being the person he was, Knud Christensen considered the matter carefully for several additional days. Jens Krag, he knew, would be glad to take him out in his boat the following Sunday after church, although in that case Knud knew he would be obligated to share in whatever he salvaged. And somehow there was the feeling that sharing in the case or its contents would somehow be a little like sharing Gustave, who, after all, had not only led him to the metal box, but had also been its guardian, so to speak, watching over it until his body had been rescued—recovered, that is. No, Knud would bring the case up alone. He would do it at night. There was no need for anyone else to know or to be involved. He could reach the spot easily in his dory and be down, up again, and back home before anyone was even aware he had been out there diving. Relieved at having reached a positive decision, Knud Christensen went to bed that night, and while he had the same dream again, somehow there was less dread in it; he assured the waiting Gustave that he would be back, to rid them both of the nightmare.

The following night, once the lights of the village began to go off one by one, Knud Christensen took his compressed-air gear and the hundred feet of rope he had prepared and carried them down to the dory. He quickly spliced the extra rope to the forty or more feet of rope the dory anchor normally carried, and then returned to the house. There would be no Jens Krag waiting for him this time, and he would be in no position to search for a drifting dory. In the darkened house he put on his wet suit, attached the new belt he had since purchased together with new knives. He would not require weights this trip, the anchor would serve that purpose. He picked up his lamp and flippers and walked quickly down to the dock.

He paused, looking about. Above him and to one side the searchlight atop the lighthouse tower revolved impersonally, lighting a swath of sea in its glow, its principal beam reflecting back from a bank of lowering clouds. A bit of rain might come later, but there was ample time for his mission beforehand. He climbed into his dory, untied it, and reached for the oars.

When he judged he was close enough to the spot where he had located the *Kirsten Christensen* and Gustave's body, he paused and looked about. The tower light still rotated evenly, but there was no indication he was being watched. Not that it really made any difference, he said to himself, and pulled on his compressed-air gear and his flippers. Then he tucked his mouthpiece in place, clipped his lamp to his belt, picked up the anchor, and leaned backwards over the gunwale, falling silently into the water.

The water was still cold, and although nowhere near as cold as it had been in January, he knew he could not stay down for very long. For one thing his determination to recover the case was not the same driving force that had willed him to recover Gustave's body. He came down in total blackness, not wanting to use his lamp until he was sure the glow of light beneath the water could not be seen from the surface or from the lighthouse walkway. When he struck it was with a painful jolt against the sharp rocks, the anchor pinned against his chest, and for a moment he feared he might have pierced his wet suit, but a swift check proved this fear unfounded. He settled the anchor firmly in the rocks, hooked the slack rope into his belt to be sure not to lose the line that led to the surface and the waiting dory, and began his search. His lamp pierced the darkness of the sea for only a few feet, and he wondered if he should have waited for daylight to make his search. But that might have brought curious neighbors. Besides, the difference in light at that depth was negligible. He felt a tug; he had reached the limit of rope. With a muttered curse he pulled himself back to the anchor, raised it, swam ahead for a few minutes, and then replaced it in the rocks, taking up the search again.

He was about to move the anchor for a second time when he saw the tangled wreckage of the two boats ahead of him. He nodded in satisfaction and swept the sea floor with his lamp. He had come upon the object of his search in time. A few more minutes and he would have had to surface and try another night. But where was the case? He frowned and then realized he had come upon the two boats from the side of the *Kirsten Christensen*. He swam to the right, skirting the wreckage, his lamp moving furiously from side to side, almost afraid to look up for fear of seeing Gustave tangled in the ropes. The feeling made him realize he was running out of time. *Where was the case?* For a moment he feared someone had been down there before him, had stolen the case from him—the case, he now felt, was his by rights—and an unreasonable anger swept him. And then, just as he was about to concede failure this first night of his search, he saw the glint of light from metal, and knew he had found it.

In the light of his electric lamp, now held close to his strange discovery, he saw that the last of the wooden casing had rotted away during the hard winter, and only a few bits of board were held clamped between the steel case beneath and metal straps that had been wrapped around the case. He locked the anchor rope to his belt, set down his lamp, and put both hands to the task of shifting the box. Even though its weight was greatly reduced under water, it was heavy, and Knud paused, thinking. Then he came to a conclusion. He cut the anchor loose and thrust the free end of the rope through the metal straps, drawing the rope tight, making a sturdy knot that held the case firmly. Then with one last look at the box he gave a firm thrust with his flippers, grasped the rope, and swiftly drew himself up through the chill waters to his dory.

He climbed aboard, slipped off his gear, and sat down, resting a bit. The only problem now, as he saw it, was whether the straps would hold the weight, or if he had abandoned a good anchor for nothing, and would have to repeat his search another time. He began hauling slowly on the rope, bringing the case from the bottom. Beneath his feet the dory dipped dangerously. Maybe he should have brought Jens Krag into the picture, he thought. With the winch on Krag's boat it would have been no job at all to handle the heavy case. But no! The case and its contents were his by right of discovery and by every other right! He would not share. He would get it ashore by himself. He pulled on the rope steadily, the case moving with greater ease as it came up from the bottom.

Christensen knew, as he slowly pulled the steel case toward him, that he would never be able to bring the case into the dory without capsizing, but that was not what he had in mind. When the side of the box bumped gently against the bottom of the dory, he looped the rope tightly around one of the dory's bollards and bent to the oars. It was hard rowing, and occasionally Knud could feel a slight bump as the heavy case swung against the dory at the end of its tether, but he was getting closer and closer to the dock. As he rowed he kept a steady look over his shoulder, judging his position constantly should the straps or the rope break and drop the case to the bottom again, requiring another dive, but it was still with him when he nudged the dory against the dock.

Christensen climbed out, secured the boat, and then waded out to his prize. He reached down with his knife and cut the rope, leaving enough slack to wind about his thick arm and allow him to drag the case to land. He paused, panting. One thing was sure; the case was heavy. Another thing was equally sure; he could not and would not ask for any help. With a deep breath and the assurance to himself that if there was anything of value in the box it would go toward a memorial to his brothers, he bent and with all the strength of his large body brought the case to his arms and staggered toward the house.

He dragged the heavy box across the sill and closed the door behind him, allowing himself to fall in near exhaustion to the floor beside it, catching his breath, feeling the strain in his muscles from the arduous job. Then he came to his feet, closed the shutters and drew the curtains before lighting a lamp. In its light he made his way to the kitchen and poured himself a large glass of aquavit. He downed it as if it were water, shuddered a moment, and then went back to the living room, staring down at the case. Whatever was in it, he certainly hoped it had been worth the effort, not to mention the cost of a new anchor for the dory, because he knew he would never dive in that area again, for his lost anchor or for anything else. How long had the box been at the bottom of the sea? There was no way of knowing. He could not recall any ship sinking in that area in his lifetime. Possibly if he were to ask Jens Krag or the lighthouse keeper, who were far older than he, one of them might remember—but that would be stupid. If he was going to keep his discovery a secret, the last thing to do would be to go around asking questions.

He went through the house and out to the barn, keeping the lantern in his hand shuttered. Inside, in the lantern's light, he found the tools he was seeking and returned to the house. With a cold chisel and a mall he carefully cut through the steel, making sure to make his entry large enough to bring out whatever was inside without cutting himself, or the contents, on the ragged edges. When he had removed a large enough panel he tried to see inside by the light of the lantern, but it was unsatisfactory. He reached in and felt around, and eventually brought out four wrapped packages.

He spread them on the floor at his side and began opening them, one by one. Each of the packages was wrapped in some type of suede leather, and inside, wrapped with equal care in tissue paper, were a huge number of beads and buttons and little circlets of wire, as well as oddly carved larger pieces made of some sort of metal he didn't recognize. Knud sat and stared at his find, wondering what on earth it was supposed to be, or why it had been so carefully packaged in a steel box. He picked up one of the larger pieces, which seemed to be a childish attempt at a mask, stared at it a few moments and then put it down again. Like the other larger pieces it seemed to be flimsy, amateurish, and while Knud recognized that he was no expert he did know what he liked, and he didn't particularly like any of the pieces. It seemed to him extremely doubtful that the things he had found could possibly have enough value to compensate him for his effort, or his lost anchor, or to leave enough for the most modest of memorials for his brothers. Most likely the stuff had a sentimental value for someone, to account for the care that had gone into wrapping and encasing the stuff. Still, they *had* gone to that trouble, so it seemed a bit early to give up all hope of eventually realizing at least a little value from his find.

But who could he ask regarding the odd material? Father Rasmussen? The father was by far the most highly educated in the village, but his education had been largely ecclesiastical, and that might or might not enable him to give a judgment as to the value of the beads, buttons, and the other larger pieces. Besides, Father Rasmussen was a noted gossip, and the chances of keeping the matter secret were the good father to be consulted were extremely remote. Per Baunsgaard, the blacksmith? The one who fixed most of the farm equipment as well as the fishing gear that required any metalwork? He might recognize what alloy the stuff was made of, but Per Baunsgaard was an even bigger gossip than Father Rasmussen. Showing him the pieces would be the same as advertising the affair in the Copenhagen newspapers, or putting it on the radio. Besides, Per Baunsgaard was a noted liar, so how could he be trusted no matter what opinion he gave?

It was a problem, and Knud Christensen had the habit of putting problems off awhile to see if possibly they might solve themselves. Certainly it wouldn't do any harm to sleep on this one, at least. Sleep, he was sure, would not be hard to come by that night, or what little was left of the night. And if he had any dreams, he only hoped they might lead him to some idea of the value of what he had discovered. Satisfied with the temporary solution to the problem, he packed the stuff back into its box, pushed it into a closet for the time being, and went to bed.

Nor was Knud Christensen wrong, for when he woke at dawn the following day he knew exactly the man to help him solve his problem. It was a distant cousin; actually the son of one of his mother's cousins. His name was Arne Nordberg and he was a professor or something of that nature at Copenhagen

University. Certainly, Knud thought, mentally chastising himself for not having thought of it at once, Nordberg would be the exact man to help him in his dilemma. Satisfied, and refreshed by not having had any dreams at all, good or bad, he got up and began to dress. Uncharacteristically, he intended to go to Copenhagen without delay and ask the advice of his cousin. He had never met the man, but he was sure that would make no difference. His mother had mentioned his cousin often enough, usually to point out the difference in his own educational ambitions as compared to those of the other. Now those educational differences were going to work for his benefit.

Whistling, he completed dressing . . .

9

From the window of his small office at Copenhagen University, overlooking the Frue Plads on one side and the Nørregade running into it, Associate Professor Arne Nordberg stared sourly at the pretty co-eds hurrying past, books in arms, their short skirts and lack of brassieres raising lewd thoughts in the professor's mind. But they were useless thoughts, he knew. For some unknown reason he never seemed to be able to impress the pretty ones, and the ugly ones didn't interest him, though he had never been able to impress them, either. His hints that favors might be returned in the form of better grades were invariably met with, at best, blank stares; at worst, by barely concealed smiles of derision.

If he had money, Nordberg assured himself, it would all be different; his shortness would be forgiven, as well as his tendency toward obesity, or the fact that at the young age of thirty-two he was rapidly losing his hair. Or if he had an international reputation like some members of the faculty, there would be, he was sure, no problem. Girls would be all over him like they were over that idiot Carl Becker, and for what? So the man won a so-called prestigious award once. It had been pure luck, those things mostly were. But the sad fact was that Arne Nordberg had very little money; he could barely afford the girls he visited over the sex shops in the Istedgade, beyond the railroad station, and then only the cheapest. And as for scholarly attainment, of the few papers he had managed to write all but one had been refused publication by the University Press, although they were constantly importuning the faculty for submissions, and seemed to print every piece of garbage sent in by anyone else. The world was against him, and that was a fact. The professor knew it was a fact, although just why the world should take this unfair attitude was beyond him.

So he was considered strict in class? Why shouldn't he be strict in class? Who did anything for him that he should do anything for others? He had also heard it said, snidely, behind his back, that he was also unintelligible in class. That, simply, was a lie. If others couldn't or wouldn't recognize erudition when they saw it or heard it, it was just too bad. So he didn't have any friends among the faculty? Why should he go out of his way to appear friendly to a bunch of louts who seemed to think friendship consisted solely of drinking another person's liquor or eating another person's food? The truth was he was as bright as anyone on the staff, although naturally nobody would admit it. He was also as educated, as intelligent, as personable. But what had it gotten him? Nothing! Take Carl Becker, for example. He would bet that Carl had been in the skirts of half the girls in his classes. And what did Becker have? Tell the truth—a laugh like a hyena, and little else!

He became aware that his intercom was buzzing and he glared at it. My God! A man couldn't even take a few minutes to cogitate, to reflect, to relax after the grind of four hours of trying to pound some historical facts into the heads of a bunch of big-breasted, succulent-bottomed numbskulls, without being constantly interrupted. He considered disregarding the intercom, but he knew that his secretary—a dessicated, flat-chested widow ten years his senior he had once considered seducing—his face flushed at the memory although he still wondered how it might have been—would continue her racket until he answered. With a scowl he flipped the proper switch downward.

"Yes? Now what?"

"There's someone here to see you, Professor." She had a voice like a crane, as if there were something wrong with her throat. Why couldn't she at least have *sounded* intriguing, even if she wasn't?

"Professor?"

He brought his mind back to the matter at hand. "Who is it?"

"He says he's a cousin of yours, Professor. Knud Christensen."

Nordberg frowned at the telephone. Christensen? It seemed faintly familiar. A cousin? Some distant relative of his mother's, as he recalled. Fishermen, weren't they? From somewhere down in Nykøbing, or Korsør, or one of those other God-forsaken villages in the south. What on earth could a fisherman cousin—not even a real cousin, but one of those hundred-times removed cousins—want of him? The answer wasn't even a problem. Money, of course. All these country yokels seemed to think if you lived in Copenhagen, you were rich. If you were a professor at the university, you were made of money. Well, little did they know! He stared at the intercom, seeing in his mind's eye his middle-aged secretary at the other end of the line, leaning over to press the intercom buttons. He tried to picture the view down her gaping blouse, and then recalled that she was flat-chested, or so he had to suppose from the tight brassieres and buttoned-up blouses she wore. Why couldn't he have had the luck to be assigned a good-looking secretary? Like Carl Becker—?

"Professor?"

He cleared his throat. "Tell him I can't see him. I'm busy."

"Yes, sir." Nordberg's hand went thankfully to push the intercom switch, but before he could do so his secretary's voice came back. "Professor, Mr. Christensen says he'll wait."

Damn! Nordberg stared about the small office. There was no escape other than the one door leading past his secretary's desk and the undoubtedly raw-boned and equally undoubtedly fish-smelling peasant outside. Nordberg thought a moment and then allowed himself a feeling of righteous anger. What did he owe this perfect stranger? Everyone was constantly trying to take advantage of him, and he wasn't going to stand for it! Enough was enough! He would simply tell this oaf he was wasting his time, and that would be that. He didn't have to explain the circumstances; he knew if he were the richest man in Denmark he would still refuse the man money. What did he owe the man, anyway? He steeled himself and glowered at the intercom.

"Tell him to come in."

The door opened and Nordberg coldly considered the man who stood there. Christensen had dressed in his Sunday best, and did not appear particularly raw-boned, although he was certainly big. He also had a thick head of curly hair, and not for the first time Nordberg resented his father's baldness that had apparently been transferred through genes to blight his son's existence. Christensen also did not smell of fish, although this, Nordberg thought sourly, would not get him one penny. Christensen carried a small cloth bag with him and smiled with a bit of uncertainty at his distant cousin. Nor was any smile going to do the lout any good, Nordberg thought with an inner sneer, and did not even offer the man a chair.

"What can I do for you?"

"I thought—" Christensen paused and looked around, finally finding a chair and sitting in it. He edged it to the desk, his small bag held firmly in his lap. Here it comes, Nordberg thought, and waited, his face expressionless. Christensen studied the ranks of books on the shelves that enclosed the tiny office, and finally brought his attention back to his cousin. Rather than speak again, he opened his bag and brought out a piece of metal, placing it on the desk. "I thought you might be able to tell me if this had any value."

Nordberg frowned. What was this? A new way to ask for money? Or an attempt to use the fiction of their relationship to peddle something? Or was it simply a case of thinking of him as one would of a pawnbroker, which was simply insulting? Or even simply asking his advice. Others on the faculty occasionally served as consultants, but they were paid for it. He picked the piece up and studied it without much interest, finally looking up at Christensen.

"Where did you get this? Do you have more?"

"I have a few more pieces with me. There's lots more at home." Christensen hastily brought out the rest of his samples and laid them on the desk. Nordberg looked at them, his interest at least piqued. They were undoubtedly old, very old. How had a mere fisherman come by them? He looked up again.

"Where did you say you found them?"

"You see—" Christensen began, and then paused. He was never very good with words. Maybe it would be better if he began at the beginning. "You see, my brothers were both drowned three months ago. There was a very bad storm—"

So he *was* going to ask for money after all! The pieces were just a lead-in; the sob-story was about to begin. Well, better to cut it off quickly.

"I'm afraid—" Nordberg began.

"I wanted to bring up the body of my youngest brother," Christensen went on. He hadn't heard the interruption; his mind was back in the icy water cutting Gustave's body loose. "He was tangled in the shrouds. So I went down and found the wreckage of the boat, and brought up his body for decent burial."

Despite himself, Nordberg was impressed. "You dove for his body—when?"

"Three months ago."

"In *January?* Where was all this?"

"Off the Gedser lighthouse. Yes, it was January," Christensen said simply. "It was cold, but it had to be done. But what I'm trying to say is that when I was down there I saw this box, this crate, made of steel. It must have come from the second boat I found, which must have been sunk a long time ago, because I never heard of the sinking, and it was less than a mile from my house. Anyway, when the weather got better— last night, in fact—I went out in my dory and I dove and brought the box up. And when I opened it I found these pieces. And a lot more."

"How much more?"

Christensen shrugged. "Much, much more. Hundreds and hundreds of pieces. Oh, most of them were small, like beads and buttons and things like that. I didn't count them. There were too many." He looked down at his samples and then up to Nordberg's face. "Do you think they have any value?"

Nordberg bent over the pieces once again, now studying them intently. There was something vaguely familiar with the piece he was looking at, a small slightly curved mask with open eyeholes, too small for an adult, probably for a child, or possibly a small woman. The material, he was sure, was gold, almost pure gold if he was not mistaken. He tried to recall where he had read about something like this. It seemed to him he had been reading or researching another matter, when he had run across something about some pieces . . . Still, he was sure it would come back to him in time. In the meantime, caution was clearly indicated in giving this peasant any information.

"Value?" He shook his head. "I doubt it. I would have to see the rest of the pieces you found to give you any idea at all. But if these pieces are representative—" He looked across the desk. "*Are* they representative?"

Christensen swallowed miserably. "The other pieces mostly are a lot smaller, but some are bigger. There's a cup . . . I think it's a cup . . . or maybe a bottle . . ."

"You see? No, I'm afraid you found something somebody probably threw away. You can see for yourself. They're obviously made of some inferior alloy. See how easily it bends. And as for the workmanship—if you can call it workmanship—it's simply childish. I doubt they would be worth more than their value as scrap. Still," Nordberg added, as if trying to put the best face on the matter, "I won't say they're totally worthless. Or at least I won't say it until I've had a chance to see the rest of what you found. Can you bring it to me?"

"I—"

"Or possibly it would be less trouble for you if I were to come over to your place?"

"You'd go to that much trouble?" Christensen asked anxiously. Nordberg shrugged modestly. "Could you come back with me? I live in Gedser, on Falster. It's only a few hours by train."

Don't rush, Nordberg told himself sternly. No show of the slightest anxiety over this freak accident. Some of these country types are shrewder than they look. And you may have fallen into something just because you were smart enough to see this yokel. Others, like Carl Becker, for example, wouldn't have wasted a minute on him.

"Today? I'm afraid not. In any event, I don't believe it's all that important," Nordberg said, and forced himself to bite back a yawn. He reached over and flipped the pages of his appointment calendar, being careful that his visitor could not see the blank pages. "Ah! How about a week from Sunday?" Even as he said it he wondered if perhaps he was being just a bit too reckless; if given too much time the man might go to someone else for an opinion.

"Not before?" Christensen could not keep the disappointment from his voice.

Nordberg flipped the pages again, and then reached for a pencil. He crossed out something on a page. "I'll postpone that," he said, half to himself, and looked up. "Saturday next, then," he said, making a great concession. "I'll drive down to your place on Saturday." He nudged the pieces on his desk. "If you wish you can leave these here with me. I can try to find out what alloy they're made of. Or you can take them back with you, whichever you prefer."

Christensen shrugged helplessly and came to his feet.

"You might as well keep them," he said, and sighed. "Until Saturday, then. Anyone in Gedser can tell you where Knud Christensen lives." He walked to the door and then paused, twisting the empty cloth bag in his hands. "And thank you," he said sincerely, remembering his manners. "Thank you for your time."

Nordberg waved the thanks away gracefully.

It came to Nordberg at three o'clock in the morning. He left his bed and padded to the front room of his small apartment, lighting a lamp, and then searching the bookshelves for the reference copy he wanted. He drew it down, the excitement in him growing, and flipped the pages until he reached the section he wanted. He found the part that had teased his memory, found the reference it made to another book, and hastily searched for the second book without bothering to replace the first. He almost tore the pages in his anxiety to find what he wanted. He thrust the page under the lamp. There it was! *There it was!* A picture of the very mask that was now locked in his desk at the university. And there! *Look there!* That diadem, with the owl's head at the end of each of the hanging chains; the owl's head of Athena! My God! Was it possible! He felt himself begin to tremble. The Schliemann treasure in the hands of a stupid fisherman from Gedser, when the entire world was convinced it was in Russia someplace, most probably at the Hermitage Museum in Leningrad? *Was it possible?*

He fell into a chair, eagerly reading a description of the treasure, and then fell back, his mind churning. He had suspected the pieces had value, but nothing like this! He forced himself to try and think clearly. Saturday was four long days away. Could he take the chance and wait that long to go to

Gedser and verify that the treasure was, indeed, the Schliemann collection? Suppose the fisherman went to someone else for advice, or an opinion, in the meanwhile? Or suppose he had listened to his words and went and disposed of it for scrap to some metal dealer who, in all probability in that part of the country, wouldn't know the difference and would bale it together with other scrap and sell it to some factory where it would all go into the furnace together, iron, steel, tin—and the Schliemann gold! The thought was too horrifying to contemplate. Or the metal dealer *would* recognize the material as gold, which was even worse!

But on the other hand, if he went down to Gedser any sooner than the following Saturday, wouldn't the peasant wonder at his early arrival? Would the clod begin to suspect that possibly the pieces he had found were of greater value than mere scrap? What excuse could he give for hurrying down to Gedser that would not arouse suspicions on the part of this Knud Christensen?

It was a most difficult problem, and one that prevented him from sleeping the rest of the night. He sat and gnawed his nails, staring at nothing, trying to find a suitable answer. And then an even greater problem formed itself in his mind, relegating the one of a reason for an early appearance at Gedser to a very minor position. He sat a bit erect as he contemplated this new, and far more frightening, possibility. Eventually, no matter what he did with the treasure, word would get out! The world would know that the Schliemann treasure had been found! *And Knud Christensen was part of that world!* There would be newspaper articles. It would be marveled at in the magazines and on the radio! Pictures would be shown. Would it be possible that with all the attendant publicity, the clod would not hear of it? And if—or, rather, when—he did hear of it, what would his reaction be?

A cold, eerie feeling gripped Nordberg. There was only one solution . . .

He came to his feet, now moving almost marionettelike, as if his actions were being controlled by an Arne Nordberg he had never known. He went to his bookshelf again, but this time to bring down his pharmacopoeia, carrying it back to the lamp. He sat and pulled the heavy volume into his lap, leafing through its pages. He would require a poison that could be introduced in liquor, for he was sure that a man like Knud Christensen drank. The poison would have to be slow-acting, for Nordberg had no intention of watching the giant die, or be caught in those frightening hands should the oaf suspect what was happening to him. And then Nordberg paused, thinking, again as if his thoughts were those of a stranger, as if he were standing to one side watching Arne Nordberg think, and being able to read those thoughts. There were certain pills, drugs of some sort, which could not—or, rather, should not—be taken with alcohol. A strong dose of one of those drugs in a bottle of liquor . . . And if, for some reason, an autopsy should be ordered, the cause of the suicide, or accidental death, would be all too evident.

He sat and coldly made his plans for the following day, but one small part of his mind kept praising him for his courage, for his ability to recognize a situation and take the necessary steps to handle it. Another portion of his mind, though, kept hoping his nerve would not fail at the proper moment.

The pharmacist who furnished him with the sleeping tablets was careful to caution him not to drink anything alcoholic while using the pills, and Arne Nordberg assured him that he was quite aware of the consequences of doing so. He next stopped by his office, which was in the next block, to advise his secretary that he had been taken ill on the way to school and would not be able to take any classes that day—which was easily believed with his high color, his feverish eyes, and his shaking hands. He then drove to the bank and withdrew two thousand kroner, which left his balance woefully thin. But there was nothing to be done about it; this was no time to be niggardly.

His next stop was at a liquor store. Again he decided not to be cheap, and purchased a quite expensive bottle of whiskey. His coldly calculating brain, now directing him almost without his volition, told him that the drugs he had purchased might well cloud the otherwise water-clear aquavit, but they would be invisible in the amber color of scotch whiskey. Besides, scotch whiskey, at those prices, made a more prestigious present.

He then got into his car and started for Gedser. At a rest area he pulled from the road, and in a secluded area he carefully opened the bottle of whiskey and inserted the pills. He recapped the bottle and shook it to dissolve the pills, and then held it to the light; there was no sediment visible. He put the bottle into his handbag and pulled back onto the highway for Gedser, forcing himself not to think of the bottle by his side, concentrating instead on what he would do when he had his hands on the treasure.

There were two choices: one, should he turn the treasure in to the authorities? There was no doubt that if he did so, his fame would be great. He could see it in all the scholarly journals, every historical or archaeological publication: *Professor Arne Nordberg, the man who discovered the long-lost Schliemann treasure!* It could and probably would mean advancement. At the very least it would mean, it had to mean, the publication of a paper on how and where the treasure had been located. He would bring in the history of the treasure, a history of the Schliemanns, Heinrich and Sophie. No university press in the world would turn *that* paper down!

On the other hand, selflessness was fine, but here he would be with a fortune in his hands, if only he had the slightest idea as to how to exploit the situation. How on earth could he make a decent sum of money from his possession of the treasure? Assuming, of course, he managed to get his hands on it—but the thought of not getting his hands on it was just too terrible to consider, so he put it out of his mind. No, he would get the treasure one way or another. But what then? As far as he knew there had never been any reward offered for the recovery of the collection. Nobody had ever considered it lost, merely taken a bit illegally by the Russians and hidden away all these years. Possibly if he were to contact someone in the Russian Embassy? But if the Russians had managed to lose the treasure, if someone had managed to steal it from them, letting them know he had it could be suicidal.

And one could scarcely put an advertisement in the newspapers saying that one had the treasure for sale, could one? Obviously, one could not. Still, there simply *had* to be some way to get at least a portion of the great value of the treasure. With the amount of money he was considering—an amount that made his head spin just thinking about it—he tried to picture all the things he could do, all the places he could go, all the girls he could have. The thought of the pleasures that could be purchased with unlimited funds brought a twinge to his loins, but he put the sensuous thoughts aside for the time. First he had to get his hands on the treasure.

His palms were damp with sweat where they gripped the steering wheel, holding it as if to sustain himself. He pressed harder on the accelerator, hurrying to Gedser, forcing himself not to think of the bottle in the bag beside him.

It was late afternoon when Nordberg finally arrived at the Christensen home. He had hesitated several times before finally stopping at the post office as being the least noticeable place at which to ask directions. Knud Christensen was fixing a harness in the barn when Nordberg pulled into the driveway, turned off his noisy engine, and climbed out. The sound of the ancient car's asthmatic wheezing brought Christensen to the doorway. He frowned and walked down to greet his unexpected guest.

"Professor Nordberg? But, I thought—"

Nordberg shrugged a bit self-deprecatingly.

"I found it was impossible for me to break my appointment for Saturday," he said lightly. "A faculty tea, and I'm expected to address them, you know. And I'm busy every other day for the next several weeks. But since I had made a sort of promise to you"—he smiled—"and since it was a nice day for a drive, I thought—" He allowed the words to slide into silence. Fortunately for him, it did happen to be a nice day, although he had not noticed it until then.

"Good! Good!" Christensen said, pleased at the professor's presence. It would save him from four more days of wondering at the possible value of his find. It did not occur to him to be suspicious in any way of this erudite man, a relative, even though a distant one. Knud Christensen was not by nature a suspicious person. He tilted his head in the direction of the house. "It's—the things—are in there."

He led the way, knowing the neighbors would think it strange for him to be having a guest who boasted a car, even an old one, but also knowing that a visit from a relative could easily be explained, especially after the tragedy he had suffered. Inside the house, the curtains drawn, Knud lit a lamp and dragged the heavy steel case from the closet. He reached in, fishing out the four packages, and carefully unwrapped them, placing their contents down in small piles. He then looked up at the professor anxiously.

"Well? What do you think?"

Nordberg could scarcely keep his hands from trembling as he reached for a small gold cup and brought it up to his eyes for closer inspection. He pursed his lips in his most professional manner, studying the cup with ill-concealed disinterest. Inside he was chortling, for he was positive he was actually looking at the missing Schliemann treasure; the night before, in Schliemann's own book *Ilios,* he had seen that same cup in illustration. But there was no indication of his feelings in his expression of disdain. He put the cup down and picked up a necklace, sure as he did so that the quadrangular beads would be seventy in number, just as Schliemann had described it. The Schliemann treasure! And he had it in his hands, practically! He would have liked to ask the clod for more details as to how he had managed to come on the treasure, although with the collection in his hands he now knew he would never turn it over to any authorities for the puerile purpose of mere academic credit. It was worth a fortune, tons of money, mountains of money! He tossed the necklace down carelessly and with a final sigh made a sort of sweeping motion with one hand, a gesture that took in the entire collection, obviously condemning it to oblivion.

"I'm sorry," he said, and actually managed to look a trifle chagrined. You should have been an actor, he said to himself, and drew his lips into a grimace of pity. "But it's what I was afraid of. You see"—his voice took on the tones of confidentiality—"after you left yesterday, I had the pieces you brought me checked by our engineering laboratory. And discovered what I suspected, that they were an alloy of tin and white metal. The cheapest sort of costume jewelry, the sort of things servants buy in the cheap bazaars. And not particularly good examples of even that. I had hoped that some of the stuff you had here might be of better quality, but it all appears to be the same sort of—of—" He hesitated and then shrugged delicately, hating to hurt the other man's feelings. "Well, to be frank, junk."

Knud's face had been slowly falling during this recitation. Although he had feared such a report, especially after his visit to Copenhagen the previous day, his disappointment was still visible. He looked at the pieces piled on the floor and shook his head disconsolately, not knowing what to say.

"I know," Nordberg went on sympathetically. "I can understand how you feel. I'm disappointed too." He looked at Christensen with what he hoped was a look of compassion. "Tell me—ah—cousin, what do you plan to do with this—this—these things?" His hand indicated the piles of pieces on the floor.

Knud raised his shoulders and tried to smile. "I have no idea. Try to sell them to the local bazaar, I suppose. Or for scrap." He stared at the pieces, wondering what insane motive had driven him to dive for them. And to sacrifice a good anchor for them. "I don't know. I honestly don't. Maybe donate them to the church for their next raffle. They ought to be worth something."

"Not very much, I'm afraid," Nordberg said, and frowned as he considered the problem. A possible solution seemed to occur to him. "I can make a suggestion, if you should be interested. I have a collection of curiosities, of junk, if you will. Things without value, such as these. Conversation pieces, you know. If you would be interested in selling them to me, they might be amusing to some of my friends—" He hurriedly raised a hand. "I couldn't pay very much, of course, but then the stuff isn't worth very much, if anything. But I'm sure it would be more than the church would ever get trying to raffle such things off. Or more than you could get from the local bazaar..."

Christensen's face began to clear. His eyes brightened a bit. "How much do you think—?"

Nordberg thought a moment and then shrugged, as if to say that after all it was only money, and money which he could easily afford, certainly more easily than his obviously poor cousin.

"Well," he said, his voice deprecating his generosity, "after all, you went to a lot of trouble diving for this stuff, bringing it up from the bottom of the sea. That alone ought to be worth something. What about—say—a thousand kroner?"

Christensen took a deep breath of relief. A thousand kroner! It wasn't, of course, what he had hoped for when he found the stuff, but it was far more, he knew, than what any bazaar would offer him for the stuff. And certainly far more than its value as scrap. It would buy a new anchor, and while what was left wouldn't pay for any memorial for his brothers, it would at least make a down-payment on some sort of metal cross to replace the crude wooden one over Gustave's grave.

"That's very generous," he said, and held out his big hand. Nordberg gripped it, his diffidence at the compliment apparent. Knud swallowed, as if ashamed, after such generosity, to be asking. "I don't suppose—?"

"You mean, can I pay you now? Of course," Nordberg said, disparagingly, as if he carried thousands of kroner with him every day. He brought out his wallet and separated a thousand kroner from the pile of bills there, allowing Christensen to note his affluence. It did strike him for a moment that it was a shame to be wasting a thousand kroner on a dead man, but he could see no other way to handle the affair. He certainly had no intention of waiting for Christensen to die and then recover the money from the body. He handed the money over. "There you are."

"Thank you!" Christensen could not believe his good fortune. "Thank you!"

"There's one thing, though," Nordberg said, almost as an afterthought. It had struck him that he really didn't know how fast the poison would work, and he didn't want the oaf to go running to the neighbors and telling them of his good fortune before it took him to bed for the last time. "I should not like my colleagues at the university to think me a fool for spending that much money on an obviously worthless collection of cheap costume jewelry. So while they may be conversation pieces, there is no need for anyone to know I went overboard in paying for them. So I would appreciate it if we could keep this business—well, just between the two of us."

"Of course! I haven't told anyone that I ever found the box, and there's no need for me to ever tell anyone." Christensen tucked the money deep into a pocket and bent to wrap the pieces roughly in their original packages. Nordberg did not stoop to help him, but when the packages were ready, he did deign to carry two of them out to his car and store them, together with the two that Christensen carried, into the trunk. He closed the trunk lid and turned to look at his distant cousin. He steeled himself. This was the moment to prove if he had the nerve to murder or not. And he knew that he did.

"I say," he said as if the thought had just occurred to him—

and again it seemed to be a different Arne Nordberg speaking. His voice sounded different even to his ears. "Do you like whiskey?"

"Very much!" Christensen said, and then seemed to realize the lack of hospitality on his part the question seemed to imply. "I never offered you a drink! I'm sorry. Here, let me get you—"

"No, no!" Nordberg waved the offer away. "I brought a bottle for you. Actually"—he tapped his stomach and smiled regretfully—"doctor's orders. No alcohol for a long, long time. But someone gave me this bottle, rather fine stuff, imported, and since I'm not allowed it, I thought you might care for it." He reached into his handbag and brought out the bottle, handing it over. "Here you are. Have some now. To—well, to sort of seal our deal."

Knud Christensen grinned as he looked at the label. "My Lord! I haven't seen anything this fine for a long, long time. Somebody's wedding, I forget whose."

"Yes, it's good stuff. Have some now."

Christensen shook his head, still grinning. "Not anything this fine, this good. This will have to wait for a proper occasion."

"No, no!" Nordberg said hurriedly, and cursed his stupidity in bringing an expensive brand. "It—I mean, it really isn't all that fancy. Have some and tell me how it is, in case—I mean, so I'll know when the day comes the doctor lets me drink again..."

"It's good. I don't need to prove that." Christensen studied the label again and then looked up, smiling gratefully. "It won't go to waste, I promise." He held out his hand. "And I want to thank you for everything."

Nordberg stood and stared, incapable of thinking of any way to get the clod to drink the whiskey. Then, unable to do anything else, he shook the outstretched hand briefly and climbed into the car as Christensen stepped back and raised his hand in a slight salute, the bottle dangling from his other fist. For a moment Nordberg thought of making one final effort, but he knew it would only look suspicious. With a frozen face he put the car into gear and drove from the yard.

But if the oaf didn't drink the whiskey today, he would drink it one of these days, certainly before any possible news of the treasure or its disposition ever got out. Maybe it was just as well that Christensen hadn't drunk the whiskey while he had been there. He had no idea of just how fast the combination of drugs and alcohol acted. And occasions as an excuse for opening a bottle of fine whiskey, Nordberg was sure, came up with a great regularity—birthdays, anniversaries, weddings, whatnot. And one nice thing about having spent that much money for an expensive brand was that it was doubtful the big man would share it with others. Not that it would have bothered Nordberg if others suffered the consequences as well. It was just the fact that sharing might dilute the strength of the combination, and that would not do at all.

And, of course, he had the idiot's promise not to mention the deal to anyone. It wasn't everything, but it was about as much as he could have hoped for—and the fact remained that in the trunk of his ancient car at that very moment as he headed back to Copenhagen, he had the famous Schliemann treasure.

That was a fact!

10

Other than the fact that Knud Christensen had not drunk the doctored liquor in his presence, and the fact that he would never know exactly when the clod did drink it since the deaths of unimportant people were not reported in the Copenhagen newspapers—and he certainly had no intention of returning to Gedser to verify the death—one might have thought Associate Professor Arne Nordberg would have been a happy man. Not only was he in possession of the Schliemann treasure, but in the week since he had brought the treasure back from Gedser and deposited the pieces trip-after-trip into two large safe-deposit boxes in his bank, he had lost ten pounds of weight. He had also saved at least a hundred kroner, since the girls in the Istedgade, for the first time since he could afford them, did not interest him in the least. His hairline, however, seemed to have receded even farther, and he wondered if worry alone could account for the fact.

What to do! *What to do!*

A fortune in his hands, a veritable king's ransom, and all it apparently was going to mean were the added expenses of two large safe-deposit boxes, a complete loss of appetite, as well as the very possible loss of his job if he didn't get his mind back onto the subject of Danish history and away from thoughts of the treasure sitting idle and for all purposes worthless in a box in a bank. He knew his lectures were suffering, but how was he supposed to be able to concentrate on the eighteenth century and the failure of Christian V in the Skåne War, or rejoice with his class over Frederick IV's victory over the dukes of Holstein-Gottorp? The chances were if he didn't find a solution to his problem soon, he would be forced by mere economic considerations to turn the treasure over to the authorities and attempt to glean what few tidbits of recognition he might from the whole affair. The thought was sickening. One morning he stared at his class without seeing them and then wordlessly left the rostrum and walked unsteadily into his office. He passed his secretary without a glance or a word, closed the door of his tiny sanctum sanctorum, fell into a chair, and pressed his head into his shaking hands.

What to do! *What to do!*

It was evident he was slowly going to pieces, or not even slowly. A solution had to be found and found quickly or he was going to suffer a complete nervous breakdown. Why had that fiendish fisherman come to *him* with the blasted treasure? Why couldn't he have enticed someone else with its potential wealth? Or, better yet, left it at the bottom of the sea? Or had the fisherman been sent? Had someone—his colleagues, possibly Becker—arranged the whole thing, knowing it would drive him mad? But this thought in itself was madness, and he still had enough control to know it. He reached into a drawer and brought out a bottle of aquavit, bringing it unsteadily to his lips, upending it, aware as he did so that any sign of drunkenness, or smell of liquor on his breath during lecture hours, could mean instant dismissal. But he was past caring. He took another drink and could feel the alcohol begin to intoxicate him. Still, it was relaxing...

There had to be a solution. If only he had money! That was the answer, of course. Money begets money. With money he was sure any number of possible solutions would press themselves upon him. All that anything ever required was money. What was it Rousseau said? *Money is the seed of money.* Or Emerson, the American—sometimes they said something wise—*The world is his who has money.* Or Pulilius Syrus, who said the same thing earlier, before the birth of Christ: *Money alone sets the world in motion.* But Diogenes Laertius, three hundred years later, had put it the most elegantly. When a man asked him the right time for supper, Diogenes said: *If you are a rich man you eat whenever you please; if you are a poor man, whenever you can.* And he, Arne Nordberg, was a poor man, and he hadn't even been eating at all lately, as a matter of fact. A classical education is fine, he told himself, feeling tears of self-pity welling behind his eyes, but what good is knowing what a lot of dead people said, or when they said it? It would never take the place of just plain, simple money.

He took another drink and yawned deeply, feeling the effects of the strong drink on his empty stomach. Then suddenly sat erect, his eyes widening dramatically, his mind snapping for a moment from its aquavit-induced torpor. He closed his eyes and shook his head violently, trying to force away the cobwebs, and instantly regretted it. He gripped the edge of his desk tightly, trying not to be sick, wondering what thought had come to bring on that ridiculous reaction, and then he remembered. Of course. *Of course!* The answer was simplicity itself. It was true that he, himself, had no money, but that didn't mean there weren't others in the world with money. Many, many, many! Hundreds! Thousands! Millions, probably! Undoubtedly! And sharing the great fortune that could be realized from the treasure with someone else was certainly better than having it sit in a bank idle and worthless—not to say a drain on his finances—and driving him half-insane in the bargain.

He leaned back, smiling, pleased with his brilliant solution, and not at all perturbed by the fact that at the moment he had no particular wealthy man in mind. That would be a matter of selection, careful selection. He would require someone, obviously, who would not be disturbed by the fact that the Schliemann gold had apparently been stolen from the Russians and somehow lost at sea, but Nordberg was sure that this in itself would present no problem. Rich men seldom accumulated their wealth by practicing excessive moral scruples. He would also have to find a man who would believe his story of how he had come into possession of the treasure, for he certainly had no intention of introducing the name of Knud Christensen into the narrative. This also seemed to be no great problem. He had all of history to select in fabricating a story of stolen material, and whatever else he was, he was definitely a scholar, not only of history, but of the classics. He would invent a story so logical that it would make the delivery of the Golden Fleece from the kingdom of Colchis seem like the normal arrival of the afternoon post; the stealing of Helen of Troy by Paris appear like picking up a girl in the Istedgade.

He realized that to a large extent it was the aquavit that was speaking in his boastful and swollen thoughts, and resolved to be sober when he did make up his story, and then to make it as simple and uncomplicated as possible. But basically, he knew his solution to the problem was right. He needed a partner; someone with money as well as contacts. And, of course, brains. Someone with nerve as well as a touch of the gambler in him. Someone, he told himself in the slowly evaporating stupor brought on by the alcohol, like himself. He smiled broadly at the idea. Not exactly like himself; someone with money. Someone who could complement his qualities, as well as duplicate them. Someone like Count Lindgren, for example.

Even as the thought came, he knew it had been a burst of pure genius. He had found the solution! Count Axel Poul Hemming-Westberg Lindgren was a trustee of the university, a man Nordberg had not only seen from a distance, but had even met on several occasions. Rich as Croesus, they said. Certainly Lindgren Castle on the outskirts of Ringsted seemed to bear that out. Nordberg had seen the castle several times. When the count was traveling he permitted the castle to be used for conducted tours with the monies, of course, going to charity. Set in two hundred rich acres, with its tessellated towers and its more than a hundred rooms filled with untold wealth in the form of paintings and statuary, the castle represented all that Nordberg had ever considered the finest in life. Just as the castle's owner and tenant represented all that Nordberg had ever hoped for in himself.

Count Lindgren's family held a revered place in Danish history. His father's ancestors had fought with Harald Blaatand, the son of King Gorm, in the completion of Denmark's unification and in the conquest of Norway. It was said another ancestor on his mother's side had been the right-hand man of Sweyn I, Harald's son, when he conquered England in 1013. No fisherman cousins in *his* line! No distant cousins living in little cottages in places like Gedser! And to make the man more attractive as a partner was the fact that Count Lindgren was a known gambler. The Copenhagen newspapers often mentioned his presence at Monte Carlo or Mar de Plata; at Las Vegas or Punta del Este. And the pictures in the society pages always showed the count visitng the casinos with a lovely lady on his arm, and always a different one. In fact, it was rumored that the reason Axel Lindgren had left the consular service was because he had been asked to. A matter, it was said, of an affair with the wife of a diplomat, a man so obsolete in his thinking as to act quite undiplomatically when he discovered the facts. So Count Lindgren had this love of the fleshly pleasures in common with Arne Nordberg, as well. Kindred souls, Nordberg thought—except, of course, for money. Yes, Count Lindgren was exactly the man to help him solve his problem. In fact, the count probably wouldn't even want money for his help. With his wealth he didn't need it. He'd probably do it just for the sport of it. Rumor had it he was just that kind of man. And according to the papers, Axel Lindgren was at home in Ringsted, which in itself could be considered a sort of favorable omen, since the count was known to travel widely.

Nordberg started to come to his feet, staggered, and sat down again. Better sober up, he told himself sternly. When you can walk a straight line, then go home, take a hot bath, get some rest, and tomorrow, when you have all your wits about you, go down to Lindgren Castle and start the ball rolling. It was such an attractive thought that he decided to have one more drink on it . . .

RINGSTED—April

The following day, Count Axel Poul Hemming-Westberg Lindgren was, indeed, home. He was in conference with his lawyer, and while the two men could not be said to be arguing—Axel Lindgren had learned early in his diplomatic career that arguing was counterproductive—it could be said they were having a serious discussion. The lawyer, Erik Trosborg, considered himself an old friend and felt he could speak freely.

"Axel," he was saying, his voice pleading, "why can't you seem to realize that the estate is entailed? It is not yours to dispose of when and as you wish! You know that as well as I do. You simply cannot go around selling off pictures, or statuary, or anything else. Why do you continually put me in the embarrassing position of rounding up these things and getting them back? I'm supposed to be a lawyer, not someone on a perpetual sort of scavenger hunt. When are you going to stop these stupidities?"

Count Lindgren shrugged. He was a handsome man in his late forties, with the build of an athlete, sharp clean features, a cleft chin, icy blue eyes, and a white streak down one side of his light brown hair that women found most attractive. He flicked ash from his thin cigar and smiled at his friend. It was a cold smile, but most things about Axel Lindgren were cold.

"I needed the money," he said simply. "Blame it on inflation. Everyone else does."

"Or gambling. Or women."

"Now there you are being unfair," Lindgren said a bit reprovingly. "My women do not cost me a krone."

"Not in hard cash. Only a Mercedes for this one, a dress shop for that one! I wish," Trosborg said fervently, "you would be smart enough to buy your women as you buy anything else. Or not to buy anything at all for a while. Axel, you simply cannot keep this up!"

"My dear Erik," Lindgren said with no attempt at apology, "I honestly have no idea where the money goes. It just goes." He glanced about a moment before returning his gaze to Trosborg's face. "Erik, do you have any idea of how much it costs just to run this place? On the veriest shoestring, I assure you. A valet who also does duty when needed as chauffeur, or even butler, a cook and an assistant, five maids and a housekeeper?"

"I have a perfect idea," Trosberg said dryly, "since I handle the bills."

"Oh. Of course." Lindgren was not in the least nonplussed. "Well, then, do you have any idea of what, say, a few new suits of clothes cost? Just the trip to London, alone, to visit the tailor—"

Trosborg shook his head in almost amused resignation.

"Axel, Axel! You have an income from this estate that would enable the most extravagant man in the world—no, since that's you let's make it the second-most extravagant man in the world—to live in absolute and total comfort. You simply must learn to live within that income. To begin with, legally you have no right to touch any part of the estate. It's entailed and you could get into serious trouble by doing so. And secondly, if you had your way, in ten years there would be no estate at all, and then, my spendthrift friend, you would *really* have something to complain about!"

"All right, all right." Lindgren smiled with amusement at the lawyer. "Don't spank. I'll try to be a good boy in the future. Now, how about lunch with me?"

"No, I have to get back to town. Handling the affairs of Count Axel Lindgren is a full-time job, believe me." Trosborg came to his feet and shook his head as he looked down at his friend. All the lectures in the world would not change Axel, he knew. He only hoped the excesses could be kept within reasonable limits. "You know, Axel," he added thoughtfully, "you might even consider working..."

Lindgren looked up, honestly surprised. "I beg your pardon?"

Trosborg laughed. "It's not a crime, you know."

"Well, it should be," Lindgren said, and smiled.

Trosborg became serious. "I mean it, Axel. Not that you need it—you'd have ample money if you didn't throw it around the way you do. But I'm serious. You're considered an expert on art, aren't you? I'm sure you could get quite a few very well-paying commissions, purchasing commissions, if you were to let people know you were interested—"

"And have all my friends realize the depths of my degradation?" Lindgren laughed. "Have everyone from Cannes to Hollywood know I was reduced to—to—labor?" He shook his head mockingly, but there was a touch of seriousness in the gesture as well. "François would begin serving me leftovers for lunch; Wilten would let my shoes go unpolished for a month. The maids would be afraid they wouldn't be paid next week."

Trosborg laughed. "What you mean, of course, is that honest labor might interfere with your traveling or with your spending time on the yachts of your poorer, but more practical, friends." He held out his hand. "I don't agree with your philosophy, but it's your life. Take care."

"I have you for that," Lindgren said with a wry smile, and shook hands. He watched his friend leave the room and leaned back, his smile gone, his cigar smoldering forgotten in the ashtray at his side. This money thing, or the lack of it, was the very devil! He supposed in a way Erik was right. The income from the estate was a fair sum, and he could imagine there were people who could live on it. But not the way he liked to live; not and travel to the places he enjoyed visiting, or dress the way he liked to dress, or be with the type of women he liked being with. And the saddest part of the whole business was that when at last he died, as even he, Axel Lindgren, had to eventually, the lovely Lindgren estates that Trosborg was so intent upon keeping intact, would not go to another Lindgren as entailed estates were supposed to go, handed down in their entirety in the blood line from father to son, but would undoubtedly end up with the government. A government, incidentally, who had fired him most unjustly for the small matter of sleeping with a lady. Who was he supposed to sleep with, for heaven's sake? His first secretary? The military attaché? The only reason he had ever gone into the consular service had been for the women he could meet . . .

But the sad fact was that two marriages had not only failed to provide Axel Lindgren with any particular satisfaction, they also had not provided him with any progeny. And Lindgren had no intention of risking a third marriage simply to furnish an heir to inherit Lindgren Castle and all it contained, or its estates, or anything else. It would be a dirty trick, he thought with a rather sour smile, to place the burden of landed poverty onto another, as it had been placed upon him.

He crushed out his cigar and was about to go in to lunch, when his butler appeared, standing discreetly at the door. He was a large man, with cold unexpressive eyes. Lindgren looked at him inquiringly. "Yes, Wilten?"

"A—a person to see you, sir."

"A person? Does he or she have a name? Or a card?"

"He has no card, sir. But he said he was an acquaintance. A Professor Nordberg. Of the Copenhagen University, sir."

Lindgren frowned. He seemed to remember Nordberg; they had met at a few university functions when the professor— assistant professor, wasn't it, or even associate?—had managed to introduce himself. A rather disgusting example of the human animal, as the count recalled. Most unattractive. Fat, short, going bald, verbose and stupid, constantly ogling the women and scratching himself while talking. What on earth was he doing here? And coming at this most inconvenient time, when lunch was about to be served. François, the cook, would be most perturbed should his carefully prepared meal be delayed, and Count Lindgren could understand that perfectly. What he could not understand was why someone as obnoxious as Nordberg should be bothering him when he had sufficient problems without additional ones from assistant—or more likely, associate—professors.

Still, Count Lindgren prided himself on always being polite, particularly with his inferiors, and it would be impolite not to see a man who had, after all, traveled the whole forty miles from Copenhagen to Ringsted, and who undoubtedly considered he had gone to the ends of the earth to see him. To the professor, at least, the reason for his hegira from the capital probably seemed important; a request to take one of his classes through the castle without paying the usual fee? And if Erik Trosborg had any idea of how little of the collected fees ever found their way to charity . . . ! The count put that thought aside and shrugged.

"Ask him in. And tell François that lunch will be delayed. But not very long. I don't imagine this will take much time."

"Sir," said the butler and retired, rather surprised that the count would see a scruffy specimen like Nordberg at all.

Count Lindgren seated himself and brought out another small cigar, lighting it, inhaling deeply, waiting for his visitor. When Nordberg appeared, looking about in wonder, obviously impressed by the luxurious appointments of the room in which he found himself—he had never seen Count Lindgren's private sitting room, which was off-limits on the guided tours—the count came to his feet smiling, as if he had lacked suitable company all morning and was pleased to find that of all people, Arne Nordberg had appeared to resolve that want. Count Lindgren had not spent years in the diplomatic service for nothing. Such dissembling had often proved profitable in the past, although the count, in all truth, could see little possibility of gain in the present circumstance.

"Ah, Professor. It's good to see you again."

"Thank you! Thank you!" Nordberg was positive now that he had been completely correct in choosing Count Lindgren to help him. What a fine gentleman! He gratefully accepted the chair the count waved him to and stared about him in awe. What beauty! What exquisite taste in everything in the room! He was brought back to earth by a polite cough from the other man. He turned to look at his host. Count Lindgren had also seated himself and was smiling at him.

"You wished to see me about—"

For the first time a touch of doubt came to Arne Nordberg. He wondered if possibly it had been the aquavit he had drunk the previous day that had made him think Count Lindgren would help him. With all the money the count had, was it not possible—in fact, likely—that the man would not be interested in helping him dispose of the collection? What could he offer Count Lindgren that Count Lindgren did not already possess? Or could not buy if he so wanted? Still, he was here, and after so many days of terrifying indecision, there was nothing for it but to tell the whole story, or at least the concocted story, and see where it led. One thing was reassuring, and that was the gentle, friendly smile on the count's face. Nordberg wet his lips, took a deep breath, and began.

"You know, I'm sure, of the Schliemann treasure, sir—?"

No muscle moved on Lindgren's face. He remained the same smiling friendly man, but within his mind a slight wonder formed. Was he going to be forced to eat a delayed lunch just because this idiot wished to discuss art objects?

"Yes," he said, anxious to terminate the pointless interview. "I'm quite familiar with the collection. Before the war I was fortunate enough to have seen it at the museum in Berlin. I was a child, but my father insisted upon my getting a very broad education. May I ask in what connection you asked about the treasure?"

Nordberg swallowed, and then to his own amazement heard the words come from his lips. He had meant to be far more circumspect in releasing the information.

"I—I have it . . ."

The smile disappeared from the count's face, replaced by a slight frown. "I beg your pardon? You said—?"

"I said I have it. I have the Schliemann treasure. In my possession." The very saying of the words seemed to bring renewed confidence to Nordberg. After all, he *did* have the treasure, and nobody else did, and that was a fact!

"Are you quite sure you know what you are saying?" Count Lindgren was now convinced he was dealing with a mentally unbalanced man. He promised himself to speak to Wilten about being more careful in whom he admitted. Wilten was usually excellent in this regard, having much experience, but—democracy was all right in its place, but letting insane people in to annoy him was quite another matter. He began to rise. "I'm sorry, but I'm afraid—"

"Please!" Nordberg's tone was pleading. Then he seemed to read something in the other man's expression. He leaned forward. The count was forced to sink back in his chair to avoid a collision. "Look, sir, please! I'm quite serious. I'm not lying, and I'm not crazy. I said I have the Schliemann treasure, and I have!" He reached into a pocket; the count's frown deepened. Was the maniac going for a gun? But before he could ring for Wilten to come and eject his unwelcome visitor, Nordberg had brought out a tissue-wrapped packet and was opening it. He reached over, handing the count a diadem. He had selected the most ornate, the most individual, for his presentation. "Have you ever seen this before, sir?"

Count Lindgren took the diadem carefully, examining it in detail. It certainly looked genuine. Was it possible that a lout like Nordberg actually had the entire collection? It seemed impossible. In fact, it seemed utterly ridiculous. Still, there was the diadem. He looked up, his interest now fully aroused. "Where did you get this piece?"

Nordberg now felt surer of himself. "It's not just that piece. I have the entire collection. Thousands of pieces," he said with confidence. "And I have them in a very safe place—"

"I asked where you got it."

"Well, I'm sure you know the treasure has been in Russia all these years since the war—"

"And I thought it was still there. You still haven't answered my question." Count Lindgren's tone was insistent, the tone of a man accustomed to being answered when he asked a question.

"Well, sir, it was stolen." Nordberg raised a hand hastily. "Oh, not by me! I've never been in Russia. It was stolen by a man who worked in the museum—it was the Hermitage, in Leningrad—and he stole the collection and defected. He got as far as Copenhagen and he needed money desperately to continue his escape. He came to me at the university and offered it to me for sale. At first I was sure it was a hoax—he wouldn't tell me how he got it out of the museum, or even how he got it out of Russia. But when I examined the pieces, and compared them with the records of the collection, the pictures and the detailed sketches in Schliemann's own book, I knew it was genuine. So I—I bought it."

Lindgren tried to comprehend the startling fact, if it was a fact, that Arne Nordberg—Nordberg, of all people!—should be in possession of the Schliemann treasure. It just did not seem possible. In fact, the more he thought about it the less possible it seemed. Still, the diadem was there. He supposed the professor's story might be true; stranger things had happened in the world. But not many. He frowned at Nordberg.

"I see. And may I ask just why you're telling me all this?"

This was the part that Nordberg had rehearsed in his mind when he first planned to present the case to the count. He had been sure it would be one of the first questions. But it really wasn't so hard. All he had to do was tell the truth.

"Well, sir," he said earnestly, "the fact is, I'm like the man who stole the treasure from the museum. He had it, but he didn't know what to do with it. That's the position I'm in. I've got it, but I don't know what to do with it. It cost me all the money I had in the world—"

"And how much was that?"

"I know it won't sound like very much to you, sir, but it cleaned out my bank account—" Nordberg hesitated as if ashamed to be mentioning such a minute sum to a man as rich as Lindgren. The count waited. "It was fifty thousand kroner, sir. But I thought it was worth it."

"I'm sure," Count Lindgren said dryly. Fifty thousand kroner for the Schliemann collection? The cost of a new Volvo for one of the greatest collections the world has ever seen? "And at the risk of being impolite and repeating myself, may I ask again, just why are you telling me this? Do you wish to resell it? I'd have to verify its authenticity—"

"No, no!" Nordberg said hastily, moving to the edge of his chair, wishing to correct this misunderstanding at once. "I had nothing like that in mind! I thought—" He hesitated. Lindgren waited. "I thought," Nordberg said at last, in a subdued tone of voice, not looking at the count but staring at the thick rug instead, "that we could be sort of—of partners, sir. That you might be able to figure out how both of us could make some money from it . . ." There! It was out, it was said!

Lindgren contemplated the man before him with outer calm, but inwardly his mind was racing. So the man wasn't as big a fool as he appeared. Nordberg was, however, still a lout, there was no doubt of that, but he was an educated lout, after a fashion, and he would scarcely have been foolish enough to pay whatever he paid—the count was positive it would not have been fifty thousand kroner or anywhere near it, but that was unimportant—for a hoax. Nor would he have been so foolish as to attempt to bring a hoax to Count Lindgren. It would have been far too dangerous to attempt anything like that with a trustee of the university where he worked. It would mean his job, if not worse. The count fully intended to verify the authenticity of the collection, but he was beginning to really believe that the miserable person facing him actually, through some weird accident of fate, had come into possession of the Schliemann treasure. The story of the Russian defector probably was the truth. It was the only way Lindgren could imagine Nordberg getting hold of it. Certainly not through his own weakling efforts.

And if Nordberg actually had the treasure, there was indeed a fortune to be made. Enough, in fact, to enable the count to return to the style of living he had unfortunately been forced to abandon for the time being. It was rather a good thing the man had not wanted to sell it; he might have been foolish enough to have given him something for it. Now, if it really existed, he was sure that somehow he could realize its value without sharing a bit of it. If, always if, it were real . . .

He became aware that Nordberg was speaking and looked up. "I'm sorry. I was thinking. You were saying—?"

Nordberg smiled nervously. "I was wondering what you were thinking, sir."

Count Lindgren smiled genially. "If the collection is genuine," he said, "and that, of course, I shall have to verify, then I think I might be interested." He laughed. "Oh, not for the money, of course, but for the sport of it. I think it might be rather a lark, you know? Interesting, in a way."

Nordberg was thrilled. He could feel the wave of emotion travel the length of his body, prickling him. He had been so right to contact Count Lindgren! So absolutely right! Not, of course, that the presence of the count automatically meant a solution to the problem, but he knew he felt better for just not being alone with the problem any longer.

"Do you have any idea, sir, of—of just how we—you— we might—?"

Lindgren waved the question away airily. "I'm sure there are many means of disposing of a collection that desirable," he said absently, and smiled, the same intimate friendly smile that had greeted Nordberg when he first arrived, admitting the professor into the warm fraternity of the rich and privileged. The count swiveled his chair to face a cabinet and brought forth a bottle of rare brandy. He poured two glasses and held one out to the professor. Nordberg could hardly believe it; he was drinking cognac with Count Axel Lindgren! He tapped his glass against the one being held out by the count, raised it to correspond to Lindgren's gesture of a toast, and sipped. My Lord, it was good! To think that with money one could drink this ambrosia of the Gods every day of the week! He finished his drink but refused a refill. It would not do to look greedy in front of his new partner. Besides, there was a more important matter to be discussed.

"How much money do you think—?"

"I shouldn't worry about that, if I were you. The Schliemann treasure should bring in a fortune," Lindgren said encouragingly, and offered Nordberg a cigar. Nordberg took it and put it to his lips; the count held a flame to it from a gold lighter. The professor did not smoke, but it would have been unthinkable to refuse an offering from the count. He smiled to hide a grimace at the unfamiliar acrid taste, and persisted.

"But, roughly, how much—?"

"Please don't worry about that," Lindgren said sincerely. "Whatever monies result from selling the treasure, I assure you will be yours. I have all the money I need. What I don't have is some project to occupy my mind. And this sounds as if it might be good sport. But first, of course, I should not wish to even become involved unless the treasure is authentic. And when may I verify that?"

"Right now, if you wish." Nordberg puffed out smoke, wondering if one could become accustomed to rich cigars. "It's in several safe-deposit boxes at my bank, the Handelsbanken in the Østergade in Copenhagen. The bank is open, and it's only an hour from here—"

"Shall we say tomorrow, instead? Suppose I meet you at the bank at eleven," Lindgren said, and came to his feet. He did it in a reluctant manner, as if he would have liked to continue the scintillating conversation with the brilliant professor for hours, but unfortunately other matters prevented him from this pleasure. The truth was he had a lot of thinking to do and he wanted his mind clear when he saw the treasure the following day. If it should turn out to be authentic, he did not want to be confused about what had to be done. He walked his guest to the door, one friendly arm about the other's shoulders, saw him properly taken over by Wilten, and made his way toward the dining room.

Professor Nordberg walked to his ancient car as if on air. It was real! It had happened! He had neither imagined it, nor dreamed it! Everything had come about exactly as he had hoped and prayed for. And what a pleasure to be associated with a gentleman like Count Lindgren! He had the count's word for it—his word!—that he would never need for anything again! The money was all to be his! Ah, to be rich. Oh, not to live in a grandiose place like Lindgren Castle, but to have a larger apartment, with a servant—a combination maid and cook... He could picture the maid he would hire when money was no problem. With a low-cut uniform that would show off her full figure to the best, short skirts for her wonderful, enticing legs. A maid who would understand the needs of a passionate man, and who would share that passion.

He climbed into his car in euphoria, started it, and listening to the engine promised himself that even before the new apartment, even before the maid, he would get himself a new car. One that would attract the attention of the girls who had refused to share his ten-year-old, battered, limping automobile...

In the dining room, for once Count Lindgren's mind was not on the food. The overdone introductory *omelette*, François' answer to tardy diners, barely was noticed. The soup, made a trifle bitter by unnecessary boiling, was consumed with equal lack of complaint. The chop, toughened by a purposeful long tenure in the pan, was merely dallied with. Count Lindgren had more important things on his mind.

Barely on the fringes of his mind, however, was the matter of Arne Nordberg, or any claim he might have to share in whatever the Schliemann collection would bring. Count Lindgren had killed in the Korean War. He had once killed in an unpublicized duel—a duel in which Wilten had acted as his second and had been in charge of seeing that the pistols were properly loaded, or at least one of them. In his youth Count Lindgren had volunteered as a mercenary in Africa just for the adventure. Count Lindgren would not have the slightest compunction about eliminating a person as distasteful as Arne Nordberg should the need arise, and Count Lindgren realized without the faintest regret that the need might very well arise. And even had Arne Nordberg not been distasteful, the count's compunction would have been no less. Axel Lindgren and his desires came first; all else was secondary.

No, Nordberg would present no problem. Nor, for that matter, would disposing of the treasure. An auction, conducted between the top museums of the world, without, obviously, revealing his identity or anything else not necessary to the negotiations. With his contacts throughout the world, it should be no problem. It would take a bit of planning, of course, but it certainly could be done. Oh, the museums would all claim, as he would have done himself, that they couldn't touch anything the slightest bit doubtful as to ownership, but they'd all manage to bid anyway, one way or another. And not only the ones brought in to bid, but others, advised of the auction by the undoubted publicity the affair would garner in the world press. Yes, it actually would be a lark, in addition, of course, to bringing his reduced finances from the pit in which they found themselves.

But all this was a bit premature. First, of course, there was the matter of getting the treasure transferred from the insecurity of bank safe-deposit boxes to the true security of Lindgren Castle's vaults. After all, safe-deposit boxes could be opened with court orders. Robbers had been known to be able to open safe-deposit boxes not only in banks but in hotels, as well. No, the proper place for the treasure was at Lindgren Castle. After all, in the more than five hundred years since the castle had been built, its security had never been breached. And it carried in its halls and on its walls a fortune in art objects as great if not greater than the Schliemann gold, not to mention the plate and other valuables in its vaults. So what better place to insure the safety of the valuable collection? And he and the lout Nordberg were, after all, partners, were they not? With the mutual interest of seeing to the treasure's safety until it could be properly and advantageously disposed of?

The count smiled coldly and reached for the trifle, heavily oversugared by an irked François...

PART FOUR

1979

11 ||

The Translation Conference Room of the new and impressive Gramercy Arms Hotel in Park Lane was slowly filling up. Ruth McVeigh, at the head of a long conference table that had been installed in place of the normal theater-seat arrangement, sat and watched her colleagues slowly file in and take the places assigned to them by their name cards. Many of those present were friends of hers, or at least acquaintances, but some new faces could be seen settling down, bringing out cigarette packets and placing them with matches beside the already-furnished pads and pencils, pulling ashtrays closer, or fiddling with the water glasses at each setting. Before each person was a small console furnished with a pair of earphones and five buttons for the five languages to be furnished in instant translation, if required.

Along the wall, as if in the position of observers, were faces she did not recognize. She assumed they were from the world press, men who had been unable to arrange space at the press tables, for the wall chairs were not furnished with translation consoles. Television cameras had been barred, and many of those along the wall were waiting patiently with notebooks on their knees, their breast pockets filled with sharpened pencils. One man, sitting along the wall in a relaxed manner, dressed

145

more informally than most in a dark jacket over a white turtleneck sweater, seemed faintly familiar to Ruth, although she
was sure she had never met him. She was sure she would have
remembered if they had. Without notebook or pencil, he appeared to only be a curious observer. Ruth leaned over to a
colleague from the Cleveland Museum, the antiquities curator,
Timothy Rubin, speaking in a low voice.

"Tim, don't just turn around and stare, but that man along
the wall, the one sitting next to that man with the stiff white
hair, the one with the turtleneck sweater. He looks familiar.
Do you know him? I expect he's from some small museum—"

Tim Rubin managed to casually look around, as if checking
the room, and then turned back, his expression one of complete
innocence, although there was a wicked glint in his eye.

"As a matter of fact, I do know him," he said, "but I
wouldn't bother with him if I were you. He comes, as you say,
from an insignificant museum. I'm surprised they even let him
in." He turned away, as if he had answered the question fully.

Ruth shook her head. "Tim! Don't be cute. Who is he?"

"He's a nobody named Gregor Kovpak, from a nothing place
called the Hermitage, or something like that, in Leningrad,"
Rubin said with a wicked grin. "Or maybe it's in Moscow.
One of those small museums, as you guessed."

Ruth's eyes widened. Of course! She had seen Gregor
Kovpak's pictures in the journals often enough. And she not
only had visited the Hermitage Museum in Leningrad several
times, she knew it to be one of the finest and most prestigious
in the world. She managed to look down the row of chairs as
if merely checking to see how close they were to starting, but
her look was for Gregor Kovpak. What was a man like Gregor
Kovpak doing here? Was it possible that the Russians were
behind the auction, after all? But that was ridiculous. If everyone there was behind the auction, it would be like Chesterton's
The Man Who Was Thursday. But whatever reason had brought
the eminent Russian archaeologist, Ruth McVeigh was suddenly glad he was here. She told herself it was because it would
give her a chance to meet the famous Dr. Kovpak at last. She
became aware that Tim Rubin was speaking to her, and looked
around.

"I'm sorry, I wasn't listening. What did you say?"

"I was merely answering you."

"Answering me?" Ruth looked at him, surprised. "I didn't ask anything."

"Yes, you did. You may have thought you just thought it, but you said it. You said, 'He's very good looking, isn't he?' And I said that I usually don't notice those things in men," Tim said dryly. "Now, if you want my opinion of that lovely from the Museo di Antichità in Turin, I'll be glad to go into details. However, for your information, I might mention that Kovpak is a widower. That's the good news. The bad news is that he's not interested in any further entangling alliances, as I understand it."

Ruth felt her face flushing. "Tim, you're an idiot! I don't believe I said a word. And I'm not interested in Dr. Kovpak other than to meet him. I've read his papers and I think he's brilliant."

"As well as good looking and single," Tim murmured, but Ruth had turned away. The room was now full. People were settling down. She saw Dr. Lopez of Madrid coming rushing in and hurrying down the table, peering over people's shoulders at name cards to see if someone might have taken his seat. He finally noticed his empty chair and dropped into it, panting. Ruth smiled. Now the last one was here the meeting could start. She glanced at the wall clock, verified the time with her wristwatch, and reached for the gavel, promising herself that this first session, an afternoon session, would be a short one. Many people were tired from travel, and she promised herself an early night as well.

She tapped the gavel several times and the noise abated, people slipping on their headsets, pressing the proper buttons. Reporters at the press table also put on their headsets while those along the wall brought out their pencils. Ruth looked about the room, waiting for silence. Dr. Kovpak, his arms folded comfortably, was watching the proceedings with what appeared to be good-natured interest and nothing more. Ruth came to her feet, tapped the gavel once again, and then set it aside with a smile.

"I'm not exactly sure how to address an august gathering such as this," she began. "Ladies and gentlemen seems a bit formal. Saying my friends seems a bit premature to say the least, although I hope by the time these sessions end we shall be, indeed, friends. So I'll merely say, my colleagues in the field of archaeology, and let it go at that."

She wondered, as she spoke, how much English, if any, Dr. Kovpak understood. It was a pity she had not known he was going to attend. She could easily have arranged a place at the table for him where he could hear her through a translator. It was pretty hard to impress a man with the brilliance of her ideas if he had no notion of what she was talking about. She brought her thoughts back to the meeting.

"This session will be a short one. It's already two o'clock and I'm sure we all are tired from our travel. But we can consider it an introductory one and take up the more serious aspects of our meetings tomorrow." She glanced at some notes and then back at her listening audience. "We all know we are here in connection with the auction of the Schliemann treasure, whether we as individual museums have been asked to bid, or not. We are unaware—I believe this is true of all of us—of exactly who is offering this collection for sale. In addition, I am sure there have been many discussions at the various museums represented here regarding the matter of legal title to the treasure. My own views on this are known to my board of directors, and in time will be known to you as well, but in the course of these discussions I expect we will hear the views of others. I shall also present certain proposals for discussion before we are finished with these meetings."

She consulted her notes once again. The room was now totally quiet. She looked up, continuing evenly.

"I am sure there is no need to go into the history of the collection, of how and where it was discovered, or by whom. We in this room are all aware of this history, and from the world press coverage of the so-called 'Auction of the Century,' I should imagine almost everyone else in the world is equally knowledgeable. Suffice it to say, I believe that few other collections in the world could evoke the interest the Schliemann treasure has, or brought together such prestigious scientists as we are privileged to have here in this room today."

There was a slight murmur of self-appreciation. Ruth waited until it had died down and then went on.

"I believe it would be best, before we make any concrete proposals, to open the floor for a general airing of views. I shall ask each speaker to limit his remarks to ten minutes. After that I'm afraid I shall have to use my authority"—she smiled and touched the gavel—"to ask him to wait until others have spoken, at which time he will be permitted to speak again. I shall not wish to embarrass myself. I shall not attempt to pretend to know everyone present today. Therefore, when a speaker is given the floor, I suggest he introduce himself, as well as the museum he represents, after which we will be pleased to hear his remarks. Who would like the floor, please?"

A hand shot up at once, ahead of several other hands. Ruth nodded to the man. He came to his feet, bending a bit to speak toward the console microphone. He spoke in German.

"I am Dr. Wilhelm Kloster, of the Museum Dahlen, in West Berlin," he said in quiet, courteous tones. "I have been listening to our charming chairperson's speech, and as I look about the room I must say I am, indeed, impressed by the quality of the people here. I am forced to give full credit for the eminence of those present to our charming chairperson, since had it been anyone less respected, less admired, than Dr. Ruth McVeigh who called us together, I should have been surprised had the meeting been this well attended."

He paused and looked about, a short, rotund man with a pleasant smile, pince-nez glasses, and wearing a high, rather formal collar.

"However," he went on in the same polite tone, "I must admit I am a bit puzzled by the presence of many of you. Of most of you, in fact. In fact, to be perfectly honest, of any of you. The Schliemann treasure, as we all know, was stolen." He turned to look directly at Kovpak as he spoke; it was evident he recognized Kovpak and was not afraid to speak his mind. At the head of the table Ruth McVeigh wondered if Kovpak understood German; not a muscle had moved in the Russian's face, he still appeared to be listening in a relaxed, easy manner. Kloster turned back to the console microphone and continued. "Stolen, as I say, from a bunker under the Berlin Zoological Station. I shall not say by whom it was stolen; this is not a political meeting. But I'm sure we all have our own thoughts on that. However, what I am trying to say, my friends, is that the treasure was taken from a part of a divided city that is today West Berlin."

He paused to take a sip of water and then wiped his lips in a rather effete manner. This done, he tucked his handkerchief away and spread his rather pudgy hands as if seeking logic from those listening to him.

"Our charming chairperson mentioned the matter of a problem of legal ownership. There is no problem, my friends. There is no question of legal ownership involved here at all. The treasure belongs to Germany, to the Museum Dahlen. There is not the slightest doubt of this at all! None!"

He paused to sip some water, his small eyes moving calmly from one person to another, his pince-nez glittering as the light struck them from different angles.

"But let us go even further and eliminate at once any pretentious arguments for ownership that may mistakenly be brought before this group. The treasure was taken to the Berlin Zoo from the Museum of Ancient History, which was a part of the Museum of Handicraft, a museum that was situated near the Potsdamer Platz, which is in West Berlin, as well. The treasure was given to that museum by Heinrich Schliemann himself, and it remained in the possession of that museum uninterruptedly, and"—a pudgy finger came up—"*unchallenged as to ownership,* I might mention, until the last war, when, as I say, it was removed for safekeeping and subsequently disappeared. The hour of safekeeping is long past. It now appears that the treasure has been found, no matter who had it all these years, or where it has been kept. Logic and law both state unequivocally that it should and must return to its proper home at the Museum Dahlen in West Berlin. And may I add"—his voice hardened perceptibly, the small eyes behind the pince-nez glittered threateningly—"that when the treasure is recovered, or is bought, no matter who buys it or thinks he has bought it, the treasure rightly belongs to us, and I'm afraid we shall take whatever steps are necessary to see that our rights are not trampled upon!"

He sat down abruptly, but another hand had been held high during his final words, and Ruth recognized its owner. A stocky woman with gray hair in a tight bun came to her feet, speaking into the console, but with her eyes roving from person to person as she spoke, also in German.

"My name is Dr. Elsa Dornbusch. I am from the Staatliche Museen zu Berlin, which comprises the Bode, the Pergamon, and the National Gallery. I have listened to Dr. Kloster with, I must admit, a touch of surprise that he did not end his pretty speech with a 'Heil Hitler!' and more than a little admiration for his utter and complete gall. While he is perfectly correct in wondering why this meeting was convened, or, rather, why any of you who are present attended, he failed to include himself in that number. I cannot imagine why Dr. Kloster is here. Certainly not, I hope, merely to fill our ears with the nonsense we have just been subjected to. He says the treasure was taken from the Berlin Zoo, which today is in West Berlin, and therefore it belongs to the Dahlen. I have seldom heard anything that ridiculous, even from Dr. Kloster. He might equally say the treasure was deposited there by a man named Herman, and therefore the treasure is his because he has an uncle named Herman!"

There was a slight titter from the audience, quickly muffled. But Dr. Elsa Dornbusch had not intended anything humorous and she frowned, her lined face remaining as uncompromising as before. Across the conference table from her, Dr. Kloster had reddened slightly, but he managed to remain calm, his thick fingers tapping nervously on the table. Dr. Dornbusch disregarded her opponent and continued.

"Dr. Kloster compounds this farcical position by stating that the treasure was given to the Museum of Ancient History—which I concede it was—and that since that museum was located in what is now West Berlin, again the Dahlen can claim ownership. On that basis they could claim ownership of just about everything in the shops on the Kurfürstendamm because that avenue is also in West Berlin. What idiocy!"

She paused to glare around, as if to dare anyone to even smile. Her audience watched her carefully, as one might watch a ticking package, wondering what might come next. She went on, satisfied with the attention she was getting.

"Now, ladies and gentlemen, let us look at some facts. The treasure was, indeed, given to the Museum of Ancient History, but that museum, of course, was not the Dahlen. The Museum of Ancient History, as we all know, was destroyed during the war and was never rebuilt. The Schliemann treasure, therefore, cannot return to that museum. But it was given to Germany, and it must therefore remain in Germany. But where? Obviously at the Staatsliche, not anywhere else. Let me explain. Prior to the war, all cultural activity in the city—the theaters, the concerts, the galleries, the museums"—she paused to look at Kloster as if challenging him—"the important ones, that is—were located in that section of Berlin—not East Berlin or West Berlin, but simply Berlin—that today is part of the German Democratic Republic. This is true. I doubt if even Dr. Kloster would deny it. And Potsdamer Platz, which Dr. Kloster went to great lengths to point out is in West Berlin, is less than half a mile from the Staatsliche, at the very edge of the zone, while being as far from the Dahlen in both distance and in conception, if we consider the museum there that no longer exists, as the moon!"

She paused to sip water and then went on in the silence.

"The proper museum—German museum—to lay claim to the treasure is the Bode, which is part of the Staatliche. Here is one of the finest collections of ancient treasures in the world, on a par with the Hermitage, the British, or the Metropolitan. It is the logical place for it. It is the moral place for it. And may I finish by saying—with less belligerency than Dr. Kloster, I hope, but with equal fervor and total intent—that that is where the Schliemann treasure is going to end."

She sat down to silence. Ruth McVeigh involuntarily glanced toward Gregor Kovpak. The white-haired man at his side was leaning over, obviously asking Kovpak something. Ruth saw Kovpak answer in apparent good nature, and then return his attention to the discussion, while the white-haired man sat back, a frown of uncertainty on his face. Ruth became aware that other hands had been raised during her lapse. She reddened a bit and wondered who had been first, finally selecting one at random. The man who rose was heavy-set, with a pock-marked face and a fierce-looking mustache, but with a rich and surprisingly friendly voice. He smiled around the table before beginning, his hands idly caressing the back of his chair as he spoke.

"My name is Dimitrios Jacoubs. I am afraid I do not represent any particular museum, nor do I have all the letters after my name that you illustrious people do. However, I represent the Greek government, so I ask your indulgence to hear me out—"

He paused, seeing the frowns of non-understanding on everyone's face, seeing hands reaching out, punching buttons on the consoles. He shrugged apologetically as the reason came to him. He had been speaking Greek, a language not on the translator. He changed to French, apologizing, and repeated himself. Then he continued.

"I have listened to the two people who have just spoken,

and I can understand their differences. I can also understand their problem. Basically, what I believe they are saying is that neither one of them has a decent claim to the collection; that this poor treasure, its former home no longer existent, is without a place to lay its head, so they both want to adopt him. Well, possibly I can resolve the problem for them, because I should like to present my case for Greek ownership of this poor orphan, which I am sure everyone here will recognize as far more legitimate than the claims presented by the previous two speakers."

He sipped water and smiled at his waiting audience as he picked up the thread of his argument.

"I should like to take you back to when the treasure was first discovered and brought to Greece. Yes, friends, it was brought to Greece and remained there for some years before it was given—without the right to give—by Heinrich Schliemann to a German museum. I say without a right to give, because the discovery of this treasure was a joint effort by Heinrich Schliemann and his wife, Sophie Engastromenos before her marriage, and a Greek. And Sophie Engastromenos wanted the treasure to be given to Greece, desperately wanted it. Her husband's will prevailed, but the desire of a husband is not necessarily a legal right, not concerning a property that was found jointly and therefore should have been disposed of jointly. Now, when Heinrich Schliemann died, Sophie was his heir, and as such was now the full owner of the treasure. But Sophie Schliemann was a dutiful wife, and although her wishes should have been the ones that dominated, she allowed the treasure to remain where it was. The Greek government, however, is under no such compulsion to allow the situation to remain."

He shrugged and spread his large hands.

"You may wonder why the Greek government has taken so long to press their claim to this collection. In the first place, at the time that Heinrich Schliemann donated the treasure to Germany—a treasure it was not his alone to donate—the German government was a powerful state, and we certainly had no intention of going to war over a collection of ancient artifacts. At that time, also, the German state was an entity. Today that is no longer the case. We have, in fact, heard representatives of the two German states arguing ownership today. The fact is, the Germany to whom Schliemann gave the treasure no longer exists. The thought that Schliemann would have given his treasure to West Germany, is doubtful; he wanted it to go to the country of his birth, and he was born in Neu Buckow, in Mecklenberg-Schwerin, which today is in East Germany. And the thought that Schliemann would have wanted his treasure to go to a Communist regime is unthinkable."

He looked about the room and shrugged again.

"And then, when there was no longer a united Germany of any kind, in 1945, there was also no longer a Schliemann collection. It had disappeared. However, now that it appears to have been rediscovered, I suggest quite strongly that the proper place for it is in Greece, a country it should never have left. It is the country where Sophie Engastromenos always wished it to be, the country where it belongs. Regarding the desires of Sophie Schliemann in this regard, I might mention, they are fully documented and I have the documents here for anyone who wishes to examine them. I will close with the statement that the Greek government intends to pursue this matter to the fullest. Thank you."

He sat down. A man who had been holding up his hand almost from the beginning of Jacoubs' statement, came to his feet slowly at Ruth's nod. He was a tall man, almost painfully thin, with sunken swarthy cheeks, and black hair cut short and combed rigidly back. He was smoking a cigarette and he contemplated it in his twiglike fingers most of the time he spoke, as if drawing some degree of comfort from it. As Jacoubs had done, he spoke in French.

"My name is Suleiman Abbas," he said, "and I represent the Archaeological Museums of Istanbul. But I am sure I speak for all Turkish museums, as well as for the Turkish government. Let me say at the very beginning that I am quite surprised at this meeting. All of you are aware, I am sure, that the so-called Schliemann treasure was taken from Turkey illegally. The *firman*—the permit issued by the Turkish government to Schliemann to dig in the Troad—was given him under certain conditions, and I can assure you those conditions did not include the right to steal from the Turkish people. It specifically indicated that all finds were to be presented for examination to a representative of the Turkish government, and that a division, based upon mutual agreement, would be made. But what actually happened? Schliemann, discovering the treasure—or his wife discovering it, if that pleases some of you—sent his workers home for the day, carried the treasure to his home by subterfuge—under his wife's skirts, the story is—and later smuggled it from Turkey to Greece. I said before the treasure was the 'so-called' Schliemann treasure, because it never belonged to Heinrich Schliemann. If you wish to call it the Troy treasure, or the Troad treasure, or the Turkish treasure—or even Priam's treasure, as some scholars think it to be—very well and good. But it is not and never was the Schliemann treasure."

He paused to flick ash from his cigarette and resumed speaking, still staring most of the time at the smoke curling from between his thin fingers.

"I am sure that all of you are not only aware of the illegality of Schliemann disregarding his *firman* and smuggling the treasure to Greece, but you are also aware of the United Nations stand on art treasures, that they belong to the country of origin. Who can deny that Turkey is the country of origin? Who can deny that Schliemann broke the rules of his permit, and then compounded his crime by smuggling the fruits of his find out of the country of Turkey?" For the first time he raised his eyes from the hypnotic wreath of smoke rising from the cigarette to look about the room, almost accusingly. "Many of you have excavated in countries under permits issued by those countries. Those who have are well aware of the rules of the game. How many would have had permits renewed, or extended, had they done what Heinrich Schliemann did? Yet the man is considered a sort of genius when he was, in fact, a mere thief. Even in Greek law, I'm sure"—he looked at Jacoubs, sitting large and silent down the table from him—"a man is not permitted to gain from something he has stolen. And the goods, when recovered, must always be returned to the party from whom they were taken."

He noticed his cigarette had burned down to the cork tip and crushed it out almost reluctantly. Without this center for his attention his dark brooding eyes moved from one listener to another, demanding their attention, their understanding, their acquiescence.

"You may ask why Turkey never made claim to the treasure before. Well, as a matter of fact, we did. Many times while

Heinrich Schliemann was alive. But after his death, with the treasure firmly in the hands of the German government, the matter seemed too difficult to resolve. As Mr. Jacoubs said, quite correctly in fact, one does not go to war—particularly against a stronger power—over a collection of ancient artifacts. Now, however, the situation is completely different. The treasure, it appears, is now in the hands of a person or persons who have no legal claim to it at all."

He looked at Ruth McVeigh, sitting at the head of the table. His voice was quiet, almost resigned.

"Dr. McVeigh, the Turkish museum will not bid in the farce of this so-called auction. We would expect that nobody would bid, but we are realistic enough to know this will not be the case. I can therefore only say we shall be most humbly and gratefully thankful to the successful bidder, whoever he may be, because he shall have to turn the treasure over to us."

He nodded toward the head of the table, a brief, short nod, pushed his chair back, and walked slowly but with dignity from the room. There was a moment's silence at his unexpected departure, and then everyone seemed to want to speak at once. Hands flashed in the air, waving frantically, people stood, calling out, leaning over at last to speak into the console microphones for attention, without waiting for permission to speak. It was bedlam, and the sharp rapping of Ruth McVeigh's gavel seemed to make little difference. She waited a moment, her gavel pounding furiously but unsuccessfully, and then reached for her purse. She brought out a police whistle, used to handle any indecent approaches, and drew her microphone toward her, turning the volume dial on it to its maximum. She then blew the whistle into the microphone with all her strength. The shrill sound, blasting almost painfully from the wall speakers and echoing loudly from all corners of the confined space, was deafening. People stopped their racket and looked up, as if at an air-raid siren. A lesser blast on the whistle completed the maneuver. People began to settle back, to quiet down. The hands that were raised now were raised quietly, respectfully. Ruth chose to ignore them.

"I think we've had enough discussion for today, our opening session," she said. "We will meet here again tomorrow at ten in the morning. I suggest in the meantime those wishing to speak write their names on a slip of paper. We will draw them from a bowl, lottery style, and they will be given the floor in that order. Thank you."

She switched off the microphone and automatically looked to where Gregor Kovpak had been sitting, but to her disappointment the chair was empty. She could see the white-haired man who had been seated next to Kovpak just making his way through the door, and she could only assume that Kovpak had preceded him. She was surprised at the depths of her disappointment. It was too bad, she would have liked to meet him. Now it would have to wait until the following day, if he remained for the next session. He might go back to Leningrad, probably feeling it to be pointless listening to speeches he could not understand. She shook her head, surprised and a bit irked with herself for her concern, slid her papers into her briefcase, and turned to find herself facing a smiling Dr. Gregor Kovpak.

"Hello," he said. "My name is Kovpak, Gregor Kovpak, and I just wanted to tell you I thought you handled that near-riot in style. Tell me, have you ever been a policeman?"

His English was excellent, tinged with only the slightest of accents. Ruth also noticed he was tall, taller than she had supposed seeing him seated. He had brown eyes, very white teeth, dark curly hair, and a wonderful smile, she thought. Someone, sometime, she thought, had broken his nose, but it only made him appear more masculine. She suddenly recalled he had asked a question.

"No," she said with a smile. "I have sat up nights with a weapon protecting a dig, though."

"As have we all," Kovpak said fervently. "I also wanted to tell you that I've read most of your papers, and enjoyed them very much. And finally, I wanted to congratulate you on your recent appointment at the Metropolitan."

"Thank you," Ruth said, and was amazed at how relieved she felt that he had not left. She felt that his candor deserved no less than her own. "I already knew who you were. The man next to me recognized you."

"Tim Rubin? An old friend. But I hope you didn't believe anything he said about me."

"I believe very little Tim says. But I did want to meet you. I'm glad you waited. I tried to meet you at the Hermitage the few times I've been there, but you always seem to be traveling. And I had no idea you would be here, or I would have seen to it you were seated at the table, with a console."

Kovpak shrugged lightly. "It was no problem. I speak both German and French, so there was no trouble in that."

"German and French? And English?"

Kovpak shrugged a bit embarrassedly, as if he disliked discussing any accomplishments he might have. "I speak German because so much is written in German that affects my work. I speak French, because"—he suddenly smiled, a smile that lit up his face, taking Ruth into his confidence—"because I like the way it sounds."

Ruth smiled with him. "And the English?"

Kovpak frowned, serious now. "The English because it's a very important language." He looked about and then back at Ruth, obviously changing the subject, his expressive face now curious. "What did you think of your meeting?"

Ruth made a face. "Hectic, is what I would call it. I had no idea—!" She looked at him. "What did you think of it?"

"Amusing," Kovpak said, and laughed. "Very amusing."

"Amusing?" It was the last answer Ruth McVeigh had expected. "In what way?"

Kovpak looked around. The room was nearly deserted; a few at the press table were putting their notes away, one reporter was painstakingly writing something in his notebook. There were a few groups around the room apparently discussing the speeches that afternoon, but the large majority of the delegates to the conference had vanished. Kovpak looked back at Ruth, smiling.

"It's a long story, far too long to go into here. Besides, it's too near the cocktail hour. I know that nobody believes that Russians drink"—he grinned—"but I'm the exception. Why don't I meet you in the bar in, say"—he consulted his watch—"half an hour? And then we can have dinner together, after that. That will give us plenty of time to talk of many things. Cabbages and kings, and treasures and things, and what I found so amusing in your meeting today."

Ruth hesitated. Some small recess of her mind reminded her of Tim Rubin's statement that Dr. Gregor Kovpak was not interested in further entanglements. He probably was still in love with the wife he had lost, she thought, and in any event, why should he possibly be interested in her? Then she had to smile at herself inwardly as she realized how ridiculous that thought was. She had met the man five minutes before, and while it was true the man was attractive, what on earth was so entangling about having a friendly drink and a dinner with a fellow archaeologist? She did it all the time. You're beginning to have the vapors, my dear, she told herself a bit sternly; doing the feminine bit a bit overmuch. She nodded at Kovpak.

"Half an hour it is. In the bar," she said, and held out her hand to be shaken in quite masculine fashion. "On second thought," she said a bit more hurriedly than she would have wanted, "let's make that an hour, instead." She wanted time to find that little perfume shop in Shepherd Market before their meeting . . .

At the press table, James Newkirk remained, writing something in his notebook in his own particular form of shorthand. James Newkirk was a tall heavy-set muscular man wearing glasses, who carried credentials as the cultural reporter for the Paris *Herald Tribune,* and he worked at the job. However, what he was writing so carefully was intended to be the basis of the report he would transmit to Langley, Virginia, in their conversation late that night.

There was no doubt in Newkirk's mind that each of the four speakers of that first afternoon session had been quite genuine in his identity, as well as in the personal conviction each carried in his own arguments, but nothing had been said in any of the impassioned speeches to indicate in any way Russian involvement in the auction. Newkirk had seen and recognized Gregor Kovpak. It had been expected that the foremost archaeologist in the Soviet Union would be attending. It had also been expected that he would be accompanied by a KGB man, and Newkirk did not have the slightest doubt that that was the role of the white-haired man at Kovpak's side.

But the interesting fact was that the noted Russian archaeologist was not seated at the main conference table. That was exceedingly interesting and would make up a large portion of his report. If the Russians were in any way behind the auction, one would think they would have arranged to be at the main table, together with the other bidders. One would think they would do this if only to dissemble. To come here as observers, which is the position one would take if they were, for example, selling the collection and wanted to see the reaction of potential buyers; that was hard to understand. It would be too open. On the other hand, possibly they were merely being subtle, expecting any foreign agent who might be present to think exactly that way. In any event, Newkirk knew it was too early to tell. More data would be required before any conclusion could be reached.

Also quite interesting, he noted in his crabbed shorthand to be included in his report, was the fact that as soon as the meeting ended, Kovpak had immediately made contact with Dr. Ruth McVeigh. There they were at this very moment, at the end of the conference table, speaking as old friends, although when Newkirk had been briefed on Dr. Kovpak and his acquaintances in the west, Ruth McVeigh had not been included. A slip-up in the agency? Possibly, but doubtful. Certainly indicating that surveillance of the two was clearly indicated. Someone would also have to keep an eye on the white-haired man, the KGB man. Newkirk thought of the possible operatives he could summon from the London office, made his choice, and finished his scribbling.

Satisfied that all was under control, and pleased with the results of the first day of the job, James Newkirk came to his feet and innocently followed Ruth McVeigh and Gregor Kovpak from the room as they left, still chatting amicably.

12

Serge Ulanov was lying on his bed, shoes off, his usual cigarette pasted in one corner of his mouth, dribbling ash on his chest. The major was reading a copy of *Playboy*, taking advantage of being abroad, when Gregor Kovpak came into the adjoining room. The major put down his magazine, got off the bed, and walked through the open connecting door. He sat down in a chair, pulled over an ashtray, and watched with a touch of interest as Kovpak opened a dresser drawer and pulled out a white shirt, examining it critically. Satisfied at last, Kovpak next went to the closet, took out his only suit and laid it on the bed, then went back to the closet to make a careful selection between the two neckties there. He put the winner on the bed with the other things and began undressing. The major smiled broadly.

"Getting dressed for dinner? With me? I'm flattered."

Kovpak smiled. "Not with you. I've got a date."

"I figured that out already. The handsome chairperson, I assume? For a confirmed bachelor," Ulanov said, flicking ash from his cigarette, "you certainly work fast."

Kovpak laughed. In the few days the two men had been together, he had grown to like the stocky KGB man. "Major, you'll become an investigator, yet, coming to such accurate conclusions so quickly. Tell me, sir—how do you do it?"

"Practice," Ulanov said modestly. "Besides, I doubt you'd go for the East German woman, that Elsa Dornbusch. She's probably old enough to be your mother."

"Or yours."

"Or mine," Ulanov conceded with a smile.

"There was another girl there," Kovpak pointed out, taking off his shoes. "A very pretty girl from Italy. It could have been her."

"Except you don't speak Italian, and she speaks nothing else. I asked," Ulanov said calmly. "Besides, you couldn't keep your eyes off the lady at the head of the table." He studied the end of his burning cigarette a moment and then added quietly, "I wouldn't get too serious about her if I were you, Gregor."

"Fortunately, Major," Kovpak said with a smile, "you're not me," and went into the bathroom for his shower. When he came out a few minutes later, toweling himself briskly, he suddenly stopped and frowned at Ulanov. "Incidentally, Major, so there won't be any misunderstanding later on, may I say that you're not invited to this dinner date of mine."

"I'm disappointed but really not surprised," Ulanov said calmly. "I didn't expect to be. Besides, I have my own date tonight."

"At your age? Or is it the effect of the *Playboy* magazine I saw you reading?" Kovpak laughed. "Which one is it? Your East German mother? Or the Italian girl?"

"Neither," Ulanov said quietly, and leaned over to crush out his cigarette. He immediately replaced it with another, lighting it from a match that appeared to come from nowhere. "It's one of the press reporters. A cultural reporter of a paper over here, and he actually is." He took his cigarette from his mouth and contemplated its end; satisfied that it was burning to his satisfaction, he replaced it, speaking around the smoke. "Of course he's also CIA. A stringer, not a regular, but still . . ."

Kovpak paused in drawing on his socks. "You're having dinner with a CIA man?"

"I didn't say that. I said I had a date with a CIA man. I didn't say he knows about it as yet. And," he added, drawing deeply on his cigarette, "if I'm properly careful, he won't know about it at all." He smiled at Kovpak brightly.

Gregor shook his head in complete non-understanding. "And how do you know he's actually CIA?"

"The same way he either knows—or at least strongly suspects—that I am KGB," Ulanov said calmly, as if it made all the sense in the world. "We try to keep track of each other's agents on a job, at least to the best of our ability. It does no harm and sometimes even helps."

Kovpak stared at the other man. "If they know you, and you know them—isn't that a bit ridiculous?"

Ulanov raised his shoulders, smiling. "I suppose it is, in a way. But that's the way the game is played."

Gregor shook his head. "Serge," he said, "tell me something. In the short time we've known each other, we've talked quite a bit. You've demonstrated to me you've got a good mind, a good technical mind. Even a sense of humor, which, frankly, surprised me. You were educated as an engineer. What made you become a security man?"

Ulanov laughed. "You mean, what's a nice girl like you doing in a place like this?" His laugh faded, and he became serious. "I became a security man because someone has to do the job, and I don't mind being the one. I agree it would be nice if there was no CIA or KGB—and I'm sure our newspaper reporter friend feels the same way. According to our reports on him, he's a very nice man. And a very good agent. Of course, he has no sense of humor, but that's an advantage in our business. But the fact is there is a CIA and a KGB, and the equivalents in every country in the world. And I'm afraid there always will be."

He tilted his head toward the door, as if to bring the conference they had attended that afternoon into the discussion.

"Now, you take this case, for example," he went on calmly. "It certainly isn't a major one. Certainly no world-shaking events depend on what we discover here, or what we do not discover here. In fact, the chances are that even if we do find out who has this treasure and is trying to auction it off, it won't help us discover exactly what weakness in CIA security allowed him to get the collection out of Langley. But we have to try. That's why we're here."

Kovpak had been dressing during this discussion. He started to button his white shirt. "And why is the CIA here in the first place?"

"Possibly to prevent us from learning anything. Or possibly for some other reason we know nothing about. Which is precisely why I shall be keeping an eye on our reportorial friend."

"And in a similar vein," Kovpak said sarcastically, tucking in the shirt, "why won't your reportorial friend be keeping an eye on you?"

Ulanov's eyebrows went up. "I should certainly be surprised if he didn't," he said, and smiled. "Or at least if he didn't try."

Kovpak shook his head in complete non-understanding of security work. He moved to the mirror and began knotting his necktie, straightening it carefully, examining it for perfection, speaking over his shoulder.

"If you're going to keep such a careful eye on your friend, hadn't you better be getting on with it?"

Ulanov smiled gently. "There's no rush. If you made a date with your Dr. McVeigh, I'm quite sure our friend was watching you do it. And was wondering just what information you were trying to squeeze out of the American. It's a suspicious business, this security work, I'm afraid. But, in any event, our friend undoubtedly decided the best way to find out what Dr. Kovpak wants from Dr. McVeigh is to keep an eye on the two of you. Which is what he will do." He shrugged, but there was a humorous glint in his eye. "Therefore, there's no need to get going, as you put it, until you yourself get going. By the way," he added artlessly, "what's your program for the evening?"

"A drink at the bar and then dinner," Kovpak said. He had put on his suit jacket and was examining himself in the mirror critically, wishing he was a person who took more interest in his clothes. Still, the suit was the best one he had and would have to do. He just hoped that Dr. Ruth McVeigh would see beyond the suit to the inner man.

"You look fine," Ulanov said dryly, reading the other man's mind. "May I make a suggestion? The hotel lounge here is fine, but while the restaurant food is decent enough, I should imagine that Dr. McVeigh will get tired of it if she eats all her meals here. Now, there's a very good place just down Curzon Street, across the way from the entrance to Shepherd Market. I'm sure she would enjoy that very much . . ."

Kovpak frowned. "Why do you want me to take her to this particular restaurant?"

Ulanov sighed. "My friend, you're overly suspicious. Leave

that to us security people. I merely suggested this restaurant—"

"Because you have a purpose in wanting us to go there," Kovpak said shortly. "All right, I'll take her there. But I really do not like playing these cloak-and-dagger games, Major."

"Cloak-and-dagger? To take a lady to a decent restaurant?" Ulanov shook his head as if hurt by the unfair accusation. He came to his feet. "Incidentally, if you don't mind, please leave the connecting door between our rooms open. I'll close it later and lock it if you should find yourself in need of"—he cleared his throat innocently—"privacy."

Kovpak laughed. "Serge, you have a filthy mind. I suppose it comes from spending your life peeping through keyholes. Do what you want with the door." He looked at his watch. "I have to be leaving. Are you coming with me, or isn't that in the best tradition of spying?"

"In the very worst tradition," Ulanov said solemnly. "You go ahead. I have a few things to do."

"I'll see you later," Kovpak said, and then paused. "By the way," he said slowly, curiously, "if I'm going to be followed, I'd like to know what my follower looks like, or what his name is, at least."

Ulanov grinned. "I'm afraid telling you would also not be in the best tradition of spying. You'd constantly be looking over your shoulder at him, and that would upset our friend very much. And it would also do you no good with your lovely lady. Women expect you to pay attention to them when you ask them to dinner."

"All right," Kovpak said. "Then I'll simply have to watch out for someone who leans over the table and turns his ear close to our mouths."

"Unless, of course, you have a deaf waiter. But generally that's the way," Ulanov said encouragingly. "And one more thing—"

Kovpak paused, his hand on the doorknob. "Yes?"

"Have a good time. Enjoy, enjoy," Ulanov said with a smile, and walked back into his own room.

Ruth McVeigh was studying herself in the mirror and liking what she saw. When she had first bought the gown she had done so in a rare spirit of adventure, aware that the gown was cut to maximally flatter her full figure, and now she was happy she had purchased it. It would have been a shame, she thought, if Dr. Kovpak had been allowed to return to Leningrad, and they never saw each other again, without his knowing that Dr. Ruth McVeigh was more than just another archaeologist, another writer of papers, but was also a woman in every respect.

She turned abruptly from the mirror, irritated with herself for her self-admiration and, unreasonably, also a bit irritated with Gregor Kovpak for making her think the thoughts she had. You would think you had never had dinner with a man before, she said to herself. It's simply a matter of eating a meal in the company of a person you respect and admire for his work, rather than eating alone. Why even get so dressed up for it? Dr. Kovpak probably won't even notice the lovely gown, or the woman inside of it. Besides, she added to herself in stern warning, if you keep standing here admiring yourself, you'll be late, and whether Dr. Kovpak will notice how beautiful you are or not, he's sure to notice if you're very late, because that's one thing that most men do *not* approve of. But you do look nice, she said to herself, turning back to the mirror for a last check on her makeup, and if Dr. Kovpak doesn't notice it, he's blind. She gave herself a wink in the mirror, grinned back at the gamine image, and left the room.

Gregor Kovpak was waiting for her at a small table for two in one corner of the dim lounge, aware of how much better dressed the men at the tables around him were in comparison with himself. He came to his feet as Ruth paused in the doorway, looking about in the gloom. He could see the eyes of almost every man turn at the same moment to take in the beautiful woman some lucky dog was going to escort that evening. Gregor fought down a tendency to grin around the room like an idiot, to show that he was that lucky dog. But then his inner exaltation faded. He knew it certainly wasn't because of his excessive charm that Ruth McVeigh had agreed to have dinner with him, but because he was a fellow scientist in her field. He wondered at his own nerve in asking her so blithely that afternoon, and instantly promised himself that as soon as he got back home he would see to it that he had a wardrobe as extensive and as colorful as Alex Pomerenko's. But he knew he wouldn't. To what purpose? Clothes had never meant a thing to him, and what difference would it make, in any event? Clothes, he was sure—or at least he hoped—were not, or could not, be important to someone as intelligent as Ruth McVeigh. Besides, he would see Ruth McVeigh tonight and possibly at the meeting the following day, and after that they would simply be distant acquaintances, reading each other's scientific papers, possibly, and—at least on his part—wondering how the other person was faring. Or who she was having dinner with...

He became aware that Ruth had made her way through the crowded lounge and the battery of admiring eyes and was standing before him. He hurried to pull out her chair, watched her sink into it, and then sat down himself, wondering at his sudden feeling of gaucherie. It's been too long, he said to himself. It's been so long since I was with a woman, certainly with a woman this lovely or this talented, that I'm acting like a sixteen-year-old on his first date. He looked up. A waiter was standing at their side, looking at them a bit impatiently. Gregor looked at Ruth inquiringly.

"A martini, very dry," she said. "With gin, not vodka."

"I'll have the same," he said, surprised to hear himself say it since he never drank gin. He waited for some word from his companion to open the conversation, but she was looking about the lounge, as if she were seeking someone. Their drinks were served in the silence that had fallen; they both sipped, set down their glasses, and spoke at the same time.

"I—" she said.

"You—" he began.

They both laughed. The ice broken, Gregor felt himself begin to relax. It's simply dinner with a fellow archaeologist, he told himself. Forget that she's beautiful, and hope she forgets you're dressed like a peasant. And forget that you'll be going back to Leningrad when she's on her way to New York. He raised his glass in the gesture of a toast and Ruth responded. They both sipped, then Gregor set down his glass.

"Now," he said firmly, "what were you going to say?"

"No, you first."

He smiled. "I was only going to say that you look very attractive in that gown. And you were going to say?"

"Thank you for the compliment," Ruth said. "I was going to ask you what you meant this afternoon when you said you thought the first session had been rather amusing."

Gregor felt his initial feeling of clumsiness slip entirely away. He was thankful that Ruth had obviously seen his insecurity and was turning the conversation in a direction where he would feel equal, a rational person discussing an event in a rational way.

"I simply meant that the arguments the four people presented each appeared logical on the surface, until the next person spoke. Then the logic seemed to change sides. But what I found amusing was the fact that all of the arguments they presented were basically completely illogical and invalid."

"Invalid?"

"Completely. But before we go into that, what did you think I meant when I said the session was amusing?"

"I thought you found the session amusing, because—" Ruth hesitated a moment and then decided to be completely frank. "Well, because you thought the whole thing of the auction was a hoax, and that the meeting was, therefore, a waste of time—"

"And I do. A complete waste of time."

"—because you knew where the treasure was all the time— in Russia—and who was auctioning it off," Ruth went on, disregarding the interruption.

"You thought that?" Gregor Kovpak shook his head. "No," he said gently, "in this you are wrong. The treasure is not in Russia, nor has it ever been. That is the truth. And as for the auction being a hoax, I'm quite convinced it is quite genuine. Since I first heard of this auction I've spoken with people I know at various museums, and they assure me the pieces they received as proof of the genuineness of the offer, were themselves quite genuine." He looked at her. "Wasn't this also your experience?"

"It was. But, in that case, why do you think this conference is a waste of time?"

Gregor hesitated, putting his thoughts in order, twisting the stem of the martini glass in his fingers, watching the contents sluggishly attempt to follow the motion of the glass but never quite catch up. At last he looked up.

"I think your conference is a waste of time," he said quietly, "because of the people you are dealing with. Consider your first session today. Four claimants, each convinced he represents the party to whom the treasure morally and legally belongs. Do you believe you can convince those four people that they are wrong? As indeed they are? And your discussions will get more disruptive, not less. Most of those present want the treasure, and they want it for themselves. If they were serious people, they would agree that each museum put up a portion of the asking price and they would buy the treasure jointly. And then decide in some kind of future lottery among themselves how each museum would exhibit it in turn. In that way—" He frowned at the expression on Ruth's face. "What's wrong? What did I say?"

"You said exactly what I said to our board of directors!" Ruth said triumphantly, and smiled at him. "That is exactly the proposition I intend to present to the conference tomorrow morning. In fact, I'm going to suggest that the four claimants, as you call them, be allowed to share without paying anything. That was my idea when I set up this conference." She felt exhilarated. "So you agree that's the best way to handle the matter. I'm sure it is."

Kovpak was frowning at her. "I do not agree at all! I said that is what would happen if you were dealing with serious people. But you are dealing with fanatics, collectors. Do you honestly believe the four who spoke today are going to relinquish their claim, just because they are given a small share of something they believe is totally theirs? Now you expect to ask the others to not only pay their own share, but to add something on for the claimants. Then you intend to tell them they possibly might not be able to exhibit the treasure for as much as fifteen or twenty years, perhaps." He shrugged. "Many of them will be dead by then."

"They could visit the museum exhibiting the treasure and see it there—"

"That would be even worse. They don't want to see the treasure, they want to own it. Many of them have already seen the treasure in Berlin, before the war. Certainly the two German museums who argued for possession today have seen it. It would be even more galling for them to travel, say, to the Metropolitan in New York, and look at a treasure they feel (a) is theirs, (b) is in the hands of someone else, and (c) they cannot show in their own museum for ten or fifteen years." He shook his head decisively. "They will never agree. Which is why I said the conference is not only amusing, but is also a waste of time."

Ruth shook her head stubbornly. "I think you're wrong. Bob Keller said the same thing as you, and I told him I thought he was wrong, too. In fact I bet him a dinner on it—"

Kovpak wondered who this Bob Keller was. For a moment he felt an unreasoning wave of jealousy, and then realized how foolish he was being. "Speaking of dinner," he said, happy to be getting away from the subject of Bob Keller, whoever he might be, "would you like another drink here, or with dinner?"

"With dinner, I think."

They finished their drinks and Gregor signed the tab. He came to his feet, helped Ruth up, and walked into the lobby with her, smiling down at her. "There's a restaurant that's been highly recommended to me. It's only a few blocks from here. It's a nice evening. We could walk over there and try it, if you don't mind."

"I don't mind at all."

They left the hotel and walked slowly along Park Lane, with the traffic pouring by on the park side, and turned into the quieter Curzon Street, not speaking, each busy with his own thoughts. The restaurant was easily identifiable, being the only one in the block across from Shepherd Market that exhibited any light at all. It occurred to Kovpak that they had no reservations, but his fears on that score were allayed when he saw the restaurant was practically deserted. If that was an indication of bad food, Kovpak said to himself, I'll have the major's scalp! On my first and probably last date with Ruth McVeigh! Not that food was all that important, but still . . .

They were seated, ordered a cocktail as well as their main meal, which was to be delayed awhile, and looked at each other in silence. Ruth could see the admiration in Gregor's eyes, and wondered if he could see the same in hers. She decided it was time to change the unspoken subject, and picked the first thing that came into her mind.

"You said before, that the arguments of those four people who made claim to the collection were completely invalid," she said. "On what basis?"

"Simply because they were. On the same basis, you could claim the treasure for the Metropolitan, or possibly the Smithsonian. After all, one made his claim on the basis of Sophie Schliemann being Greek. Well, after all, Heinrich Schliemann was a citizen of the United States at the time he discovered

Troy; not of Germany or Greece, but of the United States."

"But that's ridiculous—"

"Of course it is. As were the other arguments you heard today." He suddenly grinned. "The only valid arguments for ownership—there are two of them—would have to come from Russia."

"Russia? You're joking."

"I'm quite serious," Gregor said, his grin disappearing. "It's easy to say that Heinrich Schliemann spent the last part of his life and most of his fortune searching for Troy, or Mycenae, or anything else. The thing that enabled him to do this, instead of working as a clerk somewhere, was money. Agreed?"

"Agreed," Ruth said, wondering where he was leading.

"Money," Gregor said, repeating himself. "Money discovered the treasure, because it was money that hired the workers who did the actual excavation. It was money that paid for the equipment, for the shovels and picks and the wagons and everything else. It was money that paid for Heinrich and Sophie to travel to those places. And that money was Russian money." He saw the look on Ruth's face and nodded. "It's quite true, you know. It was money Schliemann made by holding the Russian army up to exorbitant prices during the Crimean War. Schliemann had managed a monopoly on the indigo trade in Russia, and he made the Russian army pay what even an American would call an unconscionable price for indigo at a time when the army found it an indispensable product. It was a natural product then. Indigo wasn't synthesized until many years later, and by—the word is gouging—the Russians, Schliemann became wealthy enough to indulge his passion for exploration." He shrugged. "So, on the basis that it was Russian money that financed the discovery of the treasure in the first place, one has to say the treasure properly belongs to Russia."

He paused as their drinks came. Ruth McVeigh had been listening to the argument with a slight frown on her face, wondering if Gregor Kovpak was serious, or if he was pulling her leg. They picked up their drinks and sipped. Kovpak put his glass down and went on.

"I said there were two arguments for my country to claim the treasure. The second, of course, is that the treasure was recovered by the Russians in a bunker in Berlin. That much is true. And on the basis of that find—a spoils of war—the treasure also properly belongs to Russia."

Ruth found herself drawn into the discussion despite herself. "But what about the Allied Commission on recovered art objects?"

Gregor waved that argument away as having no importance. He leaned across the table and Ruth decided he was, after all, quite serious.

"The country that was the most influential in establishing that so-called commission," he said evenly, "was the United States of America, a country, I might mention, that did not have one city bombed, or one museum looted, or one institution robbed. No one dropped bombs on the Metropolitan, or the Smithsonian." He shrugged. "It was quite easy for the Americans to decide that, since there was no chance of their participating in any spoils of war, nobody else should. Of course, the United States didn't feel that way when there *was* a chance of their participating in war spoils. They didn't feel that way after the Mexican War, when they annexed a big chunk of a neighboring country. And they didn't feel that way after the Spanish-American War, when they took over Puerto Rico—"

Ruth decided that was enough. Gregor was beginning to sound impassioned. "Look," she said quietly, reaching across the table to touch Gregor's hand. "I don't want to see a pleasant evening spoiled by a political argument. Let's change the subject." She withdrew her hand.

Gregor suddenly smiled. "I agree." He was happy he had been stopped before he had added that the Americans didn't feel that way about the Schliemann treasure, which they had in their possession, at least until recently, according to Ulanov. That would have been impolitic. "What would you like to talk about?"

It was skirting the topic they had just dropped, but Ruth was curious. "You said just now that the Russians found the treasure in a bunker in Berlin. But before, you said that the treasure wasn't in Russia and never had been..."

"That's right," Gregor said, and shook his head ruefully. "We had it in our hands, and then we lost it. It was stolen, taken from us with forged papers. Forged shipping instructions, on May 22, 1945." He looked at Ruth, his eyes twinkling. "On the other hand, if we hadn't lost it, I suppose I wouldn't be here now. With you."

Ruth McVeigh had no intention of getting off on that subject. It would be more dangerous than politics. Besides, she was intrigued by his statement. "Are you serious? About losing the treasure, I mean," she added quickly.

"Very serious. I had the story quite recently from someone who is in a position to know. It's ridiculous but, unfortunately, true. The treasure was supposedly shipped back to Russia, but the shipping instructions were false, forged. The crate was marked as captured medical equipment, to be delivered to some major on his furnishing proper identification. The crate got as far as Bad Freienwalde, a small town not very far from Berlin, and then"—he shrugged—"it just disappeared."

Ruth McVeigh frowned. It was a fascinating story, if true, and there was no doubt from Gregor's tone and mien, that at least he believed it to be true. Besides, it made sense. It could explain the auction. If the treasure was in private hands, and had been in private hands all those years, and not in the hands of the Russian government, then an auction could be explained. It was like a mystery story, and Ruth had always enjoyed those.

"But didn't your people make any effort to locate it? To recover it? They didn't simply let it go at that, did they?"

"Of course not," Gregor said, and then waited as their meal was being served. The wine he had ordered came to the table properly chilled, and he was handed a bit in his glass for approval. At his nod the waiter filled their glasses and discreetly disappeared.

Kovpak began eating and then looked around. He suddenly remembered they were supposedly being followed by some nameless unknown. He also recalled that they were eating at this particular restaurant at the insistence of Major Ulanov, although he could see no reason for that insistence. The restaurant was now more fully attended, but there were still a few empty tables in their vicinity, and nobody seemed in the slightest to be interested in them. Mostly they were couples, intent upon their own affairs. The only single person was a man seated well out of earshot, and besides, he was engrossed in a book he was reading. For a moment Kovpak wondered if perhaps Ulanov had merely been joking—if, perhaps, he had recommended the restaurant simply because it was a good one. Certainly the food was all one could ask. Or, perhaps, he had misunderstood Ulanov and had come to the wrong restaurant, and the unknown newspaper personage, as well as Ulanov, were someplace else quite different, watching some perfectly innocent couple, or even watching each other, as if anyone cared. Gregor Kovpak put the entire matter of restaurants and spies from his mind as being quite unimportant, and returned to the subject they had been discussing.

"There was an investigation of sorts at the time, as I understand it," he said quietly, "but nobody found the treasure, or any trace of it. Admittedly the investigators didn't spend as much time on it as they possibly should, but you have to remember they weren't archaeologists, or museum curators or directors, and it was right after the war with the search on for war criminals, and they weren't going to spend too much time on looking for a treasure they hadn't even known about a few weeks earlier. So they didn't waste too much time on it. But they did figure that a man named Petterssen, a Swedish national, was the one who forged the documents it took to get his hands on the treasure. He also fit the description of one of the two men who removed the crate from the train it was on. But after that"—he raised his shoulders expressively—"nothing."

Ruth McVeigh paused in her eating, her food momentarily forgotten. "That's all the investigation? Into the disappearance of the Schliemann treasure?"

"As I said, they weren't collectors. They were people from Security with a thousand things more important—at least to their minds—on their hands."

"But," Ruth said, the detective in her aroused, "if one of the men was Swedish, couldn't they possibly have taken the treasure to Sweden? Or wouldn't that be subtle enough for investigators?"

"They could have gone anywhere," Gregor said simply. "They put the treasure, in a crate, in the trunk of a car and simply drove off. The car had been waiting for them. And where they went, nobody knows. What kind of car? An official-looking car, which meant nothing then and means less today. A large black car. Period." He drank some wine, thinking. He could scarcely tell Ruth that the car most likely was the car of some American general, or that the treasure undoubtedly had ended up in America, in the hands of the OSS. It would cheat her of romance. He began eating again, speaking across the table. "Yes, I suppose they could have gone north, but both the Danish and Swedish police looked for Petterssen a long time without luck. We told them he was wanted for war crimes, not for stealing the treasure, of course."

"Why not?"

Gregor looked a trifle abashed. "Because countries do not like to admit that they've been duped, taken in by forged papers," he said, and smiled. "It's supposed to be bad for their image."

"And they don't mind people knowing now?"

Gregor shrugged humorously and stared down at his wine glass.

"I'm telling you in confidence. Besides, this auction proves rather conclusively that we do not have the treasure. Believe me," he said, looking up, "if we had had the Schliemann collection at the Hermitage all these years, we would have put it on exhibition long ago. And argued at great lengths with anyone who came up with any ridiculous reasons for taking it from us, such as we heard this afternoon! Besides," he added, smiling broadly, "can you picture any curator, any director of any museum in the world, who would allow a treasure as valuable and as unique as the Schliemann collection, to be diminished by the pieces this person—whoever he is—sent out as proof of the fact that he actually had the genuine treasure? I certainly would not have let loose of a single button. Would you?"

Ruth laughed. "Never in the world."

"Case closed," Gregor said with juridical solemnity, and went back to eating. They finished their meal in silence, each with their own thoughts, but in contentment, satisfied they had established a certain rapport, but with each secretly regretting that, in truth, their lives were worlds apart, and that in all likelihood they would never see each other again, once the conference was ended . . .

13

The properly attired waiter looking properly bored and carrying his tray in a properly gloved hand at the proper height with its whiskey bottle and glasses properly balanced, walked in the unhurried pace of floor waiters the world over down the principal corridor of the eleventh floor of the Gramercy Arms Hotel, to pause before the door of Room 1123. Had there been any observer it would simply have appeared that the waiter's other properly gloved hand had politely tapped on the door and then rested there a moment, as if awaiting permission to enter. The rapping, of course, was a pantomime. The glove held against the door actually contained a tiny microphone that was connected by a thin wire running up the waiter's sleeve and past his starched wing collar to a small amplifier mounted behind his right ear and made invisible by his stylishly long hair. Had the door opened for any reason—the room's occupant leaving for dinner, or going to the lobby for cigarettes or a journal— the tray also contained a bar bill made out to the occupant of 1133, and a brief apology for the inexcusable error would have handled the situation. Of course the man in Room 1123 would be suspicious of anything out of the ordinary, such as Room Service at the Gramercy Arms making such a mistake, but there was really nothing the occupant of Room 1123 could do about it. Russians! the waiter thought with disdain. Fortunately, the occupant did not appear, so the waiter was able to pursue his assignment in peace.

Satisfied with what he heard—the sound of a man moving about, the rattle of a newspaper, the creaking of a bed as someone sat on it, which was quite distant from the creaking of a bed when someone laid down upon it to rest, or rose from it, or any of the other things that people did that caused beds to creak—the waiter turned, looking about him innocuously, pleased that he was still without observers. For a moment he wondered that no radio or television had been turned on in the room, but he then reflected that this was undoubtedly because the occupant probably did not understand English. Satisfied with the logic of his deduction the waiter then returned to the floor-waiter's pantry, prepared to watch the door of Room 1123 from his position at the end of the long hall until he would repeat his charade with the whiskey bottle and glasses fifteen minutes hence, and at every fifteen minute interval until the occupant went to sleep, or left the room, or until the waiter received a call from James Newkirk advising him his task was complete for the evening.

Occasionally, as he watched, the floor waiter from the tenth floor, doing double duty but pleased to do so for the tip he had earned, and to be of service to the Yard—for this was his impression—would come by with a tray of something for one of the eleventh-floor rooms, giving him a wink as he passed, but at no time was anything delivered to Room 1123. And fifteen minutes later, as our waiter was about to begin his journey once again, he paused. An elderly gentleman with a dark raincoat over his dinner jacket, his gray mustache a trifle mussed, his top hat awry, a silly look on his flushed face, and more than a touch of lipstick on one corner of his mouth, had come out of a side corridor, had staggered to the lift and, eventually, into it. The waiter sighed in envy as he waited for the drunk to disappear. Then, dismissing the lecherous thoughts the man's lipsticked face had inspired, he walked down the corridor and raised his microphone once again to the door. This time he heard the creak of a bed as someone rose from it— the waiter promised himself that one day he would do a monograph on creaks—followed a short time later by the flushing of a toilet, then a rather extended but distinctly boorish belch, and the return to the bed and the newspaper. Uncouth! the waiter thought, wrinkling his nose, and walked sedately back to the pantry.

He was a young agent, and therefore had no idea he had been listening to a tape loop. It was two hours of the finest sound effect Major Serge Ulanov had been able to conceive for any curious ear...

In the lobby the elderly drunk found himself a comfortable chair that by chance happened to face the lounge and sank into it gratefully; the lipstick had been removed in the elevator under the amused glance of the young and attractive girl who ran the lift. It was evident the old gentleman was tired, for he leaned back and seemed to close his eyes, as if taking a brief rest before continuing his evening. Through his half-slitted eyelids he saw Gregor Kovpak emerge from the lounge with Ruth McVeigh at his side—and with what the watcher was sure were stars in his eyes—and escort the girl through the lobby in the direction of the street. A moment later the elderly gentleman was not greatly surprised to see James Newkirk, a thin book under his arm, turn from his contemplation of the activities-announcement board and casually move in the same direction. With a sigh the elderly man heaved himself a bit unsteadily to his feet and tottered toward the night air, obviously in need of it.

Ahead he could see Newkirk just turning into Curzon Street, but the elderly gentleman did not make the mistake of following him. Instead, he continued along Park Lane, now walking quite a bit more steadily as well as more rapidly, and turned into Pitt's Head Mews. From here he entered Shepherd Street, coming at last into Shepherd Market. A pause in a darkened store front allowed the top hat to be removed, collapsed, and tucked into his waistband. A simple cap, taken from a pocket and donned, together with a scarf that wrapped around the throat and concealed the dress shirt and black tie, completely changed the man's appearance. Now, with his gray mustache bristling, he appeared simply to be an elderly pensioner in midtown to see how his betters lived. The truth was that while Major Ulanov often decried the use of disguise in his profession, he secretly enjoyed nothing quite as much as putting on false

beards or mustaches, or pretending the effects of drunkenness—a difficult act for him, since his capacity was legendary.

He moved easily through Shepherd Market, deserted at that
late hour, and eventually found himself in the passage that
fronted on Curzon Street, across the narrow pavement from
the restaurant to which he had directed Gregor Kovpak. He
had selected the restaurant for the reason that it was easily
observed from the shadows in which he found himself, and
also because the low curtains of the establishment permitted a
view of the interior and the occupants there. To enjoy the same
anonymity in watching Newkirk and attempting to discover
what he was up to would have been impossible in the crowded
dining room of the Gramercy Arms. Never having eaten in the
restaurant, though, he only hoped the food was decent, since
he had no inclination to hear complaints when Gregor eventually returned to their rooms.

Through the window of the restaurant the major could see
Gregor and Ruth McVeigh sitting in a booth, sipping their
drinks, and apparently discussing something of interest to them
both. The Schliemann treasure, Ulanov sincerely hoped, and
not, as he feared, their personal problems. As he watched he
saw Newkirk come out of the gloom where he obviously had
been waiting, saw the reporter pause at the restaurant entrance
to glance back along the deserted Curzon Street, making sure
he had not been followed, and then open the restaurant door
and enter. Ulanov smiled slightly as he saw the waiter offer
Newkirk a table quite close to Kovpak's booth, but his smile
turned to a frown as he saw Newkirk shake his head, say something and gesture, after which the waiter led the reporter to a
table across the room and quite out of earshot of the two in
the booth. Newkirk seated himself in a chair that placed him
at right angles to the other two, spoke to the waiter, obviously
ordering something, and immediately fell to reading his book.
Ulanov shook his head. Was it possible that Newkirk was eating
in this restaurant purely by coincidence? Or that he had followed
the others in the hope that they would lead him to a decent
eating place? The thought was so ridiculous that Ulanov was
forced to smile. It certainly did not explain Newkirk's waiting
so long for the others to enter before following them.

There was the sound of footsteps on the pavement, the loud
leather-against-concrete heel sounds marching along in steady

cadence that announced the approach of a London bobby long before the blue uniform and shaped helmet could be seen. Ulanov turned and began reading the bulletin announcements posted before the window of a shuttered tobacconist, not really noting the offers of used cars in excellent condition, or clean rooms for rent by the hour, day, or week, or of photographic models with their own studios for camera buffs (no cameras needed). The even cadence of the footsteps changed as their owner paused not far from him to rattle a doorknob. They then continued evenly, crossing Curzon Street to the north side and continuing along in the direction of Lansdowne Row.

Ulanov watched the stiff back of the policeman a moment and then returned his attention to the restaurant. Newkirk was now eating his meal, a glass of wine at his elbow, not paying the slightest attention to Gregor Kovpak or Ruth McVeigh. He would pause in his eating every now and then to sip his wine or to turn a page, but otherwise his attention was on his food and his book. Suddenly Ulanov smiled. He walked back into the shadows of Shepherd Market until he located a telephone booth illuminated by a dim bulb. He dialed, listened to the phone ring followed by the rapid *bip-bip-bip*, and dropped his coin; after identifying himself to the person who answered, he gave his instructions and hung up. This chore accomplished he smiled once again, because he was now almost through working for the day. He replaced the cap with the top hat, tucked the scarf into a pocket, and once again the elderly gentleman— although far less under the influence—he marched back to Park Lane and up that avenue, past the Playboy Club, past the Dorchester, to the Gramercy Arms.

Once again he seemed to need rest, for he sat down in the lobby and leaned back, half-closing his eyes. He saw Gregor and Dr. McVeigh enter, speak a moment, and then move toward the lounge. He shrugged a tiny twitch, hoping they did not get too involved, and then bit back a smile as he remembered the imaginary girl who had put lipstick on his face. Let them get involved, he thought, only not *too* involved. He remained in his pose for a full thirty minutes, after which he came to his feet and made for the elevator, only to have another man, crossing the lobby in a hurry, bump into him and cause him to stumble to the floor. The other man was quick to help him up and brush him off, murmuring profuse apologies as he did so. Ulanov waved the entire matter off as being of no importance, and made his way to the lift. In the left he smiled at the young operator, as if proud that a bit of air along Hyde Park had prepared him for a good night's sleep or whatever else might be in store for him. The operator, returning her cab to the lobby, would have wagered it would just be a good night's sleep.

In the corridor Ulanov now walked with far more control down the main hallway. He nodded somewhat distantly at the floor waiter who was just retreating toward his pantry with a tray and a whiskey bottle, turned into a side corridor, and entered the first room on his right. He quickly closed the door behind him, entered his own room, locking the interconnecting door between his room and Gregor's, and turned off the tape recorder. From now on he would play himself in making noises to satisfy the curious waiter.

From the pocket of his burberry he withdrew the slim volume the man who had bumped into him had deposited there. From the outside it had all the appearance of one of the newer romances that were being sold at most book stalls. Inside, as Ulanov had strongly suspected, in addition to its few pages it also contained an exceedingly small but clever tape recorder, and a minute amplified pick-up set in the cover which, aimed in the direction of Gregor's booth, undoubtedly had recorded the conversation without making Newkirk noticeable at all. Ulanov grinned in satisfaction and took the machine into the bathroom; closing the door, and running the water in the tub, he ran the tape back to its beginning and then played it, holding it to his ear to listen. From the sounds that took place before the actual words became intelligible it was apparent that Newkirk had decided to wait until seated in the restaurant before beginning his taping, either because the lounge was too crowded and noisy, or possibly because it would have been inconvenient to pretend to read in its darkened interior.

Ulanov sat down on the toilet seat, reran the tape and played it once again, nodding his head as he listened to Gregor's argument for Russian possession of the treasure. But nothing he heard gave him any clue at all as to where the treasure was or who was offering it for sale. He wished that Newkirk had been clever enough to tape the conversation Gregor and the girl had had in the lounge. It might have given him a clue.

Although he supposed he could get what he wanted from Gregor himself, when he returned, or better yet, in the morning. Gregor was apt to be out late. However, at least he had come into possession of an excellent spy recorder, which was far better than anything the KGB technicians had come up with. Very clever, those Americans. Ulanov only hoped that Newkirk had not been too badly hurt in having his book taken from him.

Now that the tub was almost full, he decided to take a bath, pleased to know the waiter was probably listening to him. He removed his clothes and climbed into the tub, lying back, splashing loudly and humming an old Russian lullaby. His bath completed, he dried himself and put on his pajamas and then climbed noisily into bed. His last thought before he fell asleep was to wonder if the waiter's tiny microphone could pick up snores . . .

From a safe telephone in the American Embassy in Grosvenor Square, James Newkirk was making his report to Langley, Virginia. He was also nursing a colossal headache.

"They took everything," he was saying bitterly. "Two thugs. One stopped me and asked for a match, and the other hit me with something. When I came to, a policeman was bending over me; they wanted to take me to a hospital, but I came to the embassy, instead. They got my watch, my wallet, the book—"

"You mean that recorder we flew over to you? That was a prototype; we don't have another. Its loss will mean a lot of work and trouble! You were told to be careful with it—" Mr. Wilson, in Langley, did not sound pleased.

"I *was* careful, sir! I mean—" It seemed pointless to argue about it all night, to cry over spilt milk, as it were. How careful can a person be with something beyond holding it tightly in his hands? One would think he had invited the two thugs to knock him unconscious! Or to take his watch and wallet, as well as the recorder. Trying to put the wallet and its contents, or the watch, on his expense account, Newkirk new, would be a waste of time. Instead of getting sympathy, here he was getting a lecture! It wasn't right.

At the other end of the line Mr. Wilson also seemed to realize that Newkirk obviously had not gone out of his way to be mugged and lose the recorder. "Well, anyway," he said abruptly, "what did you learn?"

"Nothing, sir," Newkirk said unhappily. "I had it all on tape, their entire conversation in the restaurant. I had to sit far enough away from them so as not to look suspicious—"

"I know. That's why the recorder was developed." Wilson, in Langley, frowned at the telephone. "Do you think the Russians had anything to do with your getting knocked out and the recorder taken from you?"

"Not unless they have more men here than I think they have. I'm sure there's only one KGB man here, the one who arrived with Dr. Kovpak. They came in on Aeroflot yesterday afternoon. He's a white-haired man registered at the hotel as Dr. Sverdlov."

"White haired?"

"Yes, sir."

"A stiff crew cut, hair almost pure white? A stocky man in his sixties? Always smoking cigarettes?"

"Yes, sir. That's him."

"His name is Ulanov," Wilson said. "Serge Ulanov. He's a major in the KGB. A hero in the last war. He's supposed to be a good man."

"Yes, sir. But I'm fairly sure he's the only one from the KGB who's here."

"I wouldn't be surprised," Wilson said. "I doubt the Russians put too much importance on that conference in London. I'm sure they feel Ulanov can handle it." From Wilson's tone it was evident he also did not put a great deal of importance to the matter. He had been having second thoughts since the man from State had left his office, feeling he was probably wasting his time and the time of his men. "What makes you think Ulanov wasn't involved? He's supposed to be pretty clever, you know."

"I'm sure, sir. But I'm also sure he wasn't involved in this. I had a man in the hallway of his hotel, on his floor, all evening. In fact, he's still there. He's been checking this man—Ulanov?—every fifteen minutes. The waiter bit, you know, sir. I just spoke with him before I placed this call to you, sir, and he assured me that this—Ulanov?—hasn't left his room all evening. He says this—Ulanov?—just took a bath a short while ago, and now he's asleep."

"His name really is Ulanov. You needn't question it," Wilson said dryly. "What about Kovpak?"

"I don't know, sir. I left the restaurant and was walking down Curzon Street about a block behind them, and I was just passing Queen Street, when—" Newkirk paused, feeling, quite rightly, that Mr. Wilson in Langley would not be interested in hearing about the mugging twice. "But if it means anything, sir, the two of them—Dr. Kovpak and Dr. McVeigh, that is—seemed to be getting, well, interested in each other."

"It may mean something to them," Wilson said coldly, "but it doesn't mean a thing to us. You're supposed to be the cultural reporter on your paper, after information about the treasure and who has it, not the Lonely Hearts columnist." A thought came to Wilson. "You're sure that really is Dr. Gregor Kovpak? Not a ringer?"

"I'm quite sure, sir. He's very well known. I've seen him before."

There were several moments of silence as Wilson digested Newkirk's report. Newkirk might be positive that Ulanov had nothing to do with his mugging that night, but Wilson was far from that sure. Muggers took wallets and watches, of course, but how many muggers would bother taking an innocent-looking book? Unless muggers were a lot more literary in London than they were in Washington, D.C., which Wilson sincerely doubted. And if Ulanov was on to Newkirk then possibly it might be well to replace Newkirk with someone Ulanov was *not* on to. But that would take time, and Newkirk was the only one available in the area with the requisite knowledge of archaeology. Besides, the case wasn't that important in the first place, which was why they had only put a stringer on it in the first place. Even if they found out how Russian security had been breached, undoubtedly the Russians had already changed their security procedures to handle the matter. Wilson knew in their shoes that was what he would have done.

"All right," he said wearily at last. "Stay with it. Keep an eye on Ulanov and Kovpak. Keep us informed. And," he added dryly, "try not to get mugged in the future."

"Sir," Newkirk said desperately, "I certainly wasn't *trying* to get—"

But he was speaking to a dial tone. Wilson had hung up. With a heartfelt sigh Newkirk came to his feet, his head pounding, and prepared to return to the hotel and at least four badly needed aspirin tablets. There were times he wished he *was* only a reporter for the Paris edition of the *Herald Tribune*.

14

Gregor Kovpak could not sleep. Through the closed connecting door to Major Ulanov's room he could hear the faint rasping sounds that indicated that this was not the major's problem. But it was not the snoring of the major, nor even the endless sounds of traffic in Park Lane below, that kept Gregor from sleep, but his thoughts, jumbled and—a rare thing for him—unsure.

It was pointless, he tried to tell himself for the tenth or twentieth time, to think of Ruth McVeigh in any terms other than that she was a fellow scientist he had known and respected through her writings, and who he had been fortunate enough to meet in person at last. But there was no future in thinking beyond that. He had enjoyed the evening with her. Let it go at that. He had more than enjoyed the evening. He could not recall an evening he had ever enjoyed more, certainly not since Natasha had died. Which was something else to put out of his mind. Natasha had been dead eleven years, now. What had made him think of her now? Guilt? But guilt over what? He had done his mourning, and his mourning was over. Besides, there was nothing between Ruth McVeigh and him, nor could there ever be. Think of something else.

Think of your baby dinosaur and how, when it is finally

completely reconstructed and on exhibition at the Zoological Museum, next to that mammoth that was found frozen in the Siberian wilds, intact, how you will do a paper on where it was discovered and under what conditions, and be able to speculate on possible solutions the tiny bones point to, possibly resolving conflicting theories that have been riddles of those eon-old times when this world of ours was so much younger. And, hopefully, prove to Alex Pomerenko that a man does not necessarily have to direct his scientific energies in only one direction. And also—hopefully—to put some zoology professor's nose out of joint. And if, while you've been gone, he's wired up *one more bone*—!

My heavens, but the girl was beautiful! Beautiful and striking, intelligent, and—well, fascinating. Of course, there was no law that said scientists had to be ugly, or that they could not have a sense of humor, but who would have dreamed, just from reading her papers? And that dress—! But forget the dress and forget the girl inside the dress, and don't waste time trying to fathom the thoughts inside the lovely head of the girl inside the dress. But what *had* she been thinking? What was she thinking at this very moment? Certainly nothing like the thoughts he was having. She, undoubtedly, was sound asleep, which is what he should be as well. Except her face kept getting in the way—

Back to the baby dinosaur. Lucky that he had been the one who had found it in the dig; another less-delicate hand might have crushed the fragile bones. And, of course, if someone else had discovered it, the credit would have gone to him. Gregor smiled at the recognition of his own humanness—of course he would have been jealous if an assistant had come across that wonderful find on a dig he was in charge of. But he had been the lucky one. It was all luck, finding a treasure, or running into a girl . . .

But what kind of luck to see someone you'll undoubtedly never see again? That's what is known as hard luck, bad luck. What did the old song say? If it wasn't for bad luck, I'd have no luck at all. You lie here and you're forced to wonder what it will be like not seeing her again. How long to forget last night? A week? A month? A year? Ever?

Back to the baby dinosaur! What could have brought that tiny creature, certainly ugly in our eyes but just as certainly

beautiful and cute in the eyes of the mother who hatched him,
to the place where it had been found? How had it been separated
from its parents at the time of its young death, for no other
bones had been found in the area? Had the parents, facing
danger, hidden the small creature, only to have death come to
the tiny thing from some unknown source? It had hatched live;
that much the zoology professor had been able to state. Had
the parents, returning after hiding the baby, found him dead?
And if so, what had been their reaction? Or did dinosaurs have
reactions? Was it just a legend that only the human animal
truly feels sorrow at the death of a dear one?

He and Natasha had never had children. If he and Ruth were
married, do you suppose they—? What a ridiculous thought!
What an absolutely idiotic thought! Good God! One dinner
with a girl and he was having her married to him! And raising
a family, yet! Still, if he and Ruth were married, of course
they were still both young enough to have children. But the
fact was he was more than ten years older than she was. Oh,
of course ten years wasn't all that much, but when he was
sixty, an old man, she would still just be in her forties, and
without a doubt as beautiful and charming as she was now.
And when he was eighty—

He rolled over and stared at the shadowy wall. Now, really!
Stop thinking about Dr. Ruth McVeigh and think of something
else. Be serious about that. You're not a child. If not baby
dinosaurs, or babies of any species, then think about the Schliemann treasure. After all, that is what brought you to London
in the first place. Recall the conversation with Ruth—Dr.
McVeigh, that is—at dinner last night without thinking of her,
particularly. Remember what Ulanov had said about the probable—no, almost certain—destination of the treasure. But precisely how had it gotten from Bad Freienwalde to Langley,
Virginia? Ulanov had not mentioned this minor detail, assuming he even knew it, which was doubtful. Ulanov was only
interested in how it had been restolen from Langley. Well, that
was his field, his job. It would seem more interesting, if equally
unimportant, to try and trace its path from one place to another.

Most probably by way of Scandinavia, in some fashion, to
England, from which it would be the simplest thing in the
world to get it to America and Langley. He closed his eyes
and tried to picture in his imagination, the two men. They had

left the train at a darkened railway station at Bad Freienwalde in war-torn Germany, had climbed into a black official-looking car, and had disappeared. Well, they couldn't have disappeared, but where were they going? Where did one go from Bad Freienwalde, anyway? Where could one go from Bad Freienwalde? Where *was* Bad Freienwalde, as a matter of fact? It was just a name to him, heard from Ulanov, and Gregor, yawning, realized his knowledge of East German geography was sketchy, to say the least. As was his ignorance concerning Danish or Swedish geography. But at least trying to picture these unknown places had the advantage of taking his thoughts from Ruth McVeigh...

But had they? Because there she was, as he handed her down from the railway car at some unknown station—no, it wasn't unknown, for there was the name, BAD FREIENWALDE, carved in the stone sill above the doorway, and there was the car he was guiding her to, aware as he did so of the warmth of her beside him, and her faint but unforgettable perfume. And of Ulanov in the front seat, wearing a chauffeur's cap, even after he had been specifically told he had not been invited...

He slept, at last.

Ruth McVeigh was tired, and she knew she looked terrible because she hadn't slept. She was sure the rings under her eyes made her look ten years older than she was, and while that would make her only a year or so younger than Gregor, she would rather he always thought of her as being much younger than that. She sat at the head of the conference table, staring at Gregor's empty seat, while the delegates filed in and took their places around the table, fiddling with their consoles as if they had never seen them before, filling water glasses, placing cigarettes and matches in position.

Where was he? Didn't he know how much she wanted to see him, to look at him, to see that same light in his eyes when he looked at her that she knew would be in hers as soon as he walked in? Or the light she hoped would be in his eyes? To see if last night had been real or if her imagination, through the sleepless night, had added dimensions to it that did not, in reality, exist? Where was he?

She sighed and shook her head, suddenly feeling depressed. Why was she so intent upon hoping he would appear, anyway? What difference did it make? Possibly he knew the utter hopelessness of their ever being anything but friends and had taken off for Leningrad to save both of them the embarrassment of a further meeting. Or at least to save her from making a fool of herself. She had probably done or said something the night before that told him how she was beginning to feel toward him, and to save him from having to—what was the word they had used when they were in school?—jilt her, had simply gone away. Jilt, my God! She was getting positively infantile!

She looked around the room, her eye quickly jumping the blank space where Gregor had sat the day before, her cheeks red. What was she doing here, anyway? Why had she come? Why had she ever suggested this silly conference to begin with? Bob Keller was right; Gregor was right. The entire conference was pointless, useless. In fact, the entire Schliemann collection was a pointless thing. Who cared who had it, who was selling it, or who bought it? Let them all fight over it, the Germans, the Greeks, the Russians, the Turks, all of them. Let them have their next war over the silly collection. It made as much sense as any of the other things they fought about. Not more sense, but as much. She suddenly shook her head. Was this *she*, Ruth McVeigh, director of the Metropolitan Museum of Art and avid collector, thinking this way? The Schliemann treasure was extremely important, and no thoughts of a mere man should or would be allowed to obscure that fact!

Where was he?

She became aware that the elderly stocky man with the pure-white crew-cut hair had taken his chair next to the empty one Gregor had occupied the day before, and her eyes instantly went to the door to see if Gregor might have followed, but the doorman was already closing the door in a manner that indicated the meeting was closed, ready to begin. The white-haired man seemed to be considering her with a faint air of commiseration, and her cheeks felt on fire. Had Gregor discussed her with this unknown? He was a friend of Gregor's, that much she knew. Had they talked about her last night when Gregor returned from leaving her at her door? Had they discussed her girlishness, her gaucherie, and laughed together over it? Had Gregor mentioned that low-cut gown and thought of her as a bit pitiable,

throwing herself at a man? She felt flushed. The room and all
the people in it were suddenly intolerable. She became aware
that Tim Rubin had leaned over and was speaking to her. She
turned. "What did you say?"

"I said, what's the matter with you? You look like three
days in the city morgue," Tim said cheerfully. "My old grandmother, a hundred and six the day she was run over by her
father on a motorbike, and two weeks after she was buried,
looked better than you do right now." He studied her with
concern. "Why don't you go up to your room and lie down?
Let me handle the feeding of the animals? I've always wanted
to rise to an occasion."

Ruth shook her head a bit stubbornly. It was her meeting
and she was going to conduct it! She just wished that Gregor
Kovpak had not chosen to avoid the meeting. "I'll be all right."
She looked at her wristwatch and came to her feet, rapping the
gavel. Slowly the room calmed down. She pulled the microphone toward her and began, looking about the room and trying
to avoid the empty chair where Gregor had sat the day before.

"Ladies and gentlemen, I see that no names have been put
into the fishbowl as I suggested yesterday. I can only assume
that means that none of you wish to speak. Or am I incorrect
in that?"

In answer to her question there was a rush of hands held
high, a growing murmur of indistinguishable voices. She looked
at the delegates, making no attempt to use diplomacy with her
words. She felt in the mood to speak a few truths to them.

"I see. In that case I can only assume that you all want to
speak, but you do not wish to do so democratically. You all
wish to be first. The fishbowl was too chancy for you. Is that
the case?" The hands wavered and slowly dropped, although
several remained half-raised, as if to get a head start when the
chance came. "Well," Ruth went on, making no attempt to
disguise her dislike of them all, although she realized she was
being a bit unfair, taking out on the delegates her irritation
with Gregor Kovpak, "in that case I shall take advantage of
being the chairperson here, and I shall speak first. After that
I shall select the speakers as I wish, and if there are any objections to that procedure, those present have only themselves
to blame."

The room had grown quiet under her scathing tones. For a

moment she wished Gregor were there, not to see him, but for him to see her and realize she was not a person to tolerate poor manners from anyone, even good-looking archaeologists from the Hermitage! Then she put Gregor from her mind, or, rather, tucked him into a corner temporarily out of sight, and got on with her statement.

"Let me tell you all what was in my mind when I first asked you to attend this meeting. It was something I suggested to my board of directors and which they agreed should be presented to the leading museums of the world. We have already seen, in the discussions of yesterday, the diversity of opinion as to the proper ownership of the Schliemann treasure. I am sure that others here are probably prepared to offer similar arguments, and if we allow this meeting to dissolve into this type of controversy, we will be passing up a great opportunity. And that opportunity? To see that the treasure is purchased at a reasonable price from whoever is offering it for auction, and that this contention among ourselves is eliminated."

She paused. Her audience was watching her suspiciously. Well, she thought, here's where we discover if Gregor and Bob Keller were right or wrong. She sipped a bit of water to calm her a trifle before making her statement, and then went on.

"My suggestion is simplicity itself. All the museums who are interested would share the cost of the purchase price, and would also share the exhibition privileges on a basis to be determined. To begin with, this method would reduce the financial burden to each museum, and in the second—"

"No!" It was Dr. Wilhelm Kloster of the Museum Dahlen. He was on his feet, his face red as he screamed into the console. One fleshy fist was pounding on the top of the console. "It cannot be! You are very generous with something that belongs—"

Ruth rapped her gavel for order. The response was quite the opposite. The bedlam seemed to increase with everyone wanting to speak at once, some into their consoles, others on their feet merely shouting toward the head of the table. Ruth fumbled for her purse and her whistle only to remember she had left her purse in her room, bringing only the room key. She looked at Tim Rubin helplessly. He grinned, brought his microphone closer, put a finger bent at the knuckle into his mouth, and produced a whistle fully as loud and sharp as Ruth's police whistle. "Champ of the block," he murmured as the noise from the surprised delegates slowly abated to a point where the hammer of Ruth's gavel could be heard. Slowly the meeting came to order. Ruth stood and waited until the silence was complete.

"There seems to be some objection to my suggestion," she said with a faint smile. "Let's take them in order. Dr. Kloster, you can be first. And," she added warningly, "if there is another outbreak such as we just heard, the meeting will be adjourned permanently. All right, Dr. Kloster."

Kloster came to his feet, no longer attempting the suavity of the previous day.

"As I said," Kloster said heavily into the microphone, "our chairperson seems to be extremely generous in giving away something she does not own. The Museum Dahlen has no intention of permitting such misplaced generosity. When we wish to give something that rightfully belongs to us, we shall make that decision, not a bunch of—of—" He threw up his hands in disgust and sat down again. From his chair he said, "If this is what we shall be discussing, there is no sense in the Museum Dahlen even remaining here!"

"So go! Who wants you?" It was Elsa Dornbusch, glaring at him from across the table. She turned to face the chair. "The fascist is right, though! Your suggestion is ridiculous! Do you expect—"

That was as far as she got. The bedlam began again. Tim Rubin put his bent finger in his mouth, preparatory to whistling again, and then removed it. He leaned over, shouting in Ruth's ear. "It's hopeless!" An idea suddenly came. He leaned over, searching beneath the table for something and then grinned as he found the electrical outlet connecting the consoles. He pulled it from its socket, and suddenly the booming sounds from the ceiling speakers disappeared. The noise that a moment before had seemed threatening, now merely seemed foolish. The delegates stopped to look at one another, and then with what seemed to be a sudden accord, picked up their papers and briefcases and began to file from the room.

Tim and Ruth watched them go. "Well," Tim said philosophically, "I suppose it's what one should expect from museum personnel. Individualists, to the bitter end."

Ruth took a deep breath. "I should have worded it differently, perhaps. Led up to it more gradually, perhaps..."

"Led up to what more gradually?" Tim snorted. "You said what had to be said. The fact that there wasn't a wet eye in the crowd wasn't your fault. Really," Tim said, a bit chidingly, "you should have anticipated exactly what happened. Those who feel they have legitimate claims see it as a scheme to rob them of their pottage. If the meeting had gone on a little longer I was prepared to enter my claim on the basis that Schliemann changed his name from Heinrich to Henry, and Henry Ford invented the Model-T less than a hundred miles from the Cleveland Museum. But I was afraid our British colleagues might recall that they had Henrys over here in England a bit before Mr. Ford."

Ruth looked at him. "And what were the motives of the others?"

Tim shrugged. "Most are simply piggish. They want the treasure all for their lonesomes. Sharing is a dirty word. Oh, they'll loan you one of their exhibits, all right, but they want you to know that it's Theirs, do you hear, Theirs! And then, of course, there are those—there are always some—who probably thought the suggestion was a gimmick of some sort on the part of the Metropolitan, and since they couldn't figure out what that gimmick was, it made them all the more suspicious. And that's why your idea died like a dog, march on, he said."

Ruth sighed. "Well, at least it's over."

"And the Auction Stakes are back in the running." Tim changed the subject to one that was closer to his interests. "What flight are you taking back? Maybe we can travel together."

"I'm not going back for a while," Ruth heard herself say to her own complete amazement. "I—I have some work to do here. I may even take my vacation over here."

"Oh." The disappointment in Tim's voice was evident, instantly replaced by his normal cheerfulness. "Oh, well! We'll undoubtedly see you when you visit the Cleveland Museum to see the Schliemann collection on exhibit. Assuming," he added doubtfully, "that the Rockefellers didn't forget where their money came from. Or the Eatons."

Ruth smiled.

"Well," she said, "if you'll forgive me, I won't wish you

luck on that. But it was good seeing you, and thanks for that finger whistle. It's something I should have learned when I was younger. And drop in and see me the next time you're in New York."

"It's the only reason I'd come in the first place," Tim said, trying to sound arch but merely sounding sincere. "You don't imagine I'd come to see a mummy in your Egyptian Room, do you? I've got a mummy, you've got a mummy, all God's chillun—well, enough of that." He came to his feet. "So long, Ruth. Have fun. I don't suppose that, well, on your vacation over here you'll be visiting museums? Busman's holiday sort of thing? Museums like—well—the Hermitage?"

Ruth felt herself go cold. "I've seen the Hermitage," she said tightly, trying not to sound savage. Damn Tim for reminding her. "And I won't be going there this trip, thank you."

"It's better that way," Tim said quietly. He held out his hand; she took it. "God bless, Ruth." He squeezed her hand once and turned, walking quickly away.

Ruth stared after him. Why get upset with Tim Rubin? He was a nice guy, a pal, a friend. One of the men who genuinely liked her. And a very fine curator. But he shouldn't have mentioned the Hermitage. She looked around the deserted room and came to her feet. Well, Gregor and Bob Keller had been right. She had wasted her time and the time of many other museum notables. And what had she gotten out of it? She had met a man she had instantly felt a deep liking for, and he had not even bothered to try and see her a second time.

She rode the elevator to her floor, walked down to her room, opened the door, and walked in, going to the window to stare out. The meeting had been a disaster, but that was no longer important. What was important was that the Schliemann treasure was still someplace, held by someone. What could have happened to it after it had been taken from the railroad baggage car at that Bad something? According to Gregor—wasn't it even possible to think of something else without bringing him into it? Still, according to Gregor, the Russian officials had done a poor investigation at the time the treasure was stolen from them because they had other more important things on their minds. Possibly today, someone with the time and effort could find out what had happened to it, now that the turmoil of the war was long past. Certainly the one who was offering

the treasure for auction must have done exactly that. And that
person, at least, should be able to be traced. He was in the
present, not thirty-five years in the past.

How had this unknown been able to do it? He, undoubtedly,
had started at the last known place the treasure had been seen,
this place called Bad something—she was sure she would
recognize the proper name if she saw it or heard it again—
wherever that was. And what one person had been able to
accomplish, another person should be able to duplicate. And
facing this unknown with his illegal treasure, one could undoubtedly also make a deal that would bring one the treasure
for a fraction of the fifteen million the unknown was so ridic-
ulously asking for it. And what museum, faced with the treasure
actually in their possession, would fail to come up with the
required money, despite all the scruples they claimed to possess? Very few, without a doubt.

She stared down into Park Lane with its traffic and Hyde
Park beyond, covered with lawn chairs and children playing,
barely seeing them. If only Gregor were to help her, she was
sure they could dig something up that would lead to some clues
as to what had happened to the treasure thirty-five years before.
If only Gregor could help her . . . Forget Gregor Kovpak, she
told herself sternly, and if by some odd chance you happen to
run into him on some distant day in some distant place, you
will simply smile in a friendly manner and shake hands and
hope the feeling you are feeling at the moment is dead by then.

That stupid feeling! Who in her right mind would feel this
way about a man she met less than twenty-four hours before?
It was ridiculous. Oh, admittedly, she thought, I've known a
lot about him by reputation for a long time; the work he's done,
the papers he's written, the excavations he's been connected
with, but still . . . And admittedly he's attractive, but I've known
many attractive men and none ever made me feel this way.
Bob Keller's attractive, and a fine man and I like him a lot,
and moreover I know him well whereas I don't know this Dr.
Kovpak at all. But Bob Keller never made me feel this way,
while Gregor does, and it's pointless to deny it. Maybe it was
the drinks, she thought, and then smiled wryly to herself. No,
it hadn't been the drinks.

This, obviously, was no way to forget Gregor Kovpak. She
simply had to concentrate on something else, and the where-

abouts of the Schliemann treasure was as good and puzzling a subject as any. I don't know what made me tell Tim I wasn't going home right away, she thought, but it appears my subconscious knows me better than I know myself. She picked up her key and marched purposefully toward the door. And my staying here in Europe is not just to delay paying Bob Keller his dinner. In fact, probably I've been wrong in not paying more attention to Bob Keller. I'm beginning to realize for the first time how lonely I've been, whether I knew it or not. Although with something to occupy my mind I'm sure I'll get over it. And over Gregor—damn him!

Sir Mortimer Edgerton came from his chair with a bound and hurried across the room, his hands outstretched, a smile of sincere pleasure on his full face.

"Ruth, my dear! What a pleasant surprise." He took her hands in both of his and then released one in order to put an arm around her shoulders to lead her to a sofa along one wall of his large office overlooking Great Russell Street. He waited until she was seated and then sat beside her, reaching for her hand again. "I was afraid you'd be off to home without dropping by to see us." His smile faded. "I couldn't attend the meetings, but Harold Gordon told me what happened. Animals! I'm truly sorry, for your sake."

Ruth smiled. "Don't be. I must have been dreaming when I even proposed such a silly idea. But I didn't come here to be commiserated with, Sir Mortimer. I came here because I want a favor of you."

"Anything in my power, my dear." Sir Mortimer made it sound as though he would be greatly disappointed if the favor entailed anything less than slaying dragons. "What can I do for you?"

"My reader's card has expired and I want another, but I'd just as soon not have to go through the catechism they give you downstairs as to why I don't get my information some other place."

Edgerton laughed. "We have to do it, Ruth, or we'd be pushed out of the walls. The reading room of the British library here in the museum is simply too small for all the students or other people who wish to use it. Or even for all the books we have; a goodly number of them are scattered half across England." He came to his feet and walked to his desk, leaned over and scribbled something on a card. He came back, handing it over. "Here. This will do, and you won't even have to sit and submit to the terrible photography that goes on downstairs. What subject do you wish to research? We can be having tea while they dig up the books. It takes time, you know, even if they're here in the building."

Ruth took the card, tucking it into her purse. She came to her feet.

"Thank you very much, Sir Mortimer," she said with a smile that thanked him more than her words had. "But I really don't have time for tea. And I don't want to use the library, but the map room. But I do appreciate your kindness."

"Any time, Ruth." Sir Mortimer ushered Ruth to the door, a fatherly hand under her arm. "I'm glad you stopped in." He paused and smiled at her, a wise look in his eye. "I gather you'd rather not talk about the Schliemann treasure? Or what the Metropolitan plans to do about this auction?"

Ruth nodded humorously. "You're quite right. I'd rather not—anymore, I assume, than you would regarding the plans of the British Museum?"

Edgerton laughed. "I suppose we'll all be glad when this beastly auction is over and done with, and we can all go back to being friends again. Or at least until the possibility of a new major acquisition comes along, I suppose." He opened the door for her. "Good-bye, Ruth. It was nice seeing you."

He closed the door behind her, leaving her with two secretaries busily typing. Ruth sighed as she walked through the corridor and into the upper main corridor of the museum. Another nice man, Sir Mortimer, but also another rival for the Schliemann collection. And speaking of the collection, she'd better get on with trying to trace it from that Bad-something place. She knew she was being romantic. She was well aware that it was not only improbable but most likely impossible for her to discover anything new, especially after all the intervening years. But it would be good therapy, and that was what she needed.

She climbed the steps to the landing where the map room was located, and rang the bell. An elderly uniformed guard answered, studied the card she presented with a suspicious eye as not being the standard form, but finally seemed to concede that it might possibly be genuine, and allowed her to enter. He handed back the card.

"Do you know how to use the map room?" he asked, as if anyone with less than a standard reader's card would most probably not.

"Yes, I had a card here years ago." She tucked the precious card into her purse and walked into the file room. She located and withdrew the notebook containing listings for maps beginning with the letters GER and began leafing through it. There were maps for every section of Germany from the time, ages back, when the country was merely a loose federation of states and cities, up to the present, including several that had been issued that same year. Ruth located one that was cross-referenced to SCAN, and read the description. It was for northern Germany and southern Scandinavia, and was dated 1945. Precisely what she wanted! A good omen, she thought and filled out the necessary slip to have the map brought from the files. This done she replaced the notebook and went to the desk, handing her slip to the girl there. The girl started to leave the room and then returned, leafing in a basket on the desk. She nodded as she located the slip there, and looked up.

"I thought that number was familiar," she said. "I'm afraid you'll have to wait. That map is in use by that gentleman in the corner."

Ruth looked across the room and felt a shock, a tingling that seemed to start at her toes and run up her entire body. Gregor Kovpak was at a table in the far corner of the large room, leaning over a large map spread before him, studying it intently, oblivious to anything other than the map. Ruth walked across the room and stood behind him.

"Hello."

He swung about, his eyes widening in surprise, and then hurriedly came to his feet, smiling, his pleasure at seeing her evident in every facet of his expression. Why, he seems to be as happy to see me as I am to see him, Ruth thought. What an idiot I was this morning!

"I said, hello."

"I'm sorry. It was such a surprise." And I'm acting like a dolt, he thought. "What are you doing here? What about your conference?"

"You haven't heard?" Ruth made a small grimace. "The conference is over. A monumental failure."

Gregor shook his head and then ran a hand through his unruly hair. "I was afraid it was doomed to be. But"—the act of her presence was still not understood, even though he was very pleased that she was there and not someplace else—"what are you doing here?"

Ruth smiled happily. With Gregor before her, as attractive as she had remembered him, everything was all right with the world. He had not left the city without saying good-bye; he had not avoided the conference that morning for any such stupid reasons she had worked herself up with so needlessly. He was here and that was all that mattered.

"I'm here for the same reason you are," she said cheerfully. If Gregor thought the treasure could be traced, then maybe there might really be a possiblity. "To see where the treasure could have gone to, from that Bad-whatever—wherever that is."

Gregor nodded, trying to keep the profound admiration he felt for her from becoming apparent. He certainly didn't want to look gauche, not before this woman. It would be very nice if she was as happy to see him as he was in seeing her, but of course, why should she? To her he was simply a fellow scientist with whom she had had dinner once. And she was a beautiful woman, while he—well, he was a good archaeologist, if he said so himself, but that was about as far as it went. And an old, or at least ageing, archaeologist at that. He suddenly remembered his manners and pulled out a chair.

"Here, sit down." He sat down beside her. Obviously he couldn't tell her she was wasting her time, that the treasure was in Langley, Virginia; or at least it had been all these years. Now that she was in front of him, he no longer felt the need to investigate how the treasure had gotten there. Still he didn't want to waste the opportunity of spending the day with her. "So you're another detective, eh?" He decided to take a chance, prepared for failure. "I'll make a deal with you. I'll tell you where Bad Freienwalde is, and I'll even share my map with you, if you'll have lunch with me."

I thought you'd never ask, Ruth thought, although if you hadn't I should have managed it somehow. "It's a deal," she said.

"Good." Gregor leaned over the map, pointing, hiding his pleasure at her acceptance. "Here—that is Bad Freienwalde."

"Oh." Ruth sounded disappointed. Gregor looked at her questioningly. "I mean," she said, explaining, "it's almost due east of Berlin, a bit to the northeast. If they were planning on taking the treasure to Denmark or Sweden, which seems to me the logical place to go, especially since one of them was Swedish, why would they have arranged for the treasure to be put on a train that let them off in Bad—well, Bad whatever. It's certainly not the most direct way to the Baltic ports."

"The treasure ostensibly was on its way to Russia, and the trains that went to Russia did not go by way of the Baltic ports," Gregor said dryly. "That may have been the reason."

Ruth looked a bit sheepish. "Chalk one up against the lady detective," she said with an attempt at lightness, and bent over the map, irritated with herself for being so stupid in front of Gregor, especially when attempting to impress him. "So where do you think they went from Bad-whatever?"

"Bad Freienwalde. *Bad* is a watering place; actually, a bath, or a place to bathe. *Frei-en* means to woo, or to court. *Walde* is a woodland, or forest. So you might call it the Watering Place in the Courting Forest."

"The courting forest? But I thought *frei* means free. Why not the Watering Place in the Free Forest?"

"Whichever you prefer." Gregor laughed. "Possibly the forest in which you are free to court."

"While bathing." Ruth also laughed and then found herself flushing at the thoughts that had come to her mind. You're due for cold showers, girl, she told herself, if you don't snap out of it.

"I'll accept that," Gregor said lightly, and returned to the map. "Now, we have to make some basic assumptions. Let us assume, as you said, that the two men either went to Denmark or Sweden as the first step on going—wherever they eventually ended up."

Ruth looked up from the map. "You don't think they stayed there?"

Gregor was scarcely in a position to reveal Ulanov's theory that the treasure had ended up in Langley, Virginia.

"Look at it this way," he said in a reasonable tone of voice. "The police in those countries searched for them hard and long, and without success. Remember that while Denmark was in the war, she didn't suffer the disruption of the countries most actively involved, like Germany or France or Poland or Russia. And Sweden was neutral during the war and suffered nothing. So the police in both those countries, Denmark and Sweden, had a much easier time looking for people than they might have had in Europe proper at that time. And the police came up with no sign of the two. Or of the treasure. Therefore"— he raised his shoulders—"it seems likely they moved on."

Ruth considered the logic of this a moment, and then nodded.

"I'll admit it's a possibility," she said, "but they still had to get to either Sweden or Denmark before they could move on. And if we're going to trace them, we have to follow them at least to one or the other of those two countries—"

Gregor's eyebrows quirked humorously. *"We?"*

Ruth reddened a bit. "I meant, me. I forgot that you probably have to get back to your baby dinosaur and the Hermitage, but I have my vacation coming, and I think it might be fun trying to trace just exactly where the treasure did end up."

"And you think you could do it? With the trail, as detective story writers put it, thirty-five years old?"

"Well," Ruth said defensively, "you thought so, or you wouldn't be here." Gregor continued to be silent, not feeling that an explanation for his presence would be helpful. "Besides," Ruth added, "someone else did it, or there wouldn't be an auction being held in a few months."

"It's true that someone has the treasure," Gregor admitted, "but he or they undoubtedly had a great stroke of luck to come across it." He smiled. "I doubt they started their search here in the map room of the British Museum, then went straight off to Bad Freienwalde—not to take a bath or to court anyone, but to discover the next step in the puzzle, and go from there to either Denmark or Sweden, following clues thirty-five years old. Then from whichever Scandinavian country he stopped in temporarily—but where he found a further clue that led him, or them, to wherever the treasure is now, say in Canada or China or Czechoslovakia or—even in the United States."

Ruth felt herself getting red as he went on.

"You can make all the fun of it you want," she said tightly, "but I don't believe that people just stumble on treasures. They search for them, using whatever clues they can get."

"I didn't say anyone stumbled on it," Gregor said calmly. "The way I see it, whoever has the treasure and is offering it for auction, has known where it is for a good many years. And when the opportunity came along for him to get his hands on it—and get away with it—he simply took it."

Ruth shook her head stubbornly. "You mean, he's known where it was for thirty-five years, and suddenly some strange opportunity presents itself—I suppose someone forgot to lock the screen door, or left a cellar window open—and he just walked in and picked it up, saying, 'Well, well! I think I'll just auction this off.' And the ones who were holding it all these years simply shrugged their shoulders and said, 'Well, that's how it goes. You win some and you lose some.' And let it go at that?" Ruth sniffed. "And you think *my* theory has holes in it!"

"That's not exactly what I said—"

"It's close enough. I think," Ruth said argumentatively, "that he was just smarter than your Russian so-called investigators, and that he did a better job. And as a result he found the treasure. And if he could, then so can we! I mean, so can I!"

"We," Gregor corrected gently. He must have been mad trying to talk Ruth out of going on her wild-goose chase, when he had a chance to go with her! His first thought had been that it would mean her leaving London earlier than he had hoped, but if they could travel together, even for the short time it took her to realize she was wasting her time, it would be even better. No one else around to take her attention. "I can spare a few days, even a week. And," he added disingenuously, "you may be right."

"Except you don't think so. I wonder what made you change your mind," Ruth said, but her mind was not on her words but on the fact that they would be traveling together. The thought brought all sorts of possibilities to mind, but she put them away as being too dangerous. All she knew was that she was happier at that moment than she had been for a long, long time. "You really don't think so," she repeated vaguely.

"I keep an open mind on important questions like that," Gregor said lightly and returned his attention to the map. The quest would be a charade, of course, but at least he had to go through the motions as if he were serious. But she hadn't rejected his offer to accompany her, although all that meant was that she thought she could use his help, not that she was particularly interested in his being along. It was probably that she would feel safer with a man along, and a man as safe as one his age. He sighed and pointed to the map. "Let's consider the ports they might have left from. Barth or Sassnitz, I would judge. Most likely Sassnitz; it's the closest point from Trelleborg, in Sweden. Wismar, or Rostock, or Stralsund, the other major possibilities, are larger cities, and at the time of the theft from the bunker, they would have been crowded with sailors and troops, and their docks under closer military observation than a small place like Sassnitz."

"There's also that place there, Warnemünde," Ruth added, pointing. "After all, that's the closest point to Denmark."

"It's a possibility," Gregor admitted, "but it's also pretty close to Rostock. They'd be taking quite a chance going there in the hope they might get a boat of some sort."

Ruth looked at him almost pityingly. He was an attractive man, and affected her like the devil, and there was no doubt he was an eminent scientist, but the dear man could also be rather dense at times.

"They would have planned for the boat at the time they planned the theft, of course," she said almost patronizingly. "You don't suppose they planned to steal a boat, do you?"

"Why not?" Gregor said innocently. He was enjoying himself. "They stole the treasure, didn't they?"

"But they stole the treasure with a good deal of care, didn't they? They didn't just walk in with a gun and hold up the bunker. They *planned* it, down to forging documents and even passes. But you can hardly plan on stealing a boat, especially some time ahead; they don't stay in one place. And they have crews and they weigh more than a small treasure," she added dryly. "No, they either bought a boat or rented one. Probably bought it, since I'm sure they didn't plan on returning it. In any event, in that case they could have left from almost any port, including Warnemünde. And that's the closest to Denmark."

"Or Sassnitz. That's the closest to Sweden."

"But the farthest from Bad Freienwalde," Ruth pointed out. "And I don't imagine they wanted to be driving any farther than they had to. Besides, Denmark is a far better place from

which to go farther, if you're right that they merely stopped
over there. From Sweden where could they go? Norway? It's
easier to get to from Denmark. Finland? It's far too small.
They'd never feel safe there. Plus it was under Russian dom-
ination. Russia, itself? Obviously they didn't steal it from the
Russians just to go to Russia."

She was probably right in her involuted reasoning, Gregor
thought with amused admiration. The CIA man would have
taken Petterssen to the States by way of Denmark, then England, and then Langley, Virginia. And Warnemünde would
be the logical place for them to be met with a high-speed cutter
from one of the Allied intelligence forces, maybe even from
Denmark, itself. Still, he had to make it look as if there was
a choice. He wanted his travels with Ruth to last as long as
possible before she became discouraged, because he knew—
sadly—that at the end of that time he would still be going back
to Leningrad, while Ruth would be going back to New York.
And without her even knowing how he felt about her, which
was undoubtedly just as well. Elderly scientists, he told himself, do not take kindly to being laughed at by beautiful women,
even if it were done with kindness, as he was sure it would
have been.

He smiled wryly at the thought and returned to the map. "Of
course, I suppose a good deal of their decision as to which port
to leave from would depend on the state of the roads at the time.
I imagine most of them were in pretty bad shape—"

Ruth looked at him, her eyes shining. "Of course! Why
didn't we think of that before? That means that the man who
was with Petterssen had to be either a German or a Russian!"

Gregor shook his head as if to clear it of cobwebs. "What?
A German or a Russian? Why?"

"Because," Ruth said, her tone triumphant, proclaiming that
the lady detective had scored one over her more weak-minded
opponent, "who else would know the state of the roads at that
time? Only the Germans who had retreated down them a short
time before, or the Russians who had advanced over them!
Can you picture a Dane, or another Swede, knowing which
roads they might use to get *anywhere?* Or even an American
or a Frenchman? Or any of the other troops who were wandering
around Berlin at that time? They had no idea how things were
in eastern Germany at that time. They could have found them-

selves stuck somewhere, very easily. And this was *planned,* every bit of it. Including the roads they had to travel. And," she added dryly, pleased with her analysis, "they certainly couldn't call the Automobile Club and ask them where the detours were."

It was a good point, Gregor had to concede, and one that Ulanov hadn't considered, or at least hadn't mentioned. There was one other solution, however. "But they were picked up at Bad Freienwalde," Gregor pointed out mildly. "The driver might have been German, but the one with Petterssen—"

"Oh, no!" Ruth said, scotching that argument at once. "The entire thing was planned, the theft, the car, and the boat. Who had access to boats in the Baltic along the German coast at that time? Fishermen, that's who—German fishermen. And who had access to cars in eastern Germany at that time? Germans, of course—although they would have to steal one. Or Russians." She paused, her mind racing. "Of course! It was night, you said, and the car looked official. It was the German chauffeur of some Russian official, who was probably asleep at the time, and the chauffeur took the chance of getting away with using the car without being found out, because the man who was paying him, the man with Petterssen, was a former officer of his, and they were both from ODESSA—"

Gregor laughed in pure enjoyment. "And now the treasure is in Brazil or Paraguay, and they're selling it to start up a Nazi party in Bavaria, as if they don't already have one there." He shook his head in admiration. "What an imagination!"

"Well, don't laugh. They might very well be doing just that." Ruth's pout changed to a smile. "You see? We've made progress already. We know that a German and Petterssen stole the treasure. We know that they left Germany from Warnemünde, probably landing somewhere near Gedser, and from there—" She shrugged.

Gregor was considering her with a smile. "We *know?*"

"Well," she said, retreating, but not much, "we're pretty sure, and that's better than not knowing at all."

"I suppose so. So that in that case it was a good morning's work," Gregor said, and looked at his watch. "Which deserves a good afternoon's lunch. At which time we can plan our trip in pursuit of the Schliemann gold!" He made it sound very dramatic. Well, Ruth thought, it is! Or it could be...

15

From his position in one of the banks of telephone kiosks fronting the entrance to the Green Park Underground station on the park side, James Newkirk had a perfect view across Piccadilly into the Aeroflot ticket office. Beyond the broad windows with their display of small wooden dolls dressed in colorful Russian native costumes, plus, of course, the ever-present model of a Tupelov TU-144 supersonic passenger plane tilted steeply as if in take-off flight, Newkirk could see the three attendants at their counters, two of them busy with customers, one checking something on a sheet of paper. Still Newkirk waited, watching carefully through the heavy traffic, until one certain girl was the only one unoccupied with her telelphone. Then he dialed rapidly, listened for the rapid *pip-pip-pip* and pushed home his ten-pence bit, for he did not wish to be interrupted for a matter of pennies. The telephone was answered at once, the girl's voice the impersonal tone of strangers on telephones.

"Good morning, Aeroflot, Sonia speaking. May I help you?"

"Good morning," Newkirk said. Sonia's air of supercilious superiority had not changed since he had last used her services. She always sounded as if the customer were a nuisance and not even a necessary nuisance at that. As always, Newkirk wondered why Aeroflot put up with her, but then he thought of her beauty and her figure and again as always, thought he knew the answer—and she did speak excellent English. "Does Aeroflot have a direct flight from London to Kuybyshev?"

"I'm afraid not. You have to change in Moscow."

"I see. Damn! Is there much of a wait?"

"One moment, please. I'll check." There was a brief pause. "Several hours is all."

"Well, that's not too bad. What equipment flies from Moscow to Kuybyshev?"

"One moment." There was another pause. "It's an Illyushin IL-18."

"That's a prop job, isn't it?"

"It has propellers, yes, sir, but it's an excellent airplane. Are you planning a visit to Kuybyshev?"

"If I have to get there in a prop job, I'll have to think about it," Newkirk said, and hung up. And if that conversation was being recorded for any reason whatsoever, he thought with satisfaction, let someone make something of it!

He stepped from the booth and glanced at his wristwatch, and then walked past the Ritz Hotel to cross Piccadilly and strolled leisurely in the direction of Old Bond Street. He would meet Sonia for lunch at a small restaurant in White Lion Yard, and that would not be for another forty-five minutes. As he walked slowly along, pausing every now and then to glance into one shop window or another to waste a bit of time, he thought with what little satisfaction he could muster that at least he was doing something, even if that something probably wouldn't result in very much. He thought with a touch of dismay of that morning, when everyone had left the meeting and he had been forced to move out with them or look conspicuous as the only one to stay behind with Dr. McVeigh and that man from the Cleveland Museum. And then to miss her when she did come out! And Kovpak hadn't even come to the meeting. God knows what he might have been up to!

He also recalled that during the free-for-all the conference had become, he had been able to see the white-haired agent, Ulanov, look in his direction with a touch of amusement every now and then. Was it possible that Ulanov knew he had been following McVeigh and Kovpak the night before? Was it possible that, despite all his precautions, Ulanov still might have been involved in the attack on him the night before? It was extremely doubtful—one didn't want to see conspiracies behind every bush—but an even closer eye would have to be kept on the white-haired man, that was evident.

But today the agent who had covered Ulanov the night before in the guise of a waiter, had been replaced by a plain-looking woman who was also cleaning rooms, with the pleased acquiescence of the regular cleaning woman—equally plain-looking, who not only gained a day's vacation, but was well paid for it. As soon as that ridiculous conference had finally—and in Newkirk's mind, deservedly—broken up, Ulanov had moved in the direction of the elevators and up to his room. And, at last word, was still there. Newkirk wished he could ask the Special Branch to put a tap on Ulanov's phone, but he knew this would really be asking too much, despite the solid relationship between their two organizations. Fortunately, this entire business of the Schliemann collection and how it had been taken from the KGB by some smart operator was of little importance; the Russians had undoubtedly by now changed their security system, so he was probably wasting his time. Still, he had his orders, and he intended to follow them.

He came into New Bond Street, his feet still lagging, and considered with a bit of pride the code he had developed with Sonia of Aeroflot, a code that changed with every use of it, the changes given at the meeting the code had been established to arrange. This particular time the name "Kuybyshev" had meant he wished to meet her for lunch at her usual hour, one o'clock. Had it been impossible for any reason, she would have had difficulty understanding his word "Kuybyshev" and would have asked him to repeat the name. The bit about propeller-driven planes indicated where they would lunch; at a certain small restaurant in White Lion Yard they both knew, where he was always sure his reservation request for a quiet booth in one corner would be properly attended to.

He crossed Maddox Street and turned into Lancaster Court, coming almost at once to White Lion Yard and the restaurant. He had himself ushered to the proper booth and sat down, ordering a whiskey and water for himself and a very cold Finnish vodka for Sonia when she arrived, and then leaned back to wait. He only hoped the information he wished Sonia to obtain for him might be of some help, although he knew he was scraping the bottom of the barrel to even think it might. Still, one had to do something. Thank God for airline computer consoles! he thought fervently. Anyone with the physical strength to punch a few keys could ask any information from the idiot machines he wished, and the stupid computer would simply hand it over without a suspicion in the world. In fact, at the push of a button the accommodating moron of a machine even would forget you ever asked for the information in the first place. If only we could program agents that way, he thought, and then changed it slightly. Enemy agents, of course. We'd also have to be damned careful with our own, naturally.

He looked up as Sonia approached, came to his feet as she slipped into the booth and inspected herself in her compact mirror to make sure she had not changed identity on the cab trip from Piccadilly, and sat down again just as their drinks were served. Sonia did not waste time for any gestures of friendship in the form of lifted or tapped-together glasses, but drank her vodka in one steady gulp, after which she rapped her glass on the table. The waiter appeared at once, took her glass in understanding, and waited.

"We'll order a bit later," Newkirk said, and smiled across the table. "How have you been?"

"Rushed," Sonia said, and looked at the waiter in a manner that sent him hurrying to the bar. She did not expand upon her statement until the waiter had returned and hurriedly set her drink down. Sonia took a healthy sip before paying any attention to Newkirk, or expanding on her theme. "This will have to be a very quick lunch. We're busy, rushed. The British Airways strike, you know."

Newkirk grinned. "You people never go on strike, do you?"

Sonia was not amused and her expression showed it.

"We people also do not leave a thousand people stranded, sitting up all night at some airport trying to get anything that flies so that they can get home to a job, most of them without enough money to buy milk for the baby," she said coldly. Sonia certainly did not consider herself an enemy agent; the thought would have been repugnant. She merely gave information to Newkirk, or whoever appeared with the proper identification, in exchange for money, plus an occasional lunch or dinner, or—if the man were attractive enough, which James Newkirk was not—an occasional romp in bed. The information she gave was certainly innocent enough; she was not in the position of having critical information at her command, and she was positive she would have refused to pass any on if she had. If the CIA or anyone else was foolish enough to pay her sums of money for the innocuous data she passed along, well, let them. She could even manage to feel a bit patriotic, knowing that through her the CIA was helping her country's economy in a way. She hadn't asked her boss at Aeroflot for a raise in over a year.

"Sorry," Newkirk said, not a bit sorry, and finished his whiskey and water, rapping the glass on the table. Sonia took advantage of the hiatus in conversation to finish her vodka and place her glass beside Newkirk's so the waiter could make no mistake. When the waiter had taken their empty glasses and disappeared in the direction of the bar, Sonia picked up the menu, speaking over its top.

"And what do you want now?"

Newkirk did not make the mistake of lowering his menu or looking in the least conspiratorial as he answered her in conversational tones.

"Two men. Their names are Gregor Kovpak and Serge Ulanov. They arrived in England on Aeroflot from Leningrad a few days ago—"

"I know," Sonia said, interrupting almost contemptuously. "I'm the one who told you."

"Exactly," Newkirk said, not a bit nonplussed. "Now I want to know when they are leaving, if they are leaving together or separately, and where they are going. And if either or both of them will be accompanied, and if so, by whom."

Sonia thought the request was a foolish one, and her tone indicated it. "They both hold return tickets to Leningrad, with an open date."

"I'm aware of that," Newkirk said calmly. "I simply wish to know if they change them, or even if they do return to Leningrad, what day they are booked for. As well as the other information." Sonia merely nodded, and Newkirk continued in the same conversational tone as the waiter returned with their drinks. "And I think I can safely recommend the beef stroganov in this restaurant."

"In England?" Sonia asked incredulously, as she raised her glass. "Don't be ridiculous." She looked up at the waiter. "I'll have the mushroom soup to start, then the steak—the big one, not the small one, medium rare—with mashed potatoes, string beans, and a tossed salad. I'll have a pint of lager with it. I'll pick my sweet later with the coffee and a liqueur."

And how she maintains that fabulous figure on a diet like that, Newkirk thought despairingly, is beyond me; as is the question of how I'm going to present the bill for this meal on my expense account without having it appear we had an orgy. He sighed, put down his menu, and asked the waiter for a clear consomme, a cress salad, and small plate of cucumber sandwiches . . .

Serge Ulanov, his shoes off and a cigarette in one corner of his mouth, reclined on the bed in Gregor Kovpak's room with his copy of *Playboy* while he waited for his compatriot to return from wherever he was, most probably with Dr. Ruth McVeigh. Suddenly Ulanov lowered his *Playboy* and looked up with a frown. Someone was fumbling overlong at the lock of the room, as if trying first one, then another of a set of lock picks. Newkirk? Ulanov wondered, and shook his head. Newkirk was a better agent than that. He would have been sure to get a master key and not been dependent on lock picks before he would have tried to enter. He also would have called the room to be sure it was unoccupied. That inept waiter figure from the night before? Or the maid who obviously was not a maid? No matter. Ulanov slid silently from the bed, placed the *Playboy* to one side and laid his cigarette in an ashtray. He moved to stand beside the door, his stockinged feet making no sound on the thick carpeting. The sound of the key being inexpertly applied to the lock continued. Enough of this! Ulanov thought, and with a sudden motion flung the door open, and then almost went over backward as Gregor Kovpak, his arms ladened with bundles, nearly fell over him. Kovpak caught his balance and grinned at the major.

"Thanks. I was having trouble opening the door with my arms full."

"Oh," Ulanov said, feeling a bit foolish, and went to sit in a chair, retrieving his cigarette and drawing on it deeply as Kovpak unloaded his burden on the bed. Ulanov nodded. "Which reminds me, I also want to do a bit of shopping before we go back. My wife gave me a list as long as your arm. Don't ever get married."

"Before we go back..." Kovpak repeated, and rubbed his chin a bit sheepishly. "Well, that was one of the things I wanted to talk to you about, Serge. You see—"

"You're not going back with me?"

"Well, I—I mean, it's this way..."

"You're going to defect," Ulanov said in his usual humorous manner, but the normal twinkle when he said outrageous things was missing from his eye. "In that case the last person on earth you should confess this to, is a KGB man. I might drug you, wrap you in a rug from one of the fine London shops—my wife always wanted a rug of Scottish wool—and ship you back to the Hermitage in the trunk of a black—"

"—official-looking car, marked as a rare tapestry," Kovpak finished, and laughed. "No, I'm not going to defect. It's not just that my little baby dinosaur needs me," he went on more seriously, "but I think we should start to do something about this auction of the Schliemann treasure. Certainly the Hermitage must bid on it, and bid on it very seriously, and we'll have to start working on the Cultural Commission for the necessary money." This was Dr. Kovpak, the eminent archaeologist speaking, and Ulanov knew it. "It would make a perfect addition to our gold collection."

"I'm glad to hear you won't be defecting. I'd probably have the devil of a time explaining to your boss how I managed to lose one of his best scientists, and in broad daylight," Ulanov said, and was surprised at the relief he felt. Paranoia is normal in this business, he thought, but I'm beginning to go overboard. Maybe Gregor is right. Maybe I ought to try to get a job in some engineering plant, although that would probably be a bit difficult at my age. Or maybe writing jokes for *Krokodil* magazine? I could steal some from *Playboy*, except they'd never get printed. "So why aren't you going home with me? If it's a question of spending a few more days here in London, I don't blame you. Leningrad is beautiful, but I must admit it lacks the old-world charm of London. I'd be glad to spend a few more days here with you. We can go back next week."

Kovpak looked uncomfortable. "It isn't that—"

"You mean, if you must spend a few more days here, you'd rather do it in the company of someone a bit younger or more beautiful than me?" Ulanov grinned. "Someone like—well, Dr. McVeigh?"

Gregor reddened slightly. "That isn't it, either. It isn't even staying in London."

"Ah!" Ulanov looked wise. "A trip, then. To New York? Possibly to visit the Metropolitan Museum? Traveling, possibly, with Dr. McVeigh," he went on innocently. "Can she get you a visa?"

"And it certainly isn't a trip to New York. Actually," Gregor said, feeling that the truth, or at least part of it, was the best way to end what even he had recognized as a form of interrogation. "I was thinking about a trip to Germany, to East Berlin. Possibly to see the Bode Museum at the Staatsliche, since they've built up their antiquities section—"

"*Possibly* to see the Bode?" Ulanov raised his eyebrows. "Don't you think they'll let you in?"

"I mean, to *see* the Bode," Kovpak said, now thoroughly unhappy with his dissembling, or at least with his failure to do it well.

"I should imagine—" Ulanov paused to crush out his cigarette and light another at once; Kovpak wondered why the major never lit one from the other. But then, Kovpak wondered many things about the stocky major. "I should imagine," Ulanov repeated, drawing in on the cigarette and then exhaling, speaking about the smoke, "that a visit to the Bode Museum would be good for some of the other visiting curators and directors, those who don't get to Europe too frequently. People like— well, Dr. Ruth McVeigh, for instance."

"Well, as a matter of fact, we—I mean, she did mention the slight possibility, but there wasn't anything definite decided . . ."

"And when do you plan on leaving for East Berlin?"

"I—tomorrow morning, I suppose. We—I mean, I haven't made any plans, as yet."

"I see," Ulanov said, and decided to take poor Gregor off the hook. Poor lad, he thought, you may be a great archaeologist, but you've a lot to learn about successful lying. "Well, in that case all I can do is wish you a pleasant journey. Sorry we didn't get any more information at the conference, but that's the way it often goes. You have to try. In any event, let me know when you get back to Leningrad; possibly we can arrange lunch together sometime. And our department might even be able to use some influence with the Cultural Commission." He flicked ash from his cigarette and came to his feet, picking up his magazine, tucking it under his arm. "And if, by chance, you happen to run into Dr. McVeigh at the Bode, please give her my best regards and tell her I'm sorry about what happened at her conference."

He smiled genially, looked at his cigarette, decided it was short enough, and crushed it out. He held out his hand. Gregor shook it firmly. Ulanov gave him a friendly wink and moved in the direction of his own room. He paused, his hand on the knob of the connecting door. "I'll close this, if you don't mind. I think I'll do some shopping and probably eat in my own room. I'm tired. Getting old, you know. And if I'm asleep when you leave in the morning, have a good trip."

"You, too. And good-bye, Serge."

Kovpak watched the older man close the door behind him and lock it, and then heaved a sigh of relief. He had thought it would have been much tougher to shake the old boy. The last thing he wanted was to be wet-nursed, or under constant surveillance while traveling with Ruth McVeigh, but apparently that wasn't going to be a problem, thank heavens! He put such unpleasant thoughts from him and began unwrapping the packages of clothing which he hoped would make him, at least in the eyes of Ruth McVeigh, look less like a peasant and more like a man of the world. He also hoped, of course, that the salesman who had helped him select those springlike colors had been correct when he had assured him the new clothing made him look years younger...

Major Serge Ulanov made his telephone calls from the office of the military attaché at the Russian Embassy, even as he was sure that James Newkirk made his calls to Langley from the American Embassy in Grosvenor Square. The major did not know or care whether Newkirk or one of his minions had followed him there or not. Another day and Newkirk would be a thing of the past. Actually, he rather hoped that Newkirk had followed him, for a heavy rain had begun to fall, with ominous mutterings from a bank of even blacker clouds in the west, and it somehow made Ulanov feel better to think of the other man somewhere out in the rain, keeping a sharp eye on the heavy doors of the embassy.

The major's first call was to an old acquaintance, the manager of Aeroflot Airlines, in London. He spoke in Russian.

"Two people, Alexis," the major said quietly. "And all of this completely confidential, of course. A Dr. Gregor Kovpak, a Russian national, and a Dr. Ruth McVeigh, carrying an American passport. Of course, they may not be traveling by Aeroflot, but I think it possible since Kovpak already has his return on your line. But in any event, I'm sure your computer can find them. What? Going possibly to East Berlin, but not necessarily. Yes, traveling together. For sometime tomorrow morning, I'm fairly sure. What? Yes, I'll wait."

He leaned back and looked at the heavy drapes and ornate furniture of the room the military attaché had given him to use, with the inevitable pictures of heroes of the Revolution on the walls. And he undoubtedly thought he was showing me courtesy, giving me this mausoleum to use, Ulanov thought, and smiled. A little of *Playboy* art would do wonders in sprucing up the place, he thought, and then brought his attention back to the telephone, frowning in amazement.

"What? What do you mean, Aeroflot doesn't fly to East Berlin? Why not, for heavens sake? You fly to Boston, you fly to Bangkok, you fly to Belfast, and you don't fly to East Berlin?" Good God! he thought, we let all that nice hard capitalist currency go to other airlines? Typical. "What? But you found the two of them on the computer, anyway? Well, that's better; you had me frightened there for a moment. What line? Lod? I see. Leaving Heathrow at 11:50 tomorrow, arriving at Schönefeld Airport in East Berlin at 13:25 . . . Flight 286, nonstop . . . and with a car rental waiting for them at the airport. . . . Wait a minute, Alexis, let me think."

Ulanov frowned at the ceiling of the room while he sorted things out in his mind; then he smiled, a broad smile. He straightened his face as he spoke into the instrument.

"All right, Alexis, this is what I want you to do. The Lod flight was booked through your office, wasn't it? I thought so. Good. I want you to call Dr. Kovpak and Dr. McVeigh at their hotel—you have it? Good. Call them and inform them that, unfortunately, Flight 286 has been overbooked, but that you, in your infinite wisdom and skill, have managed to book them on a slightly later flight. How much later? Oh, an hour should do, I suppose. Pick out a flight like that and let me know. Oh, and also, of course, make sure there is space on the flight for them. I'll wait."

He leaned back again, wishing desperately that the Ambassador didn't have asthma, and wasn't so maniacally set against the smoking of tobacco in any form in the embassy rooms. He couldn't imagine how the others in the place could tolerate such a restriction. Probably spend 90 percent of their time in the toilets, he thought, and smiled at the picture, wondering what would happen to anyone who might want to use the rest rooms for a more legitimate purpose. Probably have to go to the pub around the corner, he thought, and then paid attention as the telephone spoke.

"What? But that leaves only fifteen minutes later! Ah! A connection in Amsterdam, eh? How long? Excellent. What line is it? KLM, and then who? Interflug? Never heard of them, but so long as their planes don't fall down. And there is space for both of them on the flight? Good! Alexis, you are a genius. What? Well, the computer is a genius, then. No, that's about it. And thanks for your trouble." Ulanov was about to hang up and go on to his next call when he suddenly remembered something; he mentally struck himself on the forehead for almost forgetting. "Alexis? Thank heaven I caught you before you hung up and went and sold those two seats to East Berlin on Lod! What? Oh, you can sell one of them, but hold the other one for me. Well, of course. What do you think this whole charade was all about, anyway?"

He hung up, thought a moment, and then placed his second call, a call to a special number in Berlin which he read from a small notebook. Knowing the bureaucracy that exists in all government departments, he hoped not everyone had already gone home. It was almost six o'clock in the evening, and not everyone, he knew, was as dedicated to their job as Serge Ulanov. The thought made him smile as he waited, but his smile disappeared when his call finally went through and he realized his fear had been well-founded, for the man who answered the telephone seemed suspicious of the call and was not inclined to accept it. Ulanov made himself heard above the voice of the international operator, who sensibly retired from the battle, leaving Ulanov on the line.

"This is Major Ulanov," he said, speaking German and putting all the authority he could muster into his voice. "I'm calling from London. Who am I speaking to?"

"Who do you want to speak to?"

Ulanov bit back his temper. "I placed this call to Colonel Franz Müeller. Is he there?"

"No." There was a click followed by a dial tone; the man at the other end had obviously disconnected.

Ulanov clenched his jaw and called for the international operator again, repeating the number. After what seemed to the impatient Ulanov to be an unconscionable wait, the telephone rang. The same voice came on the line. "Hello?"

"This is Major Ulanov again," the major said, making no attempt to disguise the fury in his voice. "Did you hang up on me?"

"You said you wanted Colonel Müeller," the voice said, attempting to appease this irascible stranger with pure logic. "He isn't here."

"Well, you listen to me! And if you hang up again, I promise you you'll be the sorriest man in all Germany, East or West! I am Major Serge Ulanov of the KGB, and when I call someone in your organization I don't expect him to hang up on me! And please don't tell me I wasn't calling you! And please don't tell me who is or isn't there! Is that understood?"

"Yes, sir!"

"Good! Now, who am I speaking to?"

"This is Corporal Burkhardt, sir." The tone was much more respectful.

"All right, Corporal," Ulanov said coldly, "listen and listen very carefully! I am arriving at Schönefeld Airport tomorrow early afternoon. Have you got that?"

"Yes, sir. I'll tell Colonel—"

"Be quiet! I'm not through. Now, I want to be met with a car—" Ulanov thought a moment and then frowned. "No, make that two cars. I want them to be—"

"Sir?"

"Wait until I finish. I want them both to be—"

"Sir?"

"If you interrupt me once again—!" Ulanov said savagely, and then resigned himself to the fact he was dealing with an idiot. "Well, what is it?"

"Sir, I can't arrange any cars. That would be the responsibility of the motor pool section, sir. Sir, I don't even have a car myself. I come to the barracks on a bicycle—"

Ulanov took a deep breath. Obviously speaking with this moron was wasting time. "Where is Colonel Müeller?"

"He's probably at the club, sir. The Officers' Club. He often stops there on the way home." The corporal's voice became confidential. "Sometimes he stays there quite late, sir. Trouble at home, I think—"

Ulanov gritted his teeth, trying to remember that just moments before he had been in the very best of humor. "Do you have the telephone number of the colonel's club?"

"Oh, I can connect you directly, sir. It's in the same building, on the top floor. It used to be in the basement, but there wasn't any view, so they moved it to the—"

"Corporal!"

"Yes, sir. I thought you wanted to talk, sir," the corporal said in a properly aggrieved tone. "I'll connect you right away, sir."

There was the sound of mingled voices accompanied with static, the usual cacophony when telephone calls are transferred, then a bit of silence—welcome to Ulanov after the corporal—after which a familiar voice came on the line.

"Colonel Müeiler here."

"Colonel? This is Major Serge Ulanov."

"Major!" Colonel Müeller sounded delighted. "When did you get in?"

"I didn't get in. I'm in London, but I'll be in Berlin tomorrow. Listen, I need your help. I get to Schönefeld at 13:25 on Lod flight 286. I want to be met with two cars. I—"

"Two cars?" The colonel chuckled; it was obvious he had been at the club some time. "Have you gotten that fat since I saw you last?"

Ulanov did not smile. "No, I'm quite the same. But I want two cars because I want to be very sure we do not lose the people we will be trailing, and if one car has to be left to trail them on foot, I want another car handy. I want both cars completely nondescript. Nothing official-looking about them, understand? And I'll want a good driver with each car, and a good man with the driver in the second car." He thought a moment. "Is it possible to get cars with some sort of telephonic communication between them?"

"Of course. How would I do for the man with the driver in the second car? I assume you'll be with the driver in the first, and getting away from my desk would be a welcome change."

"Excellent! Oh, one more thing. The man we will be trailing—at a distance, by the way; we don't want to pick him up—is named Gregor Kovpak. He's a Russian. He's arranged for a car at the airport, a rental. Is it possible—well, to put some sort of a bug on that car?"

"A homing pigeon? Certainly." The colonel paused and cleared his throat. "Major, this Kovpak—a criminal of some sort? Is he dangerous? Will we be requiring arms of any sort?"

Ulanov laughed. "No, he's not dangerous; just to secrets buried in the earth for a few thousand years. What you might bring along, though, is a cooler in each car with some bottles of beer and some sandwiches. We may have a long drive."

"Oh, Where to?"

"All I have is a silly hunch I'd be ashamed to tell you about," Ulanov said. "I'll see you tomorrow," and he hung up.

Sonia sipped her vodka and made a face. "The bottle," she said disdainfully, "says 'Finlandia' on it, but the vodka says, 'Made in Great Britain,' and in somebody's bathroom, in my opinion." She pushed the glass away from her with a distasteful grimace. "Get me a plain whiskey, please."

"Right," Newkirk said, and made his way through the evening crush to the bar. With a good deal of effort he managed to get the barmaid's attention and in a burst of genius ordered a triple, with a half-pint of lager for himself. If he had to spend most of the evening running back and forth to the bar, he was never going to get any useful information from Sonia.

He came back and placed the drink before her. If she thought it rather larger than the normal drink she received when buying her own, she made no sign of it. Probably never bought her own in her life, Newkirk thought sourly. Probably thinks a triple whiskey *is* the normal size.

"Now," he said, trying not to raise his voice, although otherwise it was almost impossible to be heard. Due to Britain's licensing law there was less than an hour in which the pub's customers could build up a glow that had to last until eleven o'clock the next morning, and the calls to the barmaid, plus the exuberant conversation in general, made communication difficult. "What have you been able to learn?"

"You mean, about your friends?" Newkirk nodded, hoping Sonia would come up with something before her triple disappeared; in fact, came up with enough to even justify the expense of the triple. She frowned, and then her face cleared. "Oh, yes. You know? You're lucky I worked last night."

"Lucky?"

"Yes. They just changed his schedule a little while ago. He's not going to Leningrad. He's to leave on the Lod plane for Berlin tomorrow—"

"Berlin? Who's going to Berlin?"

"This Gregor Kovpak. You wanted to know about him, didn't you?"

"Berlin?" Newkirk frowned. "Not Leningrad?"

"What did I say? Did I say Leningrad? I said Berlin. Do you have trouble with your ears?"

Newkirk overlooked the obvious effect of the triple on Sonia. His mind was on other things. "What do you mean, *was* scheduled?"

Sonia glared at him. "Please don't interrupt! I said he was scheduled to go on that plane, but he was put on another, one that connects in Amsterdam." She sipped her drink, hiccuped gently, and put her glass down. "I don't know why, so don't ask me."

"Ulanov, too?"

Sonia shook her head. "No, he's taken one of the seats in the Lod plane."

Newkirk wrinkled his forehead, trying to digest this odd information. "They aren't traveling together?"

"I said—!"

"I heard what you said. It was a rhetorical question." He hurried on before he could be asked to define the term. "They are both—or each, I suppose—traveling alone?"

Sonia giggled. The triple was definitely getting to her. "This Dr. Gregor Kovpak, he must be some sort of a man, huh? He's traveling with a woman, a Dr. Ruth McVeigh. Or maybe she's really a doctor, huh? If he doesn't feel so good, she puts him to bed, huh?" She grinned and then yawned deeply.

Newkirk took a deep breath. He had no idea how much

alcohol Sonia had consumed since their lunch, but it must have been a fair amount, because despite her admittedly large capacity, she was beginning to look very sleepy, and he wanted to be sure he had all the information from her, and correct and proper information, before she put her head on the table and dropped off to sleep. Or simply disregarded his questions altogether and screamed at him like a fishwife, which he was also sure she could do.

"Sonia, listen," he said, hoping the urgency in his voice would keep her awake a few moments longer. "I want to be absolutely certain I've understood you correctly. Ulanov goes to Schönefeld in East Berlin on the Lod flight first. Then Kovpak and McVeigh go to the same place, but leave later. Is that right?"

"Not later." Sonia shook her head and then caught her balance as she almost fell over. Newkirk kicked himself mentally for not having limited her drink to a double, or even a single. "They leave at almost the same time, only the two doctors have to change in Amsterdam, so they'll arrive in Berlin later. Don't you understand English?"

Newkirk considered this information. Ulanov had obviously arranged the change in Kovpak's flight. This had to mean he had arranged it in order to get to Schönefeld earlier. Had he wished to travel with the other two there would have been no problem of having some other passenger bumped to make room for him. Which, in turn, meant he wanted to get there first in order to follow Kovpak and McVeigh when they arrived. Which was certainly interesting! A surveillance by the KGB on one of Russia's top scientists? Why? Fear that he might defect? But who went to East Germany to defect from Russia? And where did the American, McVeigh, come into the picture? The only reason she would be involved had to mean the entire affair was concerned with the Schliemann treasure. Possibly, when he had been unable to keep an eye on them, they had run into some information—? And Ulanov suspected what it might be, and therefore planned to keep an eye on them without their knowing it. That had to be the answer, and if that was of such interest to the KGB, it had to be of equal interest to the CIA. A thought came.

"Sonia—Sonia! Did Kovpak arrange for a car to rent at Schönefeld?"

"Yes." She yawned deeply and blinked her eyes, not wanting to fall asleep with part of her drink unconsumed. You never knew what types you were next to in a pub, and many would not be above drinking her drink if she were asleep.

Which simply meant that he, Newkirk, had to get to Schönefeld Airport before any of the others, and with a car. And when Ulanov took off after the two archaeologists, he, James Newkirk, would fall in line—but without being seen—and find out what there was to find out. So the case was far from finished. It looked as if it might just be beginning. Which was a most interesting state of affairs, or at least might prove to be.

"Sonia! Sonia!" He shook her slightly; her eyes popped open, trying to focus. "What time does that Lod flight get into Schönefeld?"

She screwed her eyes shut, trying to recall the schedule. She opened them, smiling brightly, pleased with her extraordinary memory. "Sometime in the afternoon."

Newkirk sighed. "Is there a flight that could get me there in the morning?"

"No. It's the earliest."

Which meant he had to get to West Berlin, to Tegel Airport, in time to get a car and go through Checkpoint Charlie and get down to Schönefeld in time to be waiting when Ulanov's car passed. He was sure he would not miss that head of white hair.

"Sonia . . . Sonia! What planes are there to Tegel Airport in West Berlin that would get me there sometime tomorrow morning? Or even late tonight?"

She smiled at him and then frowned as he kept wavering before her. "What did you say?"

"I said, what planes—" He knew he was wasting time. Better to get on the phone to the airlines, or better yet, simply catch a cab to Heathrow and check out there, and take the first plane out, whenever it left. There had to be a lot of flights; it was a popular corridor. And that way he would have an excuse for not calling Langley; they might not think his trailing Ulanov and the two scientists to be as important as he knew it to be. And he had no intention of dropping the case just when it looked as if it were breaking open. He reached out, touching Sonia's arm. "Come on. I'll take you home."

She frowned at him as if he had made the most vile suggestion she had heard. "Take your hands off me! And leave this early? The pub doesn't close for almost an hour." She was slurring her words, and clutching her glass as if he might try to remove it from her hand. She put her other hand out to hold his untouched lager. "I'm staying right here. You can go wherever you want to go!"

"Look, Sonia—" Newkirk sighed and gave up. After all, he had gotten the information he needed, even if it had been like pulling teeth. He leaned over and spoke into her ear. "I'll see to it your money is mailed to you at your home. All right?"

"Right..." She leaned back, her eyes closing, her head resting against the cushion that ran along the back of the long bench that covered the pub's wall. "Right..." Her eyes opened momentarily. "You going to buy me a drink?" Her eyes closed, a faint snore came from her partially opened mouth.

Newkirk shook his head and came to his feet, walking quickly from the pub before someone might notice he had left a sleeping woman behind. It was a pity, he thought a bit savagely, that Langley didn't appreciate the sacrifices one made in this job, or the people one was forced to deal with, whether one was a regular agent or a lowly stringer...

16

From the small balcony that jutted a bit from the sheer walls
of Lindgren Castle, the view was spectacular, and Professor
Arne Nordberg, luxuriating in it, fully appreciated it; it was
his artist's soul, he knew, that delighted in beauty, and made
him proud to be himself. In the distance the sparkling spires
and glistening rooftops of Ringsted could be seen through the
leafy boughs, with the land between taken with bucolic mead-
ows in varying shades of light greens and yellows, while the
intermittent stands of pine and birch punctuated the landscape
with their darker shades. The winding road leading from the
castle to the huge gates of the estate could be seen twisting its
way like a delicate ribbon through stands of juniper and neatly
trimmed hedges foreshortened by the height. Almost beneath
the professor, as he looked down over the low balustrade, was
his ten-year-old car, parked in the parking lot, the only blot,
he told himself, on the entire scene and one he intended to
erase as soon as possible. He stepped back a bit, since looking
directly down from heights always affected him, and then turned
and walked into the living room of Count Lindgren's private
quarters.

Count Lindgren had been watching him, amused, reading

the other man's mind step by step, including the grimace on Nordberg's fat face as he had looked down. Obviously he had noted that wreck of an automobile, the count thought, and mentally smiled. Don't worry, my friend, the count silently advised his companion; you won't have to suffer that car much longer. He poured a glass of brandy for his guest and indicated with a generous wave of his hand that Nordberg should take a seat at the table across from him. The professor accepted with an eager smile, glancing over his shoulder at the balcony as he sipped.

"Wonderful!" he said, still amazed at having been invited to this sacred aerie for the fourth or fifth time. "And what a marvelous view! It never wearies, Count!"

Count Lindgren looked at the professor with sorrow, but the sorrow was directed at himself for having apparently failed to make himself understood in his role as a host. "After the time we've spent together," he said, his tone a bit chiding, "and after being partners in a most audacious scheme—my involvement being, I'll admit, but for the sport of it—you still call me Count? If I may call you Arne—and I may, may I not—?"

"Of course! Of course! Certainly! Absolutely!"

"Then you should at least call me Axel," Lindgren said, and smiled in his usual warm friendly way.

"If you wish—Axel," Nordberg said, and thought his heart would burst, it seemed to be swelling so in his breast. He was on a first-name basis with Count Axel Lindgren! Who would have believed it? Certainly not those cretins at the university, who would no more be invited into Count Lindgren's private rooms, than they would be asked to have tea at the Palace with the Queen! Still, why shouldn't Axel be his friend? After all, the count was obviously a bored man. With all his millions he had undoubtedly tasted all of life's pleasures many times, surely until they sated. Now he, Arne Nordberg, had brought the count—Axel—a most interesting proposition, one to challenge any man's ingenuity, his sporting blood, his spirit of adventure. And while the count would be deriving his satisfaction from resolving the problem, he, Professor Arne Nordberg, would be getting the money! Fifteen million dollars at the very least! It was hard to believe. He wriggled in his chair, and looked across the table. "Axel—"

"Yes?"

"Speaking of our—audacious scheme—how is it going?"

"Very well," Count Lindgren said, and decided to take his old friend Arne into his confidence. After all, his confidences would go no further. "You recall the letters that went out to the various museums?"

"Of course. But you merely said in them that further instructions for bidding would be furnished before September first. Why the delay? That's a little over two whole months away." In his petulant whine one could read his dissatisfaction with his present life, his aged automobile, as well as with the postponement of his planned increased love life, all necessitated by that delay.

Lindgren looked at him evenly. "To begin with, I wished to give ample time for the matter to be thoroughly publicized. You see, the newspapers are already calling it the 'Auction of the Century.' The meeting in London that ended in such discord, did a good deal for our cause. It brought the question of legal ownership—or lack of ownership—to the fore. That should result in even more bidders. And not only that"—he leaned forward and flicked ash from his thin cigar; in the increased intimacy of their relationship the professor had finally worked up enough nerve to confess he did not like cigars. The count leaned back, pointing with his panatela for emphasis—"but there is also the question of the time needed for the various museums to raise the money to bid against each other. They have to approach potential donors, twist arms, call up old debts, sometimes use blackmail—it all takes time." He shrugged humorously. "I've been approached, myself. By the Glyptotek Museum."

Nordberg stared at him. "What did you do?"

Lindgren laughed. "I said they could count on me for two million kroner, if they were the successful bidder." His laughter disappeared as quickly as it had come. "I'm afraid they won't be the successful bidder." He looked at Nordberg with a twinkle in his eye. "I don't mind spending a few kroner on this, just for the fun of it, but I scarcely intend to spend two million kroner for the privilege."

"Of course not!" Nordberg said, shocked at the very idea. He looked at Lindgren with even greater respect, doubly in awe of a man who could mention such huge sums without seemingly being impressed by them. "So—how do you expect to conduct the auction—well, without being identified with it? Without, in fact, being identified?"

Lindgren crushed out his cigar and leaned forward. "That was the most pleasant part of the game," he said. He was speaking now for his own benefit as much as for that of his guest. He was speaking, using the recitation to review the plan for the slightest flaw, even permitting a fool like Nordberg to listen in on the offhand chance that he might perceive an error in the scheme, much as a child might see through legerdemain whereas an adult usually would not. And with whom else could he review his plan? "As you must have been able to discern when I sent those letters to the various museums, I have contact with a reliable messenger service that asks no questions, and would not want any answers in any case. All they want is to be paid for their services, and this I do."

"I—I see no reason why the expenses to which you are being put, should not be taken from the proceeds," Nordberg said, trying to sound businesslike, and then wondered if perhaps he was being too generous. Messenger service of this type, in eight or more cities, had to run to a fair amount of money. Still, he could do no less than make the offer. Otherwise, with that much money in the offing, he might look to be miserly, or even greedy.

Count Lindgren waved the suggestion away as being of no matter.

"It's worth it to me for the pleasure I'm getting from all this," he said with his usual friendly smile, and then went on with his plan. "On the twenty-fifth of August, an advertisement will be delivered and paid for to the personal columns of the major newspapers in the major cities of the world. I am sure the word will get to every museum and interested party everywhere within hours. This advertisement will advise that a telephone conference call has been arranged for twelve noon, Greenwich time, to which any interested museum or individual can join upon request to the international telephone company, and to which the major news services of the world may also connect without cost. The conference call will last for one hour each day for three consecutive days, at the same time each day—"

"Without cost to them?" Nordberg had paled. "A worldwide conference call to which anyone can connect? For an hour each day for three days? That will cost a fortune!"

Lindgren shrugged lightly. "Fifty or sixty thousand dollars, is all. I should judge that no more than fifteen or twenty really serious bidders will enter the auction, and no more than six or seven major news services. Any lesser ones will simply be disconnected, as will anyone who does not bid. But what if it should even run to a hundred thousand dollars? Surely that is no great sum in these inflationary times, is it? For the fun of seeing an auction like this conducted? Or listening to it, rather? Believe me, it will be worth it!"

"But—if you conduct the auction, won't you be—identified? Unless," Nordberg said, thinking about it, pleased to offer a slight change in the scheme that might actually enhance it, "you pretend to be the representative of a museum—possibly raise the bidding every now and then to induce the others to—"

"And possibly end up the high bidder?" Lindgren asked dryly. "No, I shall merely be a listener—"

"But you would be cut off!"

"A listener," Lindgren repeated firmly. "The auction will be conducted by someone from Switzerland, from an unlisted number. Actually, an apartment I maintain there. That someone, I assure you, will not be me. He will be a person of confidence whose voice is unknown." The unknown, of course, would be Wilten, but there was no reason for Nordberg to know that. "I shall be listening in on an extension to that telephone from an adjoining room. And at the final hour of the conference calls—if all but one bidder has not dropped out before then—the auction will be ended. Whoever is the high bidder at one o'clock on September third, will be declared the winner."

He glanced at Nordberg, to see if the other man had seen any fault in the scheme, but the professor could only bob his balding head in profound admiration. He looks like one of those idiot dolls on a string, Lindgren thought, and then paused as a frown crossed the professor's face, indicating thought, or at least concern.

"But—what about the delivery of the treasure? And the payment, of course?"

"The height of simplicity," Lindgren said, again reviewing his plan aloud for the slightest possibility of failure. "The winner of the auction will be directed to place the proper funds in escrow to a numbered account in Switzerland. The money—"

"In escrow?"

"It means the money stays there until the treasure is delivered, after which it is turned over to the numbered account. The money is to be released from escrow to the account only when the treasure is received, or, rather, when either the museum or the high bidder—assuming it's an individual—admit that delivery has taken place, or when the delivery is reliably reported in the press, or when the collection actually goes on exhibit." He shook his head. "I do not believe that one, let alone all three of those conditions can be kept secret."

Nordberg was staring at him with stricken eyes. "But—but—"

"But what?"

"But suppose that the high bidder *never* reports delivery? Suppose it *never* comes out in the newspapers? Suppose they never exhibit it? Or not for many, many years?" The thought of an even greater ageing car, together with an even more ageing and loveless Arne Nordberg—and with millions of dollars in escrow to his account in a bank someplace—was too horrible to contemplate. It was also evident in his voice. "What then? The money could stay in escrow forever!"

At least, Lindgren thought, the dolt was listening and looking for faults. He smiled, a humorless smile, almost a contemptuous smile.

"To begin with, it will serve no purpose for the successful bidder to have his money tied up in escrow, of no use to him, and also have a collection he has paid for, but which he does not exhibit. He has the worst of two possible worlds. Nobody would be that foolish." Except a fool like you, he thought uncharitably, and continued. "In the second place, the newspapers will not only be informed as to where and when delivery is to take place, but they will be there with photographers and reporters and television and radio and everything else mankind has invented to disallow peace. We haven't planned everything else and left that matter to chance, believe me!"

"Oh!" Nordberg felt a bit foolish. This marvelous man was doing everything in his power to make him rich, and all he was doing was finding fault! He only hoped the count—Axel, that is—hadn't been irked by the question. "But—the delivery, itself?"

"The treasure will be discovered in a suitcase in the baggage-claim area of a flight that will be divulged to the winning museum, together with the fictitious passenger's name that will be on the suitcase, as well as the proper claim check. The newspapers in that city will be told—by international telex; they pay more attention to those than to anonymous calls from 'a friend'—that the denouement of the 'Auction of the Century' can be witnessed by them if they are smart enough to appear at Kennedy, or Orly, or Tegel, or wherever, at the baggage area of such-and-such terminal, for flight such-and-such on such-and-such a date at such-and-such a time." He shook his head. "No, the money will be released into the account from escrow very quickly. Within a few weeks at the most, I should judge."

Professor Arne Nordberg sipped his brandy, and set the half-filled glass down. He could see no flaw in the scheme. It was brilliant! He leaned back in his comfortable leather chair, his tiny hands clasped across the bulge of his belly, and tried to picture what it would actually be like to have fifteen million dollars in his possession! Fifteen? If that was merely the minimum bid in the auction, and if the auction went on for three consecutive days for an hour a day, giving ample time for museums to raise additional funds for bidding higher the following day—that was pure genius on Axel's part!—then the ultimate sum had to be higher, much higher!

But suppose nobody bid?

Nordberg felt a cold hand grip his stomach. No, that was not possible. Count Axel Lindgren would not have spent the time or the money on any scheme regarding the treasure that would not result in profit to his friend, the professor. It would be no game, no sport, to the count if nobody bid. But—

Suppose nobody bid?

Count Lindgren had been watching the emotions flicker across the pudgy face like indistinct images from a slide projector onto a wrinkled screen. The final expression was of unalloyed misery. Lindgren frowned in non-understanding. He did not like to be unable to fathom idiots like Nordberg.

"What now?"

Nordberg looked up in agony. "Suppose—suppose nobody bids?"

Lindgren stared at him a moment in astonishment, and then

broke into laughter of true enjoyment. "Of all the problems connected with this—what shall I call it? This sport, this game? This diversion, this amusement? This entertainment, let us say— that is the one thing I guarantee neither of us need to worry about. They will bid. They will stand in line to bid, and would have bought tickets to stand in line had I decided that was the way to go. They will step on each other's shoulders to bid. They will stay up all night and the next day to bid. They will lie, steal, cheat, and betray if necessary, in order to bid. Believe me. They are Collectors!"

Nordberg believed him. He leaned back, relieved. Where had he been in his thoughts? Oh, yes—he had been trying to picture what it would be like to be that rich. It was difficult to even imagine. Millions and millions of dollars—over *fifty million kroner!* His mind boggled at the thought. He would have to show Count Lindgren his appreciation. He would have to get him a nice gift. Not something for the castle, which seemed to have everything, but something personal. Man to man. Friend to friend. A gold cigar lighter, possibly; or a brandy flask, silver-plated and engraved with the count's name, for when the count was traveling...He became aware he was being addressed and looked up, brought from his reverie with a start.

"I beg your pardon?"

Count Lindgren's friendly smile forgave him his lapse. "I merely said, I envy you your composure."

"My composure?" The professor was confused. Had he missed something while daydreaming of the money?

"Yes," Lindgren said, and gave Nordberg a look that neatly combined congratulations with a touch of envy. "Here you are with a fortune almost in your hands—an almost assured fortune almost in your hands, you might say—and all of it depending on a very dubious location in a bank. And you sit there as if you didn't have a care in the world. I tell you," the count went on, his voice dripping sincerity, "I couldn't possibly do it. I'd be as nervous as a witch."

"I beg your pardon?" Nordberg was now thoroughly confused. "Nervous? Dubious location—?"

"You know," the count said, his tone challenging Nordberg to deny that he knew, "these bank robberies. Getting more and more prevalent. Getting more and more—well, daring? At least more technical—" He paused to take a panatela from the humidor at his elbow, held a match to it, and puffed it into life.

Nordberg frowned, still unsure of the direction the conversation had taken, but knowing it made him profoundly uneasy. He wet his lips. "Bank—bank robberies?"

"And clever, too." The count nodded at the cleverness of the current crop of bank robbers, giving credit where credit was due. "I'm sure you recall that hotel in New York that was robbed not too many years ago? Somewhere along Central Park South, I believe, or possibly somewhere else? The thieves took the doors off the safe-deposit boxes used for guests' jewelry, as if they were made of cheese. Cream cheese," he added, and frowned. "I don't recall how much money they got away with, but I believe it was nothing like the money you might be able to realize from the auction of the Schliemann treasure." He dismissed the thought with a shrug. "But, then, I suppose these people must know the chances they take when they leave their money or their jewels in one of those safe-deposit boxes."

The conversation was becoming profoundly disturbing to Arne Nordberg. "But—I thought safe-deposit boxes were the safest thing there was. Aren't they?"

The count shrugged delicately, not wishing to put banks in an unenviable position. "I suppose everything is relative. There was that case in Monte Carlo, I believe it was. I'm not sure if that was the place or if it occurred somewhere else, but no matter. You know, of course, that all banks keep a few of their safe-deposit boxes unrented in their vaults, in case some important customer comes in and requires one in a hurry? A killing at the casino, or something like that?"

"I didn't—but, of course, it makes sense . . ."

"Yes. Except in this case it didn't," the count said conversationally, "because these bandits put a gun under the bank manager's nose and made him open not only the vault, but one of those empty safe-deposit boxes. A big one. They filled it with explosive, locked the door of the safe-deposit box, left the vault and detonated the charge." The count did not explain how the bandits managed to detonate the explosive in a locked box, but he was sure it was possible.

Nordberg was watching him with wide eyes. "And what—what happened?"

"It popped all the doors of the safe-deposit boxes all along the entire wall, just like that!" The count snapped his fingers.

"The internal pressure, of course. But I'm sure you know more about that than I do, you being a scientist." He frowned off into space. "And then there was the case—"

Professor Nordberg swallowed. "But—what's safer? Than safe-deposit boxes, I mean?"

"Many things," the count said calmly, and shook ash from his cigar with a deft motion. "That's why I say I admire your composure. I must also admit," he went on as another unex-pected and rather embarrassing thought came to him, "that I'd be in a rather—well, a rather odd position should anything happen to the treasure."

"Oh, I wouldn't like that!" Nordberg said hurriedly, and then looked puzzled. "An odd position—?"

"Yes. Oh, not about the monetary value of the treasure. After all, that is your affair. But when I stop to think how I should feel if, after all the trouble I went to—trouble," he hastened to add, "that I welcomed, as I still do. But, as I say, I cannot help but wonder how I should feel if, after arranging everything as well as I have, if I say so myself, we held the auction only to discover that some thieves had staged a break-in of the boxes you showed me, and removed the treasure. I'd look a proper fool, wouldn't I?"

"I—I wouldn't want that—"

"No, I daresay you would not. No good friend would. But I'm undoubtedly exaggerating the entire thing." The count smiled self-deprecatingly. "In my case I'd be losing a bit of what the Chinese call 'face,' plus a few thousand kroner, which I can well afford. But you'd be losing much more, of course, and that would bother me. But I'm sure there's really no great worry. Banks are robbed every day without their vaults or safe-deposit boxes necessarily being disturbed. I really shouldn't have even raised the subject."

"No, no! You were quite right! But—"

Count Lindgren contemplated the pudgy professor in a kindly manner. "Yes?"

"I mean—that is—if there's a safer place . . ."

"There are many, and I'm sure you'll think of one," the count said, and brought a hand up to stifle a small yawn.

Nordberg recognized that he was being dismissed, but he certainly did not wish to leave with a matter as important as the security of the precious treasure unresolved. "But you said—"

"Yes?"

"You said there were safer places—or safer ways, I don't remember which." The professor looked about the richly appointed room, noting the valuable carvings on the shelves, the undoubtedly rare paintings on the wall. "For example, Count— I mean, Axel—how do you keep your things from—well, from being stolen? You talk about a safe-deposit box not being safe. What about your valuables, all right out in the open?" He looked a bit apologetic for pointing out the relative insecurity of the castle. "Your servants—I'm sure they're dedicated, but would they be in a position to handle a determined and large gang of thieves?"

The count stifled another yawn with a languid hand.

"My case is a bit different," he said, obviously continuing the conversation out of politeness and nothing more. "I could scarcely live the life I care to live if all the objects of beauty I need to have about me were in safe-deposit boxes. Nor should I sleep very soundly if they were. As you may or may not know, my vault below has many millions of kroners worth of silver plate. It keeps one of the maids busy just polishing it. And on the walls of the castle, as I'm sure you must have noticed, I have paintings worth many times the value of the Schliemann collection."

"I know. Oh, I know! And"—Nordberg hesitated—"you've never been—bothered?"

The count was obviously finding the conversation increasingly tiresome, but out of politeness he continued.

"You mean, robbed? No. In the olden days, the days of my ancestors, the castle was armed, of course. Armored knights and bowmen and men to handle the barrels of hot pitch and the catapults and whatever." The count bit back a yawn. It was obvious he would rather be taking his afternoon nap than discussing this wearisome subject. "Unfortunately, I'm afraid I would find my love of privacy a bit hampered by halbertmen and mace-wielding people and crossbowmen underfoot all the time. Then there was the period when the castle was overrun with servants who were, in actuality, private detectives, and they were even more objectionable, I am sure, than the bowmen." He shrugged. "Today, of course, it is all done with electronics. You may or may not know it, but you are under observation from the moment you enter the gate. Before Wilten admits you, or anyone else, he has to disconnect one of the most complete alarm systems in Denmark."

"Alarm systems?"

"Believe me," Count Lindgren said patronizingly, "if you entered without the system being deactivated, you would find yourself overwhelmed with sirens, bells, whistles, and general bedlam. In addition, the police in Ringsted would be here in moments, guns out, in case you were—as you suggested—a large determined gang of thieves." It was true, and the count still resented Erik Trosberg having insisted upon the alarm system. Without it the count might have faked a burglary and raised some needed money.

Nordberg glanced around the room, his eyes round with wonder.

"You mean—all the doors and windows?"

"Everything," the count said wearily. "Sills, stables, kitchens, even curtains, if I'm not mistaken. Plus the main vault itself, which is larger and with thicker walls than the one in your bank, where your rather vulnerable safe-deposit boxes are being guarded." The count by now could barely keep his eyes open. He came to his feet, biting back a yawn, leaned over to crush out his cigar, and then straightened up. "My dear Arne, I'm sure you will forgive me, but I had a rather long evening last night, and I'm afraid I need a bit of rest. Another party tonight, too, you know." He shrugged a bit humorously, deprecating the inevitable round of parties a man in his position had to suffer.

"Of course! Of course! I understand," Nordberg said, and came to his feet hurriedly. He downed the balance of his brandy in a gulp and moved toward the door. There he paused, unable to leave with the issue principally in his mind, unsettled. "Count Lindgren—"

"Axel," the count said, correcting him in a kindly fashion.

"Axel—I wonder—I mean . . ." Nordberg was fumbling for words.

"Yes?"

"I know it's an imposition—"

Eyebrows were raised. "An imposition?"

"I mean, I was wondering . . ." Suddenly the professor saw an out. "I mean, it would be as much for your benefit as for mine. You wouldn't have gone to all the trouble you did for nothing, in case—I mean—and I wouldn't—I mean—" Nordberg stumbled into embarrassed silence.

Count Lindgren frowned in total non-comprehension. "Arne, my dear fellow! What is it? What are you trying to say? Is there something I can do for you? Please be assured that nothing would give me greater pleasure!"

Nordberg relaxed. He should have known that Count Lindgren would not let down a friend in need. "Well, what I thought was—well, I thought that since the castle is so well protected, that—well, that we might keep the treasure here, rather than in the bank. It wouldn't take up much room," he added hastily, and suddenly remembered that it would also save him those high monthly rental fees for the boxes. A plus all around!

"Keep the treasure here?" The count frowned and rubbed his chin, staring down at the floor in deep thought. "I hadn't considered it before. The vault, of course, would be out of the question. It's loaded with plate and what not, and besides, too many people have access to it. Still—I suppose it might be done. It might be possible. We could keep it here in my study. Nobody comes in here when I'm not here, and the study, of course, enjoys the same protection as everything and everywhere else in the castle." He thought a moment more and then looked up. "Actually, now that I think about it, it's rather a good idea. I wouldn't have thought of it, myself. I must congratulate you, Arne. It's a brilliant idea."

Nordberg's face flushed with pleasure at the compliment. Which after all, he thought, was truly deserved since he actually had thought of the idea. "I'll bring it—" He started, and then he frowned. "Today is Friday; it's too late to get to the bank today. Then there's the weekend, and next week is graduation week, with faculty meetings and graduation on Wednesday—"

"Must you attend all the faculty meetings?" Lindgren said softly. "After all, in a short time you will undoubtedly be considering leaving the university—"

"True." Nordberg suddenly smiled. "You know, I keep forgetting that I'll be a rich man." He thought a moment. "Monday I really must be at the university. We clean out our desks then for the summer, and whatever we don't take, some custodian ends up with. But Tuesday—say late afternoon, I'll definitely be here. Say, five o'clock?"

"Fine!"

"And thank you, Count—I mean, Axel! Thank you!"

"It is nothing," Lindgren said modestly, and held out his hand. Nordberg shook it enthusiastically, and then dropped it as if he knew he was delaying the count's nap. He hurried to the door, anxious to allow his dear friend Axel to get his rest as soon as possible. He closed the door softly behind him, almost as if Count Lindgren had already retired to his bedroom beyond the study and was already asleep.

Lindgren watched the door close quietly behind the dumpy professor, and now wide awake again, sank back into his chair. The professor's presence had, indeed, begun to wear on him. The count poured himself a brandy and sipped it, staring contemplatively at the small balcony that the professor always favored on his visits. In four days, on Tuesday at five o'clock, the professor would bring the treasure here to Lindgren Castle. The count smiled coldly and lit a cigar, inhaling deeply and enjoying the flavor . . .

17

EAST GERMANY—July

It was a beautiful Sunday, the first day of July. The small car
that had been furnished to Gregor Kovpak at Schönefeld Airport
held a full tank of fuel, purportedly enough to take him from
one border to the other of the small country and back again.
The car was performing well. As in most of East Germany
traffic was light and automobiles were few on the autobahn,
and best of all to the mind of the man driving the car was the
fact that Ruth McVeigh sat beside him, her lovely face flushed
from the wind, looking as if she were enjoying herself. The
landscape through which they were driving was pleasant, flat
or slightly rolling countryside, neatly plowed fields, and every
now and then a herd of dairy cattle lazing in the warm sun, or
munching contentedly on grass, paying no attention to the cars
that shot past on the autobahn, as if aware of their own more
tranquil state, and quite satisfied with it.

A mile or so behind the small car, Major Serge Ulanov
relaxed, leaning back comfortably in the seat of the battered
Zis, alternately drinking from a bottle of beer, with contentment
equal to those of the cows they were passing, and consulting
a road map held in his lap. The driver at his side, forbidden
alcoholic refreshments even as minor as beer while on duty,
glanced over now and then at the drinking man a trifle chid-

ingly, but nothing could have perturbed the major less. When he had been the age of the large young man at his side, he had been happy many times to get water. He had been a partisan, probably fighting this young man's father, he thought, and put down the partially empty bottle to consult the map again.

From Schönefeld they had taken the short leg of the E-15 autobahn to the E-8, left that after thirteen kilometers to transfer to the E-74 autobahn heading north. Ulanov had to give Kovpak credit for skirting East Berlin in this fashion. The last time he had attempted to drive through the city he had become hopelessly lost, between streets that seemingly went nowhere, and those that dead-ended into the wall. While Ulanov considered the map, he also considered the fact that with the bug on Kovpak's car transmitting so well, and with the highways on which they found themselves with few intersections, and those only of very minor roads, possibly there had been no need for the two cars. Still, if and when the two people ahead left their car, it was very probable he would require all his forces to keep them adequately covered without their knowing about it. Ulanov still thought he knew their destination, but the autobahn ahead offered several alternatives, and the major saw little point in committing himself to a theory when a matter of a few minutes or a few kilometers could resolve the question.

The driver, staring ahead intently, spoke for the first time since they had left the airport. "They've turned, sir. Onto Route 2."

Ulanov consulted his map. Route 2 was a very minor road, indeed, leaving the E-74 autobahn just before the village of Bernau and passing through Eberswalde and Angermünde to skirt the Polish border and eventually return to the E-74. But at Eberswalde a turn into Route 167 would take them to Bad Freienwalde, which is where Ulanov had been sure the two had been heading all along.

His hunch, then, had been perfectly correct. Kovpak and McVeigh were starting at the last-known point where the treasure had been seen, and were attempting to trace it from there. Then they must have learned something, either from one another, or by combining information, or from some source encountered at the ill-fated conference, or from someone else in London—or it really didn't matter where or from whom—to indicate to them the route by which the Schliemann treasure had gotten to the United States and Langley, Virginia, all that distant thirty-five years before. Or—

Or? Ulanov frowned and put the "Or" aside for a moment. Whatever the two ahead of him had learned, it had been extremely naughty of Gregor Kovpak not to share that knowledge with him. Certainly a trained KGB agent would have been able to reach far more accurate conclusions than an untrained person such as Kovpak. Besides, not only was he KGB—with Kovpak on an assignment with him—but he had thought they had become friends in the short time of their acquaintance. He put that thought aside for the moment and returned to the big "Or" that had come into his mind a few moments before.

Or what? Was it possible that the two ahead knew something he did not? Was it possible that the theories of Vashugin and himself, as well as the other brains of the KGB as to what had happened to the treasure, were all wrong? Was it possible that the Schliemann treasure had *not* gone to Langley? Admittedly, the evidence indicating that the treasure had gone there was far from the type of evidence Ulanov liked to have to support a theory. On the other hand, they had seen no evidence to indicate anything contrary to the theory in all these thirty-five years. Still, the major had had enough experience to know that theories often tended to be justified by their creators as a form of self-defense.

It had occurred to Ulanov, since the announcement of the auction, that if Langley had had the treasure, it was odd that they had allowed it to be taken from them so easily. Although, he had to admit to himself, there was nothing to indicate it *had* been taken easily. It might have been a major attack, which Langley could easily keep secret. It might have been taken— or even freely given—as the result of blackmail, or the kidnapping of a major political or intelligence figure, with the treasure as ransom—something else Langley could easily keep secret. There may have been killings involved; nobody would ever need to know. Which would explain what Newkirk was doing on an unimportant conference such as the one held in London. Suppose, Ulanov thought, his mind now charging along, that someone important had been held captive, or even killed, in the losing of the treasure by Langley. Then, obviously, Newkirk, with a full complement of assistants, would have been given the assignment of tracking down those persons or that person who was responsible, who was now offering the treasure for auction...

But, in that case, would Newkirk have dropped the matter so quietly after the London conference?

Ulanov smiled to himself and stared from the car window without being aware of any of the passing scenery. You've been seeing too many movies, my friend, he told himself. Try this far more logical scenario and see how it fits: Ruth McVeigh is intrigued by the story Gregor told her in the restaurant the first night they met, the story that was recorded on the small tape-deck taken from Newkirk. She considers trying to trace the treasure, not knowing she is wasting her time. Gregor Kovpak, fully aware that Ruth McVeigh is wasting her time, is simply taking advantage of the opportunity to spend time with the girl, hoping that eventually something romantic might develop between the two. Which would explain why Gregor had said nothing to him in London. He would have been embarrassed to give his true reasons, at his age, for going to East Germany with a much younger woman. It would also explain the secrecy with which Kovpak arranged the air passages to Schönefeld Airport, as well as explaining all those fancy clothes Gregor bought for himself. The poor fool is simply falling in love, Ulanov thought, which in itself is not a particularly smiling matter, since obviously nothing can come of it.

In which case, Ulanov concluded in his discussion with himself, I am simply on a fool's errand, practically opening myself to a charge of being a Peeping Serge, and taking up the time of two security cars, two drivers, and a colonel of the East German security forces, not to mention my own time. But at least, he went on to himself, it's a lovely day, a fine day with ample refreshments, and it's a Sunday, and what better to do on a lazy Sunday if not to take a drive in the country?

He drained his bottle of beer, lit a cigarette, bent over to replace the empty bottle in the cooler to keep it from rolling around, and then glanced up at the small buzz that indicated the inter-communication unit was about to produce. He pressed a switch; the colonel's voice came on the radio speaker. There were no obvious microphones to be held and spoken into, possibly to be observed by passing motorists.

"Major?"

"Yes?"

"I think you have company."

"What!" Ulanov picked the cigarette from his lips, listening carefully.

"When you left Schönefeld, and before I picked you up and followed, another car came out of the airport parking lot and turned after you. Well, that could have been a coincidence, but I'm a suspicious person by nature, so I dropped back and gave him plenty of room. He made the same turn at E-8 and again at E-74—again it might have been someone willing to accept the extra mileage for the convenience of the autobahn, someone going north who simply didn't want to drive through the city. But when you turned into Route 2 and he followed, I thought that was enough of a coincidence to advise you..."

Ulanov had not made the mistake of looking over his shoulder, or of adjusting the driver's rearview mirror to see who might be following him. He had a pretty good idea of who it was, although he wondered how Newkirk—if it were he—had learned so quickly of his flight plans. A leak, most likely, at Aeroflot, Ulanov thought, and filed the idea away for future action. An agent at the Aeroflot London office could easily be convinced to become a double agent, which could be a useful thing. If, of course, he was really being followed, and if his tail was actually Newkirk. He continued to lean back comfortably, glancing from the window as if enjoying the view, while speaking for the benefit of the hidden microphone.

"What can you see of the car?"

"It has West Berlin plates. One person in the car. A man."

"Is it possible to get close enough to get some sort of a description without being—well, seen?"

"I can do better than that. I can drop back a bit and use my binoculars. He'll never know." There were a few moments of silence, then Colonel Müeller's voice came on again. "The car is a fairly new Ford, West German make, decent sized, and the man driving seems to be fairly tall. Wearing a dark suit. Heavy head of hair—"

"Wearing glasses?"

"I can't tell..." The colonel thought a moment. "If you could slow down suddenly—as if to avoid a small animal in the road—and pick up speed again..."

Ulanov glanced at the driver; the man obediently applied his brakes a moment, and then stepped on the accelerator again.

"That's it," Müller said into the microphone approvingly. "He put his brakes on, too, even though he's a good distance behind you. Which proves conclusively that he's following you. In any event, when he automatically looked into the side-view mirror to be sure nobody was too close to him on that side when he braked, I caught his profile. Yes, he's wearing glasses."

"His name is Newkirk," Ulanov said, and thought a moment. If Newkirk was following him, was he also merely wasting his time on a pair of love birds? Or was he onto something that he, Ulanov, didn't even suspect? He turned to his driver. "What's your rank?"

"Sergeant, sir. Non-uniformed. Sergeant Wolper."

Ulanov nodded and spoke for the benefit of the microphone and Colonel Müeller. "Franz, pass that car—don't pay any particular attention to it as you do—then pass me and take up following the two ahead. With the bug it should be no problem. Also, you can get closer to them than I could since they don't know you. When we get to Eberswalde, I'm sure they're going to turn right and go to Bad Freienwalde."

"Why?"

"It's a long story," Ulanov said wearily. "But I'm sure."

"And from there?"

"I have no idea, but from there it might be extremely important not to lose them. Follow them, but discreetly, of course. I'm going to turn left back to E-74 and then head back into Berlin."

"Taking your friend Newkirk with you, I gather. By the nose."

"Or giving it a good try. Now, Franz, what range do these police communications systems have? The one's we're using?"

"Fifteen to twenty miles, depending on the weather. Why?"

"Because after I take care of friend Newkirk, I will want to get back with you, and you may be a good deal farther away from me than the range of the set. How do I do it?"

The colonel thought a moment. "Well," he said slowly, "eventually those two are going to have to stop for the evening"—As he was speaking his car was approaching Ulanov's Zis. His driver touched the horn in warning and then the car with the colonel was past, swaying a bit as it regained the center of the narrow road, and slowing down a bit. The colonel continued to speak. He had not even glanced in their direction as they had passed—"and when they do, I'll call and leave a message for you at my office, telling you where we—and they—are. And where we can join up again. Or you call my office and let them know where you're calling from, and I'll get in touch. Either way, or both. All right?"

"Fine." Ulanov thought a moment and then wrinkled his nose. "Franz, do you have a corporal named Burkhardt on the switchboard there in the evenings? Or nights?"

"Yes," the colonel said, mystified. "I think that's his name. Why?"

"Then please leave the message with the barman at your club," Ulanov said scathingly. "I'd like to receive it." He exchanged good-byes and switched off the set, turning to his husky driver. "Sergeant, when we get to Eberswalde—"

"I know, sir," Sergeant Wolper said. "I heard."

"I know you heard," Ulanov said gently. He crushed out his cigarette. "What you didn't hear is what I'm about to tell you now..."

For some miles, now, James Newkirk had been aware of the heavy car behind him. For some time, now, he had been wondering if Ulanov had somehow been clever enough to have a second car available in case the major felt he might be followed. But, in general, Newkirk thought this doubtful. The case really wasn't that important. Still, there was that car behind him which, although he could not recall it leaving the airport after him, still had been with him for some time, now. It would get closer, and then drop back, although the road, while narrow, was still in good enough condition to permit fairly steady driving. Possibly the man was drunk, Newkirk thought, and then thought that possibly the man was not. He considered slowing down to see what reaction he would get from the car behind, but knew this could mean losing sight of Ulanov's car ahead. But his dilemma was resolved for him, because suddenly the car behind, its driver apparently deciding he had been dawdling unnecessarily, picked up speed and swept past him. He could see it racing down the road, then passing Ulanov's car, and finally disappearing in the distance. Newkirk shook his head in disgust with himself. I'm getting nerves, he informed himself

with a touch of irritation, and settled back to concentrate on
the Zis ahead.

He slowed down as they approached Eberswalde, and then
frowned as the car ahead of him swung to the left into Route
168. Newkirk had studied the area map in great detail at the
Schönefeld parking lot, and he knew that Route 168 going west
in a mile or so would either take them back on E-74, or, if
they crossed it, would have made their entire trip on Route 2
meaningless. Was it possible that Ulanov knew, or at least
suspected, that he might be being followed, and was merely
taking normal diversionary action before heading for his actual
goal? But how could that be? If Ulanov was trailing Kovpak
and the girl, how could he go anywhere except wherever they
went? Could it be that they suspected that *they* were being
followed? It was very possible, Newkirk thought. He shrugged
and settled down to the business of following the battered Zis.

He saw the car ahead pause at the entrance to E-74 and then
enter the autobahn, heading south. He frowned. Was the car
Ulanov was obviously trailing, lost? Although it would seem
strange if they were since both Kovpak and the girl must have
known exactly where they were going when they left London.
Besides, who traveled these days without a road map? He
shrugged and followed Ulanov's car into the E-74, settling
back, allowing a car or two to separate him from his quarry,
quite sure of his ability to follow another car without getting
caught at it.

They passed the Route 2 turnoff they had taken a short time
before, passed the exit to the autobahn that skirted Berlin to
connect with the Rostock road, and turned at last into Frankfurter Allee, Route 5, heading west into the heart of Berlin.
They had made three-quarters of a giant circle, and Newkirk
gave up speculating as to the reasons for the strange maneuver,
concentrating instead on keeping the other car in sight, con-
gratulating himself on not permitting the car ahead to lose him.
The city of Berlin grew about them as they plunged deeper and
deeper into the sprawling metropolis. New apartment houses,
like drab siblings, duplicated themselves in monotonous sim-
ilarity along both sides of the wide road, their lower floors
dedicated, Newkirk was sure, to equally drab stores exhibiting
dusty samples of inferior goods. At least, he thought, he was
spared the sight of the long queues; he knew all stores were

closed in Berlin on Sundays. Sunday also saw the cessation of truck traffic, which was welcome on a trailing job, although the number of automobiles increased as they approached the center of the city. Newkirk drew his car closer to that of his quarry, aware that it would be quite easy for Ulanov to evade him in the warren of streets they were passing, but the fact was that the car ahead gave no indication that it was being followed, but continued on a steady pace along the avenue.

The Frankfurter Allee became the Karl Marx Allee, leading toward the Alexander Platz and the huge television tower that dominated the skyline of Berlin on both sides of the wall. It was beginning to grow dark, and car lights were being lit on automobiles. Newkirk leaned forward and put on his parking lights, aware that while darkness would make it more difficult for him to trail Ulanov, at the same time it would make it even more difficult for Ulanov to discover he was being trailed. Under the pale glow of the street lights set very high above the wide avenue, the traffic continued to move, with Newkirk now allowing only a single car to separate him from the large Zis, and the intervening car was so small that he could almost see over it, or, on occasion, around it. Looming over them as they traveled in their tandem fashion were large office and official buildings, grim in their colorlessness and forbidding in their silence.

The Zis swung past the huge Stadt Berlin Hotel and turned into the Karl Liebknecht Strasse, continuing its even pace as it entered the Unter den Linden. Newkirk shrugged as he easily kept up. Wherever they were heading had to be fairly close since there was only a mile or so left before they would be at the Brandenburg Tor at the edge of the East Berlin zone. He leaned back, relaxed as he drove, now more sure than ever that he had not been spotted; on an avenue as broad as the Unter den Linden the car ahead might well have attempted to lose itself in the heavier traffic had it been aware of its tail. On the other hand, Newkirk had to remind himself again, Ulanov's actions were dictated by the car the KGB major was following, and by no other consideration.

The Zis suddenly turned left into the maze of side streets with their half-demolished buildings that led past the Leipziger Strasse in the direction of Checkpoint Charlie, the double-guarded gateway between East and West Berlin. Newkirk sat a bit more erect, frowning. Was it possible that Kovpak and McVeigh were heading for West Berlin with Ulanov behind them? But in that case, why hadn't the two archaeologists flown to West Berlin directly? Could it be because Kovpak had no visa for entering West Berlin? But then how could he go through the checkpoint, which was undoubtedly as exigent as the airport in the matter of visas and controls? And did Ulanov have the necessary permissions to also cross into the western zone? For Ruth McVeigh, of course, there would be no problem, any more than there would be for him; after all, they were Americans and the western checkpoint was in the American zone of the divided city. It was odd, Newkirk thought as he followed the car ahead, how most people thought there were no longer war zones in Berlin with the war so many years in the past. But there were, and at Checkpoint Charlie just that morning he had dealt—easily, with his American passport and press credentials—with an American army corporal. A sudden rather disturbing thought came: He could get back into the American zone, into West Berlin, with no trouble—but who would be there for him to trail once he got there? The delay at Checkpoint Charlie was well-known; the Germans, Newkirk thought, delayed things through sheer obstinacy, the Americans through a proper sense of security, but the result was the same. By the time he got through the checkpoint both Ulanov and the two archaeologists would have long since disappeared. It was really quite frustrating! That is, if they were really, actually, going to the checkpoint and into the western zone . . .

But, that was exactly where they were going!

He saw the Zis turn sharply into the entrance of the checkpoint and draw up to the barrier of the East German police. The husky driver leaned from the car window, exhibiting papers of some sort, spoke earnestly to the guard there for several minutes, and then put the car into gear and turned past the high wooden wall that separated the check stations of the two nations both physically and visually. So Ulanov, a KGB agent, had somehow managed to arrange papers, undoubtedly forged, to permit him entry into West Germany! Obviously, the authorities had no notion who the major really was, but he, Newkirk, would handle that lack of information as soon as he was able! Newkirk hurried his car forward, his passport in hand; his eyes were not on the guard who was examining the document with the usual intense curiosity, as if he had never seen one before, but were fixed on the spot where the Zis had disappeared about the wall. He sat in frustrated impatience as the guard checked each entry in the passport and sighed with profound relief when the passport was finally stamped and given back to him. The guard waved him through abruptly. He stepped on the gas and hoped that the American checkpoint would detain Ulanov long enough for him to be able to resume the chase. It would be hell to lose the man now!

He need not have worried.

As he swung his car around the wooden wall of the barrier toward the American post, he came very close to running into the Zis, which had been pulled across the narrow roadway, blocking his passage. The driver had obviously been waiting for him. He stepped down from the Zis and moved toward him. In the white glare of the floodlights that lit every corner of the restricted area, Newkirk could see Ulanov slide behind the wheel of the Zis and pull the car to one side out of the way of traffic. The driver, in the meantime, was leaning into the window of Newkirk's car, holding his warrant card in his hand, and Newkirk realized he was still in the East Berlin zone, although he had no fears in that regard since his papers were all in order. He looked up at the sergeant equally, quite sure of his ability to handle any contingencies.

"Yes? What is it?"

Sergeant Wolper's face might have been carved from granite. "I am a sergeant in the *Volks Polizei*. Please step down."

"May I ask why?"

"I may have to search you," the sergeant said. He tilted his head sharply in the direction of the East German barrier, invisible behind the intervening wooden wall. "You failed to declare any DDR currency you might have."

"But, they didn't ask—" Newkirk fell silent, suddenly aware of the trap into which he had been led. He got down from the car slowly, reaching into his pocket even more slowly, knowing that any quick move on his part could result in a bullet from the husky rock-faced sergeant. The *Volks Polizei* were known to be irresponsible at times. "There's no need to search me. I have some DDR marks. I bought them at the airport at Schönefeld in case I needed gasoline, or—" He knew he was wasting his time, but he had to play the silly charade to the end. "I'm sorry. The man at the barrier didn't ask and I simply forgot. I'll go back now and turn them in for West German money."

"No," the sergeant said. His voice was totally expressionless. He looked and sounded like an automaton. The effect was a bit frightening. "You are aware of the currency regulations. You have attempted to take DDR money into West Germany. This is not permitted. It says so clearly on the papers you received when you entered the Democratic Republic. You will come with me."

"Now, wait a minute, damn it!" Newkirk said testily. He made no attempt to glance in the direction of the Zis and the white-haired major he knew was watching, probably with secret amusement. "Look," Newkirk said, and then paused. Was it possible that Ulanov had no idea who he was, but was merely retaliating against a car he thought had been following them, or a car he suspected might have been following them? In that case the best bet was to act the innocent and see where it took him. "Look," he repeated, "I'm a reporter for the Paris edition of the *Herald Tribune*. I was in a hurry to get to West Berlin to file a story. So I forgot to declare a few DDR marks! My Lord!"

Sergeant Wolper might not have heard one word. "You will turn your car around and follow me. Is it understood?" He shifted his weight as he spoke, allowing his jacket to swing open; the butt of the revolver in his shoulder holster glistened momentarily under the arc lights.

"But, this is ridiculous—"

"You were smuggling currency," the sergeant said evenly. "You will turn your car—"

"Smuggling!" Newkirk exploded; not all of his irritation was acting. "Who would want to smuggle DDR money out of East Germany? What would you use it for? Outside of this country it won't buy anything, it has no exchange, it's only paper!" He took one look at the sergeant's rigid face, with the jaw muscles tightening as the diatribe went on, and sighed. "All right," he said, and added with a touch of grave-side humor, "Where are we going, in case we get separated?"

"You will follow me," the sergeant said, not amused, "and a motorcycle policeman will follow you. He is waiting now at the barrier. Come."

*   *   *

"You say you are a newspaper reporter?" the magistrate asked.

"You have my press credentials on your desk, together with my passport."

"Of course, so I have. You have visited the Democratic Republic before?"

"Many times. I cover cultural affairs for my paper. I've visited all of your museums, and plan on seeing the exhibit next month in Leipzig on the ancient—"

"Have you ever purchased DDR marks before?"

"Of course. It's the only money you can use for—"

"And when you left the German Democratic Republic in the past, did you exchange these DDR marks in accordance with the currency regulations?"

"Of course! But this time, you see—"

"This time you did not. Is that correct?"

"But, you see—"

"I asked you, this time you did not, is that correct?"

"Technically, yes. But—"

"Not technically. Actually." The magistrate eyed Newkirk sternly. "Do not take the attitude that you are being persecuted, Mr. Newkirk. We have laws. You have broken them. The degree of punishment will depend upon your purpose in so doing. That is yet to be determined. That will be all." He signaled to a uniformed policeman who had been standing rigidly to one side.

Newkirk heaved a great sigh. "May I make a telephone call?"

"Of course. All rights are respected here," the magistrate said magnanimously. "The switchboard will connect you." He came to his feet. "I will leave you alone if you wish privacy." He tipped his head toward the policeman. "The guard does not speak English."

"You can stay," Newkirk said. He knew that whether the magistrate or anyone else was in the room, his call would be thoroughly monitored in any event. He took a deep breath and put through his call. When at last it came through and he was finally connected with the man he had requested, he knew exactly what he wanted to say. "Hello, Mike? This is Jim Newkirk. I'm in East Berlin. What? In jail. That's right. The *Volks-Polizei* headquarters. Some silly mix-up with the currency regulations. It's all a mistake, but you know how these things are. I'm afraid I'll have to miss Aunt Betty's birthday party, but it can't be helped. Tell her I'm sorry. And get somebody from the paper's legal staff to start working on getting me out of here, understand . . . ?"

"Aunt Betty's birthday party!" Ulanov said, with a grin, and ordered another beer. He and Sergeant Wolper were having dinner at the Panorama restaurant on the thirty-seventh floor of the Stadt Berlin Hotel. Below them, spread out on both sides of a barbed-wire-topped wall that fortunately was hidden in the night, the lights of the city spread to the horizon. The sergeant had informed the barman at Colonel Müeller's club that any call from the colonel should be relayed here. In the meantime the two men were enjoying a pleasant meal, with the sergeant making up for his forced abstinence during the day.

The sergeant put down his stein of beer and wiped foam from his lips. "Aunt Betty's birthday party?" he asked, mystified.

"To advise his control he stepped into dung," Ulanov said. "We use Uncle Vanya's fiftieth wedding anniversary, ourselves." For a moment he thought of asking the sergeant what the East German security forces used, but felt it would be better to ask the question of Colonel Müeller, if the question had to be asked at all. He also felt that German beer was stronger than Russian beer, and yawned at the very thought.

The reply did not seem to satisfy the sergeant's curiosity, but before he could delve into the question more deeply, the head waiter was at his elbow with a telephone. The sergeant verified the source of the call and handed the instrument across the table. Ulanov took it, watching the waiter place their meal upon the table as he did so.

"Ulanov here."

"Major? Colonel Müeller. We're in Rostock, up near the Baltic. Kovpak and the girl are staying at the Warnow Hotel. So am I. I'm fairly certain they're settled here for the night. They put their car in the hotel garage, and I have my driver in my car in the same garage, so they won't go anywhere without my knowing it."

The effects of the beer, of the beers, instantly disappeared. "They went directly to Rostock?"

"No. As you surmised, they went to Bad Freienwalde, but

they didn't even get out of the car. They sat across the street
from the railroad station for about five minutes, consulting a
road map, then they turned and started back the way they had
come. They went back on Route 167, across E-74 to E-6, took
E-6 north to Neubrandenburg, and then took the road directly
to Rostock."

"One second." Ulanov cupped the receiver and looked at
Sergeant Wolper. "How far is Rostock from here?"

"About a three-hour drive." The sergeant consulted his watch
and looked at the lovely meal on the table with regret. He had
a feeling he would never get to enjoy it. "If we leave now, we
could be there by midnight."

"Thanks." Ulanov went back to the telephone. "Book me
a room at the same hotel, and get me the room numbers of
both Kovpak and the girl. If they have separate rooms, that
is—"

"They do."

So at least nothing had been consummated as yet, Ulanov
thought with a wry smile. Poor Gregor! He wiped the smile
from his face. "We'll be there by one." He disregarded the
gleam of joy that suddenly lit Wolper's eye; he also was hungry.
"Sergeant Wolper and your driver can spell each other keeping
an eye on Kovpak's car."

"Right," Müeller said. "But I wasn't finished."

Ulanov looked at his meal, getting cold while he spoke on
the telephone, while his beer got warm. He shrugged fatalis-
tically. "You weren't? Then go on." He leaned back and lit a
cigarette. If he couldn't eat at least he could smoke.

"When the two of them got to Rostock," the colonel said
in his best reportorial manner, "they stopped at the hotel and
checked in. Then they got back in their car and drove off. I
was wondering where they might possibly be going in Rostock
on a Sunday evening—believe me, if you think Berlin is dead
on a Sunday, you should see Rostock! Not even a beer hall—"
He seemed to realize he was wandering and came back to
his story. "Anyway, they drove to Warnemünde—"

"How far is that?"

"Not very far. Maybe eight miles, along the estuary, to the
Baltic."

"I see. And exactly what did they do when they got there?"

Colonel Franz Müeller's voice became slightly hesitant, as

if he was not quite sure how to explain the strange actions of the two.

"Well, Major," he said slowly, "that is what is so curious. They drove along the docks, slowly, nothing special, and then stopped and got out of the car and just stood there, facing the sea and staring about them. They actually seemed to be just two more tourists, enjoying the view of the water. And then—"

"Then?"

"Then," the colonel said, and it was obvious from his tone that he did not understand it, "then what they did was to burst into laughter. Yes, they laughed like idiots. And there wasn't anything I could see to laugh at, at least not to my eye."

"And then?"

"Then they got back into the car, still laughing, and drove back to the hotel where they are at the moment, eating dinner in the restaurant."

Which is what he wished he were doing, Ulanov thought. "You say they laughed? Just that?" Ulanov asked, now as perplexed as the colonel.

"Just that. Like maniacs," Müeller said, happy not to be alone in his mystification. "Like loons..."

And what was so comical in Warnemünde? Ulanov asked himself as he put down the telephone, crushed out his cigarette, and attacked his meal. He thought about it a moment and then desisted. That would be for tomorrow. Tonight was to enjoy a meal, even if slightly cold.

18

Across the street from the Warnow Hotel a circus was playing on the small dock that fronted the estuary. It was the only activity that seemed to be open that Sunday, and its colorful banners and cheerfully painted charabancs were a lure to the Russian in Gregor. He thought it might be fun to see, to compare with the circuses he had been raised on in Russia. Ruth McVeigh did not. While it pleased her that her Gregor—for she had come to think of him as "her" Gregor, at least for as long as she could keep him with her—while being a noted scientist could still retain traits of childishness, which gave her a slight feeling of control which was welcome, at the same time she had the feeling that if she didn't come up with at least something in some way related to the Schliemann treasure and their search for it, that her Gregor might decide that enough was enough and return to Leningrad and the Hermitage. It was a frightening, almost a sickening thought, and one that added a slight touch of emergency to her voice.

"We didn't come here to see circuses," she said, and tried not to sound like a mother lecturing a child. "It stays light until ten at night here this time of year, and Warnemünde is only a few miles away. Let's go."

"If that's what you want," Gregor said, and shrugged. He

had parked the car before the Warnow while they had registered, turned over their passports, and carried their own bags
to their respective rooms in the standard procedure of East
Germany. Now, reassembled in the hotel lobby, they had been
discussing their plans. Gregor didn't really care whether they
went to the circus or not, as long as Ruth was with him. His
fear was simply that the sooner they got to Warnemünde the
sooner Ruth would realize her quest was not only quixotic but
futile, and the sooner she would go back to New York and the
Metropolitan. It was a disturbing thought, as disturbing as the
realization that she wanted to end their trip as soon as possible.
He had thought she was enjoying herself with him.

They got back into the car and started off along the road
that curved through the town over tram tracks set in cobble-
stones to come out on a macadamed road along the south side
of the estuary leading to Warnemünde and the Baltic Sea. Ruth
McVeigh leaned back and closed her eyes, trying to picture
exactly the kind of dock they would have to look for, a small
dock with small fishing boats, the sort of dock Petterssen and
his unknown accomplice would have had to sail from. In her
mind the picture became a sort of Winslow Homer scene, with
weather-beaten wrinkled sailors sitting around a dilapidated
dock in sou'westers, scratching their chin whiskers, and puffing
on their pipes, with nets drying against the weathered shacks
and a few small boats rising and falling slowly at dockside,
their sails furled, awaiting Monday and the time to go back to
the sea and their fishing. Warnemünde had to have several
docks like that, she told herself. It was a small town and would
be sure to have more than one. And she knew she would
recognize the right one when she saw it. And those ancient
mariners sitting around and smoking, possibly—no, surely—
one of them would remember something that would be useful
to her in her search, even though it had all happened so many
years before. Sailors were known for their long memories . . .

The car braked gently to a stop. "Warnemünde docks,"
Gregor said in an enigmatic tone.

She opened her eyes and climbed down, staring about her
incredulously. In each direction huge dock cranes stretched for
miles, looking like giant gaunt prehistoric birds, their snouts
bent down, frozen in varying positions of feeding by the rite
of no-work Sunday. Behind them, rather than quaint fishing

shacks with drying nets, stood large impersonal warehouses, and between the concrete monoliths were all the welter of cases, crates, boxes, and casks in mountainous stacks that made up the life-blood of maritime commerce. On the other side of the many docks that jutted into the water, rather than worn fishing vessels bobbing lightly on the sea, were huge ocean freighters, rigid as rock, warped to the heavy dock bollards with thick rope cables. Not a soul was in sight. The only living creatures were the sea gulls that soared overhead, crying raucously, their wings startlingly white against the blue evening sky, or swooped low over the gray, choppy sea.

Gregor turned to look at Ruth, feeling sorry for her, knowing how disappointed she had to feel at seeing one of her dreams disappear, knowing that obviously this could never have been the port from which the two thieves with the treasure had sailed in 1945. Ruth's face was wrinkled as if she were fighting tears, and he wanted to go and put his arm about her to comfort her, but rather than tears a huge bark of laughter came, followed by peal after peal of laughter. He stared a moment and then saw the humor in it and joined her, the two of them staring at the huge cranes and whooping with laughter. They climbed back into the car still laughing and Gregor put the car into gear, starting back toward Rostock.

"What a scene!" Ruth said, wiping her eyes. "I pictured Warnemünde as a little fishing village like those tiny towns along the coast in Portugal, where everyone in town comes down to help haul in the nets and hang them up to dry, and then everyone goes down to the local cantina for wine, and they sing all night. I figured we'd join in with them, and when they were all mellow with us strangers, they'd tell us what we wanted to know." The very thought brought another crow of laughter. "This place looks like the New York docks, the Boston docks, and the Baltimore docks all rolled into one. If there was anyone to ask, it would have to be a committee!"

"They're big docks, all right," Gregor conceded, comparing them in his mind with the Leningrad docks which were, indeed, huge. He glanced across the car. "Ruth, tomorrow would you like to drive to Sassnitz? It isn't very far, and they might have gone from there to Sweden, you know. At least it may be worth a try..."

Ruth shook her head, her laughter now completely gone.

"No," she said quietly. It had come to her that falling in love was painful, and the sooner cured the better. "Don't humor me. I know when I'm wrong. It was only a dream in the first place, a silly notion."

There was a long silence, each busy with their own thoughts. The edge of Rostock came; they were back on the cobbled streets, swaying in the tram tracks.

"It wasn't silly," Gregor suddenly said. He kept his eyes rigidly on the street. "I doubt if anything you ever did, or ever could do, would be silly. I mean silly in the foolish sense, not in the sense of doing things that are absurd. We all do that at times and I wouldn't want you to ever stop doing them. It's part of living, of enjoying life and making it enjoyable to others." He knew time was slipping away from him, that he had to do or say something that would at least hint to her how he felt, pointless as it would be. He also knew that in all probability, now that the quest was finished, Ruth would be leaving for home very soon. And he would go back to his lonely apartment in Leningrad, an apartment that would now be lonelier than ever. He wet his lips. "Ruth—"

"Yes?"

He turned to look at her, studying the beloved features, not knowing what he had intended to say, but the words came without volition. "Do you know that you are very beautiful?"

"Do you know that you are very handsome?"

He brushed that aside impatiently. "No. I mean—"

"I know what you mean," Ruth said quietly. "You mean I'm attractive. Thank you." She turned to stare from the car window. They were approaching the hotel. She knew she had to speak now or keep quiet, but she could not leave him forever without his knowing. She spoke without looking at him. "You said before you didn't think I could ever do anything silly in the foolish sense. Well, I have. Something very foolish."

"What do you mean?"

She turned to look at this strong profile, feeling a sort of perverse satisfaction in what she was about to say, a shriving, hoping it would hasten the cure. "I've fallen in love with you."

His hand jerked wildly on the wheel. He turned to stare incredulously across the car. They bumped over the curb of the hotel entrance nearly taking down a pillar of the overhang.

He brought the car under control in time, bringing it to a stop before the hotel doors. He felt completely confused. "You— what?"

There was a touch of quiet, almost resigned amusement in her voice. "I said, I've fallen in love with you. Madly, if that makes the slightest difference."

He shook his head as if to clear it, running his hand through his thick hair. "But—that's impossible—!"

"Improbable, maybe, but unfortunately not impossible." She opened the car door and got down, bending a bit to look at him a trifle unsteadily, trying to engrave his face in her memory, although she knew she would be struggling to forget it for a long time to come, willing herself not to cry. "Thanks for the ride, and for going along with my idiocy as far as the treasure is concerned. It was a pleasure meeting you. I'll be gone in the morning. I can get an early plane from here to Berlin and fly home from there. I'll say good-bye now."

He reached across the car, taking her hand and pulling her back into the car. She came reluctantly, but there was no resisting that steady pressure, nor did she really want to resist it. It would mean a few more minutes with him, at least; a few more words with which to recall his deep voice and hurt herself with the recollection in the months ahead. Gregor reached past her to close the door and then sat back, a frown on his forehead, but a gleam of pure happiness in his eyes.

"My darling Ruth," he said quietly. "I never dreamed of such a thing—me, at my age! And you, the most lovely thing in the world! Wait—" She had begun to tug her arm free. He let her go but spoke quickly. "Listen, please! What do you think I was doing in the map room of the British Museum? I really didn't care where the Schliemann gold actually was, or how it got there. I was looking for a problem to take my mind off the fact that I was falling in love with you. Why do you think I'm here, on what is certainly a silly—in the absurd sense—attempt to chase after something we probably couldn't find if we knew where it was. We aren't trained investigators, not in something like this. I'm here because I wanted to spend as much time with you as I could before I knew we had to each go our separate ways; to just look at you, or to just know you were near me."

He smiled a bit wryly and touched the lapel of his suit.

"And why do you think I'm wearing these clothes? I'm rather an oaf where clothes are concerned. I'm wearing them because I didn't want to look like a peasant in your eyes. I'm wearing them because the salesman told me they made me look younger, which is ridiculous, but I wanted to look younger for you. Why do you think I look like an idiot when I'm with you? And talk like an idiot when I'm with you? And almost drove like an idiot a few minutes ago? I'm in love with you, Ruth. I have been almost from the minute I met you."

Ruth was staring down at her hands clasped tightly in her lap. She thought she had never felt as happy in her life, but when she looked up, rather than the radiance Gregor had expected, had hoped for, she looked almost sad.

"And now?" she asked softly.

"Now," Gregor said with a rare insight into the words the occasion seemed to call for, "I shall put the car away in the garage until morning, after which we shall have dinner, with a good wine to offset what I suspect will be a terrible meal—"

"I'm not hungry," Ruth said in a small voice, and suddenly smiled her gamine smile.

"Then we shall merely have the wine—or possibly not even that—after which"—he reached over and took her hand—"we shall go to my room and discuss many things. Including the future . . ."

They made love with a fierceness, a passion, that Gregor had thought a thing long of the past, and that Ruth had never known. Often she had tried to imagine total commitment to a person, but nothing had ever prepared her for the height of ecstacy, the sweeping fulfillment of just giving and wanting to give more, the sweet absolutes of total receiving. She clung to Gregor hungrily, part of him as he was part of her, knowing that whatever followed in their lives, nothing would or could take this moment from her. Afterward they lay quietly, holding hands like children, reveling in their feeling for each other, content to touch and to love. Ruth turned on her side, stroking his cheek.

"And now?"

He said it, attempting lightness, although he did not really believe it. It would have been more than he could ever have hoped for. "Now, as they say in the novels, we get married and live happily ever after." It could be, he said to himself fiercely. Why couldn't it be? He turned to Ruth, trying to sound convincing. "You will love Leningrad. It's truly a beautiful city. We shall work together at the Hermitage, and make trips together, and excavate in strange places together, and in the evenings"—he reached over with his free hand to touch one of her full breasts almost wonderingly—"we shall make love together. But it will always be—"

"No."

"—together." He frowned slightly, as if in non-understanding. "Did you say no?"

Ruth pulled herself up to kiss him on the lips, a long tender kiss, and then laid her head on his chest.

"Darling, you're dreaming. I couldn't possibly live in Russia. You must know that as well as I do."

"Why not?" Gregor was trying to convince himself as much as Ruth, but he could not help but sound a bit irked. "My Lord, Ruth, you don't believe those stories that we're all ignorant peasants living in caves, wearing long beards, and carrying bombs, do you? Or tossing children from the backs of troikas to satisfy the wolves? Darling, Leningrad is a beautiful, modern city. We've got traffic lights, and paved streets, and indoor toilets," he finished a bit tartly.

She laid a finger across his lips, smiling at him lovingly but sadly. "My darling, I've been to Leningrad and I know it's a beautiful, modern city—although the less said about your indoor toilets the better." Her smile disappeared; she became serious. "But you know my living there is impossible. I'm the director of the Metropolitan Museum of Art. I've worked all my life to reach that point, and I couldn't possibly leave it or give it up. The museum is my home. It's my life." A thought came, another dream as she knew, but she had to voice it. "Why don't you come to New York? I know people in Washington and I'm sure we could arrange it. And the Metropolitan could always use a fine curator—"

He grinned, but it was a tight grin. "My darling Ruth! Haven't you heard that it's bad policy to work for a relative? Unless, of course, you were planning on our living in sin." He shook his head. "I couldn't leave the Hermitage. The antiquities section is largely my work. And my plans for it mean many years of things I want to do. It's the greatest museum in the world and I'm part of it, I helped make it what it is. Besides, I have a baby dinosaur—" He stopped abruptly, feeling somehow a bit guilty. He realized he hadn't even thought of his baby dinosaur for days.

Ruth leaned over to kiss him again. Oddly enough she felt relaxed, and not at all as miserable as she would have imagined she might have felt. "My darling," she said, "neither of us can leave what we have, but we both now have something extra, something we never had before. I will always love you, I'm sure of that, and I hope you will always love me. We will meet at conferences, and archaeological congresses, and we will greet each other very formally, and discuss our respective papers in deeply scientific and dull terms, and then when we're alone"—she ran her hand lightly down his stomach to his crotch, gathering him into her hand, amazed at herself for her action but feeling completely natural and good about it—"we shall go to my room—"

"Or mine—"

"Or both, in turn, and make love all night." She kissed him again and sat up in bed, her gamine smile on her face. "And now, for reasons I cannot imagine, I'm hungry."

Gregor sighed and swung his feet from the side of the bed, shaking his head. "Maybe it's better we're not getting married," he said thoughtfully. "On my salary I probably couldn't feed you."

Their meal had been consumed with little idea of what they were eating, which was probably just as well. The only other person in the dining room with them at that late hour was a military-looking gentleman drinking schnapps with beer. The waiters in their unaccustomed stiff formal clothing would have liked nothing better than that the three would go about their business and allow them to clean up and go home, but the military-looking gentleman did not appear the type to rush without possibly undesirable consequences, so Ruth and Gregor were able to stare at each other in their increasingly growing wonder at their love, and finish their coffee and brandy without snide hints from the staff.

Ruth suddenly frowned. "It wasn't always like that."

Gregor stared. Ruth, he realized, would have been fascinating to live with. Her mind went off at odd angles without warning, like a firecracker controlled by an infant. "What wasn't always like that?"

"Warnemünde. It wasn't always like the Manhattan docks and the Boston docks and the Baltimore docks all rolled into one." She thought about it a moment and then nodded in positive conviction. "Thirty-five years ago it may have been like those Portuguese fishing villages!"

"Except, of course, for the war, which Portugal was smart enough to avoid."

Ruth refused to be distracted. "I mean, there were probably fishing docks like that thirty-five years ago. For all we know there might still be some out on the coast, past all that steel and concrete." She stared at Gregor thoughtfully, her eyes narrowing. "And the sea was pretty choppy today, wasn't it?"

Gregor pushed his empty coffee cup away and reached for his brandy. There was a glint of humor in his eyes. "Is there a connection?"

"Well, it was choppy, wasn't it? It's usually probably a lot worse, isn't it?"

"Actually," Gregor said, "not that I know what you're talking about, but the Baltic isn't a particularly rough sea. Why?"

"Well, it gets rough at times, I'll bet!" Ruth leaned toward him, conviction in every aspect of her expression. "Darling, do you want to know what happened to that fishing boat with the treasure on it?"

"I'm sure you'll tell me."

"I will, indeed. It sank!" Ruth leaned back triumphantly. *"What?"*

"Of course! That's it!" Ruth could see it all. Why hadn't it occurred to her before? It was so obvious! "That's why the treasure hasn't been seen or heard of all these years! Or Petterssen and the man with him! They've all been at the bottom of the sea!"

"And exactly who discovered the treasure in order to have this auction?" Gregor asked with gentle sarcasm. "After all, the Baltic is a pretty big sea. Was it brought up in the nets of some fisherman who happened to be an archaeology student on the side, or was some archaeologist in swimming and happened to stub his toes on it? And say to himself, 'My, my! Look what I found! This ought to be worth fifteen million dollars if it's worth a kopeck.'"

"Well," Ruth said stubbornly, "it's possible. At least it's a theory, which is more than you're offering. Maybe there was a big storm that night and the boat sank. That's happened before, hasn't it?"

"I'm sure it has."

"Well, then! Or little boats get run down in storms by big ships sometimes, don't they? And the big ship doesn't even know about it half the time. They just go on. Nobody would be on deck in a bad storm, so nobody would see it happen." She bolstered her argument. "It happened in *Captains Courageous,* and in a London book, the *Sea Wolf.*"

"And the screams of the poor sinking fishermen would be lost in the howling of the wind and the fury of the storm, and they would all go to the bottom carrying the Schliemann treasure in their arms." Gregor grinned. "Ruth, you should be the one writing books, with that imagination."

"Well, it could have happened," Ruth said obstinately. "It would certainly explain where the treasure has been all these years, and I don't hear anything from you that sounds any better." She frowned. "Where could we find out about weather conditions and storms at sea and things like that, thirty-five years ago?"

Gregor smiled and shrugged. "I have no idea."

"Probably not here in Germany," Ruth said, and frowned at her coffee. "Things must have been a mess here at the time with records destroyed and God knows what. Do you think they might have records of storms and wrecks and things like that anywhere else? In the States? Maybe Lloyds, in London! Or maybe even closer, in Denmark, possibly?"

"Possibly," Gregor conceded. A trip to Denmark, while wasting further time as far as any information regarding the treasure was concerned, would be a great excuse to spend a few more days with Ruth, and he did not wish to think beyond that point. Day by day was the only way he could handle it, and Copenhagen was a lovely city, the perfect city for lovers. Possibly that was also in Ruth's mind when she made the suggestion, although he was the first to admit he was never quite sure of what ideas were being generated in the active mind behind that lovely face. "There's one thing, though," he added in the interests of honesty. "I imagine it isn't easy to get access to their records. Have you thought of that?"

Ruth smiled at him triumphantly, and he knew that she had,

indeed, thought of that. She raised her brandy glass in a gesture of a toast, touched her glass to Gregor's. They both drank. Ruth put her glass down.

"I know a man in Denmark," she said, pleased with the way everything was working out, feeling that everything would always work out as long as she and Gregor were in love. "I knew him when I was at the Smithsonian in Washington and he was in the diplomatic corps. We'd run into each other at parties. He has all the influence anyone needs to get anything we want. He's a count—Axel Lindgren."

Major Serge Ulanov rolled over in bed and stared blankly at the drawn window shade a moment, trying to orient himself. Ah, yes. Rostock and the Warnow Hotel. And what on earth was he doing here, wet-nursing a pair of starry-eyed love birds? He yawned and sat up, swinging his feet to the floor, padding over to raise the shade and peer up at the sky, blinking at the brightness. Another nice day. At least the weather had made sense on this job if nothing else did. And he had noticed posters across the street when they had pulled into the hotel entrance the night before—or, rather, early that morning—that indicated there was a circus in town. Well, if the love birds would sit still for a day or so, maybe he could discover what they were up to—what was so comical about the Warnemünde docks—and get to see the circus as well.

He lit his usual morning cigarette, walked to the dresser, yawning, and consulted his watch there. Almost noon. Well, he had had a decent night's rest for a change, and apparently the love birds did as well, since there had been no indication from Sergeant Wolper or the colonel that their car had been taken from the garage. He washed his face in cold water to waken himself a bit more quickly, and then began to dress. He was just putting on his shoes when the telephone rang; he reached over to it and raised it.

"Yes?"

"Major? Colonel Müeller here. Did you have a good night's rest?"

"Fine, thank you. What about Kovpak and the girl?"

"They're still here. We've kept an eye on their car." Colonel Müeller hesitated a moment. As far as he had been able to tell, the case seemed to involve nothing more important than an errant husband, or an errant wife, or both. Still, of course, important state secrets were often involved in these sex cases. "Is there anything more you'd like to tell me about the nature of this affair, Major?"

"If you wish," Ulanov said pleasantly, and looked at his watch again. "I'll come down and meet you in the lobby. We'll have something to eat and I'll tell you the whole story."

Colonel Müeller frowned. "But what if Kovpak walks into the restaurant and recognizes you?"

"Then I'll simply ask him what he thinks he's up to," Ulanov said cheerfully. He had been coming to the conclusion for a long time that he had been playing it a bit more cozily than the case warranted, although there was still the fact that the CIA man, Newkirk, had considered the matter important enough to follow them all to Germany. For a moment Ulanov wondered how many days or weeks it would take Newkirk to get out of the mess in Berlin. Then with a smile he returned his attention to the colonel. "I'll see you in a few minutes." He put out his cigarette and finished dressing.

An odd security case, Colonel Müeller thought as he hung up, asking a suspect what he thinks he's up to. He shrugged and left his room, taking the elevator to the ground floor, waiting for Ulanov. As he did so he glanced into the ground-floor restaurant. Neithe Kovpak nor the girl were there, although his driver could be seen wolfing down food, indicating that Sergeant Wolper was now doing duty in the garage. At least that part was being handled properly, the colonel thought with satisfaction, and looked up as Ulanov came from the elevator. The colonel began to lead the way to the restaurant, but Ulanov stopped him.

"One minute. They haven't come down yet?"

"Not yet."

Ulanov frowned and consulted his watch again. He looked up. "What rooms do they have?"

"Four-ten and four-twelve. Why?"

The stocky major did not bother to answer but walked to the house telephone and spoke into one of them. He waited as the operator rang the number he had given her, a strange sense of unease beginning to grip him. The telephone rang and rang. Ulanov depressed the lever and raised it again, asking to be connected with the other room. Again the telephone rang without being answered. His suspicions solidifying, the major hung up and strode to the desk, a frown on his face. Of course the two might have simply gone for a walk, but he had a feeling they had not.

"Doctors Kovpak and McVeigh," he said. "Their rooms do not answer."

The girl at the desk looked at him blankly a moment and then consulted some cards. Her face cleared as the mystery was solved. "Oh," she said, looking up. "They both checked out early this morning."

The colonel leaned forward. "What! Their car is still in the garage!"

"Yes, sir. You see, it's a rental car, and we're an authorized agency to accept delivery. They turned it in this morning when they checked out."

The colonel presented his warrant card; the girl paled slightly. "All right, miss," the colonel said in his best police manner, "exactly what time did they check out?"

The cards were consulted again. "It was seven-thirty this morning, sir."

"And how did they leave? By cab?"

"I don't know, sir. They each had a small bag and they walked out the front door. I mean, we usually have to arrange a taxi for a guest the day before, and they didn't ask for one. There aren't many cabs in Rostock, sir, and—"

"Could they have picked one up outside?" Ulanov asked.

"I doubt it, sir. A cab would be here only by appointment, or if he dropped someone off here, and I remember nobody came in when they left. And cabs don't cruise in this town; gasoline, you know—"

"Then how could they have left? By walking?" the colonel asked sarcastically.

"Most probably by tram, sir. Many people travel to and from the hotel by tram, sir. It's cheap, and it runs by the bus station and the railroad station is the end of the line. It turns around there—"

Ulanov held up his hand to quiet the girl who seemed to have become compulsive in her talking since seeing the colonel's warrant card. The major led the colonel to one side. "I imagine checking on the trams is quite a job, but it has to be done. Also the cabs. They might have been lucky and found one. Also the bus station and the railroad station. They might have been recognized—after all, they're both foreigners."

"This is a seaport, Major. We have lots of foreigners here, sailors—"

"I doubt that Dr. Ruth McVeigh is ever going to be mistaken for a sailor," Ulanov said dryly. "In any event, we have to try and find them."

"But—where do you think they might have gone?"

"I have no idea. Trains and buses go everywhere." Ulanov frowned. "But in that case, why didn't they simply drive?" The answer was self-evident. Ulanov looked at the colonel accusingly. "They knew they were being followed, Colonel! They knew their car was under surveillance in the garage!" He considered the colonel coldly. "There is no other explanation."

Colonel Müeller swallowed. "I'm sorry, Major. I thought we had been most circumspect—"

"Well," Ulanov said shortly, "there's no sense in wasting any more time than has already been wasted. We're five hours behind them now. Start a check on cabs and trams, and the railroad and bus stations. And check on other car-rental agencies; they might have tried to be cute and merely rented another car. I'll meet you here at six for your report."

"Won't you be coming with me, sir?"

"No," Ulanov said. He glanced at his watch. "I'm going to get something to eat, and then I'm going to see the matinee at the circus."

He might as well accomplish at least one of the things he had hoped to do that day, he felt . . .

Major Ulanov, the usual cigarette in the corner of his lips, was consulting a one-inch map of northern East Germany while Colonel Müeller made his report. The colonel was not happy making his report, but there was nothing else he could do.

"The trams on Monday, especially at that hour, with people going to work, are like sardine tins," he said dolefully. "You know, of course, that our trams work on the honor system as far as payment for a ride is concerned; you can buy tickets at many places and when you get on the tram you put one into a machine to be punched to show the ticket has been used. The motorman doesn't see you at all, unless you happen to get on by the front door, and even then he never pays any attention."

"What you are saying," Ulanov said without looking up from the map, speaking the words around smoke, "is that wherever they went by tram—*if* they went by tram—is a total mystery."

"Yes, sir." The colonel, of course, held a higher rank in the organization of East German Security than Ulanov held in Russian State Security, but one was KGB and the other was not, and neither organization ever forgot it. "If they took a cab, we haven't been able to locate it. I think we have reports from all of them. The girl was right; there aren't very many of them. And I checked the bus station myself. Nobody recalls anyone like them."

"And the trains?"

The colonel sounded even more despondent. "The railroads are as bad if not worse than the trams on a Monday morning. People coming in from all over after the weekend to go back to work; people who should have gone home the night before all trying to get on trains and get back. You could take a herd of elephants through the Hauptbahnhof here in Rostock between six and eight or nine in the morning, and nobody would notice. In fact, it probably wouldn't even seem to be more crowded. I'm told you simply cannot move in the station or on the platforms."

"So nobody saw them, is that it?"

"Yes, sir. I mean, no, sir."

"And of course there is no record of their having rented another car." It was a statement, not a question.

"No, sir."

Ulanov sighed. He studied the map a few more minutes and then tossed it aside, looking up. "We've lost them, Colonel."

"I'm sorry, Major." A question that had been bothering the colonel for some time seemed to be forced from him. "Major, is it—are they—I mean, you never told me—is the case very important?"

"I didn't think so before, but I'm beginning to now," Ulanov said somberly, but did not expand upon the answer. He frowned into space as he tried to find a solution to their disappearance in the smoke of his cigarette. Where had they gone? And why? And how had he been so derelict as to let them get away, for although it had been the colonel who was primarily responsible, the colonel had been acting under his orders and the responsibility fell back on his shoulders and he knew it. Should he put out an all-points bulletin on them? On what basis? He'd look a proper fool if they merely gave up the car because it hadn't been running well, and had taken a train back to Berlin.

A sudden possible answer to the problem came to him, and as he examined it in detail, his frown slowly changed to a faint smile. Why not? After all, despite the occasional failings common to all security operations—as witness Newkirk forgetting the DDR currency regulations in his haste to follow the Zis— the CIA was still far from a helpless giant. He looked up at the colonel, his eyes twinkling.

"There is a man named Newkirk," Ulanov said, "being held at *Volks-Polizei* headquarters in Berlin on charges of attempting to smuggle DDR marks into West Germany—"

Now the colonel thought he understood the twinkle. "So that's how you handled it! Excellent! Is he an enemy agent? How long do you want him held—?"

"What he is," Ulanov said, answering the first question first, "is a poor, misguided newspaperman, and in thinking about it, I am ashamed of the trouble I have undoubtedly caused him. In my opinion, the German Security Forces, in their vast wisdom, their great humanity, and their exemplary generosity, should let the man go."

The colonel was puzzled. "But, if you just—"

"Should let the man go," Ulanov repeated gently, but in a manner that told the colonel he was not being requested to free Mr. Newkirk; he was being instructed. "However," Ulanov went on evenly, "since Mr. Newkirk has a habit of getting into trouble, for his own good I believe you should keep a rather careful watch over him." He looked the colonel in the eye. "A *very* careful watch. One that might contemplate the possibility that Mr. Newkirk and any car he might rent are not necessarily Siamese twins..."

Colonel Müeller could take a hint. "Yes, sir. We won't lose him. But what if—or when—he leaves the Democratic Republic?"

"Then you will advise me at once. Including his destination, if possible." The major made it sound that if the destination was not included, the colonel once more would have failed in his duty.

"Yes, sir." Colonel Müeller hesitated. "Will you be coming back to Berlin with us, sir?"

Major Ulanov put out his cigarette and sighed. "I suppose so. Once we get something to eat." Duty was a difficult decision, he thought. He had hoped to see the Warnemünde docks, not only to see what was so humorous about them—probably nothing, he thought; who could explain the laughter of starry-eyed love birds?—but because he enjoyed the sea and found sea air refreshing. He had also heard that the evening performance of the circus was quite different from the matinee. With another sigh at the exigencies of his job, he led the way into the restaurant.

It was two days before the plan of Major Ulanov bore fruit. He was lying on his bed in his room at the Stadt Berlin Hotel, his ever-present cigarette plastered to his lip, reading the last of his *Playboy* magazine and disappointed that the fiction and articles did not live up to the promise of the cartoons and photographs, when he received a call from Colonel Müeller. He put down the *Playboy* and laid aside his cigarette in the interests of clearer speech. "Yes?"

"Newkirk spent a good part of yesterday at the American Embassy," the colonel reported.

"Explaining to Langley, Virginia, how the idiotic German Democratic Republic police had picked him up for a stupid reason," Ulanov said calmly, "but were smart enough, at least, to realize one didn't fool around with newspaper reporters and let him go free in record time." He reached for his cigarette again.

"I have no idea of what went on in the American Embassy," Colonel Müeller said honestly. "We have no means of knowing what goes on there."

Ulanov's eyebrows raised. "No?" Well, the responsibility for East German security, thank heavens, was not his or his organization's. "So then what did he do?"

"He spent the day just walking around, browsing in book shops, looking at statues—typical tourist stuff. No contacts with anyone. Ate alone and went to bed early. Then today he returned to the Embassy—"

"To find out if the tentacles of the famed CIA had managed

to unearth Kovpak and McVeigh in the meantime."

"Probably," the colonel said, "because right after that he went down to the railroad station and bought a ticket to Copenhagen—"

Major Ulanov sat a bit more erect. The CIA had done his work for him in record time. He felt a bit proud of them. "Copenhagen, eh?"

"Yes, sir. The train, you know, goes right through. The railroad cars with destination Copenhagen are put on the ferry at Warnemünde, and—" The colonel suddenly realized that Ulanov was probably not too interested in the mechanics of the trip. "We can arrange a ticket on the same train if you wish; it doesn't leave until six tomorrow morning. Or we can arrange a plane ticket from Schönefeld to Kastrup Airport in Copenhagen, and you can easily get there before him."

Ulanov thought a moment, puffing on the cigarette, and then smiled as he removed it from his lips.

"No," he said. "Get me a ticket on the train for the day *after* tomorrow." This time, he said to himself, we'll let Newkirk do some of the spadework for a change. "And in the meantime, check Copenhagen hotels and find out where Kovpak and the girl are staying." He hung up and lay back in comfort once again, pleased with himself in getting Newkirk and the CIA to do his work for him. With luck, he felt, the American security organization might eventually also tell him what the case was all about, and what Kovpak and McVeigh were up to . . .

19

Count Axel Lindgren had been both surprised and greatly delighted to hear from Ruth McVeigh. In Washington he had done his best to convince Ruth that she should arrange a short vacation from the Smithsonian—or even a long one—and spend it with him in St. Croix, Cannes, or wherever she wished. Nor had he ceased his efforts once Ruth had taken over the directorship of the Metropolitan and moved to New York. His frequent telephone calls had been masterful combinations of charm and salesmanship. Nor had her constant amused refusals deterred him from continuing his efforts until, unfortunately, he had been asked to leave the Danish diplomatic service and he had returned to Lindgren Castle.

Now Ruth McVeigh was here in Copenhagen! Probably, Count Lindgren assumed, on a vacation or a rest after the debacle of the London conference, which in itself had tickled the count's sense of the absurd. If Ruth McVeigh could have known where the Schliemann treasure actually was at that moment, or who really had it! Or at least who would have it that afternoon when that disgusting Professor Nordberg delivered it.

The count had arranged a small intimate booth for the two of them for lunch at one of his favorite restaurants, the Spinderokken in the Trommesalen. He knew that most visitors to

Copenhagen preferred one of the Divan restaurants in the Tivoli Gardens, but the count wanted atmosphere and quiet in addition to good food, not the sound of hurdy-gurdy's while he pressed his suit. It had been quite a long time since the count had had a woman of the type that really pleased him, and Ruth McVeigh not only fit that category perfectly, but she was here in Copenhagen. And had called *him*. It had to mean something.

The count arrived at the restaurant early, in order to advise Sture, the Spinderokken's maître d', exactly how chilled he wished the Aalborg Export before the meal, as well as the proper selection and temperature of the wines that were to accompany the meal. Sture listened imperturbably. He had been serving aquavit and wine since the count was a small boy, but one did not argue with Count Lindgren. Especially, as Sture knew well, when the count was quite right in his orders.

"And the flowers!" Lindgren suddenly said, and frowned at Sture. "They haven't arrived!"

"They are being iced," Sture said evenly. "They will be sprayed and brought to the table as the lady is being seated."

"Good." Count Lindgren sat down and began to study the menu. As he mentally made his selections he recalled that Ruth McVeigh enjoyed her food. A proper meal, here at one of the finest restaurants in Denmark, would be a good method by which to introduce the subject of his own marvelous cook, François. And to suggest a dinner some evening at Lindgren Castle, prepared and served by the talented chef, for François had notions about serving as well as cooking. And later, seated cozily in his den, sated with food and drink, it could be found that it was rather late to return to Copenhagen. And the castle, of course, had more than ample accommodations . . .

He glanced up as the door opened and Sture moved forward, bending the least amount at the waist professionally. The count came to his feet at once as Ruth entered. He felt a small flush of pleasure; she was even more beautiful than he remembered. He started forward, both hands outstretched; and then paused, his smile tightening a bit. A man had entered behind her, obviously accompanying her, a rather handsome man in a somewhat coarse fashion, the count thought, but somehow slightly familiar. But Count Lindgren had not been a diplomat for nothing. His slight frown was instantly arrested, replaced by a brilliant smile. He took Ruth's hand, and bending over it, kissed it. Then, straightening up, he looked at the intruder.

"Ruth, it's a very great pleasure. Who is your friend?"

"Hello, Axel. It's good to see you again. I want you to meet Dr. Gregor Kovpak. He'll lunch with us." She turned to Gregor. "Darling, this is Count Lindgren I've been telling you about."

The two men shook hands, eyeing each other a bit warily. Darling, eh? Lindgren thought, and then dismissed it. Today everyone called everyone else darling; it meant little. Why did she feel it necessary to call me darling in front of this stranger? Gregor thought. Was she advising him that any relationship they had had in the past was no longer operative?

"A pleasure you could join us, Dr. Kovpak," Lindgren said heartily, and turned to Sture, who was watching with a graven face although the count suspected there was a derisive smile hidden somewhere behind the emotionless eyes. "You will set another place, please, Sture."

He led the way to the table, waited until Ruth had taken her place in the booth and Gregor had sat down beside her, and then seated himself across from them. He smiled brightly at the two of them; Axel Lindgren was a consummate actor. "Well, this is a real pleasure! I've heard much of you and all you've done at the Hermitage, Dr. Kovpak, and I'm quite impressed. On your way home to Leningrad after London, I imagine?"

"In a way," Kovpak said noncommittally, and wondered just how close this handsome but slightly forbidding man had been to Ruth McVeigh.

"It's an honor to have you as my guest for lunch. And Ruth, of course, is an old friend. A very old, dear, and close friend."

Ruth McVeigh smiled slightly. She knew Axel Lindgren very well.

"My dear Axel," she said gently, resolved to put this issue to rest at once. "You and I are old friends and I hope we always will be, but that is all we ever were. Gregor and I are lovers. We are in love."

"Ah, the honesty of young people these days! May I congratulate you both." The count's beaming expression remained, but he suddenly determined that if possible neither the Hermitage nor the Metropolitan would ever see the Schliemann collection if only for the insult to his pride. And then the count

mentally chided himself. He was being stupid and he hated
stupidity, especially in himself. Nobody had insulted him. And
as for Ruth McVeigh, with the money he would soon have,
possibly even from one of the two facing him, he could sur-
round himself with women as beautiful, as well as more ap-
preciative. It was foolish to allow emotion to interfere with
business. Instead of angling to get Ruth McVeigh in bed, the
luncheon should be used for the purpose of eliciting information. After all, he had never had the opportunity to talk the
matter over with one, if not two, of the musuems who would
actually be bidding in the auction, and it should be most interesting. He waited while Sture placed the glistening flowers
on the table and withdrew, and then went on. "I'm very glad
you called me and that I have this chance to talk with you
both," he said earnestly. "I've read about the London conference, of course, but the Danish newspapers were rather vague
as to the exact details as to what happened. Possibly one of
you could—?"

Ruth smiled, but it was a sad smile. "The less said about
the London conference, Axel, the better. About all that really
came out of it that was even faintly useful, was that the
question of legal ownership of the treasure was certainly put
in doubt."

Lindgren frowned. "But do you believe that would make
any difference as far as this so-called 'Auction of the Century'
is concerned?"

"Without a doubt," Ruth said positively. "One result is that
there undoubtedly will be more bidders than the ones who were
originally asked to participate in the auction. And that will
mean that the price will undoubtedly go very high."

Count Lindgren looked properly sympathetic. "That's too
bad! Understandably this cannot have been very welcome news
to the Metropolitan." He glanced at Kovpak. "Or the Hermitage, if they should bid. Or to anyone else."

"It isn't. If we could have gotten some co-operation from
those—those—people in London—!" Ruth seemed to realize
she was flogging a dead horse. "Axel—"

"Yes?" Count Lindgren looked up as Sture appeared with
menus. "If you will permit me to order for us all?" There was
general acceptance of this; Count Lindgren gave the orders and
turned back to his table companions. "You were saying?"

Ruth leaned a bit closer to him, unconsciously dropping her voice. "Axel, suppose I were to tell you I have a very good idea of where the treasure—the Schliemann gold—might very well be."

"What!" Count Lindgren recovered instantly, frowning in a slightly skeptical manner, although his heart was beating much faster. "What do you mean?"

"I mean I have a theory as to what happened to it. It never reached Russia in 1945. I think that can be proven. Just how is unimportant at the moment. But I think it ended up in Denmark, and with your help I think I can prove it."

"With my help?" Lindgren's mind was racing. Had Nordberg told him a bunch of lies as to how he had come upon the treasure? It was very possible. Nordberg certainly didn't look the sort to put up any great sum of money for anything. He didn't look as if he had ever had any great sum of money. And why should anyone stealing the treasure from the Hermitage and then defecting, turn to an obscure professor in Copenhagen to rid himself of the collection? He looked at Ruth, his face indicating nothing but polite curiosity. "How with my help?"

Ruth was prevented from answering by the arrival of their food. They gave the excellent cuisine the homage it deserved by refraining from any serious conversation, although Count Lindgren's brain was churning. It was not possible! Ruth had always been known for quick decisions and for outlandish conjectures, and this "theory" of hers had to be another similar case. Certainly Kovpak would know if she was only imagining things, and equally certainly Kovpak would have every reason to go along with any crazy idea of hers, since it permitted him to stay with her and make love with her and enjoy her in all the ways the count was sure the Russian was enjoying her.

But—on the other hand—what if she was on to something, something that could prove dangerous to him? What if Nordberg had been lying as to how he had gotten his hands on the treasure? Suppose he had gotten it in a manner that left a trail that could be picked up, and that now it *had* been picked up? And if that were the case the trail might not stop at Nordberg but could lead to him. Although the trail could be cut at Nordberg. Unless, of course, Nordberg had left some indication of where the treasure was. In that case, much as he admired dear Ruth and respected the good Doctor Kovpak, something would have to be done about them, and Count Axel Lindgren was not a man to have the slightest compunction in handling the situation.

But first, of course, one had to be sure. With the arrival of their coffee and brandy, Count Lindgren looked at Ruth. "You were saying I could help you? In what way?"

Ruth put down her demitasse. "Do you know anyone at the Admiralty?"

Lindgren frowned. He failed to understand the question in relation to the problem, but the one way to find out was to go along and see where it led. "As a matter fact, I do," he said. "He's head of Naval Intelligence. We were close friends when he was Naval Attaché in Lisbon and I was posted there. What would you want from him?"

"There must be records somewhere in Copenhagen, probably in the Admiralty, of storms and shipwrecks in the Baltic, aren't there?"

Lindgren thought, and what on earth was that all about? "Well," he said, "he may not have the information himself, but I'm sure he can get it for you. Why would you want it?"

Ruth smiled. "That's a secret, at least until I get the verification I want." She glanced at her watch and then at Lindgren, putting appeal in her voice. "Would it be possible to get hold of him now?"

Lindgren forced a laugh. "Impatient as ever! I'll see what I can do." He came to his feet, put down his napkin, and disappeared in the direction of the maître d's desk and the telephone there, as anxious as Ruth to move on the matter. He returned shortly, smiling. "He's in his office now. I can take you there, if you care to come now." He signaled Sture for the check.

As he led the way from the restaurant to his car, Count Lindgren hoped he would have an answer soon to the burning question of how much Ruth knew or suspected. He waited while Wilten sprang from the driver's seat to open the car doors and then close them behind the three of them. He hoped the answer would come soon, because he had an appointment later with Professor Nordberg...

The young ensign was determined to give the lady all the help he could, not just because those were his orders from the admiral, nor even because the lady was accompanied by the fabled Count Axel Lindgren, but simply because she was as beautiful a lady as the ensign could ever recall having visited the Naval Station, which was one of the problems of the naval service, the ensign thought, and laid the ledger he had procured from weather archives on his desk. He opened it and began leafing through the pages.

"May 22 and 23, 1945, I believe you said," he said briskly, as if such inquiries were routine. "Ah, here we are." He looked up, smiling brightly. "Good weather both days. A high-pressure system over the entire western Baltic."

To his surprise the beautiful lady did not seem to be pleased with the information. "Good weather? You're sure? No storms?"

The ensign checked the reports again and then looked up, slightly puzzled by the lovely lady's reaction. "No, ma'am. Excellent weather around Falster and the western end of the Baltic both days. Full moon, only scattered clouds, calm sea."

Again the lady seemed perturbed. The young ensign could not know, of course, that the lady was trying to picture a large ship running down a small fishing vessel à la some romantic sea story under a full moon that allowed perfect visibility. "Full moon, no cloud cover, calm sea," the ensign repeated and pointed to the entries, as if to remove any responsibility for the bad news from his shoulders, although why no storms and a full moon under clear skies should be bad news, was beyond him.

Count Lindgren was waiting patiently, watchfully. So far whatever Ruth McVeigh's theory was, it seemed to be lacking support, but Count Lindgren was a man who could be most patient in checking out every angle of any situation that might be threatening. Ruth looked at Gregor disconsolately, and then smiled faintly.

"It looks as if I might be wrong," she said. "Do you think that's at all possible?" She suddenly turned to the ensign, still not ready to accept the fact. "Does the naval station keep information on reported wrecks, or ships asking for assistance, or things like that? As far back as 1945?"

"Oh, yes, ma'am." While they waited Ruth and Gregor wandered to the window, staring across the water from where the Naval Station was located. They could see tourist buses lined up along the embankment while their passengers took photographs of the Little Maiden, the famed statue in the harbor from the Hans Christian Andersen story that symbolized Copenhagen for most people. A hydrofoil came into the harbor, slowing down, settling back into the water like some huge bird. In the background the spires of Copenhagen's churches could be seen outlined against the early-afternoon sky. Gregor suddenly turned from the window, lowering his voice.

"Ruth—"

"Yes, darling?"

"Look, this is all very foolish. Why don't we forget the Schliemann treasure and simply enjoy ourselves? We're wasting our time and the time of your friend, Count Lindgren. Copenhagen is beautiful. Look at all those tourists over there having a good time. Why don't we forget all this and begin to enjoy—"

He broke off as the ensign came back with another ledger, placing it on his desk. He had already checked it but had brought the ledger along for verification should the lady not be pleased with his report. Ruth, Gregor, and Axel Lindgren drew close. The ensign sighed. "There were no wrecks or ships asking assistance on those two days, ma'am." He looked unhappy that he could not satisfy the beautiful lady who somehow seemed to want storms and shipwrecks, although why she desired these unpleasant things was a mystery. He pointed to the ledger as if to ask her to check for herself if she didn't believe him. He paused. "Ma'am, if you told me exactly what you're looking for, maybe I'd know better what files to consult."

Count Lindgren drew closer, not wanting to miss a word. Gregor smiled, a sad smile.

"We're looking for a boat that my friend thinks left Warnemünde in Germany the night of May 22, 1945, or early the next morning, and that my friend believes never arrived." Gregor was getting tired of the entire affair. He wanted to be with Ruth in a more romantic setting than this dingy office searching through dusty files for things that were not there. He knew they had little time together, and he hated to waste those precious hours in this silly game. "Of course," he added, not attempting to keep the sarcasm from his voice, "we don't know that the boat never arrived, since we have no idea where it was heading."

Lindgren refused to allow himself to feel sanguine by the sketchiness of the information he was gathering. If Ruth

McVeigh put importance on a boat she felt had left Warne-münde and never arrived in Denmark, then it had importance. And if Kovpak didn't think so, then Ruth McVeigh had simply not confided everything to him, lovers or not. He continued to watch and listen, his expression one of polite interest, but nothing more.

"There is one more possibility," the ensign said hurriedly. He hated to see the lovely lady go; his small office would seem even less attractive with her departure. Besides, he honestly wanted to help her. "Wait here a minute," he said, and dashed off. He came back in a few minutes with a further file. He opened it and leafed through the pages until he found what he was looking for. He looked up. "I don't know if this is any help, but it's for that date. These are copies of the ships' logs for our patrol boats for those years. They're from the Coast Guard files. This one is from a ship named the *Elritse*. At least it's a possibility."

Ruth, Gregor, and Lindgren read the entry over the ensign's shoulder. The log had been entered in a spidery hand that seemed to be common to ships' logs. They stared at the page and then Ruth and Gregor looked at the ensign, frowning.

"What's it say?"

The ensign reddened. "Oh, I'm sorry. It's in Danish. I'll translate."

"I'll translate," Lindgren said. His voice was unconsciously harsh. He leaned over the book. "It says, '23 May. Propeller shaft twisted after hitting unknown object 2315 22 May necessitating delay and reduced speed thereafter—'"

"We're not looking for a wrecked Danish patrol boat," Ruth said, disappointed.

"No, no! Let me go on. It further says, 'At 0205 today we encountered small boat running without lights off Gedser coast. Flashed orders for her to lay to, and when it did not obey, fired several shots across her bow. In our crippled condition she could have outrun us, but unaware of the fact, elected instead to self-destruct. The *Elritse* cruised the spot where she blew up and foundered until 0300. There were no signs of survivors or anything to indicate what cargo the ship carried so precious as to cause the smuggler to blow the ship rather than to lay to and submit to search.'" Lindgren stopped and looked at Ruth. "That's it."

Ruth was beaming. "That's it, is right! *That's it!*"

Gregor sighed. "Darling," he said with a patience he was far from feeling, unhappy to be contradicting her before Lindgren and the ensign but seeing no other course, "why would they blow themselves up? It doesn't make sense. That"—he pointed to the log entry Lindgren had just read—"was probably someone running explosives or illegal arms. The chances of that having anything to do with what we're looking for are—well, infinitesimal isn't even the word. Impossible is the word."

"It isn't impossible! That's it, I tell you! That's our fishing boat!" She turned to Lindgren. "Axel, isn't Gedser that little point of land just across from Warnemünde? I thought so. Gregor, darling, that's where the train ferry docked when we were coming from Rostock here, don't you remember? We'll drive there tomorrow." She smiled at the ensign. "Thank you. I don't know how to thank you!"

The ensign blushed and tried to look as if compliments for his service were commonplace, but he knew he would remember that smile for a long time. Gregor merely shook his head in disgust. So the charade was still being played! Now that they knew they were in love with each other there was no need for excuses to be together, so why waste the time? With a shrug he nodded his thanks to the young ensign, although he would have liked to strangle the lad for being such an eager beaver and unearthing the Coast Guard log reports. As he followed Ruth and Axel Lindgren from the room he wondered which he was going to remember more once he was back in Leningrad and had only his memories to live with—the pleasure of being alone with Ruth, or the difficulty of getting to be alone with her as long as she had this mania about searching for the Schliemann treasure.

Leading the way to the car, Axel Lindgren was trying to make sense of what he had heard. It was obvious that Ruth McVeigh's theory was that the treasure had been aboard a small boat that had exploded near Gedser. If this was true, then it had been found and somehow got into the hands of Arne Nordberg. And from those hands into his. And the fact that Kovpak acted as if he did not believe it could be a sham to keep Ruth from disclosing too much. Or Kovpak could actually not believe it. That was unimportant. What was important was that Ruth McVeigh's idea was a very distinct possibility, and a very dangerous one for him. The count helped Ruth into the rear of the large car, waited until Gregor Kovpak had been seated, and then climbed in, taking a jump seat. Wilten closed the door behind him and got into the driver's seat, turning at the open divider glass to look inside inquiringly.

"The Plaza Hotel," Ruth said, and leaned back, happy.

Wilton nodded and put the car into gear. Lindgren slid the dividing glass shut and turned back to his guests.

"I really cannot allow you to hire a car for tomorrow," he said, and smiled deprecatingly. "Wilten will be very happy to drive you to Gedser or wherever you wish. He is thoroughly familiar with the road—with all the roads in our small country, as a matter of fact. And he can even take you sight-seeing afterward, if you wish."

"Oh, that's not necessary," Gregor said. "You've been more than kind as it is."

"Ruth is an old friend," Lindgren said with a smile. "I'm afraid I insist on having you use Wilten and the car! I have no plans to go anywhere tomorrow, and it would be foolish for you to hire a car. I really do insist."

Ruth smiled. "Well, you're being very sweet, and we appreciate your lunch and your help with the naval station, and everything else."

"That's what old friends are for," Lindgren said expansively, and waited as Wilten drew up expertly before the Plaza Hotel, got out, and ran around to open the door. When they were standing in front of the hotel, Count Lindgren bent over Ruth's hand in the gesture of a kiss, and straightened up, smiling. "The car will be here for you tomorrow whenever you wish."

"Would nine o'clock tomorrow morning be all right?"

"Fine!"

Ruth smiled. The day had turned out to be perfect. "Thank you, Axel."

Count Lindgren waved it away as being nothing. He waited until both Ruth and Gregor had disappeared into the hotel and then climbed into the front seat of the car beside Wilten. As the car left the hotel and started on the road back to Ringsted and Lindgren Castle, Wilten raised his eyebrows inquiringly. Lindgren nodded.

"Trouble!" he said heavily. "There's a good possibility that Nordberg was lying to me about how and where he got the treasure."

Wilten spoke without taking his eyes from the road. "You're seeing him in a while. Will you put the question to him?" There was not the normal servant/master relationship in his tone of voice, nor did Lindgren seem to expect it. The two had had a long history of roguery behind them, and Wilten was willing not only to give his Caesar his due in deference before others, or even when they were alone and not involved in schemes, but he was equally willing to always remain the lesser of co-conspirators. He lived better than any other valet-cum-butler-cum-chauffeur of his acquaintance, and he was well aware that his future welfare depended upon the largesse of his master. His ambition was simply to serve—and to gain thereby, and to date it had always worked. In the silence that had fallen, he repeated his query. "Will you charge the professor with lying?"

Lindgren shook his head. "He would only deny it. And for him to think I didn't trust him, didn't believe him, would simply put him on his guard. No, I'll stay with my present plans."

They drove for several moments in silence. Then Wilten said, "Will it make any great difference if Nordberg lied or not? What importance is it where the treasure came from? You have it. And it's genuine, isn't it?"

"Oh, it's genuine enough," Lindgren said. "But if Nordberg lied to me, there is a good possibility that that woman"—he jerked a thumb over his shoulder to indicate he meant Ruth McVeigh, who had just left the car—"may have a good idea of how to trace it to Nordberg."

"But the trail will stop there, won't it?"

"Maybe," Lindgren said, not happy about the prospects, "or maybe not. In any event, I don't believe in taking chances, you know that. You will be driving them tomorrow. You are to pick them both up at nine in the morning. I expect you to keep your ears open. If, by any chance at all, they get a lead that might bring them to Nordberg, and therefore be dangerous to me, I expect you will know what to do." He turned to look at Wilten's expressionless profile. "Do you know what I mean?"

Wilten's frozen expression loosened enough for a faint smile. "I know what you mean"—and he added, now that the decision had been made by his superior—"sir."

RINGSTED—July

From the height of the small balcony that jutted from the wall of Lindgren Castle, Count Lindgren watched with no expression as Professor Nordberg's car came rattling up the long drive. Five o'clock; the professor was on time for his appointment. The count watched the professor park the car and get out, immediately going to the trunk and taking from it a large bundle. Wilten appeared at once, offering help with the bulky package, but the professor could be seen shaking his head, and a moment later he had stumped from view into the castle, carrying the bundle protectively in his short arms.

Count Lindgren walked back into his den and sat down, coldly calculating. The sense of anticipation, the slight feeling of tenseness that always preceded a major act of violence on the part of the count, whether it might be the taking of a woman against her will, the facing of an adversary in a duel, rigged or not, the preparation for battle in war, was present. But Axel Lindgren knew from experience that the tenseness would disappear as soon as the deed was in motion.

There was a diffident rap on the door. Count Lindgren came to his feet and walked over, opening it. Nordberg stood there, puffing from his climb up the broad winding stairs with his burden, but smiling as always to know he was in the presence of his benefactor, his good friend, Count Axel Lindgren and that he knew he was welcome. The professor carefully placed the bundle down on a chair and took out a handkerchief, wiping his forehead and then his face.

"I truly appreciate this, Count Lindgren—"

"Axel," Lindgren corrected him almost mechanically and placed an arm about the professor's shoulders in seemingly friendly fashion, squeezing lightly. The thought came to him that it was somewhat like checking the body fat of an animal before slaughtering it. Still, under that fat the arms were thin, and there was not the slightest chance that the professor might struggle free of his fate. The count released the beaming professor and bent to the bundle. "Shall we see what we have here?"

"Oh, certainly." Professor Nordberg hastened to help. The

bundle was opened almost reverently, the full treasure exposed as a jumbled pile of dullish yellow. "It's all there," Nordberg said, staring down almost hypnotically. He wet his thick lips. Everything he had always wanted in life was represented by these rather unattractive bits and pieces of amateurishly fabricated metal, twisted and formed centuries and centuries ago, just to be able this day to make him rich, rich beyond anything he could ever have imagined. He watched the count check the material and then rewrap the bundle and stow it carefully in a large drawer of a cabinet against one wall. For the purpose of maintaining the general atmosphere of security, the count took a key from his pocket and locked the drawer. He tucked the key back into his pocket and patted it as if to demonstrate that everything was under control. Nordberg smiled a bit tremulously and then—as Count Lindgren had been sure he would— looked toward the balcony. "May I—?"

"Of course."

Count Lindgren watched the professor move to the balcony, to expend some of his excessive emotion on the beauty of the view. How beautifully the professor has been choreographed, Count Lindgren thought dispassionately as he reached for the brandy and two balloon glasses. Had we rehearsed this scene a dozen times he could not have taken his part better. Well, let's see if he can act out the rest of this poor comedy with equal artistry . . .

He carefully filled the balloon glasses far beyond the tiny line etched in the crystal to indicate what someone considered a proper portion, and came to his feet. The professor was staring across the trees toward the village of Ringsted, entranced, unmindful of anything but the beauty of the scene and his unbelievable relationship with the castle and with the count, a relationship that had been unthinkable such a short time before.

All feeling of tenseness, even of reality, had now left Count Lindgren, replaced with calm inexorability. He was the executioner approaching the victim with no personalities involved, an actor in a drama whose lines he could no more change than could the man he intended to kill. The count did not even feel his normal distaste for the professor at the moment. He stepped noiselessly to the balcony and raised both glasses, prepared to call out to the professor and to stumble at the same time, decanting the burning liquid into those wide inane eyes and then to quickly push the tortured disabled man over the low parapet.

He opened his mouth to call out, and then froze!

There was a loud bang on the door of his study, and then the door was rudely flung open. Lindgren swung about, the brandy in the two glasses swaying dangerously. François stood there, glowering, his assistant's ear pinched painfully between two of the chef's fingers.

"This cretin! This idiot!" the infuriated chef was saying. "He must go at once! Cumin in the vichyssoise! I shall not tolerate it! Yesterday it was paprika in the lobster bisque! Always experimenting!" He released the culprit and wiped his fingers on his mess jacket, as if to cleanse them. "You must send this one away at once, sir! Or I shall not be responsible for your meals!"

Lindgren fought down the wave of blind unreasoning fury that had swept him at the interruption. The damage was done. The professor had come back into the study as a result of the clamor and had taken one of the glasses from the count's hand in passing. Count Lindgren walked to his desk as if in a trance and pressed a button. Wilten appeared in moments, his eyes taking in the tableau, understanding it. He took François' arm gently.

"I'll take care of the matter, sir," he said to Lindgren and led the chef from the room. François, his anger expended, followed along docilely, followed at a safe distance by his assistant.

"And I'll have to go, too, Axel," Nordberg said, and emptied his glass, setting it down. "Tomorrow is graduation and tonight is rehearsal of the convocation procession." He moved to the door, and then tilted his head in the direction of the cabinet containing the treasure. "I can't thank you enough," he said sincerely, and left, closing the door softly behind him.

Count Lindgren sank into a chair. He took a deep breath and swirled the brandy in his glass as he stared at the closed door. He felt let down, deprived. It had been so close! Still, there would be other opportunities as far as Professor Arne Nordberg was concerned. Where the opportunities might be far more limited was in the case of Ruth McVeigh and Gregor

Kovpak. If they should appear to be even close to becoming a threat, any opportunities at all would have to be exploited, at any cost. It was something he would have to discuss in great detail with Wilten that very evening . . .

20 ‖

With the glass between them closed, and with Wilten sitting
rigidly in the driver's seat, Ruth and Gregor were being driven
south from Copenhagen along the coast highway. They had
skirted the Køge Bugt and had passed the small corner of the
Fakse Bugt that permitted a view of the sea below through
stands of trees; now they were approaching Vordingbord. Ruth,
studying Gregor's profile across the width of the back seat,
frowned slightly. She loved the profile. In fact, she loved the
entire face with its strong planes framed by that tangle of dark
hair. What she did not care for was the expression at the moment.

"Darling," she said quietly, "I honestly do not understand
you. We predict a boat was sunk somewhere between Warnemünde and Denmark, and we find a boat that was sunk on
the day we said it was sunk, at the place we said it was sunk.
And instead of being happy about it, you look as if you were
being driven to a funeral."

Gregor sighed. "My dear Ruth," he said dryly, "I was born
and raised in Leningrad, which is on the Gulf of Finland, which
is an arm of the Baltic Sea. In school they drummed a lot of
geography into our heads, and a lot of it dealt with the body
of water we were connected to. For your information, the Baltic

Sea is over a thousand miles long, has an average width of well over a hundred miles, and has an area of more than 160,000 square miles. It is twenty-five percent larger than all of Italy; it is five times the size of Ireland—"

"Very informative," Ruth said. "So?"

"So the chances that one sunken boat in all that vast expanse is your boat, simply because you want it to be, strikes me as being—well, ridiculous."

"So it's ridiculous. What would you rather be doing today?" She saw the sudden gleam in his eye, the quirk of his lips, and laughed. "Besides that?" Her laughter faded. She became serious. "Gregor, why don't you want this to be the boat? My boat, if you put it that way?"

Kovpak hesitated before answering. "Because," he said at last, "I don't believe there is a boat. And when this is proven to be just a boat that some smuggler was using to bring explosives, or gunpowder, into Denmark—or, what is far more likely, isn't proven to be anything—then we'll be at the end of the road." He looked across the car somberly a moment, "Then what excuse will we have for—well, for not saying good-bye and going home?"

Ruth leaned over, touching his cheek tenderly, and then sat back again. "We promised not to discuss that," she said quietly. "When it happens, it will happen. In the meantime, it's pointless to think about it."

Gregor shrugged. "If you feel that way about it."

"I feel very much that way about it. I don't see any other way to feel about it," Ruth said, and looked out the window. They had passed Nykøbing and were nearing Gedser, with an arm of the sea visible to their right beyond the railroad tracks that paralleled the highway. The land here was flat, farms running down to the edge of the waters, fields separated by hedges rather than by trees, tiny docks at the end of each bit of land, and the farmhouses were small and gaunt, built of stone, with sharply sloping roofs. Ruth turned to Gregor. "This is more what I thought Warnemünde would be like, instead of those big cranes and warehouses and all that concrete." She pointed. From the slight rise on which they found themselves a dock and sails could be seen in the distance. She nodded positively. "This is where we finish this business."

Which, Gregor thought a bit sadly, is what I'm afraid of.

Ruth leaned forward, sliding the glass divider open. "Wilten—"

"Miss?"

"That dock. I want to stop there."

"Yes, miss."

The car pulled into the town proper, past the small shops and the narrow spired church, past the large ferry slip where the train ferry from Germany landed, and turned to take a small road running in the direction of the dock they had seen, past the slight rise where the lighthouse stood. The road ran along several farms and then curved toward the dock. Sailing boats were scattered about the small harbor, white chalk marks against the slate gray of the water, each trailing a dinghy or two like piglets suckling a sow. Men were visible on the dock, repairing nets or just smoking and talking. As they approached and Wilten began to slow down at the entrance to the pier, Ruth could see that while none of them appeared to have chin whiskers, and none was wearing a sou'wester, the scene was remarkably reminiscent of the Winslow Homer scene she had pictured in Warnemünde. Maybe it's an omen, she thought hopefully, and turned to Gregor as Wilten brought the car to a halt and hurried around to open the door for her. "You stay here. I'll do the talking."

Gregor smiled faintly. "My pleasure."

A thought came to Ruth as she got down. She looked at Wilten. "Do you suppose that any of them speak English?"

"Oh, yes, miss. Almost everyone in Denmark speaks English except possibly the very old folks. It's taught in school, and school is compulsory, miss."

"Good!" Ruth said, and marched off toward the nearest group.

The men looked up at sight of the beautiful lady, and then one by one they came to their feet, wiping their hands on their trousers, wondering at the unexpected visit. The oldest, who seemed to have been elected spokesman for any unforeseen events, stepped forward a bit, frowning uncertainly. Beautiful ladies seldom visited the Gedser dock. "Miss? Is there something—?"

Ruth took a deep breath and got right to the point, looking from man to man as she spoke. "There was a ship sunk very near here, off the Gedser light," she said. "It was a long time ago, I realize. It was in 1945—May 1945. It was a small boat, probably a fishing boat. Do any of you recall anything like that?"

"1945?" The spokesman frowned and shook his head. "I wouldn't know anything about that, miss. That was a long time ago. I was in the Royal Navy at the time, stationed off Iceland." He looked around. "I don't believe any of us was around in 1945."

Ruth looked at the others. One by one they shook their heads.

"I was working in factory," one said. "In Herning. Defense industry—"

"I was army—"

"I was fishing, but off Sylt—"

"I was just a lad in 1945. Living in Korsør, going to school—"

Ruth sighed. "Let me ask you this. Would there be anyone around who might remember a ship sinking off the lighthouse in 1945? May 1945?"

The men looked at each other. The oldest shook his head slowly. "That was over thirty-five years ago, miss. Gedser wasn't much of a place in those days; not much of a place now, to tell the truth. Not much reason for anyone to be here."

"Then or now—" someone added bitterly.

The elderly man disregarded this. "How was she sunk, miss?"

"She exploded."

"In May 1945? That was just after the war," the man said thoughtfully. "Lots of ships sunk during the war between here and Germany. Lots of them exploded, too. We scuttled some ourselves, in the navy—" He studied her. "Why are you asking, miss? You a reporter for a newspaper?"

It was as good an excuse for asking questions as any. "A magazine," she said with a smile, and went back to her questioning. "Does anyone remember anyone trawling around here, say in the past four or five months, and bringing up a crate, or a box, or a case of some sort?"

"From that sunk ship, miss?"

"We think so."

The men looked at each other and then, seemingly with one accord, shook their heads. "Near the light, that would be? Nobody trawls there, miss. Lose their nets if they did. Bottom's a jumble of rocks, sharp as knives."

Ruth was running out of questions, getting a bit desperate. "Or diving, say, four or five months ago?"

"Four, five months ago?" The men grinned. "Nobody dives in water around here, miss. Oh, a little in summer, some of the younger fellows, but certainly not in winter. Water's like ice."

"Lots of times water *is* ice—"

"Man would be crazy—!"

"Except," one man suddenly said, thinking about it, "that Knud Christensen. You took him out, didn't you, Jens?"

Jens Krag nodded. He stepped forward, happy to be in the limelight, even though he considered the entire discussion to be foolish. "Man was diving for his brother's body," he said quietly. "Tried to talk him out of it, but couldn't. His only two brothers went down in a storm off the light. Never found Niels or any sign to this day, but Gustave, the youngest, was tangled in ropes. Knud, he went down for Gustave's body, not for any crate or box. Brought Gustave up, too." He said it with a touch of pride for the man's tenacity and endurance.

"Anyway, Knud Christensen ain't a man. He's a bear. A polar bear."

"He's a loony, diving in water that cold," someone else said. "Lucky he came up himself."

"Anyway, it wasn't in 1945 that the Christensen boat went down," Krag added, as if to put an end to the matter. "It was January this year, end of January." His voice became philosophical. "Knud hasn't been the same since his brothers died. Farm's going to hell."

"He should have married—"

"Who'd marry him? Sits like a log and just stares half the time. Drinks more than he should. More than he can afford, too. Going to lose the farm he doesn't wake up—"

"Don't think he cares. Anyway, going to starve first, one of these days—"

"This Knud Christensen," Ruth said suddenly. "Where does he live? I'd like to talk to him—for my article." Although, she added to herself with honesty, he doesn't sound like the man who could possibly have brought up the treasure, not if he's on the verge of starvation. Still, he might have seen something when he was bringing up his brother's body—

Jens Krag pointed. "You must have passed it on your way

here. It's back the way you came, by the light. Name's on the mailbox."

"Only he don't get no mail," someone said, and sounded sad about it.

"Thank you. Thank you all." Ruth gave them a brilliant smile that each man felt more than repaid him for the effort, and walked back to the car, climbing in. Gregor looked at her.

"Well?"

Ruth raised her shoulders. "None of them were here in 1945. They don't think anyone in Gedser was, although they're obviously wrong. We can follow up on that later, maybe at the church or at the police. They say that nobody would trawl off the light because of the sharp rocks there. The only person known to have dived in those waters in the last three or four months did it in January to bring up the body of his brother whose boat had gone down in a storm. He brought up the body, but no box."

"So where do we go from here? Church or police? Or, better yet, why not go back to Copenhagen?"

"We go to visit the man," Ruth said evenly. "We're here and he's here, and maybe he saw something when he was diving. At least he was on the bottom of the sea near our boat. Or *my* boat, if you prefer. He lives back down the road we just came on, near the lighthouse. His name is Knud Christensen, and the name is on the mailbox..." She looked at Wilten, who had been listening. "Back down the road a bit, please, Wilten. I'll tell you where to turn in."

Knud Christensen often wondered why he had wasted a good portion of the money he had gotten from his distant cousin, Professor Nordberg, on anything as silly as a new anchor. He had never taken the boat out since the night he had brought the box up. The boat had lain in the water until the wood had started to swell and the caulking had begun to dry and shred and after it had slowly filled with water and sunk to the oarlocks to rest on the bottom. He had not even taken the trouble to bail it and haul it higher on land to dry. He hated the sea for what it had taken from him and knew he would never go out on it again.

Nor had the cross he had purchased with the remainder of

the money been of long endurance. Some young fellows, driving a borrowed automobile through the cemetery one night while drunk, had torn the cross from the small base he had made for it and twisted it beyond repair. He had nailed together another cross from wood and replaced it above Gustave's grave, but neither the cheap metal cross nor the wooden one satisfied him. He had even considered using the anchor as a memorial, setting it in cement at the head of the grave, but although other graves in the small cemetery demonstrated similar memoria for those whose lives had been taken by the sea, the thought was repugnant to Knud. It would have reminded him too strongly of the body as he had seen it dangling in the shrouds. It would also have reminded him of his foolishness in buying the anchor in the first place.

What Knud Christensen would have liked to do was to buy a real stone, a large one of rough granite with a large granite cross on top, and with a polished panel on the face of it that would allow space for the names of both brothers to be engraved upon it. Or, better yet, a monument large enough to go across the heads of all the Christensen graves lined up together in the cemetery, with the names of his father and mother there as well as Gustave's, and Niels's, and a space for his own name when the time came. There would be no need for further space. There would be no further Christensens—not of their family.

He thought about the monument constantly, taking time from chores that needed doing. In his imagination he would run his calloused hands over the coarse grain of the huge gravestone and feel with his worn fingertips the cool smoothness of the highly polished panel, and pick out, like a blind man, the sharp indentations where the names had been carved. But it was an idle dream, and he knew it. Stones cost money. The block of granite as wide and thick as he wanted, finished and engraved as he wanted, would probably cost more than he could ever hope to obtain in a lifetime of hard work. Still, the longer he dreamed of the stone, the more exact the details as he pictured them, the more the project became fixed in his mind, until he had reached the point where he knew he would not settle for less, even though less would have still meant the most massive monument in the cemetery. To sell the farm? Knud Christensen was honest enough to know that in the condition it was in, the farm would bring little, certainly not enough for the memorial he wanted. And what would he do then? Where would he go? He could never leave Gedser and the cemetery.

He looked up, frowning, at the sound of an automobile being driven into the entrance to the farm, braking in the gravel of the driveway. Visitors? He never had visitors. Someone wishing directions? Let them get them elsewhere. He came to his feet heavily and walked through the living room to the front door, opening it, and watched a woman and a man come down from a car and approach while another remained in the driver's seat. His first reaction was to close the door in their faces. He had nothing to do with strangers. Let them go away and leave him in peace. But there was something about the friendly smile on the woman's face that reminded him that once he had been a part of the world, had not always been the recluse he had become in the six months since he had lost his brothers. He suddenly realized the condition of the kitchen with the dirty pans and dishes piled high in the sink, and he hurried back to close the door to that room, and then looked about as if to see if he should straighten out the living room, but the living room appeared to be all right. He never used the living room to sit and think; it faced the sea.

The woman was peering into the gloom of the living room from her place at the open door. The man, a stocky, strong-looking man, with a pleasant face, stood at her shoulder protectively. Christensen cleared his throat; it was almost as though he wondered after his long self-imposed exile from people, if he still had the power of speech. But his voice came out low and hard, even slightly suspicious.

"You want something, ma'am?"

Ruth gave him her friendliest smile, a smile that Gregor would have wagered would make any man her slave, but Christensen merely waited impassively for an answer. Ruth looked past the bulky body to the room. "We should like to talk to you a bit. May we come in?"

"Talk about what? If you're collecting for some charity, you've come to the wrong place."

"It's nothing like that. It's something important. And I think we'd all be more comfortable sitting down," Ruth said, and moved forward in such a way that Christensen automatically took a step backward. The action appeared to be an invitation to enter although all three knew it was not. Ruth sat down on a sofa; Gregor sat beside her. Christensen walked to the windows and raised the drawn shades, letting sunlight pour in through the curtains. Dust rose in the air from the unattended furniture, dancing in the shafts of light. And why should I apologize for the dust or the dirt? Christensen thought angrily. I didn't ask these people to come here! He sat down in a chair across from the two, his cold blue eyes moving from Ruth's face to Gregor's and then back again, resentful of the unwanted intrusion.

"All right," he said abruptly. "Who are you and what do you want?"

Ruth nodded, again taking the role of spokesman, knowing it was certainly all right with Gregor who hadn't even wanted to come. "My name is Ruth McVeigh and this is Dr. Kovpak. We want to talk to you about something that happened last January. You dove in the vicinity of the Gedser lighthouse, to recover the body of your brother who had gone down in a storm—"

Knud Christensen frowned. These two certainly didn't want to talk about Gustave or his recovery of Gustave's body. Why should they? Then what did they want to talk about? Obviously they wanted to talk about that case he had brought up at a later date. But how could they have known about that? He hadn't said anything. Had the professor? Or had somebody in the village become suspicious because of the money he had spent? But he had been careful not to spend the money in Gedser, knowing villages and villagers for what they were. Instead, he had taken the train to Naestved and gotten the anchor in a chandler's there, and the cross at a religious shop a block away. Still, thinking about it now, after the fact, he could see how stupid he had been. Who could have failed to notice the newness of the anchor now tied to the dinghy which had since sunk, and who could have failed to wonder where the old one had gotten to? And who could have failed to notice the twisted cross torn from Gustave's grave by those drunken vandals? The entire village had gone down to inspect the outrage, and many must have wondered at Knud Christensen's sudden affluence in buying that cross of gold. It had been gilt over welded steel, but who would have considered that?

Still, what was all the fuss about? So somebody knew or thought they knew that he had gone down again and brought

up a box from an old sunken wreck near Gustave and Niels's
fishing schooner. So what? All this to-do over a few pieces of
junk costume jewelry and a shoe box full of beads and buttons?

A sudden frightening thought came. It changed his thinking
completely. Who sent investigators to look into his finding
some poor pieces of pot metal mixed with brass? Who even
sent investigators to look into his spending a few kroner on an
anchor and a welded steel cross? *There must have been something in that old sunken wreck besides the one box he had
brought up, something of far greater value, something to interest the authorities, like drugs, or gold bars! And they thought
he had it!* He knew it would be impossible to convince these
two that he had only gone back the one time, and never again,
not even in warm spring weather, to further investigate that
sunken wreck. He knew he could never convince them that
even if he had known there was something of great value there,
that he would never go back, not even for the price of a granite
tombstone for his family; that he *could not* go back. They would
never believe him. The only thing to do, then, was to deny
everything. Deny and continue denying. He wet his lips.

"I dove to bring up my brother's body," he said through
stiff lips, his face now rigid, his hands now released from the
chair arms as being too revealing with their white clenched
knuckles, and now clasped firmly in his lap. He stared down
at them. "That's all I dove for and all I brought up. Not another
thing." His eyes came up for a moment. "Jens Krag was with
me. It was his boat. He would have seen if I'd brought up
anything more, wouldn't he? Of course he would. Go ask him.
He'll tell you. Jens Krag doesn't lie. If he isn't at the dock
he'll be there later. Go ask him—"

Knud Christensen was speaking as if by compulsion now,
sweat beginning to stand out on his brow. Ruth and Gregor
were staring, incredulous and silent.

"And I can explain the new anchor, too," Christensen said,
speaking now as if to himself. He looked up, taking the other
two into his confidence. "The cross was just welded steel with
some gold paint on it, but I didn't have much money after I
bought the anchor. He didn't give me very much, but then I
don't suppose it was worth very much." He looked down again.
"I don't know why I bought the anchor. I never used it, and I
never will. The dinghy, either. If you don't believe me, look

down at the dock. It's sunk right alongside." His eyes briefly
turned to the windows facing the sea, and then down again
quickly, in pain. "I could have gone back for the old one, but
even if the dinghy wouldn't have drifted without an anchor, I
wouldn't go back. I wouldn't!" He said it fiercely and then
returned to his thoughts. "I dove for Gustave's body—he was
hanging in the shrouds, as if he had been waiting for me to
come for him and was glad to see me..." He looked up,
desperately trying to be convincing. If he failed, he knew they
would not believe him and might even take him away, away
from his family. "But I never dove again. I never brought up
any box." He stared at the two white-faced people facing him,
confused, hurt by the unfair inquisition. "I—I'll swear to it if
I have to—"

He suddenly stumbled to his feet and walked unsteadily to
the kitchen door, throwing it open and staggering inside. The
two in the living room could hear the sound of a cupboard door
being opened, then the rattle of a bottle and a glass being taken
down. Ruth began to get to her feet, but Gregor waved her
down almost savagely. He got up silently and walked into the
kitchen, closing the door behind him. Christensen had a bottle
of aquavit in one hand, the half-full glass was at his lips and
he was drinking eagerly. Gregor waited until the glass had been
emptied and then took the bottle and glass gently from the other
man. He set them down on the cluttered counter and led the
man back to the living room. Christensen came docilely. Gregor
seated the man in his chair again and sat down opposite him
on the sofa. Ruth was still trying to fully comprehend the
possibilities inherent in the jumbled statement. She leaned forward.

"Do you mean—?" she began, but Gregor's look brought
her to a stumbling silence. Gregor turned back to the huge man
across from him, staring at Christensen with sympathy.

"Listen to me," he said softly. "We are not here to cause
you any trouble. Please believe me. We are here as your friends."
Christensen was staring at him dully, with faint curiosity as if
wondering who this man was and how he came here. Gregor
went on, his voice still soft. "This is what happened. You dove
for your brother's body and brought it up. While you were
diving, you saw another sunken ship, or what was left of it, a
ship that had been sunk many years ago. You saw a box there,

that had been there since the boat sank. You brought that up as well."

"I went back later and dove again. That's when I brought the box up." The liquor was making itself felt. Between the aquavit and the man's friendly face, Knud was feeling better, less threatened. Besides, the man already seemed to know everything, so what was the secret?

"You went back later and dove again, and on that dive you brought the box up," Gregor said, hardly believing what he was saying, or what he was hearing. Still, the wrecked ship could have been any wrecked ship, and the box could have contained anything: explosives, gunpowder... "It was a case made of welded steel inside of a wooden box, the whole thing held with steel straps, and it had lettering on it that said—"

"There was no lettering. When I brought Gustave up the wood was almost all gone; it was all gone when I went back for it. That's how I lost the anchor," Christensen said earnestly. "I had to loop the line through the straps to pull the box to the surface, and I had to cut the anchor loose to get the line free. There wasn't time to work work the knots loose, not under water, and not when the water was that cold."

"You brought the metal case to the surface," Gregor went on quietly, almost hypnotically, not wanting to break the spell. "You opened it and inside you found a treasure in gold—"

Christensen had been listening with a frown on his face, concentrating on what the man was saying. At this statement his frown deepened. So that was what they thought he had found! He shook his head violently, hoping the man would believe him, but doubting it. He knew he would hardly believe it himself.

"No!" he said hotly. "There was no gold treasure!" He looked about the room and then turned back to Gregor with a touch of grim humor. "Does all this look as if I had found a treasure?"

It did not, and Gregor had to admit it. Still, it had been quite a coincidence, a steel-case box found very close to the site where a small boat had gone down on May 22 or early on May 23, 1945. The box probably contained something quite different and obviously worthless. He leaned forward a bit, studying the blue eyes of Christensen, quite sure he was going to be told the truth. "What did you find?"

"Junk!" Christensen said bitterly. "A lot of beads and buttons and some real crude amateurish-looking lumps made into, well, like necklaces. And some masks hammered out of the stuff that looked like what children make, and a lopsided cup, I think, or maybe there were two of them." He shrugged. "He said they were made of some cheap alloy. Pot metal and brass, I think, but I'm not sure." He looked at Gregor sadly. "There was no treasure. If that's what you're looking for, it's still down there at the bottom of the sea. And it will stay there for all of me." He shook his head. "What I found was junk. He said so."

Ruth and Gregor exchanged stunned, unbelieving glances. Ruth opened her mouth to say something, but Gregor waved her down in no uncertain manner. He studied the man across from him. "He?" he asked softly.

"A cousin of mine. Not a close one, actually a distant cousin of my mother's, but still. I asked him to look at it. He's a professor at the university in Copenhagen." Christensen smiled in remembrance. "He's a nice fellow. He gave me a thousand kroner for the stuff."

With nice people like this around, Gregor thought sardonically, who needs un-nice people? "What's the name of this cousin of yours? This professor? This nice fellow?"

Christensen shook his head. "I can't tell you that. I promised I wouldn't. You see," he said, explaining, "he gave me a thousand kroner just for junk. He doesn't want anyone to know about it, of course, because he'd look foolish, and nobody likes to look foolish."

Gregor made up his mind. He took a deep breath. "Mr. Christensen, what you found was not junk. What you found was the Schliemann treasure, a collection of archaeological artifacts made of almost pure gold that was discovered by a man named Schliemann at Troy, in Turkey, over a hundred years ago. The treasure has been missing for the past thirty-five years. You found it."

Christensen had been listening, his head cocked, his forehead wrinkled, trying to understand what was being said to him. Now he shook his head. "No, it wasn't. I told you, it was only—"

"I know what you told me," Gregor said steadily. "That was the Schliemann treasure."

"*That* was a treasure?"

"That was a treasure."

"But it certainly didn't look like—"

"It was still the Schliemann treasure. Believe me."

Christensen wet his lips, still finding it difficult to comprehend. "It wasn't junk?"

"It was the farthest thing from junk."

"It was worth more than a thousand kroner?"

Gregor smiled, a cold smile. "It was and is worth millions of kroner. In fact, it has a value far beyond that of money. Every museum in the world would be happy to get their hands on it."

Christensen pressed his head into his hands, trying to understand what the man was saying. He wished now he hadn't had that full glass of aquavit; on the other hand there was nothing he would have liked more at the moment than another glass, but he knew he would not take it. Maybe later he might even break open that bottle of lovely scotch whiskey. Millions of kroner? Millions of kroner made little sense to him. He could not picture them, although he knew they were a fortune. But how could the pieces he had found be worth a fortune? It made no sense. However—he looked up.

"Look," he said earnestly. "Do you know how much a good block of granite is worth? Big enough to go across four—no, five graves? Maybe this high?" He stood, towering above them, and placed his hand across his chest, and then sat down again, looking at them anxiously. "Maybe three-feet thick, with enough stone for a cross on the top." A sudden frightening possibility occurred to him. "Do they—do they quarry granite that big?"

Gregor had no idea of how granite had come into the conversation, but there was no doubt that the man was deadly serious. "Yes," he said simply. "They quarry granite that large. They quarry it as large as you want."

"And what would a block that big cost?"

Gregor shrugged. "I'm sorry, but I have no idea."

Christensen turned to Ruth, who had been staring at both men during the conversation. "Do you know, ma'am?" Ruth could only shake her head. The giant sighed and turned back to Gregor. "I don't want a lot of money. I just want those pieces I found, if you say they're worth something, to have the value of a piece of granite that big. Including the engraving," he added hastily. "There would have to be a polished panel in the center on one side big enough for five names, though only four need to be engraved now. But there has to be enough room for all five. And enough money left over to engrave the last one," he finished, not wishing to overlook his own name once he would be beyond collectors.

Gregor sighed. "I have no idea why you want a piece of granite," he said, "but the value of the treasure you found would probably pay for every headstone in every cemetery in Denmark."

Ruth leaned forward, determined not to be left out of the conversation.

"I know why you want the granite," she said quietly. "You want it for a memorial to your family, and to the brothers you lost. If you will tell us the name of that professor cousin of yours, the museum I direct will guarantee you a reward of one hundred thousand kroner. Which will be more than the cost of your monument. If it isn't, we'll see to it that it is."

Christensen looked miserable. It would have been nice to buy the monument he had always visualized, and if anything had been left over to put the farm back into shape, because he felt with a proper headstone over the family graves, he would have been able to go back to the farming he had always liked, and even begin to live as a human being again. But it was impossible. "I can't," he said sadly. "I promised."

Gregor started to say something, but this time it was Ruth who savagely waved him to silence.

"I'll tell you who you promised," she said angrily, but her anger was not directed at Christensen but at that "nice fellow," his cousin. "You promised a man who cheated you."

"Cheated me?"

"Your cousin cheated you," Ruth said evenly. "Your professor cousin cheated you. He knew exactly what you found, and he knew its value. In fact, he is offering the treasure for auction to the leading museums of the world, asking a fortune in money." Christensen was staring at her in shocked disbelief. "It's the truth," she said flatly. "You were cheated."

"Arne Nordberg cheated me—?" Christensen looked stunned.

"Yes," Ruth said, and glanced swiftly at Gregor. The name had not been lost on Kovpak. Ruth came to her feet, looking down on Christensen with pity. "When the treasure is recovered, you will receive the hundred thousand kroner. From the Metropolitan Museum of Art in New York."

"Cheated . . ."

Ruth opened her purse and brought out money. It was all she had with her but she knew she could get more at a bank in the morning as soon as she cabled New York. "Here are two thousand kroner on account, and my card. I'm at the Plaza Hotel in the Bernstorffsgade, if there is anything I can do for you." She held out the money. "Take it and find out how much your monument will cost. I promise you'll get it, no matter what happens to the treasure."

Knud Christensen made no move to take the money. Ruth placed the small pile of notes on a table as Gregor also came to his feet. Gregor put his hand on the other man's rigid shoulder and pressed lightly in comradeship. There was no response from the large man in the chair. He continued to stare sightlessly at the floor. Gregor addressed him, although he was not sure if the other man heard him or not.

"Thank you," he said. "Thank you, Mr. Christensen. You'll get your monument, I assure you. And more." He looked around the dingy room. "Enough to begin living like a man again."

Christensen did not respond. He seemed to be stunned by everything that had been said, all that he had heard. He watched dully as the two people nodded their good-byes and walked from the room, closing the door behind them. He heard the car engine start and listened to the wheels churning in the gravel as the car swung about to leave. He stared at the door without actually seeing it, and took a deep breath.

Cheated . . . !

And not just him, but the entire Christensen family. They had been cheated of their granite memorial. Gustave had been cheated; Niels had been cheated; even his poor parents, hard-working and dead all these many years—they had all been cheated. They could have had their granite monument by this time, had they not all been cheated.

And after cheating him and his entire family, the man had presented him with an expensive bottle of scotch whiskey, of a quality so good that he had held it for an occasion . . .

He came to his feet, a lumbering, stumbling giant, and walked into the kitchen. He reached as high as he could to the top shelf of the cupboard, far to the rear, the place he had hidden the bottle to await a proper event to celebrate. His fingers fumbled blindly for a few moments and then found their target. He drew the bottle from its hiding place and carried it to the living room. He sat down and stared at it, and then looked at the two thousand kroner on the table that the lady had left.

A proper event? What was a proper event?

In the rear seat of the car, the glass divider once again closed after Wilten had been instructed to return them to Copenhagen and their hotel, Ruth and Gregor stared at each other in total disbelief while Wilten brought the car back to the main road and headed for the city. Gregor held up one of his hands; it was shaking.

"My God!" he said, almost as if in shock.

"I don't believe it," Ruth said, her voice tinged with awe.

"It isn't possible!"

"But it's true..."

"A farmer! Diving for his brother's body! And finding—!" Gregor found it impossible to even voice the words, to comprehend the enormity of their discovery. They had found out what had happened to the Schliemann treasure, after all those years, after all the conjectures undoubtedly on the part of the Americans as well as Ulanov and the KGB! It was enough to make anyone's head spin, let alone the head of a dedicated archaeologist and scientist.

"It was a game!" Ruth said in a dazed voice, almost as if speaking to herself. "A silly game. I never actually thought—"

"Neither did I," Gregor said with wonder. "Who on earth could ever have thought—?"

Ruth reached over and took Gregor's hand, squeezing it tightly and feeling him respond equally. She closed her eyes, inexplicably fighting back tears. And then opened them as the car slid to a halt before a pump in a gasoline station. Wilten leaned over, speaking to them through the speaking tube; his words echoed hollowly in the enclosed space. "Fuel..." He climbed down, gave instructions to the attendant to fill the tank and check under the hood, and then tilted his head toward the rear of the station, indicating that while the needs of the automobile were being attended to, he would attend to his own needs. He walked to the back. Beside the twin doors to the rest rooms there was a telephone booth. He squeezed his ample bulk into it, dropped a coin, and dialed.

Count Lindgren had been awaiting the call anxiously. He snatched the telephone up at the first ring. "Yes?"

"Wilten here—"

"Well?"

"First they stopped at the Gedser dock and the woman spoke to someone there. Then they had me drive them to a farmhouse nearby; the name of the man who lives there is Christensen, Knud Christensen. On the way there they said something about his diving for his brother's body. Does the name Christensen mean anything to you?"

"No. Do you know what they talked to him about?"

"I don't know, but they talked to him a long time. When they came out they seemed to be almost in shock. I kept the car's intercommunication line open, even though the glass divider was closed. They kept saying things like, 'It can't be true, but it is,' almost as if they had discovered something important." He remembered something else. "The man, the Russian, said something about a farmer, diving for his brother's body, and finding—"

"Finding what? Speak up!"

"He didn't say. And the woman said, 'It was a game. I never thought—' and that's when she stopped. Then they didn't say any more, so I stopped for gasoline, and I'm calling you from there. They can't see me."

"Did they mention Arne Nordberg?"

"No, sir."

Count Lindgren took a deep breath. His mind had been racing all through Wilten's report. "They discovered something! I'm sure they discovered something! The treasure has been under the sea, just as the girl suspected, and they have found out how it was found. It never was in Russia. She said that, and it was true! That lying Nordberg! They'll find him, and he'll lead them to us. If we let them, that is!"

"Yes, sir."

"So we won't let them." The decision made at last, the count's voice seemed to lighten. Actually, it was a decision that Lindgren had suspected would be necessary since their lunch the day before, and the information that had been given them at the naval station. It was too bad, in a way; he had liked Ruth McVeigh, and he disliked destroying anything of beauty. But where his own well-being was at stake, there was no choice. "You know what to do?"

"We discussed it last night."

"Exactly! When you're through with the police, get back here as soon as you can."

"Right."

Wilten put the telephone back in its cradle, pushed himself from the narrow booth, and walked back to the car. He paid the bill and climbed into the driver's seat, starting the engine and pulling the car back into the slack traffic pattern of the highway. In the rearview mirror he could see his two passengers holding hands tightly, looking at each other in silent wonder. With no expression at all on his fleshy face, Wilten brought his attention back to the road and stepped on the accelerator, heading north.

In the rear seat Gregor and Ruth continued to look at each other, still unable to accredit that the silly game that had begun in the map room of the British Museum had eventually led them here, to where there was an excellent possibility that they would shortly be able to actually put their hands on the Schliemann collection! It seemed so absolutely unbelievable, particularly in the first moments of their discovery, that they sat in silence, as if speaking of it might bring their remarkable success from reality to the phantasy it seemed it had to be. In their silent contemplation of the miracle that had befallen them, Gregor became aware that the car was slowing again. He looked through the window. They were at the point in the highway he remembered from their trip down, where the sea could be seen below from a point near the Fakse Bugt. Gregor leaned forward as the car left the road and came to a halt nearly out of sight of the highway on a dirt road point to the sea.

"Why are we stopping now?"

Wilten's voice came hollowly over the intercom system. "I'm afraid one of the rear tires is losing pressure, sir. I'm just going to check it now. It will just take a minute, sir."

"Oh." Gregor leaned back and watched the heavy-set Wilten get down and move out of sight behind the car. He was about to turn to Ruth and say something when he became aware that the heavy car was beginning to move, to roll down the slope, gaining momentum. Ahead in the near distance he could see the dirt road end in a turn-around guarded only by a low stone wall, and beyond that a sheer drop to the sea. He swung around, staring through the rear window. Wilten was running after the car as fast as his weight would allow, his hands outstretched. He could hear Wilten's voice, screaming.

"Oh, my God! I forgot the hand brake! Oh, my God!"

Ruth was sitting rigidly, white faced. Gregor tried the door handles; *the doors were locked!* Ahead, the edge of the cliff was coming closer and closer as the heavy car picked up momentum, the deep ruts of the worn dirt road keeping the wheels locked in their inevitable juggernaut course, the sea below frothing over rocks beneath a sheer drop. Suddenly Gregor leaned back in his seat, raising his two feet, jamming his shoes through the glass that divided the empty front seat from the enclosed rear. A moment later he had forced himself through the shards of broken glass still embedded in the frame, unaware either of the ripping of his clothes or the shredding of his skin as he slithered on his stomach across the seat and under the dashboard, pulling with all his force on the emergency brake. The car responded slowly, as if resenting this interference with its unexpected freedom, swaying from side to side as its great weight seemed determined to overcome the demands of the tightening brake bands. Gregor blanked his mind to the thought of the rapidly approaching cliff, or of Ruth sitting petrified in the rear of the car. He gritted his teeth and pulled on the emergency brake with all his power. The car shuddered under the force of that strength, swayed a bit more, and came to rest with a jarring thud against the stone wall of the turn-around, settling down with one wheel dished under by the impact.

For several seconds Gregor stayed where he was, half under the dashboard, his hands still locked tightly on the emergency brake, trembling, and then he reached up with one shaking hand to open the front car door and roll to the ground just as Wilten came panting up, his face truly white as he considered Count Lindgren's reaction to the failure of his mission.

"Thank God!" he said, trying to catch his breath. "Count Lindgren will never forgive me! You might have been killed!"

Gregor came to his feet still trembling, and opened the door to the rear of the car. Ruth still sat inside, unable to move. Gregor turned to Wilten, his jaw hard, his eyes narrowed in fury. "The doors didn't open from inside!"

"Oh, no, sir! They are locked, controlled from the front seat. For safety reasons, sir—" Wilten seemed to realize how foolish that sounded in the circumstances. "I mean—well, sir, the count never opens the door himself. The chauffeur always does that, sir. So when they are locked, the doors are arranged only to be opened from the outside. Count Lindgren often sends his car to take orphans on picnics, sir, and you know children, sir—" He brought out a handkerchief and held it out a bit tentatively toward Gregor. "Your cheek, sir. It's bleeding."

People were stopping on the highway, looking down toward the wreck; a farmer was trotting over from his fields alongside the sloping road. Wilten was pleased with his presence of mind in acting the innocent chauffeur, screamingly denouncing himself for his failure to set the hand brake. Let them think him stupid, but never let them suspect the truth. Count Lindgren, unfortunately, would not be that forgiving. It was a thought Wilten preferred not to dwell upon.

Some of the people from the highway were beginning to come down toward the wrecked car. Gregor took a deep breath, bringing himself under control, holding the handkerchief against his cut cheek. It was an accident, but at least it was over and both he and Ruth were alive. He reached into the car for Ruth's hand, bringing her to stand beside him. Her face was still pale from the fright and the thought of the death they had so narrowly escaped, but her pride in Gregor for his quick thinking that had saved them more than compensated. Gregor studied Wilten's face. There was no doubt the poor chauffeur was as upset by the affair as he had been himself. Gregor looked at the dished wheel and then back to Wilten.

"And what do we do now?"

Wilten looked at the people coming down the road to see if they could help. "I'm sure one of these people will be happy to give you a lift into Praestø, sir," he said deferentially. "You can rent a car there. I'm terribly sorry for this, sir. I'll stay with the car, if you could ask them to send a wrecker..."

"I'm sorry, too," Gregor said, feeling compunction for the

unhappy Wilten. "It was just one of those things, and I'll tell Count Lindgren that."

"I appreciate that, sir," Wilten said, although the statement did not make him appear any happier. "Count Lindgren will be very upset about this, sir. Very upset..."

21

From his corner of the Plaza Hotel, slightly hidden behind some plant although with no idea of trying to make himself invisible, Major Serge Ulanov of the KGB waited glumly for the arrival of his compatriot, Dr. Gregor Kovpak. The plant which partially protected him from view was one Major Ulanov did not recognize, but if it gave him hay fever he would not be surprised. It would be in line with the rest of his day. The major had arrived in Copenhagen that afternoon after a long, uncomfortable train ride from Berlin. He had no idea why he had not flown and preferred not to think about it as it would only make him feel worse. If there was any satisfaction to be gained at all, it was in knowing that Newkirk had suffered equally the day before. In addition, upon reporting to the Russian Embassy in the Bredgade and using their telephone facilities to report to Colonel Vasily Vashugin in Moscow, Major Ulanov had been informed that one week of his annual vacation had already been deducted, and if he were not home in two days at the most, the one week deduction would become two.

"I realize," Vashugin had said with no attempt to disguise the sarcasm, "that the fate of our country, not to mention the entire planet, rests upon the vital investigation you seem to be conducting in all the most comfortable—not to mention the most expensive—cities of Europe. Your expense account will probably deny us the importation of several thousands of tons of wheat. I don't exactly know why we began this investigation in the first place, but it was at your instigation, as I recall. We have also had several inquiries from the director of the Hermitage Museum wishing to know when we will be through requiring the services of Dr. Kovpak."

"What happened, sir—"

"My dear Major Ulanov, when I am finished I will be glad to allow you to explain your complete dereliction of duty in favor of what I believe are called, in the capitalist world, the fleshpots. I, too, in my time, have known the beauty of London, the pleasures of Berlin, the wonderful Danish food. I, too, in my time, have enjoyed the bright lights and the lesser-bright women of some of Europe's capitals. But at least I had the simple intelligence not to push a good thing to the point where I was receiving an extremely serious reprimand from my superiors!"

"Sir, you don't understand—"

"*I* don't understand?" The sarcasm disappeared instantly. "*You* don't understand, Major. I have no idea what kind of game you and this Kovpak are playing—he isn't related to you, by any chance, is he? Your sister's son, or something like that? But the two of you better have your last meal at the Tivoli, take your last shopping spree in Strøget, make your last visit to the Istedgade—yes, I know where it is—and get back home! And when you get here, Major, you better have a better story than you've given me to date!"

"Sir, I haven't had a chance to say a—"

"That will do, Major! You've wasted enough time of yours on this so-called investigation of yours without wasting any more of mine. Investigation!" The colonel snorted. "Good day!" Ulanov's ears still rang from the sound of the telephone receiver being slammed down.

Now, sitting disconsolate in his corner of the lobby of the Plaza Hotel, Major Ulanov lit a cigarette and inhaling deeply reviewed the one-sided coversation. He was forced to admit there was a certain amount of justice in the colonel's complaint. He had started out to discover why the CIA was about to auction off a certain treasure, or, if the treasure had been stolen from them, how Langley's security had been breached; but all that

seemed to have become lost in the shuffle. True, Newkirk was
still around, but that meant little. He, Ulanov, was still around
as far as that went, and only God knew why. Certainly Colonel
Vashugin didn't, and the major could hardly blame the colonel
for that.

The truth was that he had become distracted by the antics
of Ruth McVeigh and Gregor Kovpak, and they were antics
simply caused, most likely, by their having stupidly fallen in
love. Well, if that were the case, then the thing for him to do
was to speak with Kovpak like the uncle Vashugin had accused
him of being, and straighten him out. He would tell him his
duty as a Soviet citizen, ask him what the devil he had been
doing leading the KGB on a merry chase all over Europe, and
then get the two of them home as soon as possible. It was
evident to Ulanov, sitting quietly, thoughtfully considering the
actions of McVeigh and Kovpak over the past week, that they
had not necessarily tried to escape him in Rostock. They probably hadn't known he was within a thousand miles. If they
were lovers, which he strongly suspected, they probably
wouldn't have noticed him if they ran into him in one of the
Warnow Hotel's three-passenger-capacity elevators. They had
gone to Bad Freienwalde to try to follow the treasure, but then
had simply fallen in love and decided to forget the treasure and
go to Copenhagen as being a lovely city for lovers. And had
driven to Rostock as being on their way. And he, in chasing
them like an idiot, had only accomplished laying himself open
to a charge of wasting money, being derelict in his duty, and—
while it had not been said—probably opening himself up for
a demotion. It was not a pleasant prospect.

He shook ash from his cigarette and looked up as the doors
of the Plaza were opened by the ornately costumed doorman,
but again it was not his quarry. Instead he was not greatly
surprised to see James Newkirk come in looking as if he had
eaten something sour, and approach the house phones. The room
Newkirk requested apparently did not answer, and after a while
Newkirk hung up, walked over, and sat down in a chair commanding a view of the lobby and the main entrance from the
Bernstorffsgade, looking unhappy. Ulanov frowned. As far as
he knew, Newkirk had had no more success on whatever his
mission had been than Ulanov had had with his. And if Langley
was anything like Moscow, then Newkirk had probably also

been reprimanded recently for wasting time and money. In which case he was probably here to reveal himself to Ruth McVeigh, remind her of her duty as an American and ask her just what the devil she had been up to leading the CIA on a merry chase all over Europe.

On a sudden impulse, Ulanov crushed out his cigarette and came to his feet. He walked over, sitting down in a chair beside Newkirk, smiling at the man in friendly fashion. "Mr. Newkirk?"

Newkirk had been busy with his private thoughts. He looked up, startled, not recognizing Ulanov for a moment, and then reddened as he did. "I beg your pardon?"

"My name is Ulanov," the major said politely. "We might have met in London during the conference on the Schliemann treasure, but somehow it never happened. I believe we are both in a similar position. We are both following Dr. McVeigh and Dr. Kovpak to discover what they are up to. I, personally, believe they are up to nothing, but have simply fallen in love. However, I could be wrong. It occurred to me that possibly if we were to pool our efforts, we might get further."

Newkirk was looking at him as if he were insane. "I have no idea at all of what you are talking about," he said half-angrily. "I happen to be a reporter for the Paris *Herald Tribune*—"

Ulanov sighed. "I realize that," he said patiently. "I also realize that I know who and what you are, even as you know who and what I am. I merely said that possibly if we were to join our efforts—"

"I have no idea of what this is all about," Newkirk said stiffly. "You, sir, are a complete stranger to me. Pool our efforts? I never heard anything as ridiculous in my life!" What did the man take him for, anyway? A complete fool? It was, of course, a devious plot on the part of the KGB, and one that he, Newkirk, was far too intelligent to fall for. He made a motion to rise. "If you'll pardon me—"

Ulanov detained him with a gesture and came to his feet. "No," he said quietly. "I'll go back where I came from. As for my suggestion, of course it was ridiculous. It was mad. I don't deny it." He looked at the other man sadly. "I just thought it also might be fruitful."

He turned and walked back to his seat behind the plant,

wondering at the crazy impulse that had led him to approach
the CIA man. He sat down with a shrug and lit a cigarette,
wondering what his own reaction would have been had Newkirk
approached him as he had approached the CIA man. Probably
the same, he thought wearily. But at least the matter was out
in the open, he thought, puffing steadily. At least he and Newkirk would no longer have to trail each other from a distance.
Maybe, he thought with a sudden inner grin, they could even
share a car. The concept removed some of his depression and
he leaned back, smoking steadily, waiting for Kovpak.

They were driving in their rented car; Gregor's face had been
bandaged by a pharmacist in Praestø and a wrecker had been
sent for Count Lindgren's car. By mutual consent the subject
of the accident was not discussed; concentration on Arne Nordberg and the best way to handle the man was a safe antidote
to the cold feeling each had when they recalled the sight of
that cliff coming nearer, and the sea and the rocks beyond.

"My idea is this," Ruth said. "We get Nordberg's address
from the phone book, or if it isn't there, from the university,
tonight. Then tomorrow morning early, before he has a chance
to wake up completely, we walk in on him and present him
with the facts. We tell him we know he has the treasure and
can prove it. We tell him he either gives up the treasure without
any fuss, in which case the Metropolitan will see to it that he
gets an ample reward—nothing like the insane figure he was
considering, but a decent sum—or, if he's inclined to refuse,
that we will go to the authorities and he'll end up in jail. And
get nothing."

They had passed Brandbyestrand and were coming into the
southern outskirts of Copenhagen, driving along the Kalve-
boderne, the inlet from the Køge Bugt leading to the heart of
the city. Across the water they could see huge airplanes taking
off from Kastrup Airport on Amager, suddenly rising above
the apartment buildings like giant cranes frightened from their
chimney nests. The planes reminded both Ruth and Gregor that
eventually each would be taking one of those planes to his own
country, his own home. But first, as they both knew, there
was the matter of the Schliemann treasure and their unbelievable discovery of it. Gregor smiled across the car.

"All that simple, eh?" he said lightly. "And you expect that once you hand him that tough ultimatum, he'll rush to the closet, or under the bed, drag out the treasure and lay it at our feet, and then get down on his knees to thank you from the bottom of his heart for saving him from a life of crime? Is that it?"

"Well," Ruth said a bit stiffly, "maybe that isn't the scenario exactly, but it will be very close. He hasn't a lot of choice, as I see it." She frowned at Gregor. "What would you do in his shoes?"

"Me?" Gregor shrugged. "I'd say you were crazy and if you didn't get out of my house in five seconds, I'd call the police."

"*What!*"

"That's what I'd say, and that's what he'll say. He'll deny knowing what you're talking about. He'll act completely innocent. And just how are you going to prove he isn't?"

"And exactly," Ruth asked sardonically, "how will he explain Knud Christensen?"

"Why does he have to explain Knud Christensen?" Gregor sounded completely serious. He changed his voice slightly, raising it, imitating the unknown professor. "Knud who? Oh, Knud Christensen, my crazy cousin? What? He claims he found a box with a treasure in it? Well, good luck to him, he certainly can use it, if he really did find something, but he suffers delusions, you know. He *what?* He claims he sold it to *me* for a thousand kroner? I suppose he has my canceled check to prove it. What? He says I paid *cash* for it? A thousand kroner? Ma'am, do I look like a person who carries a thousand kroner in cash around with him? And when was I supposed to have done all this? And where? Earlier this year in Gedser? Gedser? I've never been in Gedser in my life. Please, Dr. McVeigh! I'm just a poor university professor. You've been listening to a sick man. I heard that ever since his two brothers were drowned, he's been a little—well, strange, to say the least. As I say, I've never been in Gedser, but I'm sure there are people there who can confirm that. What? You say if I've never been in Gedser, how do I know about his brothers drowning? Well, I happened to hear it from someone in the family. After all, we are related . . ."

Ruth had been listening to the imitation of the unknown professor with increasing irritation. "If you think my method of getting this Nordberg to confess he's got the treasure is so terrible," she said coldly, "just how would the brilliant Gregor Kovpak handle it?"

"Me?" Gregor's face lost its good humor. "I'd use a completely different approach."

"Force, I suppose. The masculine—or, rather, the macho—approach to all problems." Ruth sniffed disdainfully. "Hot needles under the fingernails, or the Iron Maiden—"

Gregor grinned. "That's us Cossacks!"

"—and if an educated man such as a university professor doesn't react to reason, what makes you think he'd react to force? And if he would call the police to throw me out after I merely talked to him, who do you think he would call to throw you out after you used muscle? And not just to throw you out of his house, but probably out of the country, as well." She shook her head decisively. "We'll try my method."

"First," Gregor said calmly.

Ruth looked at him suspiciously. "What do you mean, first?"

Gregor shrugged. "I mean, you try your approach first, and when it fails—as it will—then I get a chance to try my approach."

"I don't like force!"

"Who likes force?"

Ruth frowned at him. "Then what's your approach?"

"Ah, that's a secret! I'm not objecting to your trying your way so why object to my trying mine?"

"Because I don't trust you."

Gregor's head swung around; his eyes showed his hurt. "You don't trust me?"

"I didn't mean it that way," Ruth said hurriedly, and reached across the car to squeeze his hand on the steering wheel. "All right, darling. I'll try my method and if it doesn't work, you can try yours. I promise."

"I accept your promise," Gregor said, and pulled the car into the area before the front of the Plaza Hotel. While they waited for the doorman to come and take the car to a garage, Gregor turned to Ruth, bringing up a subject that was bothering him. "You know, darling," he said quietly, "we disagree on many things, but I love you very much. Will you please explain to me why you keep insisting on separate rooms?"

Ruth looked at him tenderly. "I love you, too, darling. We

agree on the most important thing of all—how we feel about each other. As for the separate rooms, have we lacked each other in any way?"

"In a way—"

"I don't believe so. We enjoy each other. Then, afterward, we're alone to relive the precious moments and appreciate how lucky we are to have anything at all. Besides," she added with her gamine grin, "this way I don't need to discover that you snore, or thrash around in your sleep, or hog the covers or the bathroom. This way I get the best of you."

"And leave the worst to me," Gregor said glumly, and sighed as he climbed down. He handed the car keys to the doorman and followed Ruth through the door the man was holding open. They crossed the hotel lobby to the bank of self-service elevators and waited until one appeared. Gregor ushered Ruth into the cab and followed her. They rose in silence, each with his own thoughts. Gregor reached for and held Ruth's hand as they walked down the thickly carpeted corridor to her room. He leaned over, proud and happy to feel possessive after all the years, kissing her. "I'll see you at six," he said fondly. "At the bar."

"Don't be late," she said. She squeezed his hand with a strength he hadn't known she possessed, and then she was gone, her door closing behind her, leaving Gregor standing in the hallway. He stared at the closed door a moment, as if contemplating something, then, his face inscrutable, he walked slowly down the corridor toward his own room.

Major Serge Ulanov watched the two, oblivious to anything except themselves, enter the elevator. He crushed out his cigarette and came to his feet a bit reluctantly. He liked Gregor Kovpak, and he knew the man was bound to be angry with him for needlessly interrupting what obviously was the equivalent of a honeymoon for two people who could never, or would never, marry. In his shoes, Ulanov thought, remembering when he had been courting, I'd probably take me and drop me from the roof, but duty is duty, and while I will undoubtedly lose a friend, I may save my job. He walked to the elevator bank just as James Newkirk also approached. Newkirk waited stiffly, paying no attention to the man at his side. When they entered the first car that appeared, Ulanov pressed the button for his floor and then innocently looked at Newkirk inquiringly, as one accommodating elevator passenger to another.

"Same floor," Newkirk said brusquely. Ulanov nodded and stepped back.

They rode up in silence, left the elevator together in silence, and walked down the hallway in silence. Newkirk paused before Ruth McVeigh's door and frowned at Ulanov as if wondering if he were making the same call, but Ulanov continued on without breaking his pace to Kovpak's room. He paused before the closed door and looked down the hallway. Newkirk had been waiting for Ulanov to arrive. Now both men raised their hands to knock. A farce, Ulanov thought sourly, and waited for Kovpak to open the door. It occurred to him that Gregor could well be in the girl's room, and he pitied Newkirk if he interrupted anything the two considered important, but even while the thought crossed his mind, the door opened and Kovpak was facing him. Ulanov forgot his prepared speech in light of Kovpak's appearance. From his place behind the plant in the hotel lobby he had not noticed the condition of Kovpak's face or clothing. His eyes widened; his eyebrows shot up.

"What on earth happened to you?"

"A car accident," Gregor said lightly, and waved the matter away as being minor, principally because he did not want to remember it. Then he seemed to realize who was in the room with him. To Ulanov's complete amazement, rather than show anger, Kovpak smiled at him broadly, and then winced as the movement pulled at the bandage on his cheek. "Serge! Just the man I was wishing I could see, but I never dreamed I would! Maybe if you wish for something hard enough, your wish is answered! This is wonderful!" Gregor suddenly frowned. "But what on earth are you doing here?"

Why Kovpak would have been wishing to see him was one more mystery in an affair whose mysteries did not seem to have any great importance. Ulanov would have preferred to ask after the accident that seemed to have ripped Gregor's clothes even more than his body, but it was apparent the man didn't want to talk about it. The white-haired agent decided to get the explanation of his role over with quickly.

"I've been following you and the girl," he said, and walked over to the bed, dropping down on it and fishing out a cigarette.

He waited for the explosion. He really didn't know Kovpak well enough to anticipate his reactions, and Kovpak was not only considerably younger than he was, but twice as husky. And as far as he knew, possibly as well trained in the art of self-defense. But instead of anger, Kovpak exhibited nothing except slight puzzlement.

"Following us? Then you saw the accident?"

"Not following you every minute," Ulanov said a bit sourly. "Following you from London to East Berlin, to Rostock, to Copenhagen."

"But why?" Kovpak shrugged. "Never mind. It doesn't make any difference—"

"It does make a difference," Ulanov said quietly. "In going from London to Berlin, especially after you told me a story about your motives for the trip that I didn't believe, you made me suspicious. And particularly when you went to Bad Freienwalde, it seemed to me you were obviously trying to trace the Schliemann treasure. And the treasure and its connection with the CIA is, after all, my assignment. I thought if I followed you, I might learn something. Instead," he said bitterly, remembering the tongue-lashing he had received that afternoon, "all I got was the worst reprimand of my life for chasing after a love-sick scientist, wasting my time—"

"You weren't, you know."

"—and I'll be lucky if I'm only reduced one grade and not sent back to a desk job decoding messages from our embassies around the world complaining about the quality of the vodka sent them in the diplomatic pouches!"

"I said, you haven't been wasting your time."

"At my age, too!" Ulanov went on, unhearing. "I had hoped to retire on a pension in a few years, come up to Peterhof and buy a small dasha, nothing impressive, although to tell the truth not many of them are impressive around there, mostly shacks with flattened gasoline tins to cover the holes in the roof and keep out the rain. I thought I might get in a little fishing in the summer—"

"Serge! Serge!"

"—in the winter maybe—" The man seemed to finally realize he was being addressed. He looked up, the cigarette still unlit, and then remembered to bring out a match and light it. He looked around the room and then back to Kovpak. "I'm sorry. My troubles aren't your fault. What have you been up to, Gregor?"

Kovpak grinned almost savagely. "Serge, do you know how to tap a telephone?"

"Tap a telephone?" Ulanov looked startled by the change in the conversation. He also looked disappointed. "You're having trouble so soon? You don't trust her? I wondered at the separate rooms, but it was no business of mine. But tap a telephone in a hotel—?"

"No, no! Not in a hotel! Not Ruth's telephone, for heaven's sake! In a house, or an apartment, I don't know which yet, but I will, tonight." He sat down and pulled his chair toward the man on the bed. "Well, can you do it?"

Ulanov frowned. "What is this all about?"

Kovpak took a deep breath. "Serge, we found it!"

"You found what?"

"The treasure! The Schliemann treasure! It was at the bottom of the sea all these years. A man in a town called Gedser found it when he was diving for his brother's body. He didn't know what it was, and he sold it to a professor at the university here, a man named Nordberg, for almost nothing."

Ulanov was staring. *"You found the Schliemann treasure?"*

"Yes," Gregor said simply. "We found it."

"It hasn't been in Langley all these years?" The major was trying to comprehend the enormity of what Kovpak was saying. If this was true, then Langley could not be the one auctioning off the treasure. It also meant, of course, that their security had never been breached. And to demonstrate one or the other— or neither, by implication—had been his assignment. If what Kovpak was saying was true, and could be proven, he might well wriggle off Vashugin's hook.

"It hasn't been anywhere except on the bottom of the sea, I tell you, for the past thirty-five years," Gregor said a bit impatiently. "And no, we haven't located it physically, but if you know how to tap a telephone, we soon will!"

Ulanov put aside consideration of his own problems to concentrate on what Kovpak was saying. "I assume it is the professor's telephone you want to tap. Why?"

Kovpak leaned forward. "Ruth McVeigh is a lovely woman and a brilliant one," he said, "but she doesn't know much about university professors in Europe. There is absolutely no way a

professor in a university here can possibly finance anything as
expensive as this auction. Just getting the packages delivered
to the various museums around the world would have cost more
than this Professor Nordberg probably earns in a year. And the
means of handling the actual auction, as well as the means of
guaranteeing the delivery of the treasure to the high bidder, as
well as making sure that the payment is received without revealing the identity of the person being paid—well, all of these
things cost money. And money, I'm sure, beyond the amount
this Professor Nordberg is apt to have."

Ulanov felt his hopes plummeting. "You mean, then, that
this professor does *not* have the treasure?"

"I mean, I doubt he has it in his possession," Kovpak said.
"I've thought about this all afternoon driving back. He must
have a confederate, someone with money, and undoubtedly
this confederate has the treasure—"

"A confederate?"

"Serge, you aren't thinking! He had to have someone with
enough money to finance this auction. Anyone putting up the
money isn't going to take any chances with the treasure. He's
going to keep it where he can look at it, where he knows where
it is."

Ulanov nodded. "I see. And if we can frighten this Nordberg
sufficiently, he's going to telephone this confederate—"

"If *I* can frighten him sufficiently," Kovpak said flatly.
"You're going to be in the basement, or wherever, listening in
with your tapping equipment. If you know how to do it," he
added a bit unkindly.

"Tapping a telephone is no great chore," Ulanov said, waving away the problem. "We have the equipment in the Bredgade, in our—well, let me simply say the equipment is available.
And I do know how to do it. I thought everyone did." He
paused. "When will you know where the professor lives?"

Kovpak reached for the telephone directory and began leafing through the pages. He ran his finger down a column and
looked up. "Does one need to be a trained KGB man to use a
telephone book?"

"In some cities it helps," Ulanov said with a straight face.
"In Rio de Janeiro even that doesn't help." He looked over
Kovpak's shoulder. "Nordberg, Arne, Prof. Linnesgade Num-
ber 16. That's near the center, on the Israels Plads. Not far

from the university. Those would be apartments." He smiled and came to his feet, putting out his cigarette. "I'll go and look the place over now. Tomorrow, unfortunately, their telephones will require some checking. I'll have a man with me who speaks Danish to answer any silly questions, of which I'm sure we'll get a ton—" He suddenly frowned. "What if he isn't home tomorrow?"

"A very reasonable question," Kovpak said approvingly. He checked the telephone number opposite the address, asked the hotel operator for an outside line, and dialed. He sat waiting stolidly and then suddenly came to life, smiling brightly at the receiver. "Hello? Professor Nordberg? How nice to find you in. My name is Gregor Kovpak, of the Hermitage Museum in Leningrad. What? You have? That's very kind of you, I'm sure. What? Oh, the reason for my call, Professor, is that on a recent expedition I ran across some bones which investigation proved to be those of a baby dinosaur, and which I am in the process of—You've read of it? That's extremely kind of you to say, Professor, but the truth is it was a lucky accident. No, I'm not being modest. But to get to the reason for my call, Professor; recently I came across a paper of yours in some journal—what? Oh, on history? I mean, on history, of course! It impressed me greatly, and since I find myself in Copenhagen, and also since my experience with the baby dinosaur bones has made me particularly intrigued, more and more, with the subject of history in general, I wonder if—what? Your field is Medieval Danish history? Now you're the one who is being modest, Professor. I'm sure your knowledge is far more extensive. And I would really like to discuss the age when those tiny bones were first laid down, with someone with your background. I'm sure it could make a great joint paper, if you might be interested. If you could spare me a few moments... Tomorrow morning would be fine. No, no! I'll come to you! Hotels are so impersonal. I have your address. Nine o'clock? Excellent!"

He hung up and smiled at Ulanov. Ulanov shook his head at the deceit one encountered in one's fellow man. "You said you'd read one of his papers. How did you know he'd even written one?"

"He's probably written twenty and had one published," Kovpak said with a faint smile. "Writing papers keeps professors out of mischief. It also, of course," he added, thinking about it, "often keeps them out of becoming true scientists." He glanced at his watch and hurriedly came to his feet. "And now you'll have to excuse me, Serge. I have to take a quick shower and get into some decent clothes. I have a date."

And, he said to himself as he closed the door behind Ulanov, if you and Ruth only shared the same room, you could be taking your showers together. Think of the water you'd save . . . He grinned at the thought and went into the bathroom to start the water.

Mr. James Newkirk had not received the welcome afforded Serge Ulanov by Gregor Kovpak, nor had he expected a great welcome. But James Newkirk knew his duty and fully intended to carry it out, and the fact that the lady who opened the door was frowning at him did not bother him. The lady seemed to be trying to place him in her memory as having seen him before, but then she obviously gave it up as being completely unimportant.

"Yes?" she asked.

"May I come in?"

"Certainly not! What do you want?"

Newkirk reached into his pocket and brought out his wallet, opening it to expose his warrant card. "My name is James Newkirk. I'm with the CIA. I'd like a minute of your time." He tucked the wallet away and pushed past her into the room. Ruth considered leaving the door open during any interview, but Newkirk had other ideas. He closed the door firmly and motioned toward a chair. "Have a seat, Dr. McVeigh. This may take some time."

Ruth took a deep breath. She did not appreciate strangers pushing themselves into her room and then closing the door. Still, the warrant card had been quite genuine; her years in Washington had acquainted her with the proper recognizable form of the card. She sat down, not pleased with the interruption. She wanted to take a shower and get dressed for Gregor's admiration.

"All right," she said coolly. "What do you want?"

Newkirk sat down opposite her. "Miss—I mean, Dr. McVeigh—what do you know of this man you've been traveling with—this Gregor Kovpak?" He raised his hand quickly. "I know his scientific qualifications, his reputation as an archaeologist, but what do you know of him?"

This was an easy question to answer. "What business is that of yours?"

"America is my business, Dr. McVeigh, and your business as well, I assume." Newkirk was proud of the phrase. He truly had a way with words and properly recognized it. He reminded himself to be sure to include the phrase in his report on this conversation, which unfortunately would have to be remembered since Wilson at Langley had never replaced his lost tape recorder. "Or at least I will assume that America is your business until you give me reason not to believe it."

Ruth felt her temper rising. "Are you suggesting—?"

Newkirk shrugged delicately. "I'm suggesting nothing, Doctor. The fact is that you are an American citizen traveling with a Russian national. We would like to know the reason for this—well, some might call it possible treasonable act on your part."

Ruth suddenly decided she had had enough of this. "Mr. Newkirk, do you have a warrant for my arrest?"

Newkirk smiled coldly, but inside he was triumphant. The woman was losing her temper and that was always good. When people lost their tempers they often said things better left unsaid for their own advantage. "Why, Dr. McVeigh? Do you feel you deserve to be arrested?"

"I feel—I feel you should be put away!" Ruth said, fuming, and came to her feet. "Get out!"

Newkirk was not in the least disturbed. He felt he was finally getting somewhere. An interview of this nature might have saved him a good deal of time had he conducted it earlier. It also might have saved him several days in an East German cell, not to mention several severe reprimands from Langley.

"Dr. McVeigh," he said quietly, "I am from the CIA and you are, ostensibly, an American. I can have you brought to the American Embassy here in Copenhagen on the suspicion that you are dealing with the enemy, and continue the questioning there, if you prefer." She was glaring at him, speechless. She'll reveal something soon, Newkirk thought with satisfaction. She's about to break! And she has no idea my threat is completely idle, that I have no authority in Denmark to take her to the American Embassy or anywhere else. He looked at her, his eye, he was sure, properly stern. "Well, Doctor?"

Ruth McVeigh forcibly brought herself under control, her memory beginning to work. She stared at the man with narrowed eyes and then nodded. "Mr. Newkirk, weren't you at the conference in London? At the press table?"

"Exactly." Newkirk nodded. "I represented the *Herald Tribune,* Paris edition. As cultural reporter."

"And now you're representing the CIA?"

"Precisely. Actually, I represent both."

Ruth sat down again, a move Newkirk interpreted as victory for his side as he waited for her to confess everything. She contemplated him for several moments, her mind finally beginning to recover from her blind anger, beginning to properly function. Here she was with the Schliemann treasure practically in her hands, and at this particular moment this person appears, a person who claims to be a reporter in one breath, a CIA man in the next, and then claims to be both. Even if he were truly a newspaperman—which Ruth didn't believe for a moment— any story he might elicit from her under any guise could be the cause of the Metropolitan losing sole ownership of a treasure which, after all, she alone had discovered. True, Gregor had been along, but he would be the first to admit that she was the one who had insisted the treasure was lost at sea. She was the one who insisted upon visiting Gedser, insisted upon the interview with Knud Christensen. It was her treasure, and Gregor knew it.

But this one? She suddenly remembered something else. If she wasn't mistaken this was the same man who had been sitting at a table near them when she and Gregor had first had dinner together in London. This man had been spying on her for a long time! What this man was, then, was most likely a spy for one of the other museums represented at that conference, trying to learn what he could to be used for the advantage of one of her competitors! And here she had found the Schliemann treasure and this man, this leech, this *spy,* was still right behind her! And with the guise of a CIA man to give him respectability. That could be a nuisance. He could be exposed, of course, but that would take time, and all she needed was to visit this Professor Nordberg in the morning and the treasure would be in her hands.

Newkirk had been waiting patiently—all good agents had to learn patience to be successful in their work—but it was approaching dinner time and Newkirk was hungry.

"Well, Dr. McVeigh?"

A thought came. "Mr. Newkirk, may I see your warrant card again, please?"

She was getting ready to spill! "Certainly," Newkirk said courteously—courtesy was always best once a suspect had decided to tell all. He brought out his wallet and handed it over opened to the proper cellophane slot. Ruth took it, extracted the warrant card from its snug little retreat behind its transparent panel as if to examine it better, and then methodically began to tear it into pieces. "Hey!" Newkirk said, outraged. He grabbed at his wallet. "You can't do that!"

"I just did, Mr. Newkirk." Ruth tucked the torn pieces into her bodice and smiled at him pleasantly. "And now, if you don't leave my room at once, I shall call the hotel security staff and ask for assistance."

Newkirk clenched his jaw and came to his feet. He had never seen a more blatant confession of involvement in some nefarious scheme in his entire life! This had to involve something more important than the minor Schliemann affair upon which he had started. This had to involve international intrigue of some sort, because who practically assaulted a CIA man in the performance of his duty for anything less than a major crime? And involving the Russians and the KGB, as witness the presence of that white-haired Ulanov here at the hotel! He was on to something big! Maybe he ought to thank the woman for tearing up his warrant card. It was as good as admitting complicity in something obviously vastly important. How right Wilson had been to insist that he trail the two! But even Wilson, Newkirk suspected, had no idea of how big the case was. Wilson would undoubtedly place his loss of the warrant card in the same category as the loss of the tape recorder, but that was simply because Wilson as yet did not fully comprehend the magnitude of the affair. But they would as soon as he had the complete story, which would be as soon as either Kovpak or McVeigh attempted to make contact with anyone about anything. She obviously had no idea he had been trailing her before. She would have even less in the future!

He walked to the door and turned to look at the girl with the coolness of an agent who is far from intimidated by a mere loss of warrant card. "We shall meet again, Dr. McVeigh."

"I hope not," Ruth said, and watched the door close behind the man. Then she glanced at her watch and hurried into the bathroom to start her tub.

"And what have you been doing since I last saw you, all of an hour ago?" Gregor said, looking at Ruth with admiration over the rim of his cocktail glass.

"Oh, I took a brief nap and then my bath," she said lightly, and shrugged. "Nothing important." There was no need to worry her darling Gregor with the fact that there was a spy from some other museum trying to discover their secret. She had proven she could handle amateurs like this Newkirk without any help. "And you?"

"Oh, I read a bit—rested, you know—and then took my shower." No need to bother his darling Ruth with the fact that he was certain her ploy of using reason on Professor Nordberg would be unsuccessful, and that therefore he had already taken steps to assure proper recovery of the treasure. He raised his glass. "To you, darling."

"To us," she corrected.

"To us," Gregor agreed with a smile.

They clicked their glasses and drank.

22

Professor Arne Nordberg had already changed his clothes twice, although neither change had in any way improved his appearance. He had, at first, put on his best suit and most colorful shirt and cravat. Then, sweating in the heavy heat of the morning and the stuffy apartment, he had decided that comfort was the order of the day. After all, scientists and academicians, like writers and sportsmen, were known for their disregard for fashion. It added to their bohemian image. But the sweater he had pulled on to complement his slacks was badly frayed, and the slacks themselves still had a food stain on them he had tried to remove without success. In desperation he pulled on the pants of his best suit again, promising himself the finest wardrobe known to man once the money for the treasure was in his hands, and was just pulling on his one clean sports shirt when the doorbell rang. He pressed the button releasing the latch on the street door three floors down, tucked in his shirt, slipped his bare feet into a pair of sneakers, and considered himself in the mirror. Not bad, he thought with a smile; a fitting co-author of a paper with Dr. Gregor Kovpak of the famous Hermitage Museum. My Lord, he thought, winking at his image in the glass, how things had changed in a few months!

He hurried to the door and held it open, listening to his

guest coming up the steps, and then frowned slightly as two figures instead of one appeared at the next lower landing, turning the corner to begin the final climb. One of the figures was a woman and as she raised her head to peer up the stairs, Nordberg saw that she was extraordinarily beautiful, and he was glad he had worn the clean shirt and proper pants. His eyes automatically went to the woman's cleavage, and he felt the familiar stirring in his groin. If this was Kovpak's woman, lucky Kovpak! God, to sleep with a woman like that, to run his hands at will over that lush body! He wet his lips at the salacious thought, and then suddenly felt a little shock as he recognized her. It was Dr. Ruth McVeigh of the Metropolitan Museum in New York! Her picture had certainly been in the newspapers often enough during that conference in London! All thoughts of sex disappeared, leaving only the frightening fact that here were Dr. Kovpak and Dr. McVeigh, two people vitally interested in the Schliemann treasure. He had a cold feeling that this meeting had nothing to do with dinosaurs, big or small. Nor did history play much part in it. Still, how could anyone possibly connect him with the Schliemann treasure? There was absolutely no way anyone could know! No, it simply had to be a coincidence that Dr. Kovpak wished to speak with him, and that Dr. McVeigh was along. He forced a smile of welcome onto his lips and ushered his guests into the living room of the apartment, for once more interested in the true reason for this strange visit than in the appearance of the shoddy apartment before important people.

"Dr. Kovpak? And you are Dr. McVeigh. I recognized you from your pictures in the papers. This is a very great honor." He looked from one to the other inquiringly. "Can I get you some coffee?"

"No," Ruth McVeigh said abruptly, and looked at him with open distaste. It was part of her strategy to undermine any strengths the man might have before he could build any defenses. Nordberg's smile froze on his face. There was no doubt that her unfriendly tone, combined with her look of patent dislike meant that this was far from a friendly visit. Then they had to have come to talk about the treasure. But that was impossible! There was absolutely no way they could connect him with the Schliemann gold! Still, he had to find out. He forced himself to shrug politely, as if taking her refusal merely

to mean they already had taken breakfast, and gestured toward
the sofa. Ruth sat down while Gregor moved about the room
looking at the copies of paintings on the wall. Nordberg properly interpreted this to indicate that Ruth McVeigh was the
spokesman, and sat down across from her. He tried to look
insouciant, but his heart was beating rapidly. He glanced over
his shoulder at Gregor Kovpak, still circling the room slowly.

"About that dinosaur you wished to discuss—"

"Let's not waste any time," Ruth said, rudely interrupting
him, and the professor now knew for a certainty that the subject
was the Schliemann treasure. He tried to look at her with polite
inquiry, as if requesting clarification for her desire not to waste
time, for her unfriendly attitude. "And don't look at me as if
you didn't know what I was talking about," she went on,
determined not to ease the pressure on the man for a moment.
"You have the Schliemann treasure and we know it. Your
cousin, Knud Christensen, told us all about it. He found it
while diving and you bought it from him—stole it would be
more accurate—for a thousand kroner. Well?"

Now that his worst fears had been realized, Professor Nordberg forced himself not to panic. Somehow this woman had
located Christensen, God alone knew how, and the stupid oaf
had talked. He had *not* drunk the doctored whiskey! God, why
had he bought something expensive? A cheap aquavit would
have been gone long since, and the talkative dim-witted farmer
with it! Still, it was obvious the two knew nothing of Count
Lindgren and the true location of the treasure. The thought
brought instant sanity. He looked at Ruth McVeigh with a look
of startled incredulity, as if he could not believe his ears.

"I beg your pardon?"

Ruth treated this doubt with the scorn it deserved. "Professor, please do not try to look innocent. You heard me quite
well, and you understood exactly what I was saying. You have
the Schliemann treasure, and if you don't want to spend a good
part of the rest of your life in prison, you'll admit it and we
can go on from there."

Nordberg stared at her with a perplexed frown. "How can
I admit something that isn't true?"

"It's perfectly true and you know it! If you'll simply admit
it, you can stand to gain from it."

Nordberg sighed in frustration. "My dear Dr. McVeigh,

obviously I should like to gain from anything I can, but all this nonsense—if you'll forgive me—about the Schliemann treasure is quite puzzling. I'm afraid you have me at a disadvantage—"

"I have you at a far greater disadvantage than you think," Ruth said flatly. "Let me put it to you in simple words. You have the Schliemann treasure and I mean to have it. I will guarantee you that the Metropolitan Museum will pay you a hundred thousand dollars for it. That's the equivalent of over half a million Danish kroner. If you accept my offer, I will see that you are paid in cash and that nobody beyond the three of us in this room will ever hear of it. If you refuse, then I'll have no choice but to go to the authorities and see that you are arrested. Not only for attempted extortion—because that's all this auction of yours amounts to—but also for failing to report the discovery and possession of a treasure found in Danish waters. Sovereign states frown on that sort of silence. So," Ruth finished evenly, "not only will you lose the hundred thousand dollars, the half million kroner, but you'll have a long time in prison in which to remember how foolish you were to refuse."

Nordberg had been listening to all this with a look of total disbelief on his pudgy face.

"You look like Dr. McVeigh," he said slowly, almost as if he were speaking to himself, "or at least like the newspaper photographs of her, which is possibly what turned your head. Whoever you are, you're a sick woman." He raised his voice slightly, as if now admitting the woman into the conversation. "Madame, I have no idea of what you are speaking. Of course I have heard of the Schliemann treasure and the fact that it is being auctioned off by someone—who in the world has not? But the idea that that person would be me, is absurd. It's laughable." He shook his head in amazement that any sane person could entertain such a ludicrous thought, and then obviously decided that he had had enough of this tiresome person. "I think it would be better if you were to leave—"

Ruth looked at him triumphantly. "And how do you explain Knud Christensen and the story he told us?"

"Ah, yes. The story Knud Christensen told you. I never met my cousin Knud Christensen in my life. Our mothers were distant cousins and we know each other by name. That is all.

I have no idea what story he told you. I have no idea whether he enjoys making up stories or whether the man is mad. I don't know him at all. But whatever story he told you, if it involved me in any sense, is false."

He came to his feet and moved to the front door of the apartment, obviously with the intent of opening it and politely asking his guests to leave, but Ruth remained where she was.

"Knud Christensen said his brother had drowned and he was diving for the body—"

"Madame, I'm sorry his brother drowned, if in fact he did and Christensen did not also invent that story, but I fail to see—"

"He said he was diving for his brother's body last January, and—"

"He was diving in January?" Nordberg looked amused. "Where? In Capri?"

"Off the Gedser lighthouse—"

Nordberg's amused look disappeared; he threw up his hands. "Please! This insanity must end! The waters off Gedser lighthouse would kill any man diving in them in January in minutes! I have no idea at all what your purpose was in coming here with this ridiculous story, madame, but I have had more than enough of it! You will please either leave or I shall have to call the police!" He swung the door open and waited.

Ruth stared at him, fuming. The fact that the man's actions, even his final words, had duplicated Gregor's predictions almost to the letter, did nothing to lessen her frustration. Gregor dropped his inspection of the inferior copies that decorated the apartment walls and walked over, standing over Ruth and looking down at her.

"I believe the professor is well within his rights, Ruth," he said quietly. "I tried to tell you before that you had no proof of your charge, but you insisted upon coming here with me. Why don't you go back to the hotel and wait for me? I won't be long. I should like to speak to Professor Nordberg a few moments on the subject I came to discuss with him, before you insisted upon using my introduction to the professor to accompany me here and make your—well, rather impolitic accusation—"

Ruth opened her mouth to retort, and then remembered her promise. She held little hope for Gregor's success, but she had given her word to let him try if she failed. Still, after Gregor had also failed, as she was sure he would, she fully intended to take the matter up with the authorities. She was sure that the Metropolitan could make some deal with the Danish government—especially with the influence of Count Lindgren—that would allow her to return to the Metropolitan with the treasure. The deal undoubtedly would cost more than the hundred thousand dollars that idiot, Nordberg, was refusing by pretending he didn't know what she was talking about, but the deal undoubtedly would also be far less than the fifteen million dollars the idiot, Nordberg, still thought he could realize from his auction. She came to her feet.

"Don't do anything foolish, darling," she said under her breath, and walked through the door Nordberg was holding open without a glance at him. They could hear her footsteps on the stairs and a few moments later the sound of the outer door of the building being slammed, as if in anger.

Nordberg closed the apartment door. It was with an effort that he refrained from wiping his brow in relief at having at least avoided any damaging statements. He turned to Kovpak, keeping his look of bewilderment, thinking that Count Lindgren would have been proud of his acting ability, at how well he had handled the difficult situation.

"I can't imagine where the woman ever got such an odd idea—"

"Oh, I can," Gregor said cheerfully.

"What?" This time Nordberg's bewilderment was quite genuine.

"I said, I can," Kovpak said and took the professor lightly by the arm. "Why don't you sit down, Professor, and let me explain this entire affair to you? I think I can make you understand."

He almost lowered a startled Nordberg to the sofa Ruth had so recently abandoned, and then took a chair and pulled it close to the paunchy and puzzled man. Gregor sat down and considered the professor benignly.

"You see, Professor," he said in a friendly tone which invited the other man to try and understand his point of view, "my disagreement with Dr. McVeigh was not on her facts, nor her conclusions, but on her methods. If I gave you any other impression, I'm sorry." Nordberg was staring at him half-hypnotized. He was just beginning to realize he had avoided the pendulum only to face the pit. He made a move to rise.

"You came here under false pretenses. I'll call the police—"

Gregor pushed him down, but did it very gently. "Please, Professor. I'm speaking and it's not polite to interrupt. When I am finished you can call the police if you still wish to, but in the meantime please do me the kindness of sitting quietly and listening to me, and you needn't waste time with me trying to think up denials, because quite sincerely I hope for your sake you really do have the treasure."

"For—for my sake?"

"Exactly." Gregor beamed at him, as a teacher might smile proudly at a pupil who exhibited quickness in seeing an answer. "You see, I know you have the treasure. I am quite sure, however, that you would never release it on the mere threat of prosecution by the authorities. Why should you? The proof that you have it is tenuous in the extreme, and the treasure is undoubtedly very well hidden, so that discovery of it must certainly be difficult, if not impossible. And Knud Christensen's story would never be enough, coming from a man shattered by the death of his remaining family, to convince the most sanguine jury. No, I am sure that Dr. McVeigh's threats did not bother you greatly. However"—Gregor's smiling face and suddenly raised finger asked the professor to pay even closer attention at this moment—"I believe that under modern and tested methods of interrogation, you would be more than willing to co-operate and tell us exactly where you have this treasure hidden."

Nordberg's lips were white. "But I tell you, I don't have—"

"You don't have the treasure?" Gregor's smile disappeared. He looked sad. "That would be a pity. You see, Professor, that's what I meant before when I said I hoped you had the treasure for your sake, because how can you confess you have it and tell us where it is if you really don't have it? You will suffer—that is, undergo the interrogation—for nothing, until it is too late, I'm afraid. And we will have wasted our time, although that, of course, would be no concern of yours."

Nordberg was staring. Sweat was pouring from him. "Are you—are you really Dr. Gregor Kovpak?"

"I am. Would you care to see my Hermitage pass?" Gregor

drew out his wallet and offered it to Nordberg, opened at the proper place. "It isn't a very good picture, but I suppose I'm not the best subject." He tucked the wallet back into his pocket. "The cut on my cheek, of course, doesn't help."

"You—you are a noted scientist and you're threatening to—to torture me?"

"The word I used was interrogate," Kovpak said chidingly. "And I certainly wouldn't conduct the interrogation. I'm a scientist, as you say. I would probably botch the whole thing due to my lack of experience, and lose you before—" He seemed to notice that his words were disturbing the professor and he continued a bit apologetically, as if necessary for the professor's complete understanding. "There is in Copenhagen at this moment a man from one of our Russian organizations known as the KGB. You've heard of it? Then you know. He is trained in this sort of thing. I am not. He could probably make you last for days. I'd be lucky if you didn't die on me in a matter of hours." He shrugged humorously at this admission of his own incompetence, and then suddenly changed his entire attitude; his very appearance seemed to change. "This man will do what I tell him, and I will tell him you know where the Schliemann treasure is, and that I want to know. He will get that information from you. I may or may not watch him work. I understand his methods are quite unsavory, and while I do not have a weak stomach, there are limits to everything."

He came to his feet, towering over the shaken professor.

"I will give you until noon today to decide if it is really necessary to go to such extreme limits. I know someone who wants that treasure, and that person is going to get it. You certainly will not stand in the way. I am at the Plaza Hotel. I shall expect to hear from you by noon. If not, you will be in the hands of the KGB by twelve-thirty, and calling the police will not help you. There is no escape, Professor. There is no escape!"

He walked to the door, turned to give the professor one last cold look, and left, closing the door firmly behind him. That done he hurried down the steps. At the front door of the building he paused to wedge the latch to save time in case he later had to leave and return, and then went down to the basement.

In the apartment he had left a very shaken Arne Nordberg. The professor suddenly shivered. This one was the very devil!

Those black unblinking eyes, that black hair, twisted almost like horns! That bandage, obviously hiding a sinister scar! There was no doubt the man meant every word of his threat.

Even if he told them that the treasure was at Lindgren Castle, they would never believe him, especially if the count should deny it. And why should the count not deny it? What did a man in the position of Count Lindgren have to gain by allowing himself to get involved in affairs as sinister as these? It was one thing to expect the count to handle the auction of the treasure merely as an entertainment. It was quite another to expect the count to jeopardize his position even if the alternative was the life of a mere professor of history. And if the count denied the story, as he was bound to, then nobody would believe him, and he would die.

Far better that he accept the hundred thousand dollars to give up the treasure. Certainly the count would not object to that. After all, he was just in it for sport. If he, Nordberg, wanted to give up a fortune to save his own life, certainly his good friend Count Axel Lindgren would only applaud the decision.

Still, the thought of taking a mere hundred thousand dollars when he had had his appetite whetted with thoughts of at least fifteen million, was galling. It was worse than galling, it was sickening! Certainly there had to be some means of avoiding the threatened torture, and to stay with the auction Count Lindgren had planned. There *had* to be! Only he could not think of it . . . The thing to do, he suddenly realized, was the same thing he had been clever enough to do when the question of disposing of the treasure first presented itself—ask the advice of Count Lindgren. The count might well come up with an answer where he, himself, could not.

The decision to telephone the count and tell him everything brought a certain calmness to Nordberg. He came to his feet and walked a bit unsteadily to the telephone, raised the receiver, and dialed the familiar number. But before the telephone at the other end had a chance to ring more than twice there was a heavy knock on the apartment door. Nordberg frowned blackly. Who could that be? A neighbor? But Nordberg's neighbors never bothered him. That devil Kovpak, back so soon with further demands? But what further demands could he possibly make? The heavy knock on the door was repeated. With a

muttered curse for making him postpone his call, Nordberg put
the receiver back on the hook and walked over to open the
door.

In the basement of the apartment Kovpak stood and watched
as Ulanov and another man listened patiently to their headsets.
Suddenly Ulanov looked up. He winked at Gregor. "He's di-
aling . . ." He closed his eyes as if to listen better and then
opened them to scribble some numbers on a pad. He showed
them to the large blond man who read them and nodded. Ulanov
put his attention back to his headset and then looked up, frowning. "He hung up without waiting for his call to be answered."

"Maybe he decided to go to the man instead of calling him,"
Kovpak said. "I'd better get out to my car. " A thought came;
he smiled sheepishly. "I don't even know what he's driving."

"Fortunately, we thought it might be well to know," Ulanov
said dryly. "He's driving a yellow Volvo, at least ten years
old. It's parked a block down the street, pointing north. You
can't miss it. The door on the driver's side, the street side, is
caved in and the whole thing looks as if it's being held together
with spit." He held up his hand before Kovpak could spring
for the steps. "But there's no need to rush. I have a man outside
who'll advise us when your professor leaves the apartment.
And the professor'll have a little trouble starting his car." He
grinned. "Not too much, just enough to hold him up until we
can pick him up. A loose electrical connection even he can't
miss if he has enough brains to take a look at the motor." He
returned to listening to the telephone. "Maybe he had to go to
the bathroom . : ."

The minutes passed with Ulanov wishing he could smoke
but knowing that the odor could testify to the presence of men
in the basement, and with Kovpak getting more and more
restless. Suddenly Kovpak looked up with a frown. "Major,
did you get the number he dialed?"

"Of course." Ulanov pointed to the pad.

"How long would it take to find an address for that number?
Or a name?"

Ulanov looked inquiringly at the large blond man with him.
The man considered the question a moment and then shrugged.
"Maybe half an hour." He put aside his headset without being

told, reading his orders from Ulanov's nod, and left the basement.

The two men remaining there continued their vigil. Kovpak found a couple of empty crates and dragged them over; Ulanov nodded his thanks and sat down. Kovpak slipped on the headset abandoned by the blond man. The silence continued. After fifteen more minutes Ulanov looked over at Kovpak.

"You couldn't have put much of a scare into the man," he said mildly. "Maybe I'd better go up and finish the job."

"I put enough of a scare into him," Kovpak said with a touch of irritation. "I have no idea why he isn't calling someone! Or isn't rushing to that someone right now! I don't like this..."

"Well, we'll have an address and a name in a few more minutes," Ulanov said commiseratingly.

"If you got the number right."

"If you had done your simple job as well as I do my more complicated ones," Ulanov said evenly, "we wouldn't be sitting here like a couple of dolts waiting for a telephone call it seems he isn't going to make."

"Maybe he left by the back way..."

"Maybe he went up in a balloon from the roof," Ulanov said in an unkind tone. "Or is tunneling from the third floor to the third floor of a building in the next street. Do you think you're the only person who ever heard of a back door to an apartment building? Or of having it watched?"

Gregor bit back a retort. Arguing with Ulanov wasn't going to help. And while he had been positive that Professor Nordberg had been frightened half out of his skin, the fact was that Nordberg was neither leaving nor telephoning. He was probably having a belated breakfast and laughing to himself at the puerile attempts to frighten him. Or possibly he was entertaining a woman visitor who had arrived in the past half hour. The way he looked at Ruth when she was coming up the stairs indicated he was a man who might even put a willing woman ahead of the treasure—although that seemed most unlikely. Kovpak checked his watch and muttered a curse under his breath. Where the devil was that blond genius of an assistant of Ulanov who could trace a telephone number to a name in half an hour? More than that had already passed. He probably could have done as well by simply running his finger down the list of all telephone subscribers in the country in that length of time. He checked his watch once again and made a decision. He put his headset aside, coming to his feet.

"I'll be back in a few minutes," he said quietly. "I'm going upstairs and ask our sleazy friend just why he isn't doing what he should be doing." His voice toughened. "He'll tell me, too, or else—"

Ulanov shrugged. "Or else he won't. You're talking about a lot of money, my friend. It induces silence more than physical threats." The stocky major watched his companion climb the basement steps and disappear through the door leading to the lobby. Gregor Kovpak, he decided with a sigh, did not have the proper temperament to be a successful intelligence agent. He lacked the patience for it. Although one would think that an archaeologist, working years and years on some excavation just to emerge triumphant with a few shards of pottery, or a few dessicated bones, would have the patience of Job. But it was a different type of patience, Ulanov decided, and recalled when he was a young agent and was assigned to continously stare from a window at a blank wall, simply waiting for a certain person to place a poster on it. Nobody ever did, and all he got from Vashugin when he reported had been a grunt. Still, possibly a grunt was all that particular vigil had been worth.

The minutes passed with Ulanov missing tobacco; the silence at the other end of the tapped line was beginning to make him sleepy. Then his head jerked up, alert. There had been a sound at the head of the basement steps and Ulanov assumed the attitude of a faithful member of the Danish Telephone Service, only to look and see Kovpak returning. The major looked at him inquiringly. "Well?"

"He didn't answer the door."

Major Ulanov looked at him curiously. "It took you that long to discover he didn't answer the door?"

"I went up and rapped on the door; nobody answered. I thought he might be in an inner room where he couldn't hear me knock, so I went down to the street and rang his door bell. He never answered. So then I went back upstairs and rapped on the door again—"

"And nobody answered. I heard you." The major considered his younger friend carefully. "Or else he didn't tell you what you wanted to know despite your 'or else'..."

Kovpak's face flushed. "I said he didn't answer the door!"

"If you say so, I believe you. Maybe he thought you were selling magazine subscriptions..."

There was a shadow on the steps and the blond man appeared, panting a bit and looking apologetic for the delay.

"It took longer than I thought," he said, "but here it is. The call was made to a place called Lindgren Castle. A Count Axel Lindgren lives there. It's in Ringsted. Of course, the call may have been to someone else in the household," he added, "but that is the address the call was placed to."

"Lindgren!" Gregor stared but only for a moment, then his jaw hardened. "That accident was no accident! That murdering bastard!" He stared at Ulanov, not seeing him, speaking aloud but to himself. "It makes sense when you think about it. He's important enough to have the necessary contacts throughout the world. He had the money needed to finance the operation, and he has the charm"—he smiled grimly at the use of the word—"the charm! to get a little nobody like Nordberg to hand the treasure over to him. I'm surprised Nordberg stayed alive as long as he did..."

Ulanov had been listening to this stream of consciousness politely. Now he felt he ought to speed things up. "I don't know who this Count Lindgren is, other than the fact that you don't seem to like him," he said, "but if you believe he's the one with the treasure, shouldn't we be on our way to visit him?"

"We certainly should. Let's go!"

Ulanov slipped off his headset and started to hand it to the blond man. Then he looked at Gregor, his face inscrutable. "Is there any purpose in continuing to monitor his telephone?"

"I don't think so."

"I didn't think you did," Ulanov said enigmatically, and gave instructions to the blond man. "Pack up and go home. You can leave Boris in front in case anyone comes and rings the professor's bell. Nikolai can go back with you. Reports go to the office." Ulanov turned to Gregor. "Let's go."

They climbed the steps, Gregor seething at the thought of Count Lindgren and how close he had come, through his man Wilten, in killing both himself and Ruth. He removed the wedge in the latch and unconsciously glanced up the stairway, almost

as if he could see the third-floor apartment. Then without a
word he walked quickly out to the car. Ulanov started to say
something and then thought better of it. Instead he climbed
into the car and lit a cigarette, inhaling blissfully, while studying the other's expressionless profile. Gregor paid him no mind,
studying a map of the small country's highway's a moment,
and then putting the car into motion. "We'll check for Lindgren
Castle when we get near Ringsted," he said evenly. The white-
haired major merely nodded.

They passed the ten-year-old yellow Volvo down the street
and turned into the Farimagsgade, beginning to work their way
south through the city toward the Vestergade and the road west
into the open country. Behind them James Newkirk was pleased
to see them moving at last. He had sat in his car in the hot
morning sun for over an hour, and the breeze brought on as
he drove was very welcome. At this point in the chase, Newkirk
did not particularly care if the car ahead knew he was following
them. He had no idea of what Kovpak and Ulanov had been
doing in that apartment building, but there was no doubt something was up and James Newkirk meant to know what that
something was. He had picked Ulanov up at the Russian Embassy in the Bredgade early that morning, knowing he would
stay there. He had seen him depart with three other men in
some sort of a utility truck, and had followed them to this
location. Here he had observed Ruth McVeigh and Gregor
Kovpak arrive and watched Ruth McVeigh depart alone, leaving the Russians inside. With all the characters of the drama
assembled, there was no doubt things were coming to a conclusion, and Newkirk was not to be put off from being in on
it.

Kovpak crossed the Pile Allee and entered the Roskildeveg,
heading toward the Roskilde and the turnoff to Ringsted, when
he glanced in the rearview mirror for the fourth or fifth time.
He spoke to Ulanov without turning his head.

"We're being followed!"

"Oh?" Ulanov turned to look over his shoulder and then
turned back, spewing smoke from his cigarette. "That's just
Newkirk." He bit back a yawn. He had slept poorly the night
before; he was getting too old for strange beds. And he had
had to get up early to place the bug on the professor's phone.
Maybe he ought to ask for retirement—and then he thought

that if he had any trouble on this case, any further trouble that is, he might not have to ask for retirement. It was a sad thought.

"Newkirk?" Gregor asked, mystified by the strange name.

"That CIA agent I told you about in London. Don't pay any attention to him."

Kovpak swung around, staring at Ulanov in disbelief. *"You mean he's been following us since London?"*

"No, no!" The major shook his head, dislodging ash which sprinkled his jacket. *"I've* been following you. He's been following me. Then in Germany I lost you but found him. Then when I wanted to find you I let him do it for me. Then I followed him." He shrugged. "Now he's following both of us. It isn't important."

Kovpak drew a deep breath and shook his head. "It doesn't make any sense."

"No," Ulanov said in a tired tone, agreeing. "It doesn't." He flipped his cigarette through the car window and leaned back, closing his eyes. "Try not to use the horn too much. I'm going to take a nap before we get there..."

23

Count Lindgren was in a foul mood, and the staff was well aware of it. Wilten had somehow gotten himself in the count's poor graces, and everyone suffered under those circumstances. François, cooking and serving the count's late breakfast on the terrace of Lindgren Castle, recognized that this was not time to scamp on his skills for any reason, or to make any untoward remarks on any subject. François had outdone himself on the blueberry crêpe. The count was chewing on it as if it were a mere pancake, and the chef was waiting until the precise moment to put the finishing touches on the next dish, an *omelette flambé a fine herbes Marseilles*. But as he delicately slid the *omelette* to a warmed plate and carried it proudly toward the table, he saw with dismay that Wilten, a subdued Wilten this morning, was approaching with a telephone, trailing cord behind him. Any delay in eating the *omelette*, François knew, and the dish would be ruined, and *le bon Dieu* alone knew what the count's mood would be then! A difficult man, François thought, and then saw to his dismay that the count was putting down his knife and fork and looking at Wilten. To the chef it was evident that whatever rift had developed between the master and Wilten had still not been mended. Lindgren was considering Wilten as if the other man were a stranger.

"There is a person at the other end of the line this time, I hope?"

Wilten swallowed. "Yes, sir. It's—it's that McVeigh woman..."

Lindgren stared at him a moment and then took the telephone from him, cupping the receiver while he wondered just what Ruth McVeigh might have to say. Would it be about the accident? But she had called the day before, explaining how it had not been Wilten's fault. Not Wilten's fault! Lindgren put down the taste of bile that had come to his throat at the thought, and tried to imagine what Ruth could be calling about, and just what he might say in return. Count Lindgren had spent a sleepless night alternately cursing Wilten and his failure and wondering if there was now any way in which to avoid disaster. Certainly two accidents in a row could be as bad as none. He was not dealing with complete idiots. There was, of course, the faint possibility that they had *not* traced the treasure to Nordberg; or that if they had, the brainless professor might have had enough of a spurt of intelligence to keep his big mouth shut! Well, there was only one way to find out...

He forced a smile into his voice. "Hello, Ruth! How good to hear from you! How are you?" His voice dropped. "I'm so sorry about yesterday—!"

"No, forget that. Axel, I'm worried!"

"My dear girl, what about?"

"It's Gregor," Ruth said. She sounded desperate. "I don't know where he is. We were at this man's apartment—"

Axel Lindgren felt a sudden chill. "Whose apartment?"

Ruth might not have heard him; her mind was on her story. "—and Gregor said he wanted to talk to him alone for a few minutes and would I go back to the hotel and wait for him, so I did, but Gregor never came back. I waited almost an hour and then I went back to the apartment, only this time nobody even answered the bell, and I'm afraid Gregor might have used force, and—"

"Ruth!"

"—if he did, I wonder—"

"*Ruth!*"

"I'm sorry, Axel. What is it?"

"I asked, *whose apartment?*"

"You wouldn't know him. His name is Arne Nordberg. He's

a professor at the university. It's a long story—"

"Ruth, hold on a moment." Count Lindgren cupped the receiver in one damp palm and thought furiously. Panic at this point could be fatal. Damn Wilten for failing to handle the two of them the day before, and double damn that fool Nordberg! First for lying about where he had gotten the treasure; secondly because he had undoubtedly done exactly what Kovpak had calculated the idiot would do when threatened, and that was to run to his protector, his savior, his friend, Axel Lindgren! And with Kovpak undoubtedly right behind him! There was no time to lose. He went back to the telephone. "Ruth—"

"Yes?"

"Stay in your room at the hotel and wait to hear from me. I'll be back to you as soon as I can."

"All right, Axel. But, hurry—!"

"I'll hurry," Lindgren said with grim sincerity, and hung up abruptly. He would have to find some excuse for having suddenly left the country without calling Ruth back, but at the moment that was the least of his worries. Escape came first. He came to his feet swiftly. "Wilten!"

"Sir?"

"Call Kastrup Airport. I want the first flight out on any line, to Rome, Amsterdam, London, Paris, Madrid—anyplace not in the eastern zone. Understand? I'll check the lines for the one you arrange when I get there." His tone also indicated that Wilten had better not foul up on this assignment if he knew what was good for him.

Wilton got the message. "Right away, sir."

"If anyone calls or drops in, tell them I've just gone for a short drive and should be returning shortly. Tell them they can wait if they wish." That should give him extra time.

"Yes, sir."

"And take care of things while I'm gone. I'll be in touch when I can." Count Lindgren dropped his napkin, until now held in rigid fingers, and hurried into the castle. The steps to his study were taken two at a time; a suitcase taken from a shelf over the wardrobe. The cabinet containing the treasure was opened and the treasure hastily stuffed into the suitcase. With the suitcase held rigidly in one hand, the count trotted down the steps, going at a fast walk to the stables, four of whose stalls had been requisitioned for his cars. He selected the fastest, a Ferrari open-topped two-seater, tossed the suitcase in the narrow space behind the driver's seat, and climbed in. He started the motor, allowing it to warm up for maximum performance later. Damn that bloody fool, Nordberg! Damn Wilten! Damn them all!

With a curse, Count Lindgren brought his mind back to his newly and instantly formed plan. He would go south a few miles and then cut over on a secondary road to the Vordingborg-Copenhagen road, and across to Amager and Kastrup Airport from the south; Nordberg and Kovpak undoubtedly would be taking the Copenhagen-Roskilde-Ringsted route, and this way he would avoid passing them. He took one final glance at the suitcase wedged behind him, as if to reassure himself he actually had the treasure, then he gunned the motor and roared from the stable down the curved road that twisted its way through the parklands of Lindgren Castle.

Despite his hurry, Kovpak had to stop twice to ask directions. Both times Newkirk had parked on the shoulder of the highway a few yards behind him, his engine pulsing gently, waiting patiently with a smile on his face as he noted the care with which neither man in the car ahead paid him the slightest attention. As Kovpak pulled away from the gasoline station where he had made his final inquiry, Newkirk started up as well, bringing his car up to speed to keep up with the man ahead. Kovpak jammed the gas pedal down and glared at Ulanov.

"Are we going to let that whatever-his-name-is stay ten feet behind us all the way to the front door of the castle? And listen in to everything I've got to say to that bastard, Count Lindgren, which will be plenty?"

Ulanov shrugged. He could not imagine exactly why Gregor Kovpak was so irked with this unknown count, but at least it promised for an interesting interview. And as for the car behind them—"His name is Newkirk," Ulanov said. "And I told you before, don't worry about him."

"Don't worry about him? That's ridiculous!"

"Possibly," Ulanov said equably. "What would you suggest I do? Go back and politely ask him to go home?"

"I don't know, but there must be something you can do!"

"When it occurs to me, I'll do it," Ulanov promised. "Better slow down. That must be the castle gate there." He started to lean back as Gregor braked to swing into the castle grounds, and then suddenly shot forward, pointing. *"Look out!"*

A maniac in a small roadster had come shooting around the final curve of the wooded parkland drive and was heading directly for them. Gregor swung the wheel of his car as hard as he could, stepping down on the accelerator in the hope that he might clear the roadway before the small open-topped car crashed into them. The driver of the roadster saw their car at the same time and tried desperately to avoid a collision by hitting his brakes to attempt to swing around the other car, which was still not clear of the Ferrari's projectilelike path. The roadster skidded wildly under the sudden application of the brakes at that speed. It bounced off the side of a tree; one wheel struck a rock and blew, completing the disaster. Now completely out of control, the small roadster shot erratically back across the road and crashed head-on into one of the huge stone piers that anchored the open gate. It bounced back several feet and remained there, leaning to one side like a weary animal at the end of its strength, steam spouting from its crushed radiator, dust swirling up from the torn gravel. The driver of the small Ferrari had been thrown violently forward by the impact, crushing the steering wheel, and now lay as if sleeping peacefully, his head to one side against the shattered dashboard, the column of the splintered steering wheel protruding bloodily from his back.

Gregor had braked his car with all his force once he had cleared the roadway, bringing his car to a shuddering halt, swaying, its front bumper only inches from one of the huge parkland trees. For a moment he sat there, his hands shaking at the nearness of their escape. Then he and Ulanov were out of the car, running over to see if there was anything that could be done for the driver of the roadster, but they stopped at the side of the car. It was evident the count had died almost instantly. Despite his hatred of the man, and the fact that Count Lindgren had tried to have Ruth and him killed the day before, the horrifying death the count had suffered seemed to more than pay for his crimes. He looked at Ulanov. "That's Count Lindgren."

"Who was going somewhere in a very great hurry," Ulanov said dryly. He had seen death too many times, in far more horrifying guises, to be greatly affected by the other man's death. He moved closer to the car, studying the interior, and then reached down, dragging the suitcase from its wedged position back of the twisted seat. He laid it on the ground and opened it, unwrapping the top bundle, looking up. "Would this be the treasure you've been talking so much about?"

Kovpak crouched beside him, trying to forget the gruesome sight of the count impaled on the steering wheel shaft. "Yes..." Behind them Newkirk came hurrying up. He stared with wide eyes first at the dead man in the car and then down at the open suitcase. Ulanov paid him no heed, but closed the suitcase and came to his feet. He handed the suitcase to Kovpak who had also risen.

"You'd better get in the car and get going," Ulanov said evenly. "It just occurred to me what can be done about that Newkirk person you worry so much about."

Newkirk smiled coldly. He seemed to be enjoying himself. "I don't know what you think you can do about that Newkirk person," he said, "but this isn't East Berlin. I owe you for that, Ulanov!"

"You owe me for lots of things," Ulanov said, and glared at Kovpak. "I said, get moving!"

Kovpak hesitated. He could scarcely leave a smaller Ulanov to take a beating from Newkirk, but the fact was he had the Schliemann treasure in his hand, and in a very few minutes the place would be swarming with both curiosity seekers as well as police, all drawn by the spectacular accident. And anyone around—especially with one of Count Lindgren's initialed suitcases in his hand—would have a great many questions to answer. The faint sound of a distant siren convinced him. Without another word he ran for his car. Newkirk made a move after him, but Ulanov threw himself around the taller man's legs, bringing him down, holding him tightly by the ankles as Kovpak jumped into the car and started back toward Copenhagen.

Newkirk kicked himself loose and started for his own car, but again Ulanov brought him down with a tackle. Newkirk stared at the other car, disappearing up the road, and knew he could never catch it. Still, there was something he could do that he had wanted to do for a long time. He came to his feet, his face white, and reached up, taking off his glasses and putting them away. "I'm going to beat you to a pulp, Ulanov," he said heavily. "For East Berlin——"

"Wait a minute," Ulanov said hastily, holding up a conciliatory hand. "If I'm not mistaken, your assignment was to discover who had the Schliemann treasure, and why they were auctioning it off, wasn't it? I can tell you quite frankly that that was my assignment."

Newkirk paused, his fist drawn back, uncertain as to the other man's motives in telling him all this. "What are you driving at?"

"Just this," Ulanov said, wasting time until Kovpak was well on his way and until the police could arrive and prevent him from being battered to bits, "I know that you people have always thought that we Russians had the Schliemann treasure. Well, we were always sure that you had stolen it from us. We wanted to know if you were auctioning off the treasure, why you were doing so; if someone else was auctioning it off, how they had breached your security to get their hands on it. I can only assume, since you thought we had it, that your assignment was the same. Now that we both know and can prove that neither one of us had it"—he shrugged—"well, we've completed our assignments successfully, haven't we?"

Newkirk frowned as he considered this in detail. Then his fist slowly opened, his arm dropped. The little old Russian major of the KGB was quite correct. He, Newkirk, was now in a position to demonstrate that Russian security had not been breached, and that therefore the KGB would not go about changing their systems which the CIA was on the verge of solving. Not bad for a lowly stringer! That credit alone could bring him advancement, even possibly a change to the New York *Times*. Paris was not the same since they started to put up all those skyscrapers. Looking at it in that light, this Ulanov deserved a pat on the back, not a beating, for pointing out the possible advantages of his position. Newkirk smiled at Ulanov sheepishly and held out his hand.

"I'm sorry. You're quite right."

"That's all right," Ulanov said magnanimously as he shook hands, and then, in the new spirit of friendship that had been aroused, he added, "By the way, you recall that small tape recorder you carried in that book in London? I don't suppose you happen to have any spare tapes?"

Newkirk stared at the small man a moment, speechless, and then plowed in, swinging, just as the first police car came roaring up, siren screaming.

An hour had passed since Ruth's call to Count Lindgren, and she was feeling more abandoned by the minute. She was also more worried. Her calls to Gregor's room continued to go unanswered, there had been no message for her at the desk which she checked every five minutes, and her calls to Nordberg's apartment were equally unproductive. She was about to telephone the Lindgren Castle for a second time, when there was a sharp rap on the door. She hurried over, her heart beating faster, hoping against hope it was Gregor, or at least Axel Lindgren, but when she opened the door the man facing her was a complete stranger. He was a large, heavily muscled man with a balding head, and despite the heat of the day he was dressed in a heavy tweed suit complete with vest. He was considering her politely.

"Dr. McVeigh?"

Ruth frowned. "Yes?"

"My name is Ib Rodhe. I am an inspector of police." He brought out his identification and presented it, and then neatly put it away before continuing. "May I come in?"

"Of course." Ruth led the way, closing the door after the man. Her heart was pounding; she had a premonition of disaster. She turned to face the large moon-faced man who was looking at the two chairs in the room in the manner of a person deciding which one he wished to buy. "Something's happened to Gregor, hasn't it?"

"Gregor?" The inspector finally made his selection and sank into it. It was obvious from the slight frown on his face that the name Gregor meant nothing to him. He put the matter aside to pursue the more important one that had brought him there. "Dr. McVeigh, I understand you placed a telephone call to Lindgren Castle a little over an hour ago. Is that correct?"

Ruth frowned. This was not what she had feared the police were here for. "Yes, I did. Why?"

"Count Lindgren was killed in an automobile accident only moments later. I was wondering—"

Ruth was staring at him in shock. *"Axel Lindgren is dead?"*

"Yes, ma'am. He died instantly, if that is any consolation. Now, about your call—"

"It's my fault," Ruth said miserably. "He was hurrying to get here . . ."

"No, ma'am. According to the butler, Wilten—the one who informed us of your call—Count Lindgren was on his way to the airport—"

"The *airport!* But that's impossible!"

"I'm afraid not, ma'am. I have known men like this butler, Wilten, before. While his master was alive I have no doubt that Wilten would have lied for him. But with his master dead, there was no reason for him to do anything but give us as much of the truth as he knew. I have no doubt at all that Wilten's statements are correct in every detail. Wilten said—" The inspector took a notebook from his pocket, flipped it to the page he wanted, and nodded in satisfaction. "Here we are. Wilten's exact words, ma'am. He said, 'Count Lindgren received a call from Dr. McVeigh, an American lady, at about ten-thirty o'clock. I do not know what the conversation consisted of, but when it was over Count Lindgren seemed unusually perturbed. He instructed me to call the airport and to arrange a ticket for him on the first flight out of the country to anyplace except Russia or the eastern countries. He mentioned Rome or Amsterdam or Paris or London—'"

"*What?*" Ruth was looking at him with unbelieving eyes.

The inspector returned her look apologetically. "I am only repeating Wilten's words, ma'am. He then said, and I quote," the inspector said, looking back at his notebook, " 'Count Lindgren then hurried upstairs to his study. When he came down he had a suitcase.' The inspector's eyes came up. "I asked Wilten if, which seemed logical, the suitcase contained clothing for the count's trip. He said—" The inspector went back to his notebook. "He said, quite as if I'd insulted him, 'Sir, *I* pack for Count Lindgren! When I saw him descend with a suitcase and leave the castle, I immediately checked his wardrobe. He had taken no clothes with him.'"

Ruth had been listening without a great deal of attention. Axel Lindgren dead! Gregor missing! But why was Axel going to the airport when he had told her to wait for him at the hotel? She became aware that the inspector was continuing to read from his notebook.

"So I asked him, if the suitcase hadn't contained clothes, what it might have contained, and he said, 'I surmise, sir, it was something that Professor Nordberg brought to the castle a few days ago. They were both quite protective, even secretive about it.'"

Ruth had been standing, looking down at the inspector incredulously. Now she sank to the bed, her knees suddenly weak, her mind trying to comprehend what she had heard. Professor Nordberg had brought something to Lindgren Castle, and after her call Axel Lindgren had taken something—undoubtedly the same something and equally undoubtedly the Schliemann treasure—and in attempting to leave the country with it, had been killed. In a way it *had* been her fault, not for asking him to come and help her, but in giving him the whole story, in threatening him—although she had not known it. Poor Axel! How like him to see in the treasure a means of getting a huge sum of money with which to continue his normal, extravagant, flirting ways! And now he was gone! It seemed odd to think of anyone as vibrant, as alive, as—well, as selfish—as Axel Lindgren being dead. She became aware that the inspector had been speaking to her.

"About your telephone call, ma'am—"

Something suddenly occurred to Ruth that was far more important than her telephone call. "Then the police have this suitcase?"

"No, ma'am. There was no suitcase in the car. There were two men there beginning to fight furiously when the police arrived," he said, recalling the reports. "One of them was a Russian and the other an American. It was lucky for the Russian the police got there when they did—"

"Gregor!"

The inspector wondered a bit at this constant reference to the unknown Gregor. He also seemed sad to be constantly forced to contradict the lady. "No, ma'am," he said, and referred to his notes once again. "One was named James Newkirk, who claims to be a reporter for a Paris newspaper. The other was named Serge Ulanov. He says he's an assistant curator at the Hermitage Musuem. They won't talk, at least not yet, but we have them both in custody," the inspector added in a tone of satisfaction, as if in his opinion any fighting done in his bailiwick should be done by natives. He came back to the subject that had brought him there. "Now, about your call, ma'am—"

"It's a long story," Ruth said wearily, and repeated the entire history of their locating the treasure and following it with their visit to Nordberg. "But it looks as if we were wrong," she ended. "It appears that Professor Nordberg gave the treasure to Count Lindgren. They must have been working together."

The inspector looked at her shrewdly. "And now the treasure is gone. And this Gregor is also gone. Is that the story, ma'am?"

Ruth glared. "I know what you're thinking, and you're wrong! Something has happened to Gregor, or he would have been here by now! I'm worried! I left him at this Professor Nordberg's apartment, and now the apartment telephone doesn't answer, and I'm sure Gregor must be hurt, or something—"

"This Gregor, I assume, is a good friend of yours, ma'am?"

"He is," Ruth said a bit defiantly.

"Yes. Well, then, if you will permit me to make a telephone call on your phone, we can make a trip to this professor's home and see if we can find out where your Gregor is."

He crossed the room to the telephone, got an outside line, and dialed. He spoke into the telephone in a low tone, his back turned to Ruth. All she could distinguish was a murmur. When the inspector was done, he hung up, nodded his thanks for the use of the instrument, and led the way from the room.

An unmarked police car with a driver was waiting below. They climbed in and the inspector looked at Ruth inquiringly. She gave him the professor's address and they rode through the city in silence, pulling up at last in the Israels Plad before the apartment house. A blond man leaning against the building considered them curiously. One good look at the inspector and he seemed to remember an appointment elsewhere, for he folded his newspaper, tucked it into his pocket, and began to stroll away. The inspector looked after him a moment, frowning, and then shrugged. One thing at a time. He led the way to the front door of the building and pressed the bell under the name "Nordberg." There was no response. He nodded to his driver who came from the car, his hand reaching into his pocket for a bunch of keys. Moments later the door succumbed to the driver's skill and they passed through, the inspector indicating he wished the driver to accompany them in case further locked doors were encountered.

"No point in disturbing the neighbors," the inspector said,

almost as if speaking to himself, and led the way up the stairs. The inspector rapped loudly on the door to Nordberg's apartment, waited a few minutes before repeating the knock, and nodded to the driver. A moment later he had opened the door and stepped back. Inspector Rodhe pushed the door wide and stood, looking inside. Ruth peered around his shoulder. Then she screamed. Professor Nordberg was sprawled on the sofa, his face almost black, suffused with blood, the marks of his strangling clearly visible on his neck.

For the first time in her life Ruth felt herself getting faint. "Gregor!"

The inspector looked at her sharply. "That's Gregor?"

"No. That's Professor Nordberg. I meant—" She shut her mouth resolutely.

"I see. I suggest you wait for me in the car," the inspector said politely, and tilted his head the slightest bit for the benefit of the driver, who drew Ruth back and led her down the steps as the inspector entered the room and closed the door behind him.

Ruth sat in the police car stunned, damning herself for everything she had done from the very beginning. Why had she ever wanted to find the treasure in the first place? It had resulted in Axel Lindgren's death, in Gregor killing Nordberg, and for what? A bunch of pieces of artifacts that were not worth anyone's life. And worse, why had she mentioned Gregor's name to the inspector, as much as telling him who had killed Nordberg? Oh, why hadn't Gregor listened to her when she begged him not to use force? But she hadn't begged him. There was no exculpation in that thought. She had actually promised to let him try his methods if hers failed, when she knew all along he meant to use force if nothing else worked. She wondered how long the dead man had held out before Gregor unwittingly—for nothing could make her believe he had killed the man purposely—found himself with a dead man on his hands. Had the professor begged for his life, telling the truth that Count Lindgren had the treasure, only to have Gregor continue his pressure, not believing the man?

Oh, Gregor, Gregor! she thought despondently. My darling, my love, a murderer! At this moment undoubtedly hiding someplace. And he had done it for her, for her greed for the treasure! It was all her fault, the death of Nordberg, the death of Axel Lindgren, the fact that her beloved Gregor was a murderer. He had done it for her, and the guilt would lie on her soul and her conscience for the rest of her days . . .

She looked up. Inspector Rodhe was coming from the apartment, pushing ahead of him a manacled figure. Knud Christensen was looking at her in complete non-recognition. The inspector ushered the manacled man into the front seat next to the driver and climbed in back beside Ruth.

"He was in the kitchen, drinking aquavit," the inspector said cheerfully for the benefit of the driver. "Gave me no trouble at all. Kept saying he had been cheated, and that the dead man wouldn't drink some whiskey he had brought with him, and the next thing he knew he was holding the man by the neck." He looked at the silent figure beside the driver. There was a touch of compassion in his voice. "I don't believe he's all there . . ."

Ruth felt a wave of tremendous relief, followed by a flush of shame that she could have thought her Gregor capable of killing Nordberg, followed by an equal feeling of shame that she should be happy it was poor Knud Christensen who had committed the crime. Another thought came. If Gregor was not involved, where was he? Inspector Rodhe might have been reading her mind.

"This Gregor," he said gently, almost sadly, "is his last name Kovpak?"

Ruth nodded dumbly, waiting for word of more terror. The inspector nodded to the driver. "First, the Plaza Hotel," he said, and turned back to Ruth. "I made a call from your hotel room, you may remember. I just called again from the apartment upstairs to get the results. I am an old-fashioned policeman, perhaps, but when something very valuable connected with a case disappears, and when a person connected with the same case also disappears, I tend to believe they very well might be together."

Ruth stared at him. "What do you mean?"

"I mean," the inspector said in his gentle voice, "that a man named Gregor Kovpak took a Scandinavian Airlines non-stop flight for Leningrad less than thirty minutes ago. He was carrying a very expensive suitcase; the young lady who checked him in remembered it particularly, because it was so similar to the luggage she had very often checked in for Count Lindgren on his many travels . . ."

PART FIVE

1979

24 ‖

The three weeks Ruth McVeigh had spent in Paris of a month's leave of absence, approved by cable from the board of directors of the Metropolitan, had done nothing to lessen the combination of grief and anger she still felt whenever the thought of Gregor Kovpak and/or the Schliemann treasure came to her mind. Her visits to the Louvre, once one of her greatest pleasures, were dull and purposeless. She paced the many galleries without seeing the many treasures on either side of her, feeding on her anger, unheeding, even, of where she was or why she was there. No amount of time spent in boutiques selecting clothing—all purposely high-necked and as sexless as she could find—could assuage the constant bitterness. Parisian food, once her greatest delight, was tasteless in her mouth. Her nights were lonely and sleepless, tormented with a need she tried to reject for the sake of her self-respect. Nor did the passage of time seem to ease either the grief or the anger, and when she knew her hiding from her work would never really resolve the problem—although she did not know what would—she cabled the Metropolitan that she had had enough vacation and would be back at her desk on the following Monday.

The plane trip home seemed endless, with her mind constantly revolving between the hurt she had suffered at the hands of a man who had taken advantage of her, taking her to bed under the pretense of love, making her fall in love with him, and then capping his churlishness by stealing a treasure from her—and what she intended to do to even the score once she was home. To begin with, there was no doubt it had been a common theft, a theft from the Metropolitan, as well as from her, personally. After all, *she* had traced the treasure, *she* had insisted upon their visiting Knud Christensen, when that— that—*Lothario*—had wanted to go back to Copenhagen and go to bed. She had done all the work. Dr. Kovpak had merely tagged along to get what he could get, and then when he saw the opportunity, he had stolen the treasure. A common thief! Surely there had to be a way to press charges, possibly through the State Department to the Cultural Commission in the Soviet Union—although if they were anything like Gregor Kovpak, they would probably deny any knowledge of the treasure. And how could she prove her case? At the time she had left Copenhagen, after attending Axel Lindgren's funeral, poor Knud Christensen had been put in a home for the mentally handicapped. And Count Lindgren was dead and so was Professor Nordberg. So how could she prove her story? To the police, all that Gregor Kovpak—damn the memories of the man!— had stolen was a suitcase. What it contained, nobody knew.

But she knew!

And proof or no proof, she would see to it that the entire world knew just what a libertine Gregor Kovpak was, what a cheat, despite all his fine titles and his great reputation! A common thief, a liar, despite his dark good looks and his glib tongue. She would spread the word through every archaeological society, every professional journal, to every friend she had in the entire archaeological world. She would drive the name of Gregor Kovpak down so far he would never dare to show his face anywhere except at the Hermitage, if even there! Men!

She arrived at Kennedy Airport early on that Monday morning, tired but determined to get right on with her campaign. Until she could rid herself of the incubus of her disgust with Gregor Kovpak and her equal disgust with herself for having fallen in love with a knave, she felt that she could never again lead a normal life. She dropped her suitcases off at her apartment and took a taxi at once to the Metropolitan Museum. She climbed the steps, hating Gregor Kovpak even more for taking from her the great pleasure she had always felt in walking up those steps each day. Now there was no feeling of belonging, of possession. Now there was no feeling except the need for revenge.

She stalked past the many receptionists, all of whom looked up with smiles of pleasure to see their director back again and then looked at each other in wondering surprise at not even having their greetings acknowledged. She marched down the corridors past the neat guards without seeing them or caring how they looked, and entered her office intent upon getting to her telephone and beginning her campaign. Her secretary looked up with a smile.

"Hello, Dr. McVeigh! It's good to have you back! You have a vis—"

"Later!" Ruth said brusquely, almost savagely, and moved with purpose toward her private office. The first thing to do was to get someone from the legal staff working on the matter. She pushed through the door and then stopped dead, her heart seemingly in her throat. There was a man standing looking from the window and the shoulders and back looked achingly familiar. He turned. It was Gregor Kovpak.

He smiled, his pleasure at seeing her evident in his eyes. "Hello, Ruth."

"Gregor!" She sat down abruptly, unable to believe it. "What—what are you doing here?"

He shrugged, as if his presence was the most natural thing in the world. "I'm in love with you. You are in love with me—or you were a while ago. I thought we would get married. I've defected from my country—with the help, I might mention, of a good but slightly battered friend, a retired colonel, now—and I've requested asylum in this country."

"But—but, Copenhagen—?"

"Ah, yes? You mean my sudden departure from Copenhagen with that suitcase?" Gregor grinned and then straightened his face. "Ruth, suppose I told you that when I got to Leningrad, that suitcase was empty?"

Her anger returned. "I wouldn't believe you!"

Gregor persisted. "But, suppose, even if there had been something of value in that suitcase—which I am not in a position to verify—that I honestly believed it belonged in Russia, as I once explained. And suppose I thought, considering that fact, that you might be willing to take me, instead..."

She stared at him a moment and then smiled, at first a bit ruefully and then with happiness. "I don't have much choice, do I?"

"I'm afraid not," Gregor frowned slightly. "Incidentally, where have you been? I've been in New York over a week, until they told me you would be here this morning."

"I was in Paris. Trying to forget you, as a matter of fact, but without much success." She looked at him archly, but feeling as good as she had felt miserable just minutes before. "And you waited over a week before you tried to find me?"

"I was in Copenhagen," Gregor said. "You had already left when I got there, but there was something I had to do there."

"And that was?"

"To arrange for a large granite monument," Gregor said simply. "Knud Christensen will be allowed to visit it rather frequently once it is completed."

"Oh, Gregor!" She came to her feet and into his arms, but even as they kissed, Dr. Ruth McVeigh, director of the Metropolitan Museum of Art, was trying to figure how she could get her hands on the Schliemann collection to exhibit, if only on loan. But for a decent period of time, not just for a few miserable weeks or months...

The announcement of the coming marriage of the two famous archaeologists, Dr. Ruth McVeigh, of the Metropolitan, and Dr. Gregor Kovpak, late of the Hermitage, was written up in the New York *Times* by their new cultural reporter, Mr. James Newkirk...